Also by John Updike
Published by Fawcett Books:

THE POORHOUSE FAIR
RABBIT, RUN
PIGEON FEATHERS
THE CENTAUR
OF THE FARM
COUPLES
RABBIT REDUX
A MONTH OF SUNDAYS
PICKED-UP PIECES
MARRY ME
THE COUP
TOO FAR TO GO
PROBLEMS
RABBIT IS RICH
BECH IS BACK
THE WITCHES OF EASTWICK
ROGER'S VERSION
TRUST ME
S.
SELF-CONSCIOUSNESS
RABBIT AT REST
MEMORIES OF THE FORD ADMINISTRATION
BRAZIL
THE AFTERLIFE AND OTHER STORIES

THE
AFTERLIFE
And Other Stories

John Updike

FAWCETT CREST • NEW YORK

A Fawcett Crest Book
Published by Ballantine Books
Copyright © 1994 by John Updike

All rights reserved under International and Pan-American Copyright Conventions. Published in the United States by Ballantine Books, a division of Random House, Inc., New York, and simultaneously in Canada by Random House of Canada Limited, Toronto.

Of these twenty-two stories, seventeen were first published in *The New Yorker*. "Wildlife" and "The Rumor" originally appeared in *Esquire;* "Aperto, Chiuso" and "Bluebeard in Ireland" in *Playboy;* and "The Brown Chest" in *Atlantic Monthly*. The stories were written in much the order they have here.

Library of Congress Catalog Card Number: 94-9818

ISBN 0-449-22391-4

This edition published by arrangement with Alfred A. Knopf, Inc.

Manufactured in the United States of America

First Ballantine Books Edition: November 1995

10 9 8 7 6 5 4 3 2 1

for TREVOR LEONARD UPDIKE
and KAI DANIELS FREYLEUE
newcomers to this life

Contents

THE AFTERLIFE
and Other Stories

The Afterlife

THE BILLINGSES, so settled in their ways, found in their fifties that their friends were doing sudden, surprising things. Mitch Lothrop, whom Carter and Jane had always rather poked fun at as stuffy, ran off with a young Jamaican physical therapist, and Augustina, who had seemed such a mouse all those years—obsessed with her garden and her children's educations—took it rather raucously in stride, buying herself a new wardrobe of broad-shouldered dresses, putting a prodigiously expensive new slate roof on the Weston house, and having in as a new companion another woman, a frilly little blue-eyed person who worked in Boston as a psychologist for the Department of Social Services. Ken McEvoy, on the other hand, was one day revealed in the newspapers as an embezzler who over the course of twenty years had stolen between two and five million from his brokerage firm; nobody, including the IRS, knew exactly how much. The investigation had evidently been going on for ages, during which time Ken and Molly had been showing up at cocktail parties and dinner parties and zoning hearings with not a hair out of place, smiling and looking as handsome a couple as ever. Even now, with the indictment in the paper and the plea-bargaining stage under way, they continued to appear at gatherings, Ken quite hilarious and open about it all and basking at the center of attention; he had always seemed rather

1

stiff and shy before. What had he done with all the money? It was true they had two foreign cars, and a place on the Cape, and trips to Europe in the years they didn't go to Florida; but, then, so did everybody, more or less.

And then the Billingses' very dearest friends, Frank and Lucy Eggleston, upped and moved to England. It was something, Frank confided, they had thought about for years; they detested America, the way it was going—the vulgarity, the beggary, the violence. They both, Frank and Lucy, were exceptionally soft-spoken and virtual teetotallers, with health diets and peaceable hobbies; Frank did watercolors, Lucy bird-watched. A juncture came in his career when the corporation asked him to move to Texas. He opted to take early retirement instead, and with his savings and a little inheritance of hers, plus the ridiculous price their house brought—ten times what they had paid for it in the early Sixties— they moved to England, at a time when the pound was low against the dollar. Why defer a dream, they asked the Billingses, until you're too old to enjoy it? They found a suitable house not in one of the pretty counties south of London but up in Norfolk, where, as one of Lucy's early letters put it, "The sky is as big as they say the sky of Texas is."

The letters were less frequent than the Billingses had expected, and on their side they proved slower than they had promised to arrange a visit to their trans- planted friends. Three years had gone by before they at last, after some days in London to adjust to the time change and the coinage and the left-right confusion, took a train north, got off at a station beyond Cam- bridge, and were greeted in the damp and windy spring twilight by a bouncy, bog-hatted shadow they even- tually recognized as Frank Eggleston. He had put on weight, and had acquired that rosy English complexion and an un-American way of clearing his throat several times in rapid succession. As they drove along the A-11, and then navigated twisting country roads, Carter seemed to hear Frank's accent melt, becoming less clipped and twitchy as his passengers and he talked and warmed the car's interior with their growly, drawling Americanness.

They arrived, after many a turning in the growing dark, at "Flinty Dell"—a name no natives, surely, would have given the slightly gaunt mustard-brick house, with its many gables and odd-sized, scattered windows, behind its high wall and bristlings of privet. Lucy seemed much as ever. A broad-faced strawberry blonde, she had always worn sweaters and plaid pleated skirts and low-heeled shoes for her birding walks, and here this same outfit seemed a shade more chic and less aggressively "sensible" than it had at home. Her pleasant plain looks, rather lost in the old crowd of heavily groomed suburban wives, had bloomed in this climate; her manner, as she showed them the house and their room upstairs, seemed to Carter somehow blushing, bridal. She escorted them through a maze of brightly papered rooms and awkward little hallways, up one set of stairs and down another, and on through the kitchen to a mudroom, where she and Frank outfitted themselves with scarves and Wellingtons and fat leather gloves and canes and riding crops and rakes and shovels for their dealings with the constantly invigorating out-of-doors. A barn went with the place, where they boarded horses. The village church was just across the pasture and through the wood on a path. Some obscure duke's vast estate stretched all about, with miles and miles of wonderful riding. And then there were fens, and a priory ruin, and towns where antiques could be had for almost nothing. It was all too much to take in, or to talk about, so late at night, Lucy said, especially when the Billingses must be exhausted and still on funny time.

"Oh no," Jane said. "Carter was de*ter*mined to get on your time and he wouldn't let me take even a nap that first, awful day. We walked all the way in the rain from the National Gallery to the Tate, where they had a huge retrospective of this horrid Kitchen Sink school."

"Such fun you make it sound," Lucy said, tucking her plump freckled calves under her on the tired-looking sofa. The living room was rather small, though high-ceilinged. The furniture, which they must have bought here, clustered like a threadbare, expectant audience about the tiny grated fireplace, as it vivaciously consumed chunks of wood too short to be called logs. "We thought we'd be going down to London every other day but there seems so much to do *here*."

The birding was incredible, and Lucy had become, to her own surprise, quite involved with the local church and with village good works. Frank was painting very seriously, and had joined an artists' association in Norwich, and had displayed a number of watercolors in their biannual shows. Lately he had switched from watercolors to oils. Some of his new works were hung in the living room: wet gray skies and tiny dark houses in the lee of gloomy groves scrubbed in with purple and green. Having poked the fire, and added more chunks (whose smoke smelled narcotically sweet), Frank pressed drinks upon the Billingses though, as all agreed, it was already late and tomorrow was a big day. Lucy was going to drive them to the sea while Frank rode in the local hunt. Scotch, brandy, port, Madeira, and several tints of sherry were produced; Carter remembered the Egglestons as abstemious, but English coziness seemed to have teased that out of them. Carter drank port and Jane cream sherry as they gave the American news: Mitch Lothrop and the Jamaican bodybuilder live in Bay Village and have had a baby, and Augustina has turned that big Weston place into some sort of commune, with a total of five women living in it now. Ken McEvoy is out, having served less than two years, and has been given a job by one of the big Boston banks, because now he's supposedly an expert on fraudulent bookkeeping. Though he and Molly still drive their old Jaguar and a Volvo station wagon, it's obvious he must have stashed millions away, because they're always flying off, even just for weekends, to this place they seem to own in the Bahamas. And so on.

Frank and Lucy had grown smilingly silent under this barrage of imported gossip, and when Carter stood and announced, "We're boring you," neither of them contradicted him. He had lost count of the times Frank had refreshed his port, or poured himself another brandy, and the freckles on Lucy's shins were beginning to swarm; yet he felt he was cutting something short, standing at last. All seemed to feel this—this failure, for all their good will, to remake the old connection—and it was in an atmosphere of reluctance that the guests were, sensibly, led up to bed, Lucy showing them the bathroom again and making sure they had towels.

In the night, Carter awoke and needed to go to the bathroom. All that port. A wind was blowing outside. Vague black-on-blue tree shapes were thrashing. Not turning on a light, so as not to wake Jane, he found the bedroom door, opened it softly in the dark, and took two firm steps down the hall toward where he remembered the bathroom was. On his second step, there was nothing but air beneath his foot. His sleepy brain was jolted into action; he realized he was falling down the stairs. As he soared through black space, he had time to think what a terrible noise his crashing body would make, and how the Egglestons would be awakened, and how embarrassing and troublesome it would be for them to deal with his broken body. He even had time to reflect how oddly selfless this last thought was. Then something—some*one*, he felt—hit him a solid blow in the exact center of his chest, right on the sternum, and Carter was standing upright on what seemed to be a landing partway down the stairs. He listened a moment, heard only the wind as it moaned around the strange brick house, and climbed the six or so steps back to the second floor.

He remembered now that the bathroom was reached by turning immediately left out of the bedroom and then right at the bannister that protected the stairwell, and then left again, at the second door. He crept along and pressed this door open. The white toilet and porcelain basin had a glow of their own in the moonless night, so again he did without a light. His legs were trembling and his chest ached slightly but he felt better for having emptied his bladder. However, emerging again into the dark hall, he couldn't find the way back to his bedroom. Walls as in a funhouse surrounded him. A large smooth plane held a shadowy man who actually touched him, with an abrupt oily touch, and he realized it was himself, reflected in a mirror. On the three other sides of him there were opaque surfaces panelled like doors. Then one of the doors developed a crack of dim blue light and seemed to slide diagonally away; Carter's eyes were adjusted to the dark enough to register wallpaper—faintly abrasive and warm to his touch— and the shiny straight gleam, as of a railroad track, of the bannister. He reversed his direction. There seemed many doors along the hall, but the one he pushed open did indeed reveal his bedroom. The wind was muttering, fidgeting at the stout English window sash, and as Carter drew closer to the bed he could hear Jane

breathe. He crept in beside her and in the same motion
fell asleep.

Next morning, as he examined the site of his adventure, he marvelled that he had not been killed. The oval
knob of a newel post at the turn in the stairs must have
been what struck him on the chest; had he fallen a
slightly different way, it would have hit him in the
face—smashed in his front teeth, or ripped out an
eye—or he could have missed it entirely and broken his
neck against the landing wall. He had no memory of
grabbing anything, or of righting himself. But how had
he regained his feet? Either his memory had a gap or he
had been knocked bolt upright. If the latter, it seemed a
miracle; but Jane, when he confided the event to her,
took the occasion not for marvelling but for showing
him, as one would show a stupid child, how to turn on
the hall light, with one of those British toggle switches
that look like a stumpy rapier with a button on its tip.

Carter felt rebuffed; he had told her of his nocturnal
adventure, while they were still in bed, in hushed tones
much like hers when, thirty years ago, she would confide a suspicion that she was pregnant. The Egglestons,
downstairs at breakfast, responded more appropriately;
they expressed amazement and relief that he hadn't
been hurt. "You might have been *killed*!" Lucy said,
with a rising inflection that in America had never been
quite so pert, so boldly birdlike.

"Exactly," Carter said. "And at the time, even as I
was in midair, I thought, 'What a nuisance for the poor
Egglestons!' "

"Damn white of you," Frank said, lifting his teacup
to his face. He was in a hurry to be off to his hunt; he
had been up for several hours, doing a painting that
needed dawn light, and there were blue and yellow on
his fingernails. "Not to pop off on us," he finished.

"It happens," Carter told him. "More and more, you

see your contemporaries in the *Globe* obituaries. The Big Guy is getting our range." This outburst of theology was so unexpected that the three others stared at him with a silence in which the chimneys could be heard to moan and the breakfast china to click. Carter felt, however, unembarrassed, and supernaturally serene. The world to which he had awoken, from the English details of the orange-juice-less, marmalade-laden breakfast set before him to the muddy green windswept landscape framed in the thick-sashed and playfully various windows, reminded him of children's books he had read over fifty years ago, and had the charm of the timeless.

He squeezed his feet into Lucy's Wellingtons and walked out with Frank to admire the horses. This Norfolk earth was littered with flint—chalky, sharp-edged pebbles. He picked one up and held it in his hand. It felt warm. A limestone layer, porous like bone, had wrapped itself around a shiny bluish core. He tried to imagine the geological event—some immense vanished ocean—that had precipitated this hail of bonelike fragments. The abundant flint, the tufty grass so bursting with green, the radiant gray sky, the strong smells of horse and leather and feed and hay all bore in upon Carter's revitalized senses with novel force; there seemed a cosmic joke beneath mundane appearances, and in the air a release of pressure which enabled the trees, the beeches and oaks, to attain the size of thunderheads. The air was raw—rawer than he had expected England in April to be. "Is the wind always like this?" he asked the other man.

"Pretty much. It's been a tardy spring." Frank, in a hunting coat and jodhpurs, had saddled a horse in its stall and was fiddling with the bridle, making the long chestnut head of the animal, with its rubbery gray muzzle and rolling gelatinous eyeball, jerk resentfully. The physical fact of a horse—the pungent, assaultive hugeness of the animal and the sense of a tiny spark, a gleam of skittish and limited intelligence, within its monstrous long skull—was not a fact that Carter had often confronted in his other life.

"Doesn't it get on your nerves?"

"Does 'em good," Frank said with his acquired brisk bluffness. "Scours you out."

"Yes," Carter said, "I can feel that." He felt delicate, alert, excited. The center of his chest was slightly sore. His toes were numb and scrunched inside Lucy's boots. With a terrible shuffling of hooves and heaving of glossy mass, the horse was led from the barn and suddenly Frank was up on it, transformed, majestic, his pink face crowned by his round black hat, he and the horse a single new creature. The two women came out of the mustard-brick house to watch its master ride off, at a stately pace, down the flinty driveway to the path through the wood. The trees, not yet in full leaf, were stippled all over with leaflets and catkins, like a swathe of dotted swiss. Frank, thus veiled, slowly vanished. "A stirring sight," Carter said. It came upon him that some such entertainment, astonishing yet harmless, would be his steady diet here. He was weightless, as if, in that moment of flight headlong down the stairs, he had put on wings.

Lucy asked them which they would like first, the walk to the river or the drive to the sea. Then she decided the two should be combined, and a supply of boots and overshoes was tossed into the car. Carter got in the back of the little Austin—red, though it had looked black at the station last night—and let the two women sit up front together. Jane occupied what in America would have been the driver's seat, so that Carter felt startled and imperilled when she turned her head aside or gestured with both hands. Lucy seemed quite accustomed to the wrong side of the road, and drove with a heedless dash. "Here is the village, these few houses," she said. "And the church just beyond—you can't see it very well because of that huge old chestnut. Incredibly old, they say the tree is. The church isn't so old."

On the other side of the road, there were sheep, dusted all over with spots of color and mingled with gamboling lambs. The river was not far off, and Lucy parked by an iron bridge where water poured in steady cold pleats down the slant face of a concrete weir. Embankments had been built by stacking bags of cement and letting natural processes dampen and harden them. Lucy led the way along a muddy path between the riverbank and a field that had been recently plowed; the pale soil, littered to the horizon with bonelike bits of flint, was visibly lifting into the silvery, tumbling sky. The wind was scouring dark trails of soil upward, across the plowed miles.

"It's been almost a drought," Lucy said, her voice uplifted, her kerchief flattened against her freckled cheek. Her eyes, squinting, were a pale color between blue and green, and this beryl, beneath this wild sky, had an uncanny brilliance. "Oh, look!" she cried, pointing. "A little marsh tit, doing his acrobatics! Last week, closer to the woods, I saw a pair of waxwings. They generally go back to the continent by this time of year. Am I boring you both? Really, the wind is frightful, but I want you to see my gray heron. His nest *must* be in the woods somewhere, but Frank and I have never been able to spot it. We asked Sedgewick—that's the duke's gamekeeper—where to look for it, and he said if we got downwind we would *smell* it. They eat meat, you know—rodents and snakes."

"Oh dear," Jane said, for something to say. Carter couldn't take his eyes from the distant dark lines of lifting earth, the Texas-like dust storm. As the three made their way along the river, the little black-capped tit capered in the air above them, and as they approached the woods, out flocked starlings, speckled and black and raucous.

"Look—the kingfisher!" Lucy cried. This bird was brilliant, ruddy-breasted and green-headed, with a steel-blue tail. It flicked the tail back and forth, then whirred along the river's glittering surface. But the gray heron was not showing himself, though they trod the margin of the woods for what seemed half a mile. They could hear tree trunks groaning as the wind twisted their layered crowns; the tallest and leafiest trees seemed not merely to heave but to harbor several small explosions at once, which whitened their tossing branches in patches. Carter's eyes watered, and Jane held her hands in their fat, borrowed gloves in front of her face.

At last, their hostess halted. She announced, "We better get on with it—what a disappointment," and led them back to the car.

As they drew close to the glittering, pleated, roaring weir, Carter had the sudden distinct feeling that he should look behind him. And there was the heron, sailing out of the woods toward them, against the wind, held, indeed, motionless within the wind, standing in midair with his six-foot wing-spread—an angel.

The wind got worse as they drove toward the sea. On the map, it looked a long way off, but Lucy assured them she had often done it and returned by teatime. As she whipped along the narrow roads, Carter in the back seat could not distinguish between her tugs on the steering wheel and the tugs of the wind as it buffeted the Austin. A measured, prissy voice on the radio spoke of a gale from the Irish Sea and of conditions that were "near-cyclonic," and Jane and Carter laughed. Lucy merely smiled and said that they often used that expression. In a village especially dear to her, especially historical and picturesque, a group of people were standing on the sidewalk at the crest of a hill, near the wall of a churchyard. The church was Norman, with ornamental arcs and borders of red pebbles worked into the masonry. Lucy drove the car rather slowly past, to see if there had been an accident.

"I think," Carter offered, "they're watching the tree." A tall tree that leaned out from within the churchyard was swaying in the wind.

"Bother," Lucy said. "I've driven too far—what I wanted to show you was back in the middle of the village." She turned around, and as they drove by again several of the little crowd, recognizing the car, seemed amused. A policeman, wearing a rain cape, was pedalling his bicycle up the hill, very energetically, head down.

What Lucy wanted the Billingses to see in the village was a side street of sixteenth-century houses, all of them half-timbered and no two skewed from plumb at the same angle.

"Who lives in them?" Carter wanted to know.

"Oh, people—though I daresay more and more it's trendy younger people who open up shops on the ground floor." Lucy backed around again and this time, coming up the hill, they met a police barricade, and the tall tree fallen flat across the road. Just half of the tree, actually; its crotch had been low to the earth, and the other half, with a splintery white wound in its side, still stood.

The three Americans, sealed into their car, shrieked in excitement, understanding now why the villagers had been amused to see them drive past under the tree again. "You'd think *some*body," Jane said, "might have shouted something, to warn us."

"Well, I suppose they thought," said Lucy, "we had

eyes to see as well as they. That's how they are. They don't give anything away; you have to go to them." And she described, as they bounced between thorny hedgerows and dry-stone walls, her church work, her charity work in the area. It was astonishing, how much incest there was, and drunkenness, and hopelessness. "These people just can't envision any better future for themselves. They would never *dream*, for example, of going to London, even for a day. They're just totally locked into their little world."

Jane asked, "What about television?"

"Oh, they watch it, but don't see that it has anything to do with them. They're taken care of, you see, and compared with their fathers and grandfathers aren't so badly off. The *cru*elty of the old system of hired agricultural labor is almost beyond imagining; they worked people absolutely to death. Picking flint, for instance. Every spring they'd all get out there and pick the flint off the fields."

That didn't seem, to Carter, so very cruel. He had picked up bits of flint on his own, spontaneously. They were porous, pale, intricate, everlasting. His mind wandered as Lucy went on about the Norfolk villagers and Jane chimed in with her own concerns—her wish, now that the children were out of the house, to get out herself and to be of some service, not exactly jump into the ghetto with wild-eyed good intentions but do something *use*ful, something with *peo*ple. . . .

Carter had been nodding off, and the emphasized words pierced his doze. He felt he had been useful enough, in his life, and had seen enough people. At the office now—he was a lawyer—he was conscious of a curious lag, like the lag built into radio talk shows so that obscenities wouldn't get on the air. Just two or three seconds, between challenge and response, between achievement and gratification, but enough to tell him that something was out of sync. He was going through the motions, and all the younger people around him knew it. When he spoke, his voice sounded dubbed, not quite his own. There were, it had recently come to him, vast areas of the world he no longer cared about—Henry James, for example, and professional ice hockey, and nuclear disarmament. He did not doubt that within these areas much excitement could be generated, but not for him, nevermore. The two women in front of him—Lucy's strawberry-blond braids twitching as she emphasized a point and Jane's gray-peppered brunette curls softly bouncing as she nodded in eager empathy—seemed alien creatures, like the horse, or the marsh tit with his little black-capped head. The two wives sounded as stirred up and twittery as if their lives had just begun—as if courtship and husbands and childbearing were a preamble to some triumphant menopausal ministry among the disenfranchised and incestuous. They loved each other, Carter reflected wearily. Women had the passion of conspirators, the energy of any underground, supplied by hope of seizing power. Lucy seemed hardly to notice, while talking and counselling Jane, that she had more than once steered around the wreckage of tree limbs littering the road. Through the car windows Carter watched trees thrash in odd slow motion and overhead wires sway as if the earth itself had lost its moorings.

Then, out of the bruised and scrambled sky, rain pelted down with such fury that the wipers couldn't keep the windshield clear; it became like frosted glass, and the car roof thrummed. Lucy lifted her voice: "There's a lovely old inn right in the next village. Would this be a good time to stop and have a bite?"

Just in dashing the few yards from the parking lot to the shelter of the inn, the three of them got soaked. Inside, all was idyllic: big old blackened fireplace crackling and hissing and exuding that sweet scent of local woodsmoke, carved beams bowed down almost to Carter's head, buffet of salmon mousse and Scotch eggs and shepherd's pie served by a willing lad and blushing lass, at whose backs the rain beat like a stage effect on the thick bottle panes. The middle-aged trio ate, and drank beer and tea; over Lucy's protests, Carter paid.

Next door, an antique shop tempted tourists through a communicating archway, and while the storm continued, Lucy and her visitors browsed among the polished surfaces, the silver and mirrors, the framed prints and marquetry tables. Carter was struck by a lustrous large bureau, veneered in a wood that looked like many blurred paw prints left by a party of golden cats. "Elm burl, early eighteenth century," the ticket said, along with a price in the thousands of pounds. He asked Jane if she would like it—as if one more piece of furniture might keep her at home, away from good works.

"Darling, it's lovely," she said, "but so expensive, and so big."

Elm burl: perhaps that was the charm, the touch of attractive fantasy. In America, the elms were dead, as dead as the anonymous workman who had laid on this still-glamorous veneer.

"They ship," he responded, after a few seconds' lag. "And if it doesn't fit anywhere we can sell it on Charles Street for a profit." His voice didn't sound quite like his own, but only he seemed to notice. The women's conversation in the car had obligated him to make a show of power, male power.

Lucy, intensifying her hint of a British accent, courteously haggled with the manager—a straggly fat woman with a runny red nose and a gypsyish shawl she held tight around her throat—and got four hundred pounds knocked off the price. Carter's plunge into this purchase frightened him, momentarily, as he realized how big the mark-up must be, to absorb such a discount so casually.

There were forms to sign, and credit cards to authenticate over the telephone; as these transactions were pursued, the storm on the roof abated. The three buyers stepped out into a stunning sunlit lapse in the weather. Raindrops glistened everywhere like a coating of ice, and the sidewalk slates echoed the violet of the near-cyclonic sky.

"Darling, that was so debonair and dashing and untypical of you," Jane said.

"Ever so larky," Lucy agreed.

"Kind of a game," he admitted. "What are the odds we'll ever see that chest again?"

Lucy took mild offense, as if her adopted fellow-countrymen were being impugned. "Oh they're very honest and reputable. Frank and I have dealt with these people a few times ourselves."

A miraculous lacquer lay upon everything, beading each roadside twig, each reed of thatch in the cottage roofs, each tiny daisy trembling in the grass by the lichen-stained field walls. Then clouds swept in again, and the landscape was dipped in shadow. Many trees were fallen or split. Little clusters of workmen, in raincoats that were pumpkin-colored instead of, as they would have been in America, yellow or Day-Glo orange, buzzed with saws and pulled with ropes at limbs that intruded into the road. Waiting to be signalled past such work parties took time, while the little Austin gently rocked in the wind, as if being nudged by a giant hand. Carter caressed the sensitive center of his chest, under his necktie: his secret, the seal of his nocturnal pact, his passport to this day like no other. It had felt, in the dark, like a father's rough impatient saving blow. "How much farther to the sea?" he asked.

"Well might you ask," Lucy said. "On a day of smooth sailing, we'd be there by now." The cars ahead of them slowed and then stopped entirely. A policeman with a young round face explained that lines were down across the road.

"That does rather tear it," Lucy allowed. The detour would add fifteen miles at least to their journey. The landscape looked dyed, now, in an ink that rolled across the pale speckled fields in waves of varying intensity. Along a far ridge, skeletal power-line towers marched in a procession, their latticework etched with a ghostly delicacy against the black sky. A band of angels.

Jane consoled Lucy: "Really, dear, if I saw too many more charming villages I might burst."

"And we see the sea all the time when we're on the Cape," Carter added.

"But not *our* sea," Lucy said. "The *North* Sea."

"Isn't it just ugly and cold and full of oil?" asked Jane.

"Not for much longer, they tell us. Full of oil, I mean. Well, if you two don't really mind, I suppose there's nothing to do but go back. Frank *does* like an early supper after he's been on a hunt."

It was growing dark by the time they reached Flinty Dell. Exposing to view a small, drab Victorian church, the ancient chestnut had blown down—a giant shaggy corpse with a tall stump torn like a shriek, pointing at the heavens. The tree had fallen across a churchyard wall and crushed it, the outer courses of sturdy-seeming brick spilling a formless interior of rubble and sand.

Frank came out into the driveway to meet them; in the dusk, his face looked white, and his voice was not amused. "My God, where have you people *been*? I couldn't believe you'd be out driving around in this! The hunt was called off, the radio's been cancelling everything and telling people for Christ's sake to *stay off the roads*!" He rested a trembling hand on the sill of the rolled-down car window; his little fingernail still bore an azure fleck of today's dawn.

"In this bit of a breeze?" Lucy cooed.

Jane said, "Why, Frank darling, how nice of you to be worried."

And Carter, too, was surprised and amused that Frank didn't know they were beyond all that now.

Wildlife

THE TOWN WAS SEXY, or so it had always seemed to Ferris. He had lived there for years, and his former wife still lived there. It was a town by the sea, with marshes and a broad beach; summer had been a fête of sunburn and short skirts and cookouts and insect bites. Not only mosquitoes and midges and gnats but a curious plenitude of ticks and green-headed, bloodthirsty flies bred in the marshes and the winding saltwater channels. An air of siege persisted through the other seasons—fall pinching in with an ever-earlier darkness, winter when on the crooked slick roads cars slid into one another with a dreamlike slow motion, spring with its raw east wind and bouts of flu and considerable human irritability.

The town was not for everybody; it had no country club, its politics were unedifying, its schools were only fair, its tax base needed broadening. Up-and-coming young commuters to Boston, or hi-tech engineers employed along Route 128, moved elsewhere, to more proper towns—one with a pretty blue harbor lined in granite and adorned with the yacht club's domed gazebo, another equipped with horses and stables and a weekly fox hunt, a third boasting a precious historic district of early-Federal homes, a fourth full of grand estates waiting to be subdivided. All of these towns were more suitable and sounder investments for the aspiring than the ragged, raffish settlement where Ferris had lived in his physical prime.

Its natural beauty had verged on wildness and could overflow into violence. Marital scandals would suddenly rip through the school board or the Methodist choir. Early-morning murder-suicides would bestow a blasted aura upon a pale-green house hitherto innocuous in its row. Weather would hit oddly hard, so that power would be lost for the week after a nor'easter that had hardly touched the rest of the coast, or a drought would dry up the private wells and expose the gravel bottom of the town reservoir. Fires were common in this old town built almost entirely of wood. In the years after Ferris left, first one white Congregational church burned down—an irreplaceable example of carpenter Gothic—and then another, a noble Greek Revival edifice erected in a parish schism in 1842. The movie house, with its quaint Arabian Nights décor from the 1930s, vanished in yet another holocaust, along with the adjacent paint store, its cans of turpentine and Williamsburg colors exploding like rapid artillery. Ferris's growing children reported these disasters to him, along with their own. He had remarried and lived in Boston.

Returning to the town, to take a child to dinner or to consult his dentist, who was aging along with him, he never failed to be uplifted by the local ambience into a sexier, more buoyant self. His very step became more youthful, and the rub of his shirt against his skin took on a suggestive nervous tension. Almost no one, after ten years, knew Ferris—even the corner drugstores, once operated by rival selectmen, had changed hands—but he was greeted by the familiar proportions of the buildings, the erratic layout of the streets, and unexpected souvenirs of his past: an antique store still offered, it appeared, the same sun-baked furniture in the window, a gray-haired postman was still doing his

rounds, a graceful great elm hadn't died yet, a straggling stretch of dirt sidewalk hadn't yet been paved.
The town was patchy, informal, with seams where the
true stuff of life—dirt, sex, saltwater, death—kept leaking through. Even the town's children and dogs, as Ferris saw them, were scruffier and cannier than those of
better-organized, more antiseptic communities.

In the ten years since he had left, a further plague had
been visited upon the town—a plague of deer. Even
while he had been a resident, housewives along the
beach road would complain that in the night deer had
consumed all their tulips and that their newly planted
dogwoods and crabapples had been fatally girdled by
deer nibbling the bark. But the marauders were furtive
and shy, and it was considered a treat for the children,
better than a trip to the zoo, when an October walk on
the beach yielded a glimpse of deer, their white tails
flicking, bounding away into the dunes.

Ferris still remembered a moment, freighted with
guilt and rapture, early in his separation from his wife,
when the property where he had lived still called forth
his husbandry. He had come out from Boston and he
and his son, Jamie, then in his mid-teens, were up on
the tennis court, readying it for winter by placing two-
by-fours on the tapes and weighting them with rocks.
Otherwise, the freezing and thawing of the clay lifted
the aluminum nails during the winter. Ferris happened
to glance up. At the far edge of the shaggy field a family of deer had emerged from the woods. It was an unseasonably warm day in November, misty, and in this
mist the forms of the three deer—the stag, the doe, and
the smallest, no longer a fawn—hesitated as if posed in
a soft old photograph, elegant gray-brown creatures
from the dignified prehuman world.

"Look!" Ferris told his son quietly, but even this
whispered utterance sent the ghostly forms racing,

bounding across the wet unmowed field to the patch of woods in the opposite corner of the property, where the tidal creek turned. Ferris had not felt entitled, that haggard guilty day on the edge of winter, to so magical a sight, and had pressed it upon his son as if in compensation for his coming years of absence.

Now his son, in his mid-twenties and called James or Jim, had grown accustomed to his absence, and the deer had become a famous civic problem, which Ferris read about in the Boston newspapers. They multiplied while the undeveloped land around them diminished; starving, they robbed the dunes of vegetation and ravished the landscaping of the expensive seaview homes being built above the marshes. A Christmas tree tossed out into the snow was stripped of needles by the frantic animals, even in daylight; at night, high-school couples parking on the beach lot found themselves surrounded by a crowd of deer standing mute and mendicant around the car. The deer in their delicate heraldic beauty had become as pestilential as rats, and the town, with its curious flair for scandal, where another town might have found a quiet solution, debated the issue into a storm of publicity. Nature-lovers from the other end of the commonwealth came to protest the selectmen's proposal to import hired Army sharpshooters to reduce the herds. Irate women threatened to mingle, dressed in deerskin, with the animals on the scheduled day, thus sacrificing their own lives to the ideal of unpolluted natural process. Several veterinarians came to testify that starvation is relatively painless and weeds out the weak; others counter-testified that it is agony and selectively destroys the young. There were meetings, picketing, interviews on television. Meanwhile, throughout large regions of the town—and these the most fashionable and expensive—garbage cans were kicked open, azalea bushes eaten leafless, and dead deer bodies found frozen out by the bird feeders.

Then, worse yet, it developed that the deer population was crawling with the tiny tick *Ixodes dammini*, which in turn harbored the spirochetes of Lyme disease, named after the town in Connecticut where it first was recognized. Round red lesions, malaise and fatigue, chills and fever and stiff neck: these are its symptoms. Its final results can be heart damage and lifelong arthritis. We live in plague times. As our species covers the earth like a scum, the bacteria and viruses and parasites inventively thrive. When Ferris lived in the town, no thought was given, for example, to venereal disease. Herpes and AIDS and chlamydia were unheard of; sexual affairs involved a spiritual and economic peril only. Men and women tasted one another as if at a smorgasbord of uncontaminated dishes, a tumble of treats, some steaming, some chilled, some nutritious, some not, but all clean.

The deer-lovers were overruled, and on appointed days the sharpshooters descended on the dunes. But cases of Lyme disease continued to trickle into the local hospital from all along the beach road, where property values, always high, had been soaring, and now dipped.

Ferris's old property was not on the beach road, but on a road off of it, that led nowhere. The road went over a small arched bridge that spanned a tidal creek, passed a few more houses, and then became a turn-around of packed dirt amid the encroaching marsh grass, with its bleached litter of beer cans and horseshoe-crab shells. The road was paved as far as the bridge, and Ferris knew every turn, sway, and jolt in the ride; it, too, seemed sexy, and brought back younger days. It had been a woman's town, dominated by female energy. To find oneself, of a weekday afternoon, in bed with another man's wife was to have achieved a certain membership—an accreditation in primordial coin, a basic value within an Amazonian tribe. At parties, there were four kinds of people: women who had known a number of the men, men who had known a number of the women, and men and women who were innocent. Sometimes the latter were married to the uninnocent, and that produced sadness and divorce. Ferris was returning to visit Jamie, who was house-sitting while the former Mrs. Ferris was off for a week in Nova Scotia with the latest of the series of lovers and attendants that for ten years had failed to yield another husband. Ferris for all his failings had proved to be irreplaceable.

The boy greeted his father with complaints, and looked exhausted. He stooped, and had not shaved for a day or two, so that black whiskers of an alarming virility stood out on his jaw and chin. "I've been trying to impose some order on the bushes," he explained. "Mom just lets everything grow. She has this philosophy that every plant has a right to live."

Yes, Ferris recalled, that had been the local philosophy; while the women of surrounding, proper towns tended their gardens and joined Garden Clubs, the housewives here went off to the beach to deepen their already savage-looking tans. Personal cultivation had been the style, and horticultural neglect a token of liberation. Once Ferris had tried to prune a giant wisteria vine that was prying clapboards off the house, and his wife had accused him of being a butcher, a killer. All he had craved had been a little order. She had thought dandelions and burdock rather pretty and allowed the forsythia bush to swallow the yew hedge. The lawn had been mown primarily for croquet games and had emitted a different aroma in each month of summer—that of a spicy fresh salad in June, of a well's deep walls in July, and of dry hay in August, with scuffed patches of earth around the improvised soccer goals, and oil-stains where the children had worked on their bicycles.

August was Ferris's favorite month. It was August now. "Jimmy, just don't get into the poison ivy," he warned his son, who as a boy had had a fearful case of it, his eyes swollen shut above scarlet, oozing cheeks. "Shiny leaves, always in sets of three. Not serrated and feathery, like Virginia creeper. Shiny, with a pinkish stem."

"That reminds me, Dad. I have something to show you."

"What?" Ferris's heart skipped a beat.

"I'll show you inside."

Ferris took this as an invitation to survey the outdoors first. He and this boy who had replaced him as the man of the place walked up through the remnants of a onetime orchard to the neglected tennis court. The wire fencing that had once been virgin and rust-free, stapled to bolt-upright posts fragrant with creosote, now sagged under the burden of entwined honeysuckle. Rotten old sails had been spread along the edges, to suppress the weeds that invaded from the field. Ferris looked up toward the place in the field where he had once seen the deer, but saw only forest, taller and coming closer. Old photographs of this region showed clean curves of land, stripped for firewood and cropped by sheep, and a view clear across low drumlins to the sea. Now shaggy groves covered the high ground, and the saltwater of the channel merely glinted through, with the noise of motorboats and of teenagers gleefully shouting.

"A big job," he sighed to his son. In August, there came a scratching in the air, an unlocatable buzzing undercurrent that people called crickets or cicadas but that Ferris associated with the sound that a bedside electric clock makes beside an insomniac's head in the night.

"And the dumb pear trees," his son went on, in that affronted voice children use, "keep producing all these pears to drop into the grass to gum up the mower." His tone was a child's but his timbre adult, an aggrieved baritone that went with the black whiskers, the thick powerful legs, the big-boned wrists and hands. Ferris had trouble understanding the sex lives of his adult children. He had met some of this son's girlfriends; they were presentable young women with well-conditioned figures, oily bleached ringlets, bright eyes, relaxed and sympathetic manners, and mouths curved in expectation of being amused. Yet, no sooner had Ferris mastered the name of one, and the rudiments of her geographical and educational background, than she was gone. None of them lasted, none of them apparently excited that romantic wish so common to men of Ferris's generation, the wish to marry—to claim in the sight of church and state this female body, to enter into formalized intimacy as if into a territory to be conquered, tamed, sown, and harvested. The wife at the kitchen sink, the wife at the cocktail party or the entr'acte buffet, the wife showering to go out or coming back from shopping with sore feet, the wife docile on one's arm or excitingly quarrelsome in the back of a taxi: the romance that, for Ferris, had attached to these images and made him want to marry not once but repeatedly had quite vanished from American culture—a casualty, perhaps, of co-ed dormitories or the impossible prices of starter housing. His deep-voiced son, for example, lived here for months at a time, with his lonely mother and her overgrown peony beds.

Dogs bounded around the two men as they crossed the lank brown lawn to the kitchen door. Inside, the animals clattered and slid about on the linoleum in hope of being fed. There were three dogs, disparate mongrels acquired by Ferris's former family at various impulsive moments and now collected here, along with a neighbor's dog that had attached itself to the pack. Their hair was everywhere, on rugs and sofas and in little balls collected along the baseboards like tumbleweed along a barbed-wire fence. The furniture, much of it once joint property, seemed to float in temporary arrangement, not rooted in place but at rest—Fifties modern grown old and worn. The teak arms of the Danish chairs were cracked; the glass tabletops looked permanently smeared. His ex-wife had scattered garish throw pillows and squares of Indian cloth about as if to distract the eye, and these many festive patches intensified the air of dishevelment, of carefree improvisation, an air that made the shirt on Ferris's chest and the very trousers on his legs caress his skin with an excited slither.

His son at his side fetched a weary sigh. "I was going to paint the woodwork for a project but just keeping it halfways tidy in here and the kitchen seems to take all my time."

Ferris asked, "What did you want to show me?"

"Oh yeah. I, er, have to lower my britches."

"Really? Well, do, I guess. Don't be shy. I used to change your diapers." Ferris's blood raced with the mystery of it.

Beneath his khaki pants his son wore boxer shorts, such as Ferris associated with old men. His father had worn such baggy underpants. Ferris wore Jockeys, the snugger the better. "On the back of my right thigh, Dad. Up high. See it?"

"A big round red spot. How long have you had it?"

"A while. I remember, about two weeks ago, this little critter bit me. A tiny tick—smaller than a dog tick. I didn't think much about it but now this terrible itching and this *hot* feeling are there, where I can't quite see it even with the mirror."

Ferris asked, though he knew the answer, "You've been working in the bushes?"

"I *had* to," the child whined. "They were coming into the yard. There was hardly any yard left. I've been feeling exhausted lately, too."

"Chills and fever?"

"Chills once in a while. I don't know about fever. The thermometer's broken."

"Is your neck stiff?"

"Only in the mornings, a little sometimes."

"Jamie, you poor guy. We must get you to a doctor." As Ferris bent lower to re-examine the symptom, he tried to suppress the happy thought that he had got out just in time.

Brother Grasshopper

FRED EMMET—swarthy and thick-set, with humorless straight eyebrows almost meeting above his nose—had been an only child. If he ever fantasized a sibling for himself, it was a sister, not a brother. His father had had a brother, an older brother, who, he let it be known, had dominated him cruelly. Yet into even his more resentful reminiscences crept a warmth that Fred envied, as he tried to imagine the games of catch, decades ago, on the vacant lots of a city that no longer had vacant lots, and the shared paper route in snow that was deeper and more dramatic than any snow today is, with a different scent—the scent of wet leather and of damp wool knickers. Though his father's brother had deliberately thrown the ball too hard, and finished delivering papers to his side of the street first and never came back to help but instead waited inside the warm candy store, a brother was something his father had *had*, augmenting his existence, giving it an additional dimension available to him all his life. "My brother down in Deerfield Beach," he would drop into a conversation, or "If you were to express that view to my brother, he'd tell you flat out you're crazy." And, though the brothers lived over a thousand miles apart, one in Florida and the other in New Jersey, and saw each other less than once a year, they died within a few months of each other,

Fred's father following his older brother as if into one more vacant lot, to shag flies for him.

But this was years later, when Fred's own children were grown, or nearly. He had married early, right after Harvard, supplying himself with another roommate, as it were, rather than launching into life alone. He envied siblings their imagined power of consultation, of conspiring against parents who otherwise would be too powerful. Not the least of the charms his future wife held for him was her sister—a younger sister also at Radcliffe, with her own circle of friends. Germaine was more animated, more gregarious, and more obviously pretty than Fred's sensible Betsy. Among her numerous suitors the most conspicuous was Carlyle Saughterfield, a tall bony New Englander with a careless, potent manner.

Fred had been sickly and much-protected as a child, and even his late growth spurt had left him well under six feet tall. He found Carlyle, who was two years older than he and a student at the Business School across the river, exotic and intimidating—a grown man with his own car, a green Studebaker convertible, and confident access to the skills and equipment of expensive sports like sailing, skiing, climbing, and hunting. Carlyle and his B-School friends would load up his snappy green convertible with skis and boots and beer and sleeping bags and head north into snow country with the top down. Details of their mountain adventures made Fred shudder—sheer ice, blinding fog, tainted venison that left them all vomiting, ski trails bearing terrible names like Devil's Head and Suicide Ravine. Climbing in the White Mountains one summer, Carlyle had seen a friend fall, turning in the air a few feet away as Carlyle pressed into the cliff and gripped the pitons.

"What was the expression on his face?" Fred asked.

Carlyle's somewhat protuberant eyes appeared to

moisten, as he visualized the fatal moment. "Impassive," he said.

His voice, husky and hard to hear, as if strained through something like baleen, was the one weak thing about him; but even this impressed Fred. Back in New Jersey, the big men, gangsters and police chiefs and Knights of Columbus, spoke softly, forcing others to listen.

As their courtship of the Terwilliger sisters proceeded in parallel, Fred and Carlyle spent an accumulating number of hours together. In the spring, waiting for the girls to come out of their dorms, they played catch in the Quad with a squash ball; Carlyle's throws made Fred's hands sting and revived his childhood fear of being hit in the face and having an eye or a tooth knocked out. The strength stored in the other man's long arms and wide, sloping shoulders was amazing—a whippy, excessive strength almost burdensome, Fred imagined, to carry. Carlyle had been a jock at prep school, but in college had disdained organized sports; a tendency to veer away from the expected was perhaps another weakness of his. Behind the Business School, across from Harvard Stadium, a soccer field existed where the future financiers played touch football. Carlyle passed for immense distances, sometimes into Fred's eagerly reaching hands, and protectively saw to it that his timorous and undersized brother in courtship usually played on his team.

In March of the year that Fred and Betsy graduated, the two couples went skiing, and Carlyle was as patient as a professional instructor, teaching Fred the snowplow and stem christie and carefully bringing him down, at the end of the day, through the shadows of the intermediate slope. All these upper-class skills involved danger, Fred noticed. That summer, after he and Betsy had married, Carlyle took them and Germaine sailing on Buzzards Bay and, while the two sisters stretched out in their underwear for sunbaths on the bow, commanded in his reedy voice that Fred take the tiller and hold the mainsheet—take all this responsibility into his hands!

"Take it. Push it left to make the prow move to the right. The prow's the thing in front."

"I'd just as soon rather not. I'm happy being a passenger."

"Take it, Freddy."

The huge boat leaned terrifyingly under gusts of invisible pressure, the monstrous sail rippling and the mast impaling the sun and the keel slapping blindly through the treacherous water, nothing firm under them, even the horizon and its islands skidding and shifty. Nevertheless, the boat did not capsize. Fred gradually got a slight feel for it—for the sun and salt air and rocking horizon. Germaine's breasts in their bra were bigger than Betsy's, her pubic bush made a shadowy cushion under her underpants as the sisters lazily, trustfully chattered. Carlyle's face, uplifted to the sun with bulging closed eyelids, had a betranced look; his colorless fair hair, already thinning, and longer than a businessman's should be, streamed behind him in the wind. *This bastard,* Fred thought, as the boat sickeningly heeled, *is trying to make a man of me.*

When, the following summer, Germaine graduated and married Carlyle, the groom chose Fred over all his old skiing and hunting buddies to be his best man, perhaps in courteous symmetry with Betsy, the matron-of-honor. He bought Fred a beige suit to match his own; the coat hung loose on Fred's narrow shoulders, and the sleeves were too long, but he felt flattered nonetheless. Betsy was five months pregnant, so her ceremonial dress, of royal-blue silk, was too tight. Between them, they joked, it came out even. So young, they were already launched on creating another generation.

A strange incident clouded this wedding, foreshadowing trouble to come. Carlyle and Germaine were married in New Hampshire, at a summer lodge beyond Franconia belonging to Carlyle's family, and with sentimental associations for him. The Terwilliger parents were getting a divorce at the time and were too unorganized to insist on having the event on their territory, in northwestern Connecticut. With the noon hour set for the service drawing closer, Carlyle disappeared, and it was reported that he was taking a bath down at the dam—an icy little pond in the woods, created every summer by damming a mountain trickle. Mrs. Terwilliger, rendered distraught by this apparent additional defection—her own husband was not present, having been forbidden to come if he brought his youthful mistress—appealed to Fred to go down and fetch the groom. Fred supposed that in his role of best man he could not shy from this awkward duty. In his black shoes and floppy new suit—double-breasted, with those wide Fifties lapels, and a white rosebud pinned in one of them—he walked down the dirt road to the dam. His fingers kept testing his right-hand coat pocket, to see if the wedding ring was still there—its adamant little weight, its cool curved edge. The road was really two dusty paths beside a central mane of weeds and grass, shadowed even toward noon by hemlocks and birches. Bears supposedly lived in these woods, which stretched endlessly, gloomily, in every direction, claustrophobic as a cave. Suppose Carlyle had fled! Suppose he had gone crazy, and with his excessive, careless strength would knock his best man unconscious!

Carlyle was coming up the road, in his identical beige suit, his long wet hair combed flat, his ritual bachelor ablutions at last completed. Fred was relieved; he had been afraid of, among other things, seeing his soon-to-be brother-in-law naked. The road slanted down, to the creek, so their heads for a moment were on the same level, and in this moment Carlyle gave Fred, or Fred happened to catch, a look, a watery warm-eyed look. What did it mean? *Get me out of this?* Or was the look just a flare, a droplet, of the wordless pagan wisdom that brothers somehow shared?

"They sent me after you."

"I see that, Freddy."

Carlyle's eyes were an uncanny pale green, with thin pink lids, and prominent, so that his long face gave the impression of being a single smooth tender surface, his nose so small as to be negligible. When he looked intent, as now, his eyes went flat across the top, the upper eyelid swallowing its own lashes.

In the years to come, the brothers-in-law looked each other in the eyes rather rarely. Not that they lacked occasion: though they lived, with their wives and children, in separate towns, and eventually on different coasts of the continent, Carlyle saw to it that they all spent at least several weeks of the year as one family. There was the Franconia place at first, and when Carlyle's mother, widowed early by a heart attack that carried off his father—the Saughterfields had fragile hearts—sold it, there were summer houses rented jointly, or two rented side by side, or Christmases spent in one or the other's home, the floor beneath the tree heaped embarrassingly high with the presents for their combined children. There were nine children, in the end: Fred and Betsy's three, Carlyle and Germaine's six. Six! Even in those years before ecology-mindedness, that was a lot, for non-Catholics. Fred and Betsy speculated that, his own father dying so young and his mother remarrying and moving to Paris (her new husband worked for American Express), Carlyle was afraid of running out of family; his New Hampshire cousins depressed him and his only sibling was a much older sister whom he never mentioned, and who lived in Hawaii with an alcoholic jerk of a husband.

The Emmets sometimes found the joint vacations heavy going. Their children were outnumbered two to one and everyone was benevolently bullied into expeditions—to the beach, to an amusement park, to some mountain trail—whose ultimate purpose seemed to be to create photo opportunities for Carlyle. He had become a fervent photographer, first with Nikons and then with Leicas, until he discovered that an even more expensive camera could be bought—a Hasselblad. Its chunky shutter sound sucked them up, sealed them in, captured them in sunshine and rain, parkas and bathing suits, the boys in their baseball caps and the girls in their ribbons and braids. One cherished photo, turned into the Saughterfields' Christmas card, showed all nine children squeezed into the Emmets' old workhorse of a Fairlane station wagon, each hot little grinning face smeared by an ice-cream cone. What the photo did not show was the drive away from the ice-cream stand: the cones melted too rapidly in the August heat and had to be thrown out the window when they became, in the mass of flesh, impossibly liquid. "Over the side!" Carlyle called from behind the wheel, and an answering voice would pipe, "Over the side!," and another gob of ice cream would spatter on the receding highway, to gales of childish glee. Conspicuous waste pained Fred, but seemed to exhilarate Carlyle.

As it worked out, Carlyle was often driving Fred's cars, and commandeering Betsy's kitchen for meals he would cook, dirtying every pan. He made the Emmets feel squeezed, not least with his acts of *largesse*—plastic-foam boxes of frozen steaks that would arrive before a visit, mail-ordered from Omaha, and heavy parcels of post-visit prints, glossily processed by a film laboratory in West Germany that Carlyle used. All these fond, proprietary gestures, Fred felt, spelled power and entitlement. Even taking the photographs placed Carlyle on a level above them, as an all-seeing appropriator of their fleeting lives.

Once, on Martha's Vineyard, when Fred needed his car to get to a tennis date in Chilmark and Carlyle had taken it up to Oak Bluffs to buy his daughters and nieces elephant-hair bracelets, and then to Vineyard Haven for the matinée of a Jerry Lewis movie, with miniature golf on the way home, Fred let his temper fly. He felt his face flush; he heard his shrill voice flail and crack. Carlyle, who had returned from his long expedition with bags of farmstand vegetables, pounds of unfilleted fish, and a case of imported beer, stared at Fred with his uncanny green eyes for some seconds and then cheerfully laughed. It was a laugh of such genuine, unmalicious, good-tempered amusement that Fred had to join in. Through his brother-in-law's eyes he saw himself clearly, as a shrill and defensive pipsqueak. It was, he imagined, this sort of honest illumination—this sort of brusque restoration to one's true measure—that siblings offer one another. As an only child, Fred had never been made to confront his limits.

In bed he asked Betsy, "Why does he need to do it—all this playing Santa Claus?"

"Because," she answered, "he doesn't have enough else to do."

What Carlyle did professionally became vaguer with the years. After business school there had been business—putting on a suit in the morning, working for other men, travelling in airplanes to meet with more men in suits. One company he worked for made fine leather goods—purses, belts, aviator-style jackets as items of high fashion—and another a kind of machinery that stamped gold and silver foil on things, on books and photograph albums and attaché cases and such. Neither job lasted long. Carlyle's weakness, perhaps, was his artistic side. His Harvard major had been not economics but fine arts; he took photographs and bought expensive art books so big no shelves could hold them; he could not be in his house, or the Emmets', a minute without filling the air with loud music, usually opera. When his mother's sudden death—she was hit by a taxi in Paris, on the Boulevard St Germain—brought him some additional money, he became a partner in an avant-garde furniture store in the Back Bay: chairs and tables of molded plastic, sofas in the form of arcs of a circle, waterbeds. The store did well—it was the Sixties, there was plenty of money around, and plenty of questing for new lifestyles—but Carlyle got bored, and became a partner in a Los Angeles firm that manufactured kinetic gadgets of Plexiglas and chemical fluids. This firm went bust, but not before Carlyle fell in fatal love with California—its spaghetti of flowing thruways, its pink and palmy sprawl, its endless sunshine and perilous sense of being on the edge. He moved his growing family there in 1965. As his children grew and his hair thinned, Carlyle himself seemed increasingly on the edge—on the edge of the stock market, on the edge of the movie industry, on the edge of some unspecified breakthrough. His clothes became cheerfully bizarre—bell-bottom pants, jackets of fringed buckskin, a beret. His name appeared as co-producer of a low-budget film about runaway adolescents (seen romantically, roving against the night lights of Hollywood and sleeping in colorful shacks up in the canyons) that received favorable reviews back east and even turned up in the Coolidge Corner movie complex not far from where Fred and Betsy lived in Brookline.

Fred, unromantically, worked in real estate. After splitting off from the management company that trained him,

he bet his life on the future of drab, run-down inner-city
neighborhoods that, by the sheer laws of demographics
and transportation, had to come up in the world. His bet
was working, but slowly, and in the meantime the Emmet Realty Corporation absorbed his days in thankless
maintenance and squabbles with tenants and the meticu-
lous game, which Fred rather enjoyed, of maximizing the
bank's investment and thereby increasing his own leverage. That is, twenty thousand of his own equity, plus a
hundred-thousand-dollar mortgage, meant a profit of two
hundred percent if the building's worth climbed by a
third. He was, like many only children, naturally metic-
ulous and secretive, and it warmed him to think that his
growing personal wealth was cunningly hidden, annually
amplified by perfectly legal depreciation write-offs, in
these drab holdings—in Dorchester three-deckers and
South End brick bowfronts, in asphalt-shingled Somer-
ville duplexes and in Allston apartment buildings so
anonymous and plain as to seem ownerless. He was the
patient ant, he felt, and Carlyle more and more the foolish grasshopper.

Yet, when, ten years into his marriage, Fred found
himself swept up in a reckless romance, it was his
brother-in-law that he confessed to. The seethe of his
predicament—Betsy's innocence, and the children's,
and the other woman's; glittering detached details of
her, her eyes and mouth, her voice and tears, her breasts
and hair—foamed in him like champagne overflowing a
glass. It was delicious, terrible; Fred had never felt so
alive. One muggy July afternoon he found himself alone
with Carlyle in the ramshackle Chatham house that the
Saughterfields and the Emmets were jointly renting.
The wives and children were at the beach. Carlyle came
into the living room, where Fred was working up some
figures, and sat himself stolidly down opposite the desk,
on the sandy, briny green fold-out sofa that came with

the house. Carlyle had put weight on his big bones, and moved now with the deliberation of someone considerably older than his brother-in-law. Tennis and worry had trimmed Fred down, given him an edge—for the first time in his life, he felt handsome. Carlyle was wearing a kind of southern-California safari suit, a loose cotton jacket with matching pants, suggesting pajamas or a doctor's antiseptic outfit when he operates. He sat there benignly, immovably. To relieve the oppressive silence, Fred began to talk.

As Carlyle listened, his eyes went watery with the gravity of the crisis; yet his remarks were gracefully light, even casual. "Well, Freddy—if I could see you with the woman, I might say, 'What the hell, go to it,' " he pronounced at one point in his reedy voice, and at another point he likened the sexual drive to an automobile, volunteering of himself, "I know it's in there, in the garage, just raring to be revved up."

Though Carlyle seemed, if anything, to advise that Fred follow his heart ("My doc keeps telling me we only live once"), and with his noncommittal calmness did relieve his brother-in-law's agitation and guilt, Fred was left with the impression that it would be absurd of him to leave the children and Betsy and the share of the Emmet Corporation her lawyers would demand. Would Carlyle, if he ever *did* see him with the other woman, be enough impressed? Was not erotic passion in truth as mechanical as an internal-combustion engine? Perhaps, in giving him reason to talk of her to Carlyle, to brag, as it were, to the older, taller, stronger man of his conquest, the other woman had served much of her purpose. Looking back, years later, Fred wondered if the sisters hadn't known more than they seemed to, and hadn't urged Carlyle to come and have this brotherly consultation, there in the empty Chatham house sticky with salt air.

* * *

The marriages, and the families, went on. So many outings, to build up their children's childhood—beaches, mountains, shopping malls, Disney World. So much shared sunshine. Why, then, did Fred's scattered memories of Carlyle tend to be shadowy? One Christmastime in Brookline, Fred, responding to a ruthless battering sound from below, went into his cellar and discovered his brother-in-law, sinisterly half-lit by the fluorescent tubes above the workbench, pounding something glittering gripped in the vise. The other man's eyes, looking up and squinting with the change of focus, had that watery, warm—was it sheepish?—look they had worn that day of his wedding, as he came up the shady road beneath the hemlocks and birches. "Santa's workshop," he explained huskily. He hid with his body what he was doing. He looked demonic, or damned, in the flickering basement light. Fred backed up the stairs, as embarrassed as if he had surprised the other man undressed.

Betsy explained it to him later, in bed. To save money, Carlyle was making some of their Christmas presents this year—silver dollars drilled through and beaten into rings for the boys, and strung into necklaces for the girls. It was the sort of thing he used to do as a boy; he had been creative, artistic. It was sweet, Betsy thought.

To Fred, even this exercise in thrift savored of extravagance—silver dollars! "Are they that hard up?" he asked. "What's happened to all Carlyle's money?" He had always resented it that Carlyle had simply *had* money, whereas he had had to make it, a crumb at a time.

Well, according to what Betsy had gathered from Germaine, who out of loyalty of course didn't like to say much, six children in private schools and colleges aren't cheap, and the stock market had been off under Nixon, and Carlyle had trouble trimming his expensive tastes—the M.G. convertible, the English suits ordered tailor-made from London even though he rarely wore suits, the beach house in Malibu in addition to their seven-bedroom Mission-style home in Bel Air. The people he dealt with expected him to have these things.

"Who *does* he deal with?" Fred asked.

"*You* know," Betsy said, in the voice of one who didn't exactly know, either. "Movie people. He's involved in a movie now, Germaine did allow, that's just *sucking* the money out of him. He's in with this guy, Lanny somebody, who was supposed to make a low-budget blue movie with an adventure theme as well, so it would not just be for the triple-X theatres but could get into the softer-core drive-ins, but who without asking or telling Carlyle went and rented one of those sound stages that cost twenty-five thousand a day or something fantastic for these episodes that don't exactly tie in yet, since he doesn't have a real script, it's all in his head. He even bought an old frame house somewhere and burned it down for one scene. Germaine thinks Carlyle is being taken for a *hor*rible ride but is too proud to say anything. You remember all that buddy-buddy skiing and hunting he used to do?—those people used to take advantage of him, too. He has this old-fashioned sense of honor and can't defend himself. He gets caught up in a macho sort of thing. Furthermore, he likes being around these movie people, especially the little porno starlets. She wishes *you'd* talk to him."

"Me? What would I say?" Fred's stomach pinched, there in the dark. He was still afraid of Carlyle, slightly—those flat-lidded eyes, the way he could throw a ball that made your hands hurt.

"Just open the subject. Let him tell you how it is."

"The tried-and-true talking cure," he said bitterly. A decade later, he still missed the woman he had given up—dreamed of her, in amazing, all-but-forgotten detail. He would never love anyone that much again. He had come to see that the heart, like a rubber ball, loses bounce, and eventually goes dead. He did feel a faint pity, smelling his brother-in-law's pain in the house. There had been a physical deterioration as well as a financial. Carlyle's doctor had told him to take afternoon naps, and it seemed he was often upstairs, in a kind of hibernation, from which he would emerge red-eyed, wearing soft moccasins. To his counterculture clothes his health problems had added a macrobiotic diet, and the clothes hung loose on his reduced, big-boned frame.

One day between Christmas and New Year's, when all the others had gone ice-skating on the Brookline Reservoir, Fred walked into the kitchen, where Carlyle was heating water for a cup of herbal tea, and asked, "How's it going?"

The other man wore an embroidered green dashiki hanging loose outside dirty old painter pants. His hair had vanished on top, and he had let it grow long at the back; with the long graying wisps straggling at the nape of his neck, he seemed a dazed old woman, fussing at her broth. His bare arms looked white and chilly. Years in California had thinned his blood. Fred said, "If you'd like to borrow a sweater, I have plenty."

"Actually, I just turned up the thermostat." Carlyle looked over at him mischievously, knowing that thrifty Fred would resent this, and continued his aggressive tack. "Everything's going great," he said. "Life's all *samsara*, Freddy. The Terwilliger girls may have been stirring you up about this particular film project I have in the works, but, like they say, no sweat. It's money in the bank. When you bring your gang out this summer, we should have a rough print to show you."

"That would be nice," Fred said. To be brotherly, he was wearing the ring Carlyle had given him; its roughly pounded edges scratched his skin, and an inspection of the basement had disclosed that a number of his drill bits, meant for wood and not silver alloy, had been ruinously dulled.

The film, when they saw it that June in L.A., also seemed crudely made. The young flesh, photographed in too hard a light, in rooms rented by the hour, had a repulsive sheen, a smooth falseness as of tinted and perfumed candles. The adventure parts of the film failed to link up. The burning house was on the screen only a few garish, orange seconds. Fred was struck by the actors' and actresses' voices, recorded with a curious flat echo that made him realize how filtered, how trained, the voices in real movies are. Carlyle's profile had been fascinating in the dark, the screen's bright moments glittering in the corner of his eye. When the lights came on, his tender-skinned face was flushed. He said sheepishly to his in-laws, "Hope it wasn't too blue for you."

"Maybe not blue enough," Fred allowed himself to say. It was the nearest to a negative word he had ever dared, since that time on the Vineyard when Carlyle had laughed at his pipsqueak indignation.

Now it was his turn to be amused, when, at dinner afterwards, over Hawaiian drinks and Chinese food, while the wives held tensely silent, Carlyle hoped aloud that Fred would consider investing in the film, toward distribution and advertising costs, which were all that was left to get the package off the ground. One more boost and the movie would make everybody a bundle. He could offer eighteen-percent annual interest, just like MasterCard in reverse, or up to a quarter of the net profits, depending on how many hundred thousand Fred could see his way clear to invest. Plus, he promised, he would pay Fred's principal back right off the top, before he even paid himself. He knew Boston real estate had been going through the roof lately and Fred must be desperate for a little diversification.

Carlyle's mien, in the shadowy restaurant with its guttering hurricane lamps and pseudo-Polynesian idols, wasn't easy to read; his strained-sounding voice, almost inaudible, wheezed on doggedly, and a watery fixation glazed over the old glint—the guilty glance from the bottom of something—that Fred had caught or imagined on the hemlock-shaded road twenty-five years before.

Fred didn't laugh. He said he would think about it and talk it over with Betsy. Naturally, she had a stake in all his business decisions and was always consulted. In private he asked her, "How important is it to you as a sister, if this would bail Germaine out?"

She said, "It isn't, and I don't think it would anyway."

Fred felt contaminated by the other man's naked plea, and could hardly wait until he got away, safely back to his own coast. He was too cowardly to turn Carlyle down himself. He left it to the Terwilliger sisters, Betsy to Germaine via long-distance telephone, to pass him the word: No way. Fred Emmet, too, could give a brotherly lesson in limits.

When Carlyle Saughterfield, less than a decade after his failed film had emptied his pockets, died, it was in a movie theatre. The girl next to him—not a date; they had just been introduced—noticed him at one point softly thumping his own chest, and when the lights went up the tall man was slumped as if asleep. Impassive. Wearing a green dashiki, and not much older than his father had been.

Germaine and he, some years before, had gotten divorced, and Fred and Betsy, too, as the Terwilliger sisters continued their lives in parallel. Betsy had never really forgiven him for the insult of that old affair. Germaine, a week after Betsy had phoned Fred with the stunning news, called him herself to invite him to a pagan ceremony, a scattering of Carlyle's ashes in a tidal creek north of Boston where the dead man used to sail and swim as a boy.

This scattering had been his idea, as was Fred's being invited. Germaine said, "He loved you," which sounded right, since families teach us how love exists in a realm above liking or disliking, coexisting with indifference, rivalry, and even antipathy. What with his health troubles, ominous family history, and nothing much else to do, Carlyle had done a lot of thinking about his own death: from beyond the grave, it appeared, he was trying to arrange one more group photo. The children were adult and dispersed, most on the coasts but one in Chicago and another in New Mexico. A ragged group gathered on an appointed wooden bridge, on a February day so clear it did not feel cold.

Fred dipped his hand into the box of calcium bits that had been Carlyle's big bones and, imitating the others, carefully dropped them over the rough, green-painted rail. He had imagined that the tide would carry these fragments called ashes toward the sea, but in fact they sank, like chips of shell, tugged but not floated by the pellucid ebbing water. Sinking, doing a slow twirling dance, they caught the light. Two of Fred's nieces— young women in defiant bloom, with ruddy faces and blond hair and pale eyes flat across the top—beamed at him forgivingly, knowingly. The sunshine seemed a lesson being administered, a universal moral; it glinted off of everyone's protein strands of hair and wool hats and sweaters and chilly nailed hands and the splintered green boards of the bridge and the clustered, drifting, turning little fragments in the icy sky-blue tide. In this instant of illumination all those old photographs and those old conglomerate times Carlyle had insisted upon were revealed to Fred as priceless—treasure, stored up against the winter that had arrived.

Conjunction

GEOFFREY PARRISH, approaching sixty, had long enjoyed an uneasy relationship with the stars. In childhood, when we assume the world to have been elaborately arrayed for our own benefit, with a virtual eternity allowed for inspection of its many large and mysterious parts, he had taken the stars, like the clouds overhead, for granted. His mother knew the Big Dipper, and Orion, and on a summer evening might point out, in a voice of unaccountable excitement, Venus—a white shining puncture in the blue that was deepening above the gory sunset. For a moment or two at night, he might become aware, as a skater is suddenly aware of the dark water he skims across, of the speckled heavens, a dust of distant worlds, between the massy silhouettes of the black treetops. But in his back yard, where such revelations would find him, he was generally intent upon catching fireflies or feeling the throb of his breath and heartbeat as he ran, late for his bedtime, toward the tall lit windows of the house.

Wynken, Blynken, and Nod, illustrated by Vernon Grant, had been one of the big thin books, smelling like the oilcloth on the kitchen table, that his mother would read to him at bedtime, and somehow it seemed to be taking place among the stars:

> The little stars were the herring fish
> That lived in that beautiful sea. . . .

46

The image upset him, conveying a seethe of activity
that went on without him, all night:

> All night long their nets they threw
> To the stars in the twinkling foam. . . .

Wynken and Blynken turned out to be his, the listener's,
two little eyes, and Nod his little head. It was a hideous
thought, like two eggs and a cabbage bouncing around
in this glimmering soup, and in merciful escape from
the unthinkable he let himself be lulled by his mother's
enclosing voice as it read aloud, in a grave voice sweet-
ened by the approach of the end:

> So shut your eyes while mother sings
> Of wonderful sights that be,
> And you shall see the beautiful things
> As you rock in the misty sea. . . .

High school and college brought him word of what
the stars really were, how senselessly large and distant
and numerous, but such intellectual shocks were cush-
ioned by the distractions of co-education—the female
bodies with their supple heft, their powdered and perfumed auras, their fuzzy sweaters and silken blouses,
and the glimpses, at the edges, of elastic underwear.
Why do girls wear skirts, with their strange nether
openness and vulnerability, while boys get to wear trousers? And why do girls like to talk so much, and what
do they say to each other all the time? Such questions,
and courtship, and marriage, eclipsed the stars, which
yet seemed to hang waiting for Geoffrey to get to know
them. One summer, while renting a seaside place with a
long deck, he had purchased a pocket guide to the heavens and (with difficulty, for the blazing points strewn
across the black dome overhead made a poor match
with the little diagrams picked out by dying flashlight)

taught himself the summer triangle of bright stars, Deneb and Altair and Vega, and a few prominent constellations—Andromeda's flying V, and cruciform Cygnus, and boxy little Lyra, and Cepheus, shaped like a house in a child's drawing.

In these decipherings—the planks of the deck rough beneath his bare feet, the shingled house alive with lights and the voices of his wife and children talking to one another—Parrish felt united with ancient generations. Man no sooner had attained erect posture than he began to try to unriddle the stars, to name them after gods and animals, and then to construct huge rings and pyramids of stone as if to demonstrate a placatory harmony with the cycles of the heavenly machine. Who was the first man—a creature scarcely more than ape— who realized that the frozen spatter above turned through the night like an off-center disc? And who were those wakeful wise men who first noticed the planets, the wanderers keeping their own slow looping paths across the surface of this disc? The stars were the fathers of speculation, of philosophy. Under Parrish's gaze, as if he were suspended by his heels above an abysmal bowl, the stars seemed to sing, to scream in chorus. In actuality, he heard lonely sounds from the deck—the sea breaking on a distant beach, a bell buoy rocking outside the harbor, crickets droning in the dry grass. He would become dizzy, staring up. His neck would begin to hurt. His patience and his sense of spatial relations were limited, and, having satisfied himself with a few chronic identifications, or having, out of the corner of his eye, seemed to see a meteor fall, he would leave the deck to go back into the house, into the womanly warmth, the electric light.

And then the summer was over, the heavens mostly unlearned, and a new season of constellations sent to bewilder the eyes. Decades went by in which his acquaintance with the stars failed to advance. He read about them now and then in the newspapers—eclipses, meteor showers, astronomical discoveries of gigantic vacancies in the web of galaxies and of a mysterious apparent arc millions of light-years in length. Scanning the comic strips one day, while his wife tried to make breakfast conversation, he noticed a small article, with an illustration, stating that Jupiter and Mars were to undergo, this winter, a rare conjunction.

That evening, in spite of the cold, he took the torn-out illustration into his side yard, and there, above treetops that by coincidence closely matched the schematic ones in the drawing, shone the conjunction just as diagrammed—Jupiter bright and bluish, Mars smaller and red-tinged, a bit lower and to the right. He had studied the stars but not knowingly looked at a planet since the summer evenings, a half-century ago—could it be that long?—when his mother would dramatically gesture toward Venus. As he gazed, the stars surrounding the two conjoined planets swarmed into his vision, more and more of them as he looked, as if he were film in a developing pan; but he had no trouble finding the two planets again, their close pairing distinctive as a signature. The redness of Mars was lodged in its twinkle, a perhaps hallucinatory spark, whereas Jupiter's blue glow appeared cool and steady. Parrish's eyesight had deteriorated over the years. Without his glasses, near things blurred and far ones looked double. He needed a telescope. He began by suggesting to his wife that she might want to get him one for Christmas.

"Why don't you get it for yourself?" Berenice asked.

"I might get the wrong kind."

"You're as much an expert as I am," he told her. "It's

like everything else—you go by the money. The more it costs, the better it probably is."

"It would feel like a test you're setting me. I'd be scared to get any except the most expensive, and then you'll say I spent too much money."

He wondered if this were just. True, everything she did lately seemed to him slightly excessive or insufficient, a bit too determined and rigid or else irritatingly casual and heedless; yet he imagined his irritation to be invisible within the vast context of their decades together, their children and now grandchildren, their ever-expanding, circumambient troth. They had met at college and married in a wave of passion; she was still a junior and he a poor graduate student. Aeons later, it turned out that she had resented truncating her education and sitting home mired in pregnancy and motherhood while he paraded off in a business suit to a glamorous world of credit-card lunches and smartly dressed young female lackeys. Well, he could not help feeling in response, he didn't make the world, and he didn't ask to be born a male, with a male's responsibilities and prerogatives. Their children grew and went away, their automobiles became foreign and expensive, their houses increased in price and suburban remove, and at the center of all this centrifugal movement the cinder of her resentment remained, paired with his resentment of her resentment. He had laid his life at her feet, and all she cared about was gender politics.

She went on, "Everybody says how financially timid women are, the ones who aren't extravagant, but look at the figures: your firm charges two hundred dollars an hour for your time and mine is absolutely worthless; I have to go give it away in volunteer work."

"Or else stay in bed," he said, "while I'm having a great time fighting the tunnel traffic."

* * *

Parrish bought himself the telescope, wrapping it and putting it beneath the tree with a card saying "Love, Berenice." The children and the grandchildren were impressed, and greedily took turns with it spying on their neighbors' windows and bringing closer the distant skyscrapers of Boston. But in fact it was not a very expensive telescope; his wife's uncertainties over the proper price to pay had infected him and made him cautious. Also, the very expensive ones looked too complicated. What he wanted was a tube that he would look into at one end and that would deliver reality, enlarged, at the other. This was not as easy as he had hoped. His own tremor jiggled the image, and the plastic eyepiece clicked against his glasses. A boat far from shore, a mere hyphen in the gray water, would reveal, in sudden focus, amazing detail—railings, and a pilothouse that needed paint, and a man in a watch cap and dark slicker standing on the forward deck within an eerie windless silence, an eerie ignorance of being seen. There was a bubble around things thus captured, a hermetic breathlessness and a pressure that squeezed the perspective flat.

On a clear night early in the new year, Parrish took the tripod and the telescope outdoors, and set it up on the snowy driveway, and aimed it at the conjunction. Through even this weak telescope the stars multiplied confusingly; Mars and Jupiter, though obvious to his naked eye, took a lot of calibrated groping to center in the lens. Tremors, not just his own but those of invisible events within the transparent atmosphere, beset the planets. Mars, at the maximum enlargement, remained disappointing—no canals, no red deserts, no polar icecaps, not even the impression of a sphere. Just a stubborn small hole, spitting red, in space. But Jupiter, that big smear of pallor nearby, did, unmistakably, thrillingly, resolve into a disc, a world calling out with its solemn white roundness across the deeps of space. He could not make out the churning stripes or the big oblong spot so vivid in Voyager photographs, but there *was* something unexpected—off to the side, four bright dots in a curving line, a kind of plume lifted upward, to the left. Could these be the famous moons, whose observation by Galileo marked the end of Ptolemaic astronomy? Parrish would not have expected them to extend so far out from the body of the mother globe, or to be so distinct, and organized in so smooth an arc. When he lifted his head and looked with the naked eye, Jupiter was still there but they were gone; when he peered again through the telescope, they had returned, in their unexpected pattern and vividness—a small school of the herring fish that lived in that beautiful sea.

His face and fingers and feet ached with the cold; tears in his eyes now added to the difficulties of vision. He took his equipment back into the house, keen to share the triumph of discovery; but his wife had already drifted into sleep. Though he did not again trouble to set up the telescope outdoors, all winter he would glance toward that section of sky he had explored, and watch twinkling red Mars slowly climb level with coolly glowing Jupiter and then imperceptibly, inexorably pull away, as if tracing some movement of titanic gears. The gap between them, once less than the moon's breadth, opened as the smaller planet ascended, yet Parrish had no trouble keeping track of these specks of light. He had worn a small comfortable place in the spangled void where his gaze could rest as he stepped from the car, home from a party, a meeting, a trip.

He and Berenice had the habit, as spring approached, of travelling to a warm island for several weeks, to reward themselves for having endured another New England winter; even though now she was afraid of skin cancer, and stayed in their cabaña while he went to the beach, they still made the trip, with its flavor of honeymoon. The tropical stars were different—the few constellations he knew sprawled crazily at one side of the sky, distended by their new relation to the horizon. Yet the air was familiar, the humid fraught air of summer. Sitting after dinner on the hotel terrace while a steel band played beneath the stars, Parrish suddenly again saw, as if an inner telescope had zoomed, his wife and himself, before they married, on the flat pebbled roof of the Cambridge row house where he had lived as a graduate student. Rules had been numerous in that dark age, and she had come to him illegally, lying to her housemother so that she could spend the night. The sudden May heat was so great in his airless room they took blankets up to the pebbled roof, close to the stars, which their luminous bodies seemed to join; the spine of the galaxy bent above them like an immense torn pale rainbow. Wherever his eyes travelled on her body, splendor glimmered.

He asked Berenice to dance.

"To this music? We don't know how."

"You just shuffle, from the look of it."

"Let the young people do it, Geoff. Don't put me to the test."

The test? Her face, white on the dim starlit terrace, while the black band poured forth its practiced jubilation, did not look old to him, but somehow closed, too firmly knit, as if her life, her life with him, were a wound that had nearly healed at last. Behind her, the warm dark sea, struck by the light of a full moon, seemed to lift in a bulge toward the other heavenly body's cold brightness.

Back home, where the snow had all melted, Parrish stepped from the car and glanced toward the sky, and could find neither Mars nor Jupiter. They had parted and lost themselves among the less wandering stars. He could not believe it, and searched for minutes. His wife had taken the keys and gone into the house, turning on the switches, filling window after window with artificial light. Conscious of his breath, conscious of his heart-beat, he followed her in.

The Journey to the Dead

LIVING ALONE after nearly thirty married years, Martin Fredericks was beset with occasional importunities. A college friend of his former wife's—a jaunty, sturdy comp.-lit. major named Arlene Quint—telephoned him one early-spring day and asked him to drive her to the hospital. He wasn't sure he understood. "Now?"

"Pretty soon, yeah, if you could." The plea in her voice was braced by something firm and ceremonious he remembered from college days. "I thought, you have that little car parked out behind your building, and in this city when you call a taxi it takes hours and then they drive like maniacs. I need to be driven gently."

"You do?"

"Yes, Marty," she said. "None of your sudden stops and starts."

They had recently remet, after many years, at a party in an artist's loft a few blocks away in town; she was less surprised to see him than he her, since she had been in touch with his former wife, Harriet, and knew he had moved in from the suburbs. She, too, lived in town now. She and Sherman Quint—a chem. major—had been divorced for several years. She loved being in the city, and free, Arlene told Fredericks. She looked sallow, and her pulled-back black hair had gone gray in strange distinct bands, but she seemed much as he remembered her, solid and energetic, with a certain air of benign defiance. Like his former wife, she had been a collegiate artsy type, in a pony tail and peasant skirt. Now, still pony-tailed, she sat up on a table swinging her plump legs in sheer happiness, it seemed, at being alive and single and here.

The table was a heavy harvest table that the artist, a small goateed man, worked on; it was peppered with thumbtack holes and covered with accidents of ink and paint. At Arlene's back hung tacked-up charcoal sketches of idealized male nudes. At her side, space fell away through a big steel-mullioned industrial window onto the lights of the city, amber and platinum and blurred dabs of neon red, stretching far away; the city was not New York but Boston, and nothing in this direction looked higher than their own windows, the streets and brick rows streaming beneath them like the lights of an airport during takeoff. Her happiness glowed through her not quite healthy skin and her legs kept kicking friskily—the drumstick-shaped calves, the little round-toed Capezio flats. Those shoes dated her; Frederick's former wife, too, had worn ballerina shoes in all weathers, in rain or snow, as if life at any moment might become a dance.

The crowd at this party seemed young—young would-be artists with ugly punk haircuts, shaved above the ears and tinted in pastel tufts, boys and girls alike, wearing baggy sweaters and getting louder and shriller as they sipped wine from cheap plastic glasses. One boy took a flexible stack of these glasses and pretended to play it like an accordion. Their host's voice, nasal and gleeful, cut through the noise. Only the host, and his Japanese boy friend, seemed close to Fredericks's age, and though this troubled him the youthfulness of the gathering seemed to add to Arlene's happiness, her aimless, kicking happiness like that of a little girl perched up on a high wall. "Hey. I think I'll, as they say, split," he said at last to her, in slight parody of her own eager assimilation to this youthful scene. "Want to be walked home?"

Her eyes abruptly focused on him. Shadows beneath them betrayed fatigue. "Oh no, Marty, it's much too early!" Her voice came out high and as if from far away. Her lips were slow to close back over her teeth, which protruded a bit and were stained like a smoker's, though she no longer smoked. "You're sweet, but I can walk alone. This section of town is quite safe."

He was glad to be rejected; he was involved with another woman and had made the offer in a truly protective spirit, and as an obscure gesture toward his former wife. Because the two girls had been close, a taboo as of incest had come between him and Arlene in college; it was strange to feel that taboo lifted, and a queasy freedom fallen over them all, relatively late in life. Freedom—that was what her plump kicking legs expressed. But Americans are oversold on freedom, Fredericks thought, and availability does not equal attractiveness. There was a glaze of unhealth on Arlene, and she had grown thick around the middle.

When he described the encounter to Harriet over the phone, she told him that Arlene had had a cancer scare but the chemotherapy seemed to have worked. The disease figured in his mind as another reason to let Arlene alone. She was taken. It slowly ebbed from his mind that she lived a half-mile away, working part-time in an art-supplies store near the local university, until this sudden phone call.

It was late afternoon, becoming evening. The downtown skyscrapers visible from his window were broken into great blocks of shadow and orange glare as the sun sank over the Fens. By the time he had made his way to his automobile—a decrepit Karmann-Ghia convertible, its left fender dented, its canvas top slashed one night by a thief looking for drugs or an expensive radio—it was dark enough to use his headlights. Irritated and flattered, he inched through the rush-hour traffic to the address Arlene had given him.

She was standing in the vestibule of her building, and came out carrying a little suitcase, walking very carefully, with short slow steps. When he jackknifed awkwardly up out of the car and moved around it to take her bag, she lifted a hand in alarm, as if fearful he would bump against her. She wore a loose heavy cloth coat, but, even so, he could see that her shape was not right—her middle was not just thick but swollen. The street lights didn't help her color; her face looked greenish, waxy, with hollows like thumb-marks in wax beneath her eyes. She smiled at the intensity of his inspection. Arlene, whose mother's parents had emigrated from Macedonia, had a certain stiff old-world mannerliness, and Fredericks sensed her determination to make this mannerliness see them through. Though his car, double-parked, forced the street's two lanes of traffic to squeeze into one, with some indignant honking, he made his own movements as unhurried as hers, and set the suitcase in the back seat as gently as if it contained her pain.

She slammed the door on her side but remained a bit hunched forward, her profile silhouetted against the side window, beneath the slashed and taped canvas: her sharp high-bridged nose, her lips' prim set over her slightly protuberant teeth. He asked, before easing in the clutch, "O.K.?"

"Just fine," she said, in a voice surprising in its normality. "You're sweet to do this, Marty."

"Not at all. Which hospital?"

She named one a mile away. The rush hour was at its worst, as darkness deepened, and there were many stops and starts. She rested a hand on the dashboard at one point, as if to brace herself, then abandoned the posture, as perhaps more uncomfortable than it was worth. The car was rusty and old and gave a jerky ride however delicately he shifted. "Sorry," he said, more than once.

"You're doing fine," she said, almost condescendingly.

He couldn't believe a taxi wouldn't have been better. It was as if she had decided to accept, now, his rejected invitation to see her home. "Sorry the car's cold; the heater should come on any minute."

"I don't feel the cold."

"Is your—is this, ah, a sudden thing?"

"It's been coming on."

"They know at the hospital you're coming?"

"Oh yes. They do."

"Is it going to be a long stay?"

"That's up to them. My assignment is to deliver the body."

The body. "I'm sorry," he said.

"About what, Marty?" They had broken free of the traffic for a block and were gliding along smoothly, between four-story bowfronts, beneath trees that in a month would have leaves.

"That your body's, uh, acting up."

The glide ended; a cross street, a principal artery, was jammed solid. "I expect it will all be all right," Arlene said, after a second of tense silence in which she saw that the stop was not going to be jarring. Her voice had the false, light tempo of someone issuing reassurances to a child.

"I do hope so," Fredericks said, feeling foolish and puny relative to the immense motions, the revolutions of mortality, taking place inside her, next to him in the shuddering, cold, slashed cave of the car.

She said, more conversationally, "You adjust. You come to terms with it."

"Really?"

"Oh yes," Arlene said simply, as if he were in on the secret now—as if he and she were now on the same side of the mystery growing within her. But he couldn't imagine death's having a human size, finite enough to come to terms with. The car heater was producing heat at last, as the hospital's lights came into sight. She directed him to a curved side street that became a ramp. As he gently pulled up at the entrance, Fredericks had the impression of bustling all-hours brightness that an airport gives, or a railroad terminal in the old days—a constant grand liveliness of comings and goings.

He said, scrambling to extricate himself from behind the wheel, "Let me get the door for you."

"I can manage." She popped the door latch and was standing at the side of the car when he came around for the suitcase. She had that waistless stiff look women of the Balkans have, in their layered peasant outfits. She was reverting. Her face was turned toward the light pouring through the glass doors of the hospital lobby.

"Shall I walk you in?"

"No." The answer was so abrupt she tried to soften it. "You can't park here. I can manage." Hearing the repetition, she insisted on it: "I want to manage. I've chosen to be on my own." She looked at him quickly, with a suspicious slide of her eyes, and gave him her gracious, buck-toothed, matter-of-fact smile. "Thanks, Marty. That was a nice ride."

"Do you want visitors?"

"I'll have plenty, thanks. All those children we had for some reason."

"Call me up when you're done and I can come for you."

Her lips slowly closed over her teeth. "I should be up to a taxi by then." There was no offer of a pecked kiss goodbye, though he would have been careful not to bump against her. But if her own body was betraying her, Fredericks thought, why should she trust him? She passed through the glass doors and did not look back. From behind, she seemed, with her little suitcase and bulky coat, an immigrant, just arrived.

Arlene was not the first dying woman his own age that Fredericks had known. In the suburb where he and Harriet had lived together, a mutual friend, the merriest wife in their circle, had a breast removed in her early forties. For years, that seemed to have solved the problem; then she raucously confided to them, outside the doors of the local supermarket, "The damn stuff's come back!" The last time they saw her, it was at a small barbecue lunch that all the guests tacitly knew, though none would admit aloud, to be a farewell to their hostess.

On that summer Sunday, as Fredericks and his wife in their car pulled into the property, a new green hose, stretched to reach a flower bed, lay across the asphalt driveway, and he braked. Their hostess, in a sun hat and gaudy muu-muu, was standing on her lawn and vigorously waving him forward onto a section of grass set aside for parking. Hesitantly he eased the car—a Volvo station wagon, which felt stiff as a truck to drive—forward into the spot she was marking, fearful his foot might slip and his front bumper strike this woman already stricken by disease.

He got out and kissed her on her upturned face, which in illness had become round and shiny, and explained that he hadn't wanted to run over the hose. "Ach, the hose!" she exclaimed with startling guttural force and a sweeping, humorous gesture. "Phooey to the hose!"

Nevertheless, Fredericks went back and moved the hose so the next car would not run over it, at the same time trying to imagine how these appurtenances to our daily living, as patiently treasured and stored and coiled and repaired as if their usefulness were eternal, must look to someone whose death is imminent. The hose. The flowers. The abandoned trowel whose canary-yellow handle winks within weeds in the phlox border. The grass itself, and the sun and sky and trees like massive scuffed-up stage flats—phooey to them. Their value was about to undergo a revision so vast and crushing Fredericks could not imagine it. Certainly he could not imagine it in relation to the merry presence who entertained them, sitting with her guests on the screened porch while her husband cooked at the grill outside, in a cloud of gnats. As a concession to her debility she lay on an aluminum chaise longue, her feet in thick wool slipper-socks though the day was warm, and still wearing her sun hat, perhaps to hide her chemotherapy-blasted hair. The party, as the guests drank wine, became ever more relaxed and hilarious, the hostess urging the conversation into mundane channels—local zoning problems, and movies they had seen. She elaborated so feelingly on the horrors of a proposed condominium development that they forgot she would not be there to see it or to contend with the parking problems it would pose. When another woman objected that all the movies seemed to be about—with emphasis—*sleaze*, the dying woman quickly joked, "*Gesundheit!*" and then, merrily, added, "I love sleaze. Sleaze," she said, "is truth. Sleaze," she went on, excited to a crescendo by the laughter surrounding her, "shall set us free!"

A season later, attending her funeral, trying to picture her moving somewhere from strength to strength as the service claimed, Fredericks wondered that none of them that afternoon had been able to find a topic more elevated, more affectionately valedictory, than condominiums and sleazy movies, and wondered where that garden hose of which he had been so solicitous now lay coiled.

The dying, he marvelled, do not seem to inhabit a world much different from ours. His elderly neighbors in this suburb plucked with rakes at the leaves on their lawn, walked their old lame dogs, and talked of this winter's scheduled trip to Florida as if in death's very gateway there was nothing to do but keep living, living in the same old rut. They gossiped, they pottered, they watched television. No radical insights heightened their conversation, though Fredericks listened expectantly. In college he had been a classics major, and dimly recalled the section of *The Odyssey* in which the dead stare mutely at Odysseus, unable to speak until they have drunk of the sheep's blood with which the hero has filled, by Circe's prescription, a pit a cubit square and a cubit deep. The hero's own mother, Anticleia, crouches wordless and distraught until he allows her to drink "the storm-dark blood." The dead in Homer feel themselves inferior, even—in the T. E. Lawrence translation—silly. Dead Achilles tauntingly asks Odysseus, "How will you find some madder adventure to cap this coming down alive to Hades among the silly dead, the worn-out mockeries of men?" And Aeneas, in Virgil's Avernus, cannot elicit a word from angry Dido, who listens to his entreaties and apologies with fixed eyes and a countenance of stone, and who flees still hating him—*inimica*—back to the shadowy groves where Sychaeus, her former husband, responds to her cares and equals her love— *inimica refugit / in nemus umbriferum coniunx ubi pristinus illi / respondet curis aequatque Sychaeus amorem.* Virgil's version of the underworld becomes implausibly detailed, with the future of Rome set forth at length by Anchises, and various rings and compartments all laid out as if in anticipation of Dante's defin-itive mapping. Whereas Gilgamesh, an older journeyer still, found only, as far as the broken tablets of his tale can be deciphered, confusion and evasion at the end of his passionate quest: "Sorrow has come into my belly. I fear death; I roam over the hills. I will seize the road; quickly I will go to the house of Utnapishtim, offspring of Ubaratutu. . . ."

Utnapishtim answers Gilgamesh in broken clay, "Since there is no . . . There is no word of advice . . . From the beginning there is no permanence. . . . As for death, its time is hidden. The time of life is shown plain."

Fredericks was shy about calling Arlene, lest it seem to be a kind of courtship. Yet in decency he should ask, after their perilous ride together, how she was doing. For several weeks, her phone didn't answer; then, one day, it was picked up. "Oh," she responded, with a thoughtful, chiming, lazy lilt to her voice which seemed new, "not bad. There are good days and bad days. They have me on a mixture of things, and for a while there the mix was all wrong. But it's settled down now. I feel pretty good, Marty."

"You're home now," he said, as if to fix a fact in this flux of unimaginable therapy. The wandering drugged sound of her voice awakened firmness in his. "Are you going to work, too?"

"Yesterday, which was so sunny, I trotted over to the art store, and they were happy to see me, but I'm really not ready yet to be on my feet all day. Some afternoon next week is my goal. You learn to set goals."

"Yes." His firmness seemed to miscarry—a punch at empty air. "Well, take things a day at a time."

There was a pause. "I don't mind visitors," she said. He thought of the artist's loft and that noisy crowd and how happy she had been to be among them, and felt spiteful. If they were all so great, where were they now? "Well, I could come by some day," he said. "If it wouldn't tire you out."

"Oh no, Marty," she said. "It would be cheery."

Fredericks felt uncomfortably obliged to set a time, late one afternoon, after his own work. He did not feel, in this single interim of his life, quite free—the woman he was involved with was possessive of his time, and kept watch on it. His life seemed destined to be never wholly his own. By his choice, of course. Arlene had told him, *I've chosen to be on my own.*

At the hour when he drove to Arlene's address, cars were leaving the streets to return to the suburbs, and he had no trouble finding an empty space at a meter. Every day, the sunlight clung to the city a few minutes longer. Her house was a bowfront brownstone, handsomer than his brick tenement, and faced not the downtown's little knot of skyscrapers but a strip of old-fashioned park, part of the Fens, with iron lamp standards and a stone footbridge arched over a marshy creek dotted with beer cans and snow-white Styrofoam takeout boxes. A wide-spreading beech tree whose roots drank at the edge of the creek was coming into bud. *The time of life is shown plain.*

Arlene greeted him at the elevator, unexpectedly, so that he nearly bumped into her. As he kissed her cheek, she stayed hunched over, so it was awkward to plant his lips. Her cheek felt dry and a bit too warm.

She was wearing a kind of navy-blue running suit, and looked much thinner. The sallow skin of her face had tightened, and her eyes—a surprising light brown, a flecked candy color—peered out of their deepened sockets suspiciously, around a phantom corner. Hunched and shuffling her feet, she led him toward the front room and its view of the park. From her windows he could see through the budding beech a diagonal path and, in the middle distance, an iron bandstand. Her apartment was on a higher floor than his own, though not so high as the artist's loft, and abundantly furnished with surprisingly expensive furniture: loot from her marriage, he thought. She let Fredericks make himself a drink while she lay on a brocaded sofa, with her feet up, and sipped Perrier water. "What a *lovely* place," he said, and then feared that his emphasis betrayed his assumption that she lived shabbily, in bohemian style.

"I missed it those weeks I was away. My plants were so happy to see me. A cyclamen died, though I had asked the super's wife to come in twice a week and water."

"Has Harriet ever been here?"

"Oh yes—a number of times. She likes it. She says she hates being stuck out there in that big rambling place of yours. I mean, that the two of you had."

"The children aren't quite flown. And if she moves into town, too, we'll have an overpopulation problem."

"Oh, Marty, you know she never will. Harriet needs all that showy country space. She needs animals."

The conversation began to excite him. He sat in a chair so unexpectedly soft he nearly spilled his drink. From the low angle, Arlene's front windows were full of sky, sky only, with white spring clouds set close as flagstones and hurrying thus close-packed in a direction that made the room itself seem to be travelling, smoothly pulling its walls and furniture and late-afternoon shadows backward, toward the past, toward the time when they were all in college and young and freshly acquainted, and the elms weren't blighted and cars were enormous and the Army-McCarthy hearings fascinatingly droned over the radio into the spring afternoons when they should have been studying Chaucer. And then later, still keeping in touch, Arlene and

Sherman and Harriet and Martin shared the astounding feat of making babies—creating new people, citizens, out of nothing but their own bodies—and the scarcely less marvellous accomplishments of owning houses, and tending them, and having friends who were sometimes wicked, and giving cocktail parties. Though they lived in different towns, in different circles, they had occasionally entertained each other. The Quints had installed a pool, and Fredericks remembered Sunday cookouts on the patchy lawn where the recent excavation had left scars, beneath a sky marred by charcoal smoke and the lazy *bop-pop* of tennis drifting in from their neighbor's clay court. The sun of youth dappled their reminiscences, as Arlene stiffly adjusted her legs on the sofa from time to time and Fredericks sank lower into the chair and into alcoholic benignity, and the sky with its travelling clouds sank into evening blue. Arlene's voice had a high distant quality as if she were reading words from a card held almost out of eyesight. "Harriet took a shine to our minister," she said, Fredericks having recalled the cookouts.

"She did?" Though he had become adept at receiving the signals women sent out, he had never thought of Harriet as sending out any.

Arlene laughed, on a high thin prolonged note, and then her lips closed slowly over her prominent teeth. She said, "Reverend Propper—not that he *was* so proper, it turned out. He was a Unitarian, of course. Harriet even in college liked that kind of boy—a *serious* boy. You weren't *serious* enough for her, Marty."

"She did? I wasn't?" He blamed himself for their breakup, and was pleasantly startled to hear that the rejection hadn't been all on his side.

"Not really. She adored idealists. Union leaders and renegade priests and Erik Erikson—these healer types. That's what drew her to Sherm, before she discovered he was just one more chem. nerd. I guess we didn't have the word 'nerd' then, did we?"

"I had forgotten that she went out with him for a little while."

"A *lit*tle while! The whole sophomore year. That's how I met him, through her."

"Did I know that?"

"You must have, Marty. She used to say she loved the way his hair was going thin even in college. She thought that was a sign of seriousness. It showed his brain was working to save mankind. All those soc.-rel. majors wanted to save the world."

He had even forgotten that Harriet had majored in social relations—not forgotten, exactly, but not had the fact brought back to life. There had been a time, in those Fifties, when sociology, combining psychology, anthropology, history, and statistics, seemed likely to save the world from those shaggy old beasts tribalism and religion. Harriet had been, with her pearly shy smile and pony tail and tatty tennis sneakers, an apostle of light, in those unfocused pre-protest days. "I hadn't realized that she and Sherm had been that serious."

"*Serious*. You said it. He never smiled, unless you told him something was a joke. God, it was good to get away at last. It was *such* bliss, Marty—and yet there really was almost nothing to complain of about the man."

He didn't want to talk about Sherman. "Did you ever notice," he asked, "how white Harriet's teeth were?"

"I *did*. She knew it, too. She used to tell me I was staining my teeth with my cigarettes. Maybe I should have listened. Nobody believed in cancer in those days."

The word was especially shocking, coming from her. He said, "But it isn't your lungs . . ."

"Oh, it's all related, don't you think?" Arlene said breezily. "And probably basically psychosomatic. I was too happy, being out from under Sherm. My body couldn't handle my happiness. It freaked out."

Fredericks laughed, trying to push up out of his soft, unresisting chair. "Remember how they used to tell us smoking stunted your growth? Listen, Arlene, I must run. Somebody's expecting me to check in. This has been lovely, though. Maybe I could swing by again."

"Please do," the woman said, squinting off as if to read an especially distant prompt card. "I'll be here."

But sometimes when he called she was absent—at the art-supplies store, perhaps, or visiting her children, who were adult, and living within a fifty-mile radius. Or else she was too sick to answer the phone. She had ups and downs, but the trend seemed down. Perhaps he saw her six or seven times in the course of the summer; each time, there was something of the initial enchantment— the day changing tone through the big windows, her thin and distant but agile voice evoking those old days, those Fifties and early Sixties when you moved toward your life with an unstressed freedom no one could understand, now, who had not been young then. There was less outside to that world—less money, fewer cars and people and buildings—and more inside, more blood and hopefulness. Nothing, really, had cost much, relative to now, and nothing, not love or politics, was half so hyped as now. There was a look, of Capezios in the slush, that summed up for Fredericks a careless and unpremeditated something, a bland grace, from those years. There were names he had all but forgotten, until Arlene would casually mention them. "And then Brett Helmerich, the section man in Chaucer, he was another Harriet had her eye on. . . ."

"She did? Brett . . . Helmerich. Wait. I *do* remember him. Leather elbow patches, and always wore a long red muffler wrapped a couple times around his neck, and a red nose like Punch's, sort of."

She softly nodded, looking off in her far-gazing way, her jaundiced face half in window light. Her feet, in thick, striped athletic socks, rested on a pillow, her knees up. Her ankles and wrists and face had been swollen at one phase of her body's struggles with its invader, and then her frame had subsided toward emaciation. She moved more and more stiffly, hunched over. While he drank whiskey or gin, she sipped at a cup of tea so weak as to be mere water turning tepid. But her mention of Brett Helmerich would conjure up the vanished throngs that once stampeded in and out of the Chaucer lectures, given by a wall-eyed professor who over the decades of teaching this course had become more and more medieval, more gruff and scatological and visionary. "You really think she had her eye on Brett? But he was ten years older than we were, with a wife and babies."

"Other people's babies aren't very real to you, until you've had some of your own. Or wives, even, until you've been one. Even then . . . Ex-wives are the worst, the way they hang on to the men's heads."

Arlene on the subject of Harriet fascinated Fredericks, as if his former wife could be displayed to him in a whole new light—resurrected, as it were, by a fresh perspective. She who had seemed to him so shy and sexually clumsy in fact had juggled a number of relationships and flirtations in those college years, and in the years of their young marriage had not been entirely preoccupied by him and their dear babies. Fredericks asked, "There really was something between her and Reverend Propper?"

Arlene's mouth opened wide but her laugh was inaudible, like a bat's cry. "Oh, I don't know if it ever got to the physical stage, but didn't you ever wonder why she would drive twenty-five miles each way to sing in our little off-key choir?"

"I thought it was because of her friendship for you—it gave her a chance to keep in touch with you."

"She kept in touch with me when it suited her," Arlene said, and sipped her weak cold tea, and made a small thrusting gesture with her lips as if to register an unquenchable dryness of mouth. "And still does."

"Harriet's in touch?"

"She calls. Often enough."

"Often enough for what?"

"To hear about you."

"Me? No!"

"Yes."

"But she's so happily remarried."

"I suppose. But a woman is like a spider, Marty. She has her web. She likes to feel the different threads vibrate."

Her phone rang, on the table a few feet from her head, but Arlene let it ring until, at last, the ringing stopped. He wondered how often he had been the person on the other end, assuming she was out or too sick to reach for the phone. Several times when she did answer, her voice croaked and dragged, and he knew that he had pulled her from a narcotic sleep. He would apologize and offer to call again, but she would say it was *cheery* to hear from him, and her voice would slowly clear into animation.

Just before Labor Day, though, she answered on the ring when he had been about to hang up, and he could hear her gasp for breath after each phrase. The medicine she had been taking had "gone crazy." Two days ago her daughter had driven in from a far suburb and gotten her to the hospital just in time. "Scary." Arlene had never before mentioned fear to Fredericks. He asked her if she would like him to swing around for a quick visit.

She said, almost scoldingly, "Marty, I just can't do Harriet for you today. I'm too tired and full of pills. I'm worn out."

Do Harriet? Hanging up, he marvelled that that was what he had been having her do. Harriet when young, and that whole vast kingdom of the dead, including himself when young. His face felt hot with embarrassment, and a certain anger at Arlene's rebuff and its tone. It was not as if he had nothing else to do but pay sick calls.

It was Harriet who told him, over the phone, that Arlene had had a stroke and was in the hospital.

"For good?"

"It looks like for that."

"Have you seen her?"

"Once. I should go in more, but . . ." She didn't need to explain; he understood. She lived too far away, the living are busier than the dying, it was scary.

He, too, did not want to visit Arlene in the hospital; her apartment—its air of shadowy expectant luxury, like a theatre where a performance was arranged for him— had been one of the attractions. But Harriet urged him to go, "for the both of us," and so he found himself making his way out of a great damp concrete edifice full of inclined ramps and parked cars. He rode down in an elevator whose interior was painted red, and followed yellow arrows through murky corridors of cement and tile. Emerging briefly aboveground, he recognized that curved stretch of side street to which, six months ago, Arlene had guided his Karmann-Ghia. The car since then had fallen apart, its body so rusted he could see the asphalt skimming by beneath his feet, but the cavernous hospital lobby still radiated its look of sanitary furor, of well-lit comings and goings, of immigrants arriving on a bustling shore.

Fredericks pushed through the glass doors, made inquiries, and tried to follow directions. He threaded his way through corridors milling with pale spectres—white-clad nurses in thick-soled shoes, doctors with cotton lab coats flapping, unconscious patients pushed on gurneys like boats with IV poles for masts, stricken visitors clinging to one other in family clumps and looking lost and pasty in the harsh fluorescent light. *There beset me ten thousand seely ghosts, crying inhumanly.* Though the hospital was twelve stories tall, it all felt underground, mazelike. He passed flower shops, stores stocking magazines and candy and droll get-well cards, a cafeteria entrance, endless numbered doors, and several sighing, clanking elevator banks. He entered an elevator, and was crushed against his fellow-passengers by the entry, at the next floor, of a person in a wheelchair, a shrivelled man with a tube in his nose, pushed by an obese orderly. On the eleventh floor, stepping into a bewildering confusion of desks, he asked for Arlene. He was told a number and pointed in a direction.

The door was ajar. He pushed it open lightly, and saw first an empty bed and a big metal-framed window overlooking the city from a height even greater than that of the artist's loft many months ago. But the prospect was dominated by a great ugly iron bridge spotted with red rustproofing paint and crawling with cars.

She was around the edge of the door, sitting in a chair by the bed. Her close-cut hair seemed mostly white, and a catastrophe had overtaken her face: one side of it, eyelid and mouth-corner, had been pulled sharply down. Her Macedonian eyes burned at him from within a startled, stony fury. She could not speak. The stroke had taken away her nimble power of speech. In her lap and scattered on the bed were a number of children's books and some handmade cards each holding a letter of the alphabet.

Fredericks understood. She was trying to learn to read, to express herself. Her children—parents, now, with children of their own—had lovingly made the alphabet cards, and provided the books. He understood all this but he could not speak, either. His tongue froze after a few words, much too loud, of greeting, and when she held up some of the letters as if to indicate words, he could not make out what she was spelling.

Frantically he tried to make conversation for them both. "Harriet told me you were here. I'm so sorry. It must be—it must be hard. When will you be getting out? You have a terrific view."

In an attempt to respond to his question—he blushed at his own stupidity in asking a question she must try to answer—she pointed at the clock on her bedside table, and then shuffled the cards in her lap, looking for one she could not find. She held one up the wrong way around, and then with a grimace on the side of her mouth that was not dead she flipped it away. He remembered the gesture. *Phooey.*

In a virtual panic, blushing and stammering, he talked inanely, finding, when he reached into himself for a subject that he and Arlene had in common, only the hospital itself, its complexity and strangeness to him, and the grim comedy of being crushed in the elevator by the wheelchair and the pushing fat man. "We all could have been squeezed to death. One girl had a cardboard tray full of coffee cups and had to hold it up toward the ceiling." He imitated the heroic, Statue of Liberty–like pose, and then lowered his arm, shamed by the shining unblinking fury of Arlene's eyes, one eye half shut. The dead hate us, and we hate the dead. *I went pale with fear, lest awful Persephone send me from Hades the Gorgon's head, that fabulous horror.* Standing, he felt some liquid otherworldly element spill from him rapidly, cooling the skin of his legs. "I'm afraid I have to, as they say, split." Fredericks wondered if she would remember his saying that long ago, with faint sarcasm, and try to smile. Arlene unsmilingly stared. *None of your sudden stops and starts.* He promised, insincerely, to come again, and, like heroes before him, fled.

The Man Who Became a Soprano

ALL THINGS have a beginning and an end. The recorder group began in the domestic warmth of the Weisses' marriage, a model marriage of dark and light, firmness and delicacy, shining on top of their little hill as if for all the town to see. Andrea was a slightly skinny blonde with ironed-looking long straight hair both before and after such hair was the fashion, and pale-blue eyes that developed pink lids when she was tired or emotionally stimulated. Fritz was a dark, almost heavy man with wide hairy-backed hands that, like his tenacious scientist's mind, took up everything in a grip of steel. From a musical family of physicists, he had played the bass recorder since childhood, having been trained in this instrument to round out a quartet consisting of his father (tenor), mother (soprano), and sister (alto). But the bass was a doleful mumbly instrument played alone, and for their seventh anniversary he bought Andrea a quality soprano recorder, of dark-striped pale pearwood—a Moeck. Slowly, obediently, she learned to play it, her hesitant piping echoing through the boxy bare rooms of their white, clapboarded house—rooms rather underfurnished, their friends thought, with an austere mix of glass tables and Danish modern (Fritz's taste) and imitation-Shaker chairs and handwoven wool rugs (Andrea's). She owned a loom as big as a small room, and spent afternoons at it, before the three children (girl, boy, girl) came home from school. There was a shy and stubborn expertise to all she did, though on the soprano recorder she tended to panic at any note higher than the G at the top of the staff, and when a trill involved moving more than one finger on the stops, she fluttered off into blushing silence. When she blushed, her cheeks suddenly matched the tint of her lids and lips, and the rose color sank into her throat and the décolletage of her peasant blouse.

There is little music arranged for the bass and the soprano in duet, though some of the Bach fugues build to a certain passion without the middle voices. The Weisses' three children, some nights, would be kept awake as the couple moved the theme back and forth, from low to high to low, and at intervals beat time in silence, or held harmonic whole notes, while the absent instruments possessed the melody. The sounds carried beyond the house. Another couple, the Bridgetons, had moved to town, and lived along the beach road at the base of the Weisses' hill, close enough to hear them these spring nights, now that the storm windows were off. In the crowded high-school corridor as they waited to be checked in at the May town meeting, Terry Bridgeton mentioned the music to Fritz (they knew each other by sight, from the train platform and Little League games) and said how lovely it sounded from afar. Terry allowed that he was a musical ignoramus but his wife, Jessie, was a kind of marvel; she could play anything— piano, guitar, church organ, even the clarinet when she was a girl.

Fritz told him, "The recorder is the easiest instrument in the world to learn, next to the triangle and the tambourine. And I suppose the maracas." There was a German pedantry to Fritz.

"Well," Terry said, blushing with his own effrontery,

or from the heat of the high-school hall, "we could both try to learn, if you'd tell us what instruments to get."

"Alto and tenor," Fritz said, firmly, then, suspecting he had allowed himself to get in too deep, added, "Of course, you and your wife may not take to the instruments."

Jessie, an olive-skinned, short, plumpish, eagerly smiling woman in bangs, somewhat alarmingly clad in a fringed shawl and a tangle of gold and turquoise pendants, spoke up behind them. "Oh, we'll take to them. We're desperate to do *some*thing and meet some *peo*ple."

It was high summer before the Bridgetons, having put themselves to school with Mario Duschenes's *Method for the Recorder* and Marguerite Dubbé's *First Recorder Book*, dared present themselves to the Weisses one agreed-upon evening; Andrea had suggested they come for dessert and coffee and then "give it a try." The newborn quartet was able to make its way, with many halts and restarts, through a Bach fugue without flats and sharps, several Corelli gigues, and the first sheet of a Byrd fantasia before the clock struck ten and it was time for cigarettes and beer and a social exchange. After their immersion in music, a warmth remained. The two couples had more in common than their relaxed costumes—Terry was an artist in an ad agency, and dressed after work in frayed jeans and logo'd T-shirts. But, though they promised to meet again, and again, it was uncomfortable—somehow too naked. Each player, alone on his or her part, was embarrassed whenever he or she became lost and the whole quartet had to stagger to a halt. Musical Jessie, confidently warbling on her alto, rarely slipped and tried to keep the tempo up, and Fritz in his steely way persevered on the bass, which made so low and indistinct a noise that it scarcely mattered if he was in time with the others or not. But Terry,

as he had admitted, was a musical novice, and sometimes intently went along measure after measure on his
tenor without realizing that he was a beat behind and
generating dissonance on every chord. Andrea, though
more practiced than he, was almost too sensitive to play
the soprano, which by virtue of its pitch had to carry the
melody, and yet whose high notes she heard as painfully
shrill, a wet strained squeaking she preferred to put out
of its misery, lowering her recorder to her lap and en-
folding it with her long, pale, pink-knuckled hands.
Terry loved her in those moments, grateful that someone else was causing the quartet to founder. They had
become the clumsy children, and their spouses the for-
midable parents.

The group needed more players; and, magically,
more did appear, like dewdrops on a spider web. Carolyn Homer, a tall auburn-haired woman who held aer-
obics classes in the parish hall of the Congregational
church, turned out to have taught herself the recorder
while enrolled, years ago, in a course at the New England Conservatory in Renaissance music; she brought
a well-exercised alto instrument, the color worn from
its mouthpiece and finger-holes, to the group. Dick
McHoagland, the squat and scowling leader of the local high-school band (and the typing instructor as
well), brought a tenor instrument; he and Fritz, both
being martinets, hit it off well and played side by side,
leaving Terry next to the alto section. Both Dick and
Carolyn were married, to unmusical spouses, but the
town was rich in divorcées and men on the loose, and
now these began to adhere. Alice Arsenault, a nervous
little rounded thing who for some reason had been
married to Skip Arsenault, an uproarious town fireman,
former athlete, and hard drinker, showed up one night
in Carolyn's shadow with a soprano recorder and an
earnestly annotated copy of the Trapp Family Singers'

instruction manual. Maury Sutherland, a stooping, sexually undecided country gentleman (whom Terry had
always supposed, from the way he tilted his head and
spoke in cautious fragmented sentences, to be hard of
hearing), produced from his inherited treasures an alto
recorder acquired by his great-aunt Esther—on the Je-
kyll side—while sightseeing in Austria and northern Italy before the First World War. "Do tell," he would say
in response to a lengthy disquisition, with an expression of amiable bafflement. "Beats me."

This made three altos, and soon there were three
sopranos, since somehow in Maury's orbit there materialized, one bitterly cold night just before Christmas, a
vivid woman newly escaped from Boston, propelled
into this far suburb by the repulsive force of the
crack-up of her long-term relationship with an anchor-
person whose handsome ochre visage was known from
Provincetown to Pittsfield, from Salisbury to South
Dartmouth. Toula Jaxon, as she presently called herself,
had emerged with a cathode-ray glow from her discon-
tinued relationship—a luminosity that made the men of
the group stare and the women squint. She was a study
in high contrast; her white forehead flashed between her
eyebrows and hairline, her eyes were black lights encir-
cled by ink, even the parting in her blue-black hair
seemed incandescent. Her lips and fingernails were
painted in slashes of purple. Her clothes, though she
tried to tone them down as the sessions ensued through
the drab winter, were city-slick—tight skirts well above
the knee, and rippling silk blouses, and Hermès scarves
swirled at the throat. As if colorized, she jarred among
the earth-tones of the suburban women, and although
there was something chastened and shyly willing to
please about her social manner, she played the recorder
the way she looked—loud and too expressive. Much
defter than one would have thought possible from the

length of her fingernails, Toula had no fear of high fast
notes; her flair, mounted between Andrea's perfectionist
reserve and Alice's novice awkwardness, seemed all too
displayed. Her recorder, a stylish artifact of high-density
plastic produced in Japan, didn't sound like the other
instruments and glistened above their resonant merge
like oil making its rainbows on water.

In the alto section, tweedy Maury Sutherland did indeed prove to be hard of hearing, or blunderingly insen-
sitive, for his alto, fed out of his large male lungs,
arrhythmically overpowered the instruments of the two
females; Jessie had to sit next to him, since Carolyn
from the start assumed the position of priority, next to
the sopranos. Terry, glancing over past Maury, saw an
expression of suppressed wincing on his wife's usually
cheerful face, with its long bangs and gypsy complexion. In the privacy of their home Jessie almost wept.
"He just *blows*," she complained, "every note, as loud
as he can. Tonight, on the little Purcell, I *very* tactfully
pointed out to him all the pianissimos and diminuendos,
and he nodded, that obtuse handsome way he has of
nodding, and then when the time came blasted away as
if he was pouring buckshot into some poor trembling
quail. And on top of everything else he's a disgusting
racist fascist!" During the beer and cigarettes tonight
they had discussed politics; these after-sessions, as they
all got to know each other, were getting longer and
longer, so that sometimes they broke up not short of
midnight, even though the recorder playing always
ended on the stroke of ten, as chimed by the clock in
the hall—a tall case clock of walnut and pine, with a
pewter face, that Terry associated with Andrea's half of
the furnishings, and that he loved for having her quiet
elegance and soft severity.

"Darling," he said to Jessie, of Maury, "he's just a

small-town conservative—a good old boy, Yankee-style."

She looked at him warily; ever since meeting at a Seabrook sit-in, they had always been in perfect political agreement. Now Terry found her, he was implying, priggishly liberal. And he had noticed that as they all played together he could distinguish the three sopranos—iridescently warbling Toula, fumbling Alice, and Andrea dropping away on the high notes, receding and vanishing into her seductive distance—and even hear Carolyn steadfastly keeping the alto beat amid Maury's oblivious wandering, but he could never quite hear Jessie, his own wife, playing. He could see her lips prehensile on the fipple, her slightly protruding chocolate-colored eyes intent on the sheet music, her slightly thick coarse eyebrows arched in concentration, her stubby-nailed, practical fingers twitching on the stops, and not hear her. The effect was mysterious but not unpleasant. Caught between Maury's alto and Dick McHoagland's onrolling tenor, Terry felt inaudible himself. However, it was comforting to know that he could lose his place and Dick would march on; and when a third tenor joined them, a divorced accountant named Jim Keel, with a port-wine stain on the side of his face that Terry couldn't see, Terry felt his own notes blending into an ecstatic whole, a kind of blessed nonexistence such as Buddhists talk about.

For what bliss, when all is said and done, and after its musical inadequacies are all confessed, the recorder group was! Arrival was bliss, especially on winter nights when it had been a slippery battle to get the car up the Weisses' snowy driveway, and an exciting uncertainty obtained whether or not one could get safely down at midnight. Scarves, mittens, down vests piled up on the Shaker settee in the front hall; boots accumulated under it. Cold fingers unfolded the steel music stands and assembled the wooden flutes. Cork joints were rubbed with a dainty ointment kept in cannisters smaller than pillboxes; chilled mouthpieces were tenderly warmed, held in an armpit or against open lips. In a bliss of anticipation the players would settle into the arranged arc of dining-room chairs, while the Weisses' wood stove cracklingly digested another log in its belly and the black night pressed on the frost-feathered panes and the footsteps of the Weisses' three children scurried overhead, on the other side of the ceiling. Preliminarily, there were scales and little abortive riffs, impudent snatches of jazz tune and hymn picked out by ear; then, when all were in place, a fidgety cough, the crushing of a last cigarette, a nervous giggle, and a premature toot. Finally, at Fritz's firmly whispered "*One*, two, three, four," there was a unified intake of breath and the astounding manifestation, the mellow exclamatory blended upwelling, of the first note. They were off, stumbling, weaving, squinting, blowing, tapping time with feet no two of which tapped alike.

If you looked (and Terry, often lost and dropped out, did look), some feet kept time just by flexing the big toe (Carolyn, who wore sandals to minimize her height, favored this method), some by snapping the ankle sideways (gangly Jim Keel, right under Terry's left eye), and some by stoutly, thumpingly bouncing the heel (Maury, and also, in her insecurity, Alice). During the universal rests that came in some dramatic codas, you could hear tapping feet like a shuffling of soldiers breaking stride across a bridge.

Rarely they made it to the end of a piece without falling apart and collapsing, as Toula, Carolyn, Fritz, and Dick, the last to give up, fluttered on for another stubborn, show-offy few measures. With Jim Keel's arrival that second winter, they had become ten in number, and unwieldy; yet no one seemed disposed to drop out or even to miss a single evening. They met even though the day's news had brought disasters (a Beirut massacre, the Challenger blow-up); they met during the seventh game of a Red Sox World Series, whose progress the men periodically checked on a television set chattering to itself in the kitchen. Once they convened on the fringes of a hurricane called Gayle; her winds stripped leaves from trees and lifted doghouses while the group generated its own breeze this side of the shuddering windows. Andrea, cleaning up afterwards, complained to Fritz of the fortnightly intrusion: "It's become a brawl, and the beer and potato chips cost us twenty dollars every time."

"Perhaps we could say different people should be the host. The group should rotate."

"That'll make it even more of a social brawl. I know *just* when the music stopped being the point. When Maury brought Toula, without even asking any of us first!"

"But Toula's the only one of you sopranos willing to attack the high notes. If she'd just get rid of that futuristic Japanese piece of plastic—"

"No. It's not that. She plays everything like a solo. I don't feel I can *grow*, as long as she's there, doing everything so flashily. And you love her. All the men love her."

"*Liebchen.* Don't cry. Recorders were meant to be *fun.*"

"They're *not* fun and never were. They're your attempt to make me something I'm not. I've never been an aural person, I've always been visual. You know that."

He was abashed, by an unexpected emotion that seemed less a matter of cause and effect than of a simultaneous wave and particle, a single photon passing through two slits at once. "You didn't have to try to learn to play," he said.

"How could I *not*?" Andrea cried. "It was such a lovely anniversary present. So *visually* lovely. The sweet little phallic shape of it, and the stripes of the pearwood grain."

Judging the curve of her tears to have peaked, Fritz's mind slid off on a practical track. "I've been thinking," he said, "the sessions might go better if somebody could stand up to lead. The tempo tends to drag. Sometimes by the end of a piece it feels like the Doppler effect, we've all slowed down so."

"You *can't* stand up to lead. You're the only bass."

"Maybe we could convert another player to the bass."

Andrea stared at her husband with narrowed blue eyes; her eyelids were pink. "Who?"

Fritz shrugged. "Toula might enjoy the challenge."

Her eyelids flared open. "Darling!" she exclaimed. "You're brilliant! Get her away from me!"

By the third winter, they were rotating houses and had acquired a leader—a barrel-shaped little spinster, Miss Eleanor Hart, whom Carolyn knew from the Congregational church. Also, Toula acquired a bass. She said, with her brave brightness, "It will suit me better, at this low time of my life," and was undaunted by either the change of clef, from G to F, or the change of fingering system, from C to F. She took the chair next to Fritz, leaving him on the end in his traditional position of leadership, and separating Fritz and Dick. Miss Hart, scarcely five feet tall and quite waistless, and dolled up in lace-trimmed layers of velvet, would lift her stubby arms and the chattering row of players would grow silent; a curt clenched hand—she conducted with her fists—would descend, and that first marvellous upwelling note would be born, and another, and then many overlapping others. She kept a clear beat and seemed curiously engaged, like a mother with secret plans for her children. She had taught the piano for decades and for a mysterious period long ago had lived in Cairo—perhaps, Terry speculated one evening over beer after she had gone, as a member of King Farouk's harem. "What does she see in us?" he asked aloud.

"An evening out," said Andrea, after a silence. Terry had noticed that she often seemed the only one in the group listening to him. "Anything's better than sitting home," she added, she who had always seemed so ideally domestic. "Most people, when you come down to it, are lonely."

Miss Hart always left after one drink of diet cherry Coke, a lone stray can of which the Weisses had found in the back of the refrigerator when she refused beer, the first time she came to lead them. This became, then, her drink, and as the group rotated from house to house each host or hostess went to the trouble of buying a six-pack of diet cherry Coke, of which only one can was drunk until Miss Hart came round again, in four months, and drank another.

Toula's brilliance was suitably muffled in the bass section, though she had found an eccentric instrument of bleached mahogany with aluminum fittings. She and Fritz became a musical pair; their hands in synchrony roamed the length of the romantic instruments, and with identical vigorous gestures, between numbers, they shook the spit from their tubular curved mouthpieces. Without Toula, Andrea and Alice did not quite blossom, however; their timidity of attack truncated, as it were, the rising climaxes that Bach and Pachelbel had so methodically arranged, and drained some of the Renaissance dances of lilt and verve. And now that they had a leader—an authority figure, a focus for their arc of chairs—a restless chemistry possessed the group. As it met in one house after another (even Jim Keel played host when his turn came, in his bachelor condo on the river, with its purple shag rug, triangular kitchenette, and bedroom that his surprisingly ambitious bed, a four-poster, entirely filled) the old chair arrangements seemed no longer sacred. Dick McHoagland, his he-man, can-do solidarity with Fritz broken by Toula's appearing at their end of the arc, moved around Terry and Jim in the tenor section (leaving Jim next to Toula, on the side with his port-wine stain) to sit next to Carolyn, who in an answering move had jumped over Jessie and Maury, rendering Jessie even less audible to Terry and her pained expression even richer in accumulating grievance against male afflatus.

"I can't *stand* it another night," she told Terry in the privacy of their home. "Every time he blasts in my ear I think of his position on the Contras and I could scream."

"He wouldn't hurt a fly, really," Terry said, ostensibly by way of comfort but really to irritate her, to provoke her to greater, more alienating fury.

"*Pfou,*" she said, expelling smoke; she had taken up smoking again, claiming she was becoming too fat without it. "He has this complacent image of himself as a New England gentleman but in fact he's a lowbrow klutz who if he hadn't been born with money would have no idea how to make it. He can't even talk in complete sentences. 'That so?' he says, and 'Do tell?' The whole recorder group irritates me, in fact. Everybody's gotten silly and full of secrets, somehow."

"What's *your* secret?" Terry innocently asked.

"I just told you. I don't like anybody."

"Not even me?"

"Less and less," Jessie rather surprisingly confessed, bringing tears to her eyes and a twinkle of gratification to his.

He drew her closer to him on the sofa where they had been talking. "Tell you what," he said, letting his voice, *largo*, deepen and resonate. "I'll give you my tenor. Come join the boys."

"You'll swap for my alto?" she asked. "There're already too many, with Maury playing loud enough for two."

"Carolyn has the alto part under control, and anyway I'm not musical enough to go from a C-instrument to an F-one. I've been thinking of becoming a soprano. They need rescuing."

From within his accustomed arms Jessie looked up askance out of her slightly protuberant chocolate eyes, from beneath her long bangs and thick brows, and asked, perhaps innocently, "You sure you're up to it?"

Terry bought himself not a Moeck but, less expensively, an Adler, a smooth small instrument that felt in his hands like his tenor transposed to a daintier scale. It responded much more readily to his breath, with what seemed a certain excitement, especially when he set his nail in the thumb-hole and attacked a note above G, where Andrea tended to give out, and shy Alice never aspired. He became a specialist in high notes. The secret was to pinch the thumb-hole truly small, as if closing it with the back of the thumbnail, and to blow into the mouthpiece quickly and sharply, like checking when skiing on ice. Hit it, and ski on. Don't panic or look too far ahead. It also helped to pronounce *tu* instead of *du* into the mouthpiece, and to think of your mouth as tiny and dry. The high A was easy, involving only two closed finger-holes, and the B not too bad, since to these two the right hand merely added two more, and the C possible, subtracting merely one, but the high D, using four fingers spaced apart, was a note he had never struck to his own satisfaction. Nor had he ever seen it called for in a piece of recorder music.

Alice or Andrea would turn to him afterwards and say, "You're wonderful." "Wonderful" was not in their leader's vocabulary, but when the treble part began to move above the staff Miss Hart's neckless, many-chinned head turned with a touching expectancy toward the end of the arc where Terry sat, on the extreme right, and in the lower left corner of his vision he could see Andrea's blurred white hands docilely lower to her lap. Only a maestro could have hit the high notes softly, so Terry's single instrument had volume enough for these dizzying moments when he strained alone at the top of the scale. For all his androgynous name and diffident slouching slenderness, there was a sharp passion in him, which the high notes now expressed. As they rang in the drum of his skull his senses were besieged by the shine of Andrea's fair hair in the side of his vision, the scent of her shampoo and bath gel in his nostrils, the rustle of her sheet music and scuffle of her feet in his ears. In the summer, that third summer after the summer of the group's beginning, he was aware of the scent of her sun-tan lotion, of the salt and chlorine dried in her hair, of an ice-creamy, cottony, dusty essence of summer rising from her, even of the musk from between her legs. Perhaps her musk was on his fingers as they twiddled on the stops; by August he and she had become lovers, and sometimes on the day of a recorder session would have met at a beach or motel halfway to Boston, in a storm of bodily fluids, including tears. But long before her surrender he had felt her body beside him like an immense word on the verge of being spoken, while they played in unison or whisperingly compared trill fingerings. When they went to bed together the first time, she instinctively lay on his left, and he on her right. Ever since he had taken up the soprano, he had felt her peripheral presence pull at him like a vacuum. Men and women in need distort the space around them, and Terry near Andrea in any circumstance, even at a May town meeting or accidentally met in the gourmet section of the supermarket on Saturday with their children in tow, felt marvellously enlarged—his voice resonant, his aura extended as if in a wavy mirror.

Nor was theirs the only warping within the group. The spectacular and able Toula, shining among them like an electronic wraith, had imperceptibly turned from Fritz, whose hairy, metallic nature did indeed have something repulsive about it, to the vividly stained face on her other side; both she and Jim Keel were excessively vivid, out of sync, singled out. And Jessie, guilty Terry observed, now that Carolyn had abandoned her to be next to Dick McHoagland (both of them married and doomed to respectability but nevertheless touching elbows and interpenetrated by their alto/tenor harmonies), was trying with a certain maternal breadth to suffer Maury's primitive political views during the beer-and-chitchat part of the evening, when his musical squalling had died down; she seemed to look upon him a bit tenderly, her wounded dark eyes shining, as on some rough beast who was nevertheless *there*, as Terry was never there for her any more. But Maury, deaf to this change of emotional tune, was tipping his big, primly combed head with old-fashioned gallantry to catch what soft-voiced little Alice Arsenault, beaten and abandoned by one of the town's agents of protective order, was shyly offering to say. "Do tell? That so?" They were all trying to listen to one another. It seemed to Terry—inflamed by love and distress as his psyche was—that they were making music even without the recorders and in their interaction catching at something splendid, just as individual notes, bare of nuance, in combination gain meaning and mount to an expression of otherwise inexpressible completeness and resolve. He hated to go home and face the tired babysitter, and the poor children lying sprawled in the muss of sleep, and Jessie in her ghastly aggrieved silence.

Whichever house they played in now, the trees at the windows were blood and brass; New England's autumnal climax swelled and faded. Miss Hart was excited and proud; the Golden Agers of her church had invited the group to give a Christmas concert. They must do it, they all agreed in furtive phone conversations; she had been so kind. Andrea and Jessie, Terry and Fritz had stopped speaking but communicated through others. The affair, which had burned through to common knowledge, cast over their rehearsals a pall of which only their stout leader was oblivious; her stubby arms lifted again and again in a flurry of yellowed lace as the group repeatedly flubbed the difficult time-change into 9/8 and then 6/4 toward the end of "The Leaves Be Green." Adson's "Courtly Masquing Ayres" had two soprano parts, and Alice was in a panic over holding down the second descant line by herself while the lovers clung to the same part. Her former husband, the fireman and athlete, was paying her ardent attentions again and had expressed nothing but blazing scorn for the recorder group and its snobs like Maury Sutherland; drunk, Skip Arsenault once with a contemptuous laugh tossed her instrument into the fireplace, and the acrid taste of char wouldn't leave the fipple. Every time she put it in her mouth, Alice felt a sexual shudder of ambivalence.

Toula was moving back to the city, where Jim was also thinking of getting an apartment, and they began to miss rehearsals. Maury went off on a two-week sailing trip to Bermuda, and Dick became preoccupied by the football season and the needs of marching bands. The

Weisses had considered themselves a perfect couple and held true to their perfectionism to the end. The idea that they were now flawed and must be divorced had been taken up by Fritz's mind in a grip of steel. No legal steps were to be initiated until after the concert. Since the other players were nervously shying away, the Weisses steadfastly hosted the meetings, as they had at the beginning. On these terminal evenings, before the other players arrived, Andrea would try, across the chaste space of their underfurnished living room, as Fritz fetched in the dining-room chairs, to punish herself by feeling some tenderness for her husband; but the very rigor with which he arranged the chairs in a mathematical arc, and the grim ironic courtesy he had shown her ever since the night when she had revealed her secret in a flood of tears, merely confirmed her in her bleak coldness. "Stop acting so righteous," she might blurt out, maddened by his calm. "You began it, enticing Toula into the basses. I was so insulted and upset, and you never noticed."

"That was a sound move," Fritz would insist. "It gave us much better balance."

"It meant Terry had to become a soprano, for everybody's good."

"He didn't at all. You could have carried the section if you'd tried."

"I did try," she said, "I *did*," happy to feel tears coming again—her eyelids were always pink these days—for their blinding action seemed to absolve her. On recorder evenings, Fritz always changed out of his professorial clothes into corduroy pants, the same cardigan sweater with elbow patches, and a pair of green espadrilles such as old European men wear; the sight of these espadrilles senilely shuffling on the striped carpet her young fingers had once woven seemed to absolve her further.

The concert consisted of the well-worn Byrd; two surefire Bach fugues; "My Robin Is to the Greenwood Gone" and "And Will He Not Come Again?" from Kenneth Meek's contemporary setting of Ophelia's songs; "Patourelles Joliettes" and "Je l'Ay, Je l'Ay la Gente Fleur," by Claude Le Jeune (1528–1601); three of the "ayres" by John Adson (b. ?, d. 1640); a bit of Bartók and Hindemith to wake the crowd up; and, perhaps ill-advisedly, some Purcell "Music to Dioclesian," chock-full of flats and dotted sixteenths. The program was too ambitious; Miss Hart flailed away at the spottily attended rehearsals sensing that the glue had gone out of her group but not knowing why. Jessie, catching a glimpse of, just beyond Alice, Andrea's pink-and-white profile next to her animatedly bobbing husband's, would find her lips trembling and her breath raw in her throat like vomit. Grimly Fritz clamped down on the stops and puffed wind into his metal mouthpiece as if pinching curses from the side of his mouth. By unspoken agreement, the Bridgetons would leave the Weisses' house early, before the beer, even before Miss Hart had downed her diet cherry Coke.

Yet the concert was a success. The elderly crowd in the Congregational church's parish hall didn't know what recorders were supposed to sound like, and accepted the dissonance and awry counterpoint as one more proof that music, like everything else in this world, has progressed. What they heard was what the group itself had heard on all those evenings of gathering: the sudden stunning beauty of the first note, blown through a little forest of wooden flutes. And the players, the men in gray suits and the women in formal dresses, looked so relatively young, so handsome and vital and pretty, and were so obliging to be here, under poor dear Eleanor's direction, that the applause thundered in. The group played all the encores it had prepared—"Drink to

Me Only with Thine Eyes," a saucy Handel bourrée, and, finally, "Silent Night."

Infected by the warmth of the audience, the ten members of the group joined their sweaty hands and bowed. In front of these old faces, and amid the crowd afterwards, they felt cherished as children are cherished, just for being themselves. Jessie gave Andrea, over by the bowl of pink punch, a curious hysterical kiss; neither had slept much last night. In their crisis Andrea had become skinnier and Jessie plumper. Terry felt hot and exhausted and exalted, on the eve of a new life. Nobody peeking in the tall parish-hall windows at the performers and listeners mingling in a steamy atmosphere of congratulation and relief beneath the mistletoe and red and green streamers would have guessed that the recorder group was dead.

Short Easter

FOGEL could not remember its ever happening before—
the advent of Daylight Saving Time clipping an hour off
Easter. Church bells rang in the dark; the pious would
be scrambling about in their topcoats and hats turning
the clocks ahead. All day, the reluctantly budding earth
would wear its crown of cloudy firmament a bit awry.
Easter had always struck Fogel as a holiday without real
punch, though there was, among the more vivid of his
childhood memories, a magical peep into a big sugar
egg; it had been at his aunt's house, in Connecticut,
where the houses seemed cleaner than in New Jersey,
the people wealthier, the daffodils a brighter yellow. Inside the egg, paper silhouettes spelled out a kind of
landscape—a thatch-roofed cottage, a rabbit wearing a
vest, a fringe of purple flowers, a receding path and paper mountains—all bathed in an unexpectedly brilliant
light. Where had the light come from? There must have
been a hole in the egg besides the one he peeped into,
a kind of skylight, admitting to this miniature world a
celestial illumination.

But, generally, the festivity that should attend the day
had fallen rather flat: quarrelsome and embarrassed
family church attendances, with nobody quite comfortable in pristine Easter clothes; melancholy egg hunts in
some muddy back yard, the smallest child confused and
victimized; headachy brunches where the champagne

punch tasted sour and conversation lagged. Perhaps if Fogel had not been led to live north of Boston, where at Eastertide croci and daffodils poked up through dead lawns like consciously brave thoughts and even forsythia was shy of blooming, nature might have encouraged the ostensible mood of hope and beginning again. But the day was usually raw, and today was no exception—a day of drizzle and chill, only an hour less of it.

Fogel was sixty-two, and felt retirement drawing closer. In the daily rub he discovered all sorts of fresh reasons for irritation. The line at the post office was held up by people buying money orders, and the line at the grocery store by people buying state lottery tickets. It seemed to him sheer willful obstructionism. Why didn't these people have checking accounts, and do their gambling on the stock market, as he did? Driving to work, on those days when he did not take the commuter train, Fogel resented being tailgated, and especially by young drivers, and very especially by young men in sunglasses, their identity further shielded by tinted windshields and newly fashionable opaque side windows. One morning, the car behind him, a low scarlet sports model, wore a kind of mask or muzzle of dark vinyl over its grille, and this ultra-chic, ultra-protective touch infuriated him, just as did cardboard sunshields in parked cars, and leather-ridged, fingertipless driving gloves, and fuzz-busters blatantly fastened above dashboards, and bumper stickers declaring SHIT HAPPENS or ironically commanding SUPPORT WILDLIFE—THROW A PARTY. The vinyl-faced car was frantic to pass, and nosed toward the right and, finding there an onrolling eighteen-wheeler, nosed back and swerved left, into a lane that in a few hundred yards terminated in a blinking yellow arrow. Fogel pressed on the accelerator, to keep abreast of the boy and hold him out in the doomed lane. Fogel smiled behind the wheel, picturing the other car's satisfying crash into the great arrow—the raucous grating of metal, the misty explosion of glass, and himself sailing serenely on in his middle lane. But the boy, getting the picture, cut in so sharply that Fogel had to brake or hit him; he chose to hit the brakes, and the youthful driver, steering one-handed, held up the middle finger of the other hand for Fogel to see as the red car, belching, pulled away.

If Fogel's stately Mercedes had been equipped with a button that annihilated other vehicles, he would have used it three or four times a mile. Almost every other automobile on the road—those that passed him, those so slow he had to pass them, those going just his speed and hanging in his side mirrors like pursuing furies— seemed a deliberate affront, restricting his freedom and being somehow *pretentious* about it. What was the point of that sinister Darth Vader–like mask over a grille? No point, just pure intimidation. Which was, he had come through sixty years to realize, the aim of eighty-five percent of all human behavior.

His body's accumulating failures also angered him. His eyelashes kept falling into his eyes, and the presbyopia of late middle age prevented him from seeing, in the mirror, his own eyes well enough to take the lashes out. A tantalizing refusal of focus, like the pressure of water that keeps us from seizing a tempting shell on the sandy bottom of six feet of crystalline sea, frustrated him, and when he put on his reading glasses he could see the dark curved foreign body but not get his fingers and the corner of a handkerchief in behind the lenses to remove it. So he would blink and grimace and curse and wish he had a young wife; his wife's vision was no better than his own, and dismissingly she said things like "It will work its way out" or "Maybe it just *feels*

like an eyelash." His mother, he could not help but remember, would deftly stab away with a folded piece of
toilet paper a fleck of dirt that was tormenting his sensitive cornea. But his mother, he realized now, at the
time had been half his present age, though she had
seemed ageless, enormous, and omnipotent.

Flying back from New York to Boston late one afternoon this past winter, he had sat across the aisle from a
young man and woman, both about thirty, who evidently had not known each other before taking seats
side by side. The man was a bit beefy, with a reddish-
blond mustache and thinning pale hair; the woman, all
but eclipsed from Fogel's angle, held a large cardboard
folder and seemed to be in a state of some excitement.
Her hands, gesturing and flickering in front of the oval
airplane window, appeared ringless and agitated. Her
voice, as she explained herself—the advertising agency
she was taking the folder to, her mixed feelings about
living in New York, her roommate's sayings and comi-
cal attitude toward life—did a penetrating dance, tireless and insistent, though her voice was high and light.
Perhaps she was less than thirty—just starting out, testing her powers. She talked incessantly but, as it were,
abashedly, throwing her words out in a feathery way, as
if to soften their impact. "Yeahhh?" she would add,
nonsensically, to a sentence, and she put on a soft quick
giggle, a captivating titter, a kind of shimmer of shyness
in which she wrapped her unrelenting verbal assault
upon her seatmate, who responded—how could he
not?—with ever more murmurous and authoritative re-
plies, concerning cities and work and all other areas
where he might be supposed to wield male expertise.
This man's chunky pale hands began to gesture, to chop
the air; he pompously crossed and recrossed his legs
and preeningly lifted his shoe, rotating the tip; his voice
grew gravelly and confiding as the feathery, ques-

tioning, giggling, excited voice of the other assaulted his ear and, unintentionally, Fogel's.

Fogel had been talked to, in the course of his life, by a woman in a voice exactly like this. It had been a bath, her voice, in which he grew weightless, an iridescent bubbly uplifting in which floated always a question, the lilting teasing female question, to which his maleness, clumsy and slow to comprehend though it was, was the only answer. He and this woman, Fogel further remembered, had come, twenty-some years ago, to an unhappy end, which had seemed tragic and hard to swallow at the time but which now, to this elderly man sitting above the clouds while the engines droned and the stewardesses struggled to distribute drinks and the girl across the aisle deliciously prattled and her naked hands flickered against the deepening darkness of the airplane window, appeared merely inevitable, since all things end. One small side-effect still rankled: their affair ended in the springtime, and his former mistress declined to invite him and his family to an Easter-egg hunt she and her husband annually gave. His children's feelings were hurt, and for consolation they were taken out, after church, to eat at the local International House of Pancakes. Heaps of pancakes, Fogel remembered—buckwheat, buttermilk, blueberry—that seemed, soaked in syrup, almost unswallowably sweet.

And yet, when the plane landed and the scramble to retrieve things from the overhead rack took over, Fogel forgot to look, as he had been intending, at the young woman, to check out her height, her hips, her face full on, her lovely long lively hands, to see if they were truly ringless. While his attention was elsewhere or nowhere she must have stood and brushed her backside past his and out of his life forever. She remained with him only as a voice, the perennial voice of flirtation.

* * *

Fogel's absent-mindedness was becoming alarming. On this strangely short Easter, as bells prodded the air in the town below the hill where he lived, he walked to his mailbox to retrieve the morning *Globe*, and his old gray-muzzled dog, a Labrador retriever, flushed the six or so mourning doves that gathered on a warm open slope, amid scrub brush, above the curving driveway. Every weekend morning, Saturday and Sunday, this happened, the dog ponderously charging forward and the mourning doves thrashing into the air with an abrupt whistle and merged beating of wings, and yet Fogel always forgot it would happen and was startled, so that his heart raced, his blood leaping like another dove. His heart would keep thumping as he walked back up the hill with the many-sectioned, pretentious, intimidating Sunday newspaper in his arms. The thumping felt dangerous, and he felt endangered when his wife, at breakfast, proposed that he help her with the spring raking. "We were unfor*giv*ably sloppy last fall," she said. "We left leaves under all the bushes and over by the rocks, and now they'll smother the new growth if we don't dig them out." She was a native of these Northern parts, and knew the ways of its weather. "You can't trust the lawn boys to do it; it was their stupid useless blower that put the leaves there in the first place. They didn't have these leafblowers when I was a girl; my father's gardeners *raked*."

Unlike those of the girl on the plane, this woman's powers were long established, and she felt no need to test them. She moved back and forth between kitchen island and sink, between sink and refrigerator and stove, with an insatiable silver-haired energy. As Fogel sat at the breakfast table with the newspaper, trying to remember which sections he had already read, he felt pushed from behind, tailgated. How did she know he hadn't, sentimentally, decided to go to church? "I'll never forget," she went on, "the year we went to Morocco and didn't get the leaves off the front beds until May and the poor tulips had all grown *inches* under the mulch—horrible, these pathetic white snaky stems growing sideways! Once the sun got to them they straightened up but all summer until they died back were shaped like the letter L. They all had elbows!" This monologue, he recognized, was a matured version, hardened into jagged edges and points that prodded and hurt, of the young woman's feathery, immersing discourse across the airplane aisle—a version of that female insistence upon getting male attention, a force as irresistible as the ability of freezing water to split rocks.

"I'm trying to read the paper," Fogel pointed out.

"I think it's grotesque, it's absolutely *dod*dery," she said, "the way you've taken to dawdling over the paper, even the real-estate section, even the cooking tips! It's a bad habit you've gotten into from killing time on the train. Nobody expects you to read *ev*erything—they just want you to glance at the ads."

"Isn't it rather cold and dismal outdoors?" he asked.

"No more so than it ever is this time of year. The longer we work, the warmer it will get. If you think about it, darling, the sun this time of year is as strong as an August sun, though it doesn't feel that way. Don't be a doddery dawdler; come *on*—one hour of good stiff yard work and then the Allisons' brunch and you can watch the football playoffs."

"They're over."

"Are they honestly? I thought they were endless."

"You were confused by the Hula Bowl. It's hockey and basketball now."

"How can you tell? It's all just ugly brutes bashing into each other. It's horrible, the way television has turned violence into a joke." She had suddenly left the kitchen.

Meekly, draggingly, Fogel followed. Pulling moist compacted oak leaves from underneath the forsythia and lilacs, careful not to let a budding twig poke his eye, Fogel was reminded of an Easter-egg hunt, and in his reverie, while his wife swooped back and forth with sheets of last year's leaves and bundles of brisk directives, his brooding mind warmed his old indignation at not having been invited to that party given by his then recently forsaken inamorata. She could have trusted him. He would have stood off to one side and been distant and discreet while his children hunted and his wife mixed it up socially. Insult was added to injury when, some months later, at a third family's house, he was shown home movies of the day—the scampering children, their faces in close-up smeared with chocolate and anxiety at not getting their share; the men in business suits and pastel shirts, standing on the brown lawn in little conferences of three or four, holding wine glasses and pâté-laden crackers; and the women, all in miniskirts in that era, swooping about after their children with brown paper bags and discarded sweaters. It was a familiar scene, year after year, except that this year he was not in it; no matter how the camera panned and skidded from group to group, Fogel was invisible. His former mistress wore a glistening purple dress, he seemed to remember, that just barely covered her bustling hindquarters, and she clowned for the camera when it came her way, her lips moving to frame a gay feathery voice that was inaudible.

How tenacious, really, forsythia is of last fall's leaves! And the English ivy was worse yet, more clingy and snaggy. The teeth of Fogel's little bamboo rake kept snapping in the struggle with hostile vegetation. One of his fantasies was a kind of ray gun that, directed at a plant or tree, would not only kill it but instantly vaporize it into a fine, fertilizing ash. Agricultural labor, this endless plucking of weeds and replowing of fields, had always seemed to him the essence of futility; after sixty years he was coming to realize that all work, legal or medical or, like his own, financial, was also a Sisyphean matter of recycling, of pushing inert and thankless matter back and forth, of turning over (in his case) the profoundly rich compost of corporate debt. All labor was tied to human life, life as pointless as that of any new little jade-green weed already joyously sprouting beneath the damp-blackened leaves.

The Allisons' brunch was also pointless—the same dozen aging couples, with three widows and a bachelor, that they saw every weekend. Throughout the gathering Fogel kept trying to glimpse, out of the corners of his eyes, the shoulders of his navy-blue blazer, and brushing at the white hairs that kept appearing there; he was shedding. To get himself through a strenuous conversation on the future of yachting after this winter's debacle in San Diego, he accepted a second Bloody Mary. Then he prudently switched to the faintly sour, platinum-colored champagne punch. One widow told him he should take his cholesterol count very seriously; if her husband had, she wouldn't be a widow now. Tears suddenly troubled her eyes, with their cobalt-blue contact lenses. Another woman, in a purplish dress, came up to Fogel and pressed her wrinkled face upward toward him as if straining to see through a besmirched skylight, and launched her voice into an insistent sweet sing-song. He regretted that no movie camera—a video camera was what they used now, with a built-in sound track—was at work recording the fact that he was here, at this party: that he had been invited. He and his wife left at two-thirty, which felt nearer noon than that. Because the clocks had been jumped ahead, the day kept feeling in retard of where it actually was. It was later than he thought. The cold drizzle intensified, and discouraged returning to the yard work; the bursitis in his shoulders ached from all that reaching with the rake. He found some golf on television. The tour had moved east from the desert events, with lavender mountains in the background and emerald fairways imposed upon sand and cactus and with ancient Hollywood comedians as tournament sponsors, to courses in the American South, with trees in tender first leaf and azaleas in lurid bloom. Young blond men putted, over and over, for birdies. A tremendous drowsiness seized Fogel as he watched within his easy chair. The fresh air and yard work, the gin and tomato juice, the champagne and the effort to be sociable all added up to a crushing accumulation.

Stealthily, avoiding his own bedroom, where his wife could be heard chattering on the telephone to one of her myriad of woman friends, he took a section of the newspaper that perhaps he had not already read and lay down on the bed in their younger son's old room. Posters of European cars and American rock stars were still on the walls, though the boy had left for college over ten years ago. His mother liked to keep the room as he had left it, as some fanatical religious sects keep a room ready in case Jesus returns and asks to be a guest. A pipe rattled—fresh steam hitting condensation in an iron elbow. Fogel had become sensitive to his house, identifying with its creaks, its corners of decay, its irreversible expenditures of energy. He tried to study the section, the financial section. "THE DEFICIT PROBLEM—IS IT ALL IN OUR MINDS?" one headline read. Interest rates, restructuring, soft markets, debt, debt . . .

He rested the paper on the floor beside his son's narrow bed and fell headlong asleep, while drizzle flecked the windowpanes and steam ticked in the radiators. He dreamed, in the deep colors of true weariness. Electricity wandered through his brain, activating now one set of memory cells and now another. A wash of buried emotion rounded these phantoms into light and shadow, and called up tears and outcries of indignation from Fogel's phantom self; he presided above the busy lit stage of his subconscious as prompter and playwright, audience and *deus ex machina* as well as hero. His parents hove into view—his father a coarse man, who worked with his hands, and his mother a virgin in her simplicity of mind, her narrow passion to defend as if sacred the little space her family had borrowed from the world. He hugged his pet teddy bear, Bruno. Bruno had a glass eye, on a long wire stem, like a toy flower. His parents were talking above him, urgently to each other, in a language he didn't know. In their vicinity, Fogel became heavy in every cell, so dense that he fell through into wakefulness, though the dream world tried to cling to his warm body, amid that unnatural ache of resurrection—the weight, the atrocious weight, of coming again to life!

His mouth felt parched, and a dribble from the downward corner of his lips had moistened the pillow. The air of the room was dusky. He did not at first know what room it was, of the many his long life had occupied. A fur of shadow had grown on every surface, even that of the sleek posters. The hour was indeterminate; yet Fogel knew at once that the day was still Easter. How long had he slept, so solidly? Naps were not something he liked to do. Better to store up sleep, at his age, for the night. He listened for his wife's voice from their bedroom and heard nothing. He was frightened. He lay half curled up on the narrow bed like a fetus that has lost flexibility. A curve of terror chilled his abdomen, silvery and sore; had he been the phantom self of his dreams, he would have cried out aloud with the sensation. His eyes checked the items of the room—shiny posters, vacant fireplace, light plug, bookcase of abandoned schoolbooks, rack of obsolete cassettes, stolen NO PARKING sign, stuffed rabbit wearing a vest—one by one. Everything seemed still in place, yet something was immensely missing.

A Sandstone Farmhouse

JOEY'S FIRST GLIMPSE of the house was cloudy in his memory, like an old photo mottled by mildew. During World War Two, his family owned no car, and renting one, for their infrequent excursions out of the compact brick city where his father worked, so embarrassed the twelve-year-old boy that he didn't see clearly through the windows, and wasn't conscious of much beyond his internal struggle not to be car-sick. He fought the swaying, jiggling motion, which was mixed with the warm confluent smells of rubber floormat and petroleum combustion and the patient pale veiny look of his father's hand on the gearshift knob. Farm country, miles of it, poured past. Depressing, monotonous fields moved up and down beneath their hazy burden of crops. A winding asphalt highway climbed a hill, passed a lumpy stone church, then settled into a flat stretch where they slowed to turn left down a dirt washboard road that shook the car sickeningly. Not a building in sight. No sign of civilization but telephone poles carrying a single wire. Another turn, right this time, down an even smaller dirt road, and they stopped, and in the sudden flood of fresh air as Joey opened the car door the green of the grass rose waxy and bright to greet his giddiness, his nausea. In his cloudy memory, they went up to the house and there were people in it, farm people, wearing workclothes and muddy shoes, shyly trying to get out of

107

their way, like animals. There was a front porch, he remembered that much. With a bannister upheld by boards jigsawed into an ornamental shape, and a secret space underneath, of weeds and pebbly dirt. A space where chickens could scratch, and dogs could lie and pant during hot weather, the kind of space that is friendly and inviting to a boy of the age he was just outgrowing.

By the time they had bought the house with its surrounding eighty acres and moved in, he was thirteen, and the front porch had vanished, leaving a space between the front of the house and the cement walk where they eventually planted croci and tulips and erected a grape arbor. Joey as an adult could not remember how or when it had happened, their tearing down the rotten old porch. Pieces of it remained in the barn—segments of bannister, and ornamental balusters cut of inch-thick pine. Once he even took a baluster home with him, back to New York City, as some kind of memento, or sample of folk art. The pattern held a circle in the center, a circle with a hole, between two shapes jigsawed into the wood, one like an arrow and one like a fish. Different-colored flakes fell dryly from it, brittle layers of old-time lead paint. The object, not quite of art, rested sideways on the black-marble mantel of his apartment for a while, then found its way to the back of a closet, with broken squash rackets and college textbooks and table lamps that might some day be made to glow again. Like his mother, he had trouble throwing anything away.

If he and his father and grandfather had torn the porch down themselves, he would have remembered so heroic a labor, as he did the smashing of the lath-and-plaster partition that separated the two small parlors downstairs, making one big living room, or the tearing out of the big stone kitchen fireplace and its chimney, right up into the attic. He remembered swinging the great stones out the attic window, he and his grandfather pushing, trying not to pinch their fingers, while his father, his face white with the effort, held the rope of a makeshift pulley rigged over a rafter. Once clear of the sill, the heavy stones fell with a strange slowness, seen from above, and accumulated into a kind of mountain it became Joey's summer job to clear away. He learned a valuable lesson that first summer on the farm, while he turned fourteen: even if you manage to wrestle only one stone into the wheelbarrow and sweatily, staggeringly trundle it down to the swampy area this side of the springhouse, eventually the entire mountain will be taken away. On the same principle, an invisible giant, removing only one day at a time, will eventually dispose of an entire life.

When, over forty years after that summer of 1946, his mother died, and the at last uninhabited house yielded up its long-buried treasures, he came upon a photograph of her at the age of ten, posing in front of the porch. Someone in pencil, in a flowing handwriting not his mother's—hers was tiny, and cramped, and back-slanted—had marked on the back, *Taken August 1914. Enlarged August 1917.* Someone had loved this snapshot enough to have it enlarged and mounted on thick gray cardboard: who?

His mother, wearing a low-waisted dress, dark stockings, and black shoes with big, thick heels, her hair done up in a long braid that hangs over one shoulder, is holding the collar of a young medium-sized dog, part collie. Both the child and the dog are looking straight into the camera with similar half-smiles and wide-spaced, trusting eyes. They are standing on a cement walk that is still there, uncracked; behind them the porch balusters repeat their simple, artful pattern and a small rose bush blooms. The long-dead dog and the recently dead human female look identically happy. Joey would hardly have recognized his mother but for the thick abundance of her hair—a cheerful chestless little girl in old woman's shoes. Beyond the edge of the barn to her right, ghostly in the enlargement, are fences and trees of which no trace remains and, just barely visible, an entire building that has vanished—a tobacco shed, perhaps. The lawn is edged around the walk, and the fences look trim. This was the private paradise, then, to which she attempted to return, buying back the old sandstone farmhouse that her parents, feeling full enough of tobacco profits to retire, had sold while she was innocently off at normal school. Precocious, she had been skipped up through the local schools, and was sent away at the age of twelve, and hated it, hated it all, including the hour-long trolley ride to Kutztown. The swaying, the ozone, the drunk men who sat down beside her made her sick.

She loved the old house; she loved the *idea* of it. For most of her life, except for the twenty years of exile in her young womanhood, when she went to normal school, then to college, and married a man she met there, and travelled with him until the Depression cost him his travelling job, and bore him a son, in the heart of the Depression, while they were all living with her parents in the brick city house—except for these twenty years, she happily inhabited an idea. The sandstone house had been built, her fond research discovered, in 1812. In that era teams of masons and stonelayers roamed the countryside, erecting these Pennsylvania farmhouses on principles of an elegant simplicity. Their ground-plan was square, set square to the compass. The south face basked in the maximum of sunshine; the east windows framed the sunrise, and the west the sunset.

The cornerstones were cut at a slightly acute angle, to emphasize the edge. The stout scaffolding was rooted in holes in the thirty-inch walls as they rose, and these holes were plugged with stones four inches square when the masonry was pointed, and the scaffolding dismantled, from the top down. In the mortar, lime from the lime kiln was mixed with sand from creek beds, to match the stones. Though the size of the stones raised and fitted into place was prodigious, the real feats of leverage occurred in the quarrying. Sandstone exposed in an outcropping was rendered useless by weather, but underneath the earth the sound stone slept, to be painstakingly split by star drills and wedges and "feathers" of steel, and then hauled out by teams of horses, on wagons or sleds. Sometimes a wagon shattered under the load of a single great stone. But the vast hauling and lifting continued, a movement as tidal as that of the glaciers which here and there, in this area of the last ice age's most southerly advance, had deposited huge moraines—acres frightening in their sheer stoniness; heaped-up depths of boulders in which no tree could take root, though forest surrounded them; lakes of barrenness fascinating and bewildering to nineteenth-century minds eager to perceive God's hand everywhere.

For sensitive, asthmatic Joey, removed from a brick semi-detached city house where he had felt snug— where he could hear through his bedroom walls the neighbors stirring as he awoke, and the milk being delivered on the porch, and the trolley cars clanging at the corner a block away—the silent thickness of stones just behind the old plaster and wallpaper, and the rough hearths and fireplaces visible within the country house, seemed to harbor nature's damp and cold. A sullen held breath dwelled in the walls. The summer's heat brought swarms of wasps, millipedes, carpenter ants, and silverfish out from the crannies. That first winter in the house, before an oil furnace was installed in the basement, a kerosene-burning stove in the living room provided the only heat. Joey remembered the stove clearly; it was painted chocolate-brown, and stood on little bent legs on an asbestos sheet papered with imitation wood grain. He spent days huddled in blankets next to this stove, on a grease-spotted sofa that had been brought close. With his chronic cold, he missed days of school, and hated to, for it was warm in school, and there was running water, and flush toilets. And girls in long pleated skirts and fuzzy sweaters and bobby socks, who belonged to the modern era, to civilization. He clung to civilization by reading; huddled in the brown stove's aromatic aura of coal oil, he read anything—P. G. Wodehouse, Ellery Queen, John Dickson Carr, Thorne Smith—that savored of cities and took him out of this damp, cold little stone house.

His mother remembered that first winter with rueful pleasure, as a set of tribulations blithely overcome. "It was really very hard, I suppose, on everybody—you were *so* sick, and your father had to struggle to get to work in that old Chevrolet that was all we could afford, and for my parents it was a terrible defeat, to come back to the farm after they had gotten away; they would hide together in the corner just like children—but I was so happy to be here I hardly noticed. The movers had broken the large pane of glass in the front door, and for some reason that whole first winter we never managed to replace it; we lived with a sheet of cardboard wedged over the hole. It's incredible that we survived." And she would laugh, remembering. "We tried to light fires in the living-room fireplace but all the wood the Schellenbargers had left us in the basement was moldy elm, and that fireplace never did draw well, even when the swifts' nests weren't plugging it up. Smoke leaks out into the room, I've never understood quite why. If you look up the flue with a flashlight, the stonework has a twist to it."

Joey seemed to remember, though, waking upstairs and putting his feet onto the bare wood floor and grabbing his school clothes and hurrying in his pajamas down the narrow stairs—the treads worn in two troughs by generations of footsteps, the nailheads protruding and shiny and dangerous—to dress in front of the fireplace, where logs were crackling. The freezing upstairs air would lick at his skin like flame, like the endless conversations between his mother and her parents, incessant flowing exchanges that would ripple into quarrel and chuckle back again into calm while he focused, when he was home, into the pages of a book. His grandfather had a beautiful, patient, elocutionary voice; his grandmother spoke little, in guttural responses. His mother, unlike most adults, hadn't parted from her parents, and clung to them with old tales and grievances, like someone adding up the same set of figures day after day and forever expecting a different answer. While Joey, sick, huddled by the stove, heated conversations were in his ears as the smell of coal oil was in his nostrils, but always, those five years (only five!) that he lived in the sandstone house with four adults, his attention was aimed elsewhere—on schoolwork, on the future. He tried to ignore what was around him. The house, even when plumbing and central heating and a telephone were installed, and new wallpaper made the repainted rooms pretty, embarrassed him.

He was never more embarrassed than in that summer before they moved in, before they owned even the erratic old Chevrolet. The war was still on, the Pacific part of it. Several times, his mother made him travel with her by bus out to the farm they already owned. She had a vision of a windbreak of pines rimming the big field, along the road, and she and Joey carried seedlings in boxes, and shovels, and pruners, and a watering can—all this humiliating apparatus dragged onto a city bus by a red-faced middle-aged woman and a skinny boy with ears that stuck out and dungarees that were too short. His mother wore a checked shirt like a man's and a straw sun hat and a pair of light-blue overalls with a bib; she looked like a farmer in a Hollywood musical comedy. There was no space inside the bus for the shovels; the driver had to store them in the luggage compartment and then stop and get out in the middle of nowhere to hand the tools over. It was a relief when the bus, headed south toward Washington, D.C., disappeared around a bend in the highway.

Joey and his mother walked down the dirt washboard road in the heat, carrying their equipment. He had never been so humiliated, and vowed never to be again. He couldn't blame his mother, he still needed her too much, so he blamed the place—its hazy, buggy fields, its clouds of blowing pollen that made him sneeze and his eyes water, its little sandstone house like a cube of brown sugar melting in the heat, in a dip of hillside beneath an overgrown, half-dead apple orchard. All through noon and into the afternoon they cleared small spaces at the edge of the field, where the Schellenbargers' last crop of field corn was pushing up in limp green rows, and cut away burdock and poison ivy and honeysuckle, and dug holes, and set in each hole a six-inch puff of pine seedling, and sprinkled water over the sandy red earth. Moving a few paces farther on to plant the next tree, Joey could no longer see the last one amid the weeds and wild grass. The work seemed hopeless. Yet, when the afternoon breeze came up, he heard a purity of silence that didn't exist in his beloved street of semi-detached houses. Perhaps one car an hour passed, the people staring at this woman and boy dressed in clothes suitable for neither country nor city. And he felt a kind of heroism in his periodic trudge, with the empty sprinkling can, for the half-mile along the edge of the cornfields to the empty house, with its rusty iron pump on the back porch, and then the long haul back, the sloshing can as heavy now as a stone.

He felt heroic to himself. Space for heroism existed out here; his being had been transposed to a new scale. He was determined to impress his mother—to win her back, since here on this farm he for the first time encountered something she apparently loved as much as she loved him.

At last, the weeds threw feathery long shadows upon one another and the tiny pines were all planted in the hopeless roadside jungle and it was time to walk back up the dusty washboard road to wait for the bus from Washington to round the corner. Having gone and come so far, the bus could be as much as an hour late, and their eyes would sting, staring down the gray highway for it, and his stomach would sink at the thought that they had missed it and were stranded. But not even this possibility daunted him, for he had forged a mood of defiant collusion in which he was numbed to embarrassment and played a role both stoic and comic, co-starring with his mother in her straw sun hat and their lanky, sharp-faced sidekicks, the clippers and the shovel. Years later, he could even laugh with her about it, the memory of those awkward hot trips to plant a line of trees most of which never thrived, choked by thistles and bindweed or severed in a year or two by a careless sweep of a scythe.

Yet a few of the pines, perhaps six or seven, did live to tower along the roadbank—shaggy-headed apparitions taller than a ship's mast, swaying in the wind. By this time, the dirt road was macadamized and hummed with traffic, and the bus route to Washington had long ago been abandoned as unprofitable.

Five years after the September when they had moved, Joey went to college. Essentially, he never returned. He married in his senior year, and after graduation moved to New York City. Another of his mother's visions, along with that of the farm as paradise, was of him as a poet; he fulfilled this heroic task as best he could, by going to work for an ad agency and devoting himself to the search for the arresting phrase and image, on the edge of the indecent, that incites people to buy—that gives them permission, from the mythic world of fabricated symbols, to spend. The business was like poetry in that you needed only a few lucky hits, and he had his share, and couldn't complain. He never again had to get on a bus with a shovel.

The numbers attached to the years and decades slowly changed, and with them the numbers in his bank account and on his apartment building. His first marriage took place in three different apartments, his turbulent second in four, his short-lived third in only one, and now he wondered if women had been not quite his thing all along. He had always felt most at ease, come to think of it, in the company of men, especially those who reminded him of his quiet, uncomplaining father. But it was the AIDS-conscious Eighties by then, and his hair had passed through gray into virtual white, and he was content to share his life with his books, his CDs (compact discs, certificates of deposit), and his modest little art collection, mixed of watery commercialism and icy minimalism. On the other side of the white walls of his apartment he could hear the mumble and thump of his neighbors, and he liked that. He had come home, in the Fifties, to semi-detached living.

Three hours away, his widowed mother lived alone in the sandstone house. Joey had been the first to depart. A few years later, his grandfather died, suddenly, with a stroke like a thunderclap, and then, after a bedridden year, his grandmother. This created an extra room upstairs, so Joey and his first wife and young children, when they came to visit in the Sixties, no longer had to camp out downstairs, on cots and the sofa spotted by the peanut-butter crackers he used to eat when condemned to reading the days away. The upstairs had two real bedrooms, to which the doors could be closed, and a kind of hallway beside the head of the stairs where he had slept for five years, listening to the four adults rustle and snore and creak while girls and prayers and the beginnings of poems all ran together in his brain. His grandfather, on his way downstairs in the early morning, would ruffle the hair on the sleeping boy's head, and the gathering sounds of family breakfast, as Joey's grandmother and parents followed, would rise under him with the smell of toast, a doughy warmth of life rising beneath the cold bare floorboards of soft old pine.

There was a fourth room, a small room in the northwest corner, where his mother had once been born, in a long agony of labor—a rural calvary, as Joey imagined it, with flickering lamps and steaming kettles and ministering cousins arriving by horse and buggy—that shaped her relations with her own mother into, it seemed, a ferocious apology, a futile undying adhesion in an attempt to make amends. She nursed her mother in the old woman's long paralysis of dying, but not always patiently, or tenderly, and when the ordeal at last was over she was left with additional cause for self-blame. "I spent my whole life," she concluded, "trying to please my mother, and never did."

Joey would ask, irritated by these repeated surges of self-dramatization, "Did she ever say so?"

"No, but you knew her. She never said anything."

"Unlike *my* mother," he said, with an ironic pretense of gallantry.

She heard the irony. "Yes, I inherited Pop's gift of gab," she admitted. "It's been a curse, really. If you talk enough, you don't feel you have to *do* anything."

This fourth room had become the bathroom, with a tub but no shower, a basin but no cabinet. Toothpaste, sun lotion, hand creams, razors, dental floss, slivers of soap thriftily stuck together all accumulated on the deep sill overlooking the blackening shingles of the back-porch roof. After his father died, in the early Seventies, the house gradually lost the power to purge itself of accumulation. The family's occupancy, which had begun with removal of the porch, the inner wall, and the chimney stones, now silted the attic and cellar and windowsills full of souvenirs of his mother's lengthening residence.

On the theory that it would save the wild birds from being eaten, she had fed a stray cat that came to the back porch; this cat then became several, and the several became as many as forty. The kitchen became choked with stacked cases of cat food, and a site in the woods, at the end of a path overgrown with raspberry canes, became a mountain of empty cat-food cans. Tin Mountain, Joey's children called it. Magazines and junk mail and church pamphlets sat around on tables and chairs waiting to be bundled and taken to the barn, to wait there for the Boy Scouts' next paper drive. Photographs of Joey and his children and wives, Christmas cards and valentines from relations and neighbors piled up on available spaces like a kind of moss. Even the table where his mother ate had room eventually for only one plate and cup and saucer, her own. The house was clogging up, Joey felt, much as her heart—coronary angiography had revealed—was plugging with arteriosclerosis, and her weakly pumped lungs were filling with water.

His arrivals, as the years went on, seemed to accumulate, one on top of another. He would park his car by the barn and pick his way across the line of stepping stones that in the decades since they were laid (even Granny, stiff and bent over, helping with the crowbar) had been silted over by the sandy soil and its crabgrass. On the back porch there would be a puddle of cats and kittens mewing to be fed. Entering the back door, he would try not to grimace at the stench of cat food and damp cardboard. His mother saved, in separate sections of the floor, the empty cans, and the plastic bags the supermarket bagged her groceries in, and slippery stacks of mail-order catalogues, and string and twine snarled in a galvanized bucket. Joey recognized in this accumulation a superstition he had to fight within himself—the belief that everything has value. The birds in the trees, the sunflower at the edge of the orchard, the clumsily pasted-up valentine received years ago from a distant grandchild—all have a worth which might, at any moment, be called into account. It was a way of advertising that one's own life was infinitely precious.

There would be a peck of a kiss at the door, and he would carry the suitcase upstairs, past the dog; the last of the series of dogs was a whirling, nipping mongrel bitch who was thrilled to have a man in the house. The guest room had been his parents' bedroom. When she became a widow, his mother had moved into her parents' old room, closer to the room in which she had been born. The move was part, Joey felt, of an obscure religious system that had nothing to do with Christianity. He remembered how, in a surprising rite of that system, his parents on the day after his grandmother died took her stained, urine-soaked mattress outdoors and burned it, down near the stones he had dumped, darkening the sky all morning with the smoke.

Here, in this guest room, at night, without a wife to distract and comfort him, he would begin to fight for his breath. The bed sagged so that his back hurt. The pillow felt heavy and dense. The sandstone hearth of the never-used fireplace in the room would emit an outdoor dampness. Birds and bats and mice would stir in the porous walls, and his mother's motions would make her bed on the other side of the thin wall creak. Was she awake, or asleep? Which was he? He could truly relax only in the dawn light, when the dog would wake her, scrabbling on the bare boards with her claws, and the two females would slowly, noisily head downstairs, and the can-opener would rhythmically begin to chew through the first installment of cat-food cans.

The guest room for some reason had no curtains; in the dead of the night the moon burned on the wide sills as if calling to him, calling him back to a phase his whole adult life had been an effort to obliterate. The asthma, the effect of inner tightening and complication, wasn't so bad, usually, the first two nights; he might manage five or six hours of sleep each, if he then could get away, back to cozy, salubrious New York. But on long holiday weekends he would struggle through the whole third night with the accumulated house-dust and pollen in his lungs, and with the damp hard pillow, and with the obdurate moonlight, so accusatory in its white silence.

He was aware of his mother and himself, lying each in bed, as survivors of a larger party that had once occupied this house. It was as if, on a snowy pass, they had killed and eaten the others, and now one of the two remaining must perish next. She, too, in her eighties, had breathing problems, and slept with her head up on two pillows. One night she woke him, with the soft words, "Joey. I'm not doing so well. Put on your daddy's old overcoat and come downstairs with me."

He was awake, his head clear as moonlight, in an instant. "Shall we call the hospital?"

"No, I just need to sit up. You know which overcoat, it hangs at the foot of the stairs."

It had hung there for years, one of those curious comforting rags his father would acquire in thrift shops or outlet stores. Joey had often seen it on him, in the last year of the old man's life, when his legs turned white and phlebitic and his nose turned blue with poor circulation and his eyes sank deeper and deeper into his head and his deafness worsened. But to the end his father had held his head high, and took an academic interest in the world. Once a social-science teacher, he continued to read fat books of contemporary history, and wrote Joey, in one of his rare letters, in his patient, legible schoolteacher's hand, that being deaf made it easier for him to concentrate.

Joey wondered why his mother was being so insistent about the coat, but obediently put it on. It had a fuzziness unusual in dark overcoats, and was big for him, since his father had been bigger than he. She was right; once it was on, over his pajamas, he became a child again, and calm, and trusting. They went downstairs and turned up the thermostat and sat in the dark living room together, he on the sofa and she in her television-viewing chair, and he watched her struggle for breath, in little sudden shuddering gasps like the desperate heaves of a bird caught in the chimney.

"Do you hurt?" he asked.

She had little breath for speaking, and shook her head No, and her head underwent again the convulsion, as if trying to keep above water. "It's like," she gasped, "a squeezing."

"Sure you wouldn't like to drive to the hospital?"

A vigorous headshake again. "What can they do? But torture you."

So he sat there, in his father's overcoat, fighting sleepiness, wondering if his mother would die before his eyes. The dog, agitated at first by this pre-dawn rising, wheezed and resettled on the floor. The moonlight weakened on the sills across the room, with their potted geraniums and violets and a night-blooming cereus that had been allowed to grow grotesquely long, so that its stem filled the window. His mother's shudders lessened, and eventually she told him to go upstairs, she would sit here a while longer. In her old age she had become almost grafted onto this chair of hers. On a previous visit, she had shocked him by refusing, when the evening run of television comedies that she faithfully watched was over, to come upstairs at all; morning found her still sitting there, in her clothes. This irritated him, along with her television-watching. "Why do you watch all these idiots?" he once asked her. "They seem realer to you than I am."

She did not deny it. "Well," she had answered, "they're always here."

Now, her crisis past, he accepted her dismissal gratefully and yet reluctantly. He went upstairs feeling that this hour had been the most purely companionable he had ever spent with her in this house. To Joey in his father's fuzzy, overlarge coat, as he silently watched his mother struggle and the dog stir and doze and the night-blooming cereus cast its gawky shadow in the deep window recess beyond the tasselled bridge lamp and the upright piano, it had been like one of those scenes we witness in childhood, from under the table or over the edge of the crib, understanding nothing except that large forces are in motion around us—that there is a heavy heedless dynamism from which we are, as children, momentarily sheltered.

* * *

When she had her next attack of breathlessness, he was not there, and she called the neighbors, and they called the township ambulance, which came at five in the morning. For all her talk of "torture," she seemed to settle gratefully into the hospital's ministrations. "They said I was quite blue, the oxygen in my blood was down to nothing." Rather gaily, she described the emergency-room doctors thrusting some violent sucking instrument down her throat and into her lungs.

Her bathrobe was turquoise with a maroon hem; she ordered her clothes from catalogues now and was attracted to loud colors. With her white hair all about her on the pillow, and the baby-blue oxygen tubes making a mustache, and the identification bracelet looped on her wrist, she looked festive and hectic and feminized. All day, young men in antiseptic garb came and tended to her, cutting her toenails, interrogating her bowels. Her bowels, to Joey's embarrassment, had become a topic of supreme fascination to her. Her insides in general were brought uncomfortably close to the surface by the erosion of her body. His father's method of coping with what seemed to Joey her unaccountable whims, including moving them all to the farm, had been to say, "She's a femme. Your mother's a real femme. What can you do?" He would shrug, and sometimes add, "I should have put her on the burleycue stage."

This had seemed one of the man's lofty, pained jokes; but now her femininity, which Joey's father and then his succession of wives had shielded him from, was upon him. In her slightly dishevelled, revealing gowns, in her gracefully accepted helplessness and fragility, in this atmosphere of frank bodily event, his mother had her sex on her mind. She told him, remembering the first years of her marriage, in Pittsburgh, "There was this young doctor, Dr. Langhorne over on Sixth Street, who, when

I went to him with these pains on my chest I couldn't understand, told me to take off my clothes. Well, I trusted him, and did, and he looked me over for the longest time, and then told me, 'You're not obese.' That was all he said."

Her conviction, prior to Joey's birth, that she couldn't do such a normal thing as conceive and bear a child recurred in her self-accounting; old Dr. Mull, who kept brusquely calming her fears, who treated her as a normal woman and not as the monstrous product of her own mother's agony, emerged as a kind of erotic hero, who swept her off her feet. "He told me to stop talking nonsense and trust in nature, and so I did, and the result was this beautiful boy!" Joey suddenly saw that his own self, which he had imagined she cherished for qualities all his own, was lovable to her above all as a piece of her body, as a living proof of her womanhood.

And she recalled, of those straitened Depression days when he was an infant, how she left him in the care of his grandparents and went off on the trolley car to work in the drapes department of the department store downtown. She had lost a tooth, a bicuspid, and the upper partial plate containing its replacement was uncomfortable, and one day she didn't wear it to work and was chastised by the department manager, Mr. Wertheimer, for not wearing it. The image of her missing tooth, this tidy black hole leaping up within her young woman's smile, seemed erotic, too, along with the thought of his then-slender mother's charm as a saleswoman. "On my good days," she claimed, "I could sell anything. But then the people would bring it all back for exchange on Monday. As if I had bewitched them. Mr. Wertheimer said there was such a thing as being *too* good."

But not all her days were good days, she told Joey. She took her periods too hard, they knocked her flat for thirty-six, forty-eight hours; and this brought the conversation back to her body, her body arching over his life like a firmament, and he would leave the hospital building and find relief in the body of the city, Alton with its close-packed suburbs, a city he loved as his mother loved her farm, because it had formed his first impressions, when the wax was soft. He ate at aluminum diners where each booth still had its individual jukebox, shopped at hardware stores for parts and tools the sandstone farmhouse in its decrepitude needed, and bought a new vacuum cleaner to replace his mother's old Hoover, which had on its front a little electric light like that of his toy electric train as it circled the Christmas tree. He got himself a haircut in a front-parlor barber shop, the kind of shop, with a radio playing and a baby crying in rooms out of sight, and a spiral pole out front, that he thought had disappeared, because such shops had disappeared in New York. A small child of his, years ago, had knocked the porcelain lid off the toilet water tank and it had shattered. Now, between visits to his mother, he went about the city with the cardboard box of fragments, dusty and cobweb-ridden after years in the attic, to plumbing supply houses, where overweight, hard-smoking, not quite sardonic men would return from digging in their cavernous storerooms and give him, for a few dollars, old spare lids that did not, it would turn out, quite fit. He kept trying. Alton had lost factories and population since he was a boy, and appeared in smaller letters on the maps of Pennsylvania, but it was still a place where things were made and handled, where brute matter got its honest due. He still shared the city's blue-collar faith in hardware and industry and repair, a humble faith that had survived all his heady traffic in sheer imagery—slogans, graphics, layouts.

What was life at bottom but plumbing? After a week, the hospital had cleared out his mother's lungs, and now the cardiologists wanted to operate on the malfunctioning heart that had let the pulmonary edema occur. The angiography had revealed coronary arteries stenosed all but shut. "Oh, Joey—I could go any day," she blurted to him after the test results had been described to her. She showed him with a forefinger and thumb how small and pinched the lumen had become. "Worse than they thought." She was sitting on the bed with her hair wild and one shoulder bared by a loose tie in the hospital johnny. Her facial expression was girlish, womanhood's acquired composure all dissolved. Their intermittently shared life was being lifted into new octaves, and mother and son seemed in these moments of hospital conference simply a man and a woman, both with more white hairs than dark, taking counsel because no one else whose advice would count was left on earth.

To his relief, she did not want the open-heart operation, thus sparing him the trouble, the expense, the tests, the trips to Philadelphia. He tried to suppress his relief and to argue for the coronary bypass that was recommended, though she was well over eighty. She said, making a wryly twisted mouth just as her father used to when discussing the county's politicians, "Of course, *they* recommend it. It's what they have to sell. They're in business, just like their fathers, only peddling different things. They pass me around, one to another; I've yet to see a Christian."

In the frankness that her closeness to death allowed, as her composed womanhood melted, an anti-Semitism was one of the things that emerged. She could not see the predominantly Jewish doctors as saviors and allies but only as opportunists and exploiters. She even developed with one solemn young cardiologist a banter that cast her as a Palestinian: "You've taken me away from my village," she said. Joey was dismayed; his third wife, the briefest one, had been Jewish, and she and his mother had seemed especially friendly, and as he imagined now his mother's unspoken feelings in those years it was like seeing silverfish tumble out of old books. On her less lucid days, she seemed to think that the doctors and their allies ("One big fella, looked just like Danny Thomas, came and cut my toenails; now, how much do you think *that's* going to add to the bill?") were scheming to do her out of her house and its priceless eighty acres—that she was territory they wanted to seize and develop. Each day she spent in the hospital, the little sandstone house pulled at her harder. "Get me home," she begged Joey.

"And then what?"

"Then we'll take what comes." Her eyes widened, watching his, and her mouth as it clamped shut over "what comes" was very like a child's, stubborn in its fright. For, however close their consultations, however fervent their agreements, both were aware that she was the star and he merely the prompter: though his turn would come, the spotlight burned upon her. She was center stage, in this drama whose climax everyone knows.

When, six months later, she died—instantly, it seemed to the coroner—in the kitchen, just under the room where she had been born, the neighbors, who were patient Mennonites and Lutherans, took a day to discover her body and another twelve hours to find him in at his apartment telephone number. He had been working late. It was midnight when he let himself into the old farmhouse. The door keys had been lost long ago, in that distant, fabulous era after they had moved. When his mother was to be away for more than a day, she would lock the doors from the inside and go out through the cellar bulkhead. Her neighbors knew this and had left the house like that after her body was removed. Joey had brought no flashlight; after parking the car by the barn, he walked to the slanted cellar doors by moonlight, and within the dark cellar was guided by memory. A Lally column here, a pyramid of paint cans there. His father and he had laid this cement floor one frantic day when three cubic yards of ready-mixed concrete were delivered in a giant gob by a truck. He would have been fifteen or so, his father in his late forties. The cellar floor of these old farmhouses was typically dirt, the red clay of the region packed more or less hard, except when the foundation walls wept in the spring and it turned to mud. His father had talked with construction men, and set out boards to frame the platform for the furnace, and dug a clay pipe into the dirt for drainage, and stretched strings here and there to determine the level and pitch, but none of these preparations encompassed the alarming dimensions of the slowly hardening concrete when it arrived early that Saturday morning. With rakes and shovels and boards and trowels they pushed and tugged the sluggish stuff level, into the far corners, under the cellar stairs, and up to the mouth of the drainage pipe. His father's face went white with effort, as it had when he struggled with the chimney stones several years before, and the ordeal went on and on, by the light of a few bare bulbs, this panicky race with time and matter, as the concrete grew stiffer and stiffer, and in drying pushed its water toward the surface, and exuded its sonorous underground odor, its secretive smell of stone. The floor had come out surprisingly well, out of that day's sweaty panic—smooth and gray and delicately sloped so that hardly a puddle lingered after a flooding. It sometimes seemed, in the mottled perspectives of hindsight, that there had been a third man in the cellar with them, something of a professional, for it seemed unlikely that he and his father, a would-be poet and a soc.-sci. teacher, could have made such a satisfactory cellar floor. But if there had been such a man, Joey had mentally erased him, jealous of this arduous day at his father's side fending off disaster, doing a man's job. He was just becoming a man, and his father was wearying of being one; this was the last project so ambitious that he tackled around the house.

In the basement's absolute blackness, Joey's city shoes slithered on the smooth floor, and then thumped on the wooden cellar stairs; he pushed the door open into the moon-striped kitchen. A warm whimpering hairy body hurtled up against him, and he thought that his mother had not died after all. But it was the dog, who took his hand in her mouth and unstoppably whimpered and whined as if telling him a long story, the story of her hours alone in the house with her mistress, with the unresponsive, cooling body, with her doggy hunger and bafflement.

Things work out. One of Joey's former wives, Peggy, who had remarried into the Connecticut suburbs, agreed to take the dog. The cats a man from the county humane society came and trapped and carried away to be gassed, a few each day, frantically fighting the cage. Joey stacked the magazines and catalogues and Christmas cards and tied them with baling twine from the bucket and carried them to the barn to be trucked by a Mennonite neighbor to a landfill. The Boy Scouts no longer collected paper and bottles; nothing was precious any more, there was too much of everything. As his family assembled, Joey impressed them with his efficiency, portioning out the furniture and heirlooms among his children, his ex-wives, the local auctioneer, the junkman.

For himself he kept little but odd small items that reached back into his boyhood in the brick house from which they moved to the farm—a brass tiger that sat on the piano there, when he still took piano lessons, and a curved leather-backed brush he remembered his grandfather using on his black hightop shoes before setting off on foot to the Lutheran church. He kept some of his father's college notebooks, preserved in the attic, penned in a more rounded version of his legible schoolteacherish hand. He kept a set of Shakespeare, with limp maroon covers, of which the silverfish had nibbled some pages into lace.

His mother as a young woman, a feminine purchaser of slips and stockings and jewelry, drew suddenly close to him, after the decades in which she had been old. Inexpensive pieces of silver and turquoise and jade, Art Deco–ish, from the Twenties and Thirties, in surprising quantity, testified to a certain vanity, a voluptuous need for ornament. His mother's many country sun hats were hard to throw away, though none of the assembled females wanted them. Joey's two daughters sorted through the clothes for him. He couldn't bear to touch and discard the dresses hanging in the closet, dozens of garments pressed together in an anthology of past fashions, all the way back to a fox-trimmed spring coat whose collar he remembered with an odd vividness, its tingling black-tipped red-brown hairs close to her face: his mother was carrying him, against her shoulder.

In the toolhouse, where his father had left a pathetic legacy of rusty screws and nails neatly arranged in jars, and oily tools, half of them broken, mounted on rotting pegboard, there were also antique implements worn like prehistoric artifacts: an ancient oblong pink whetstone pointed at either end and soapily warped by all its use, and an old-fashioned square hoe worn into a lopsided metal oval, its edges had struck so many stones. Such wear couldn't have occurred in the merely forty years they were here, but must have been the work of generations; these tools had travelled back and forth across the country, surviving many moves, to end in his impatient hands. They seemed sacred—runes no one else could decipher. He was the last of his line to have ever hoed a row of kohlrabi or sharpened a scythe while standing knee-deep in the nodding damp grass of an orchard.

Relatives and neighbors spoke to him with a soft gravity, as if he were fragile in grief. He knew he and his mother were regarded as having been unusually, perhaps unnaturally close; when in fact between themselves the fear was that they were not close enough. Why grieve? She was old, in pain, worn-out. She was too frail in her last half-year to walk to the mailbox or lift a case of cat food or pull a clump of burdock: it was time; dying is the last favor we do the world, the last tax we pay. He cried only once, during the funeral, quite unexpectedly, having taken his seat at the head of his raggedly extended family, suddenly free, for the moment, of arrangements and decisions. An arm's reach away from him gleamed the cherry-wood casket he had picked out in the undertaker's satiny basement showroom three days before. The lustrous well-joined wood, soon to be buried—the sumptuous waste of it. She was in there, and in his mind there appeared a mother conceived out of his earliest memories of her, a young slim woman dressed in a navy-blue suit, with white at her throat, dressed to go off to her job at the downtown department store, hurrying to catch the trolley car. She had once reminisced, "Oh, how you'd run, and if you just missed it, there wouldn't be another for twenty minutes, and you wanted to cry." She had laughed, remembering.

His tears came and kept coming, in a kind of triumph, a breakthrough, a torrent of empathy and pity for that lost young woman running past the Pennsylvania row houses, under the buttonwood trees, running to catch the trolley, the world of the Thirties shabby and solid around her, the porches, the blue mid-summer hydrangeas, this tiny well-dressed figure in her diminishing pocket of time, her future unknown, her death, her farm, far from her mind. This was the mother, apparently, that he had loved, the young woman living with him and others in a brick semi-detached house, a woman of the world, youthfully finding her way. During the war she worked in a parachute factory, wearing a bandanna on her head like the other women, plump like them by this time, merging with them and their chatter one lunch break when he, somehow, had bicycled to the side entrance to see her. She was not like them, the tough other women, he knew, but for the moment had blended with them, did a job alongside them, and this too renewed his tears, his naïve pride in her then, when he was ten or eleven. She had tried to be a person, she had lived. There was something amazing, something immortal to him in the image of her running. He remembered, from their first years on the farm, a crisis with the roof; it was being reshingled by a team of Amishmen and they had left it partially open to the weather on the night of a thunderstorm. Crashes, flashes. Joey's parents and grandparents were all awake, and he, boy though he still was, was expected now to wake and help, too; they rushed up and down the attic stairs with buckets, to save the plaster of the walls and ceilings below. There was a tarpaulin in the barn that might help; he found himself outdoors, in the downpour, and he had retained an image of his mother running across the lawn in a flash of lightning that caught the white of her bare legs. She would not have been much over forty, and was still athletic; perhaps his father was included in this unsteady glimpse; there was a hilarity to it all, a violent health.

Working his way, after her death, through all the accumulated souvenirs of her life, Joey was fascinated by the college yearbooks that preserved her girlish image. Group photographs showed his mother as part of the hockey team, the hiking club. With a magnifying glass he studied her unsmiling, competitive face, with her hair in two balls at her ears and a headband over her bangs. Her face seemed slightly larger than the other girls', a childlike oval broadest at the brow, its defenses relatively unevolved. As he sat there beside the cherry casket crying, his former wives and adult children stealing nervous peeks at him, the young woman ran for the trolley car, her breath catching, her panting mixed with a sighing laughter at herself, and the image was as potent, as fertile, as a classic advertisement, which endlessly taps something deep and needy within us. The image of her running down the street, away from him, trailed like a comet's tail the maternal enactments of those misty years when he was a child—crayoning with him on the living-room floor, sewing him Halloween costumes in the shape of Disney creatures, having him lift what she called the "skirts" of the bushes in the lawn while she pushed the old reel mower under them—but from her point of view; he seemed to feel from within his mother's head the situation, herself and this small son, this defenseless gurgling hatched creature, and the tentative motions of her mind and instincts as she, as new to mothering as he was to being alive, explored the terrain between them. In the attic he had found a padded baby-blue scrapbook, conscientiously maintained, containing his first words, the date of his first crawl, and his hospital birth certificate imprinted with his inky day-old feet. The baths. The cod-liver oil. The calls to the doctor, the subscriptions to children's magazines, the sweaters she knit. Trying to do the right thing, the normal thing, running toward her farm, her death. In his vision of her running she was bright and quick and small, like an animal caught in a gunsight. This was the mother Joey had loved, the mother before they moved, before she betrayed him with the farm and its sandstone house.

Ruthlessly, vengefully, weekend by weekend, he cleaned the place out—disconnecting the phone, giving the auctioneer the run of the attic, seeing the refrigerator and stove hauled off for a few dollars each, by a truck that got stuck in the muddy winter lawn. With his new vacuum cleaner Joey attacked the emptying rooms, sucking up the allergen-rich dust from the cracks between the floorboards, sweeping the walls and ceilings clean of their veils of cobwebs upon cobwebs. How satisfying this was, one room after another that he would not have to do again. Joey discovered that his mother had been far from alone in the house; while the cats mewed and milled outside on the porch, a tribe of mice, year after year, ancestors and descendants, had been fed sunflower seeds, whose accumulated stored husks burst forth by the bucketful from behind where the stained-pine corner cupboard had stood, and from the back of the dish-towel drawer of the kitchen sink. He set traps for the mice. He set out d-Con, and the next weekend tossed the small stiff bodies, held gingerly by the tail, down into the swamp, where the chimney rocks, and the ashes of his grandmother's mattress, had joined earth's stately recycling.

The old house had curious small cabinets built into the stone thickness, and they disgorged packets of his father's index cards, riddled with anxious reminder notes to himself, and pads of old high-school permission slips, and small boxes of dull pencils and hardened erasers, and playing cards from the remote days when he and his parents played three-handed pinochle at the dining table. At first, he could scarcely hold the cards, sixteen fanned in one little hand, and would stifle tears when his meld was poor and he lost. Once at the farm, they were too busy to play cards again. There were animals of petrified Play-Doh made by Joey's children, and useless pretty vases and bowls sent distractedly as seasonal gifts from Bloomingdale's, and plush-bound old-fashioned albums, with little mildewed mirrors on the covers, of stiffly posed ancestors he could not identify. His mother had offered, over the years, to teach him their names and exact relation to him, but he had not been interested, and now she was not there to ask, and his ancestors floated free and nameless, like angels.

There were things she had offered to tell him he had not wanted to hear. "What didn't you like about him?" he had once asked her—a bit impatiently, tiring of her voice—about his father.

Sitting in her television-watching chair, her weight and strength so wasted that only her mouth and mind could move, she had been telling him about her youthful romantic life. She had gone to a one-room country school—when she was dead, he came upon a photograph of the student body and its corpulent mustachioed instructor, his mother's broad little face squinting toward the camera under a ponderous crown of wound braids. Among the other children there had been a dark-haired, dark-eyed boy whom she had fancied, and who had fancied her. But her parents had disapproved of the boy's "people," and of several other dark-eyed substitutes that over the years she had offered them. Not until Joey's blondish, pale-eyed father did she bring home a suitor they could endorse. "They liked him, and he liked them. I'll say this for your father, not every man could have lived with his in-laws that cheerfully all those years. He really admired my mother, that style of little woman. Energetic little women—he loved them. He thought they could make money for him. It's true, Mother was a money-maker. She was the one who got up in the dark to drive the cart into Alton to market. The tobacco they retired on had been her project. But admiring Mother was no reason to marry me. I was *big*. It was a mistake, and we both knew it. We knew it the first day of our honeymoon." Joey had often heard his mother's views on little women, how they have the best of it, and take the men from the big women like herself, big women who have tortured their little mothers in the birthing. Behind these formulations there was something—about sex, he believed—that he didn't want, as a boy or a man, to hear. *A real femme.* Even as a very small child he had been aware of a weight of anger his mother carried; he had quickly evolved—first word, first crawl—an adroitness at staying out of her way when she was heavy with it, and a wish to amuse her, to keep her light. But now, as they were nearing the end of their time together, and her flesh was dissolving and her inner self rising to the surface, his responses had become more daring, less catering, even challenging. Her own pale eyes, a blue faintly milky though she had never needed a cataract operation, widened at his question as if she were seeing ghosts over his shoulder. "Oh, Joey," she said, "don't ask. It was un*speak*able."

He had to smile at the old-fashioned concept. "Unspeakable? Daddy?"

A bit of flush had crept into her colorless creased cheeks. She was getting angry, once again. She kept staring, not so much at him as at the space in his vicinity. She knew from watching television what the talk shows permitted people to say these days. "Well, maybe you're old enough. Maybe I *should* speak it."

"Oh no, no thanks, that's all right," he said, jumping up from his chair and heading into the kitchen, much as his father used to in the middle of a marital exchange. *Poor Daddy,* was his thought. *Let the dead alone.* Now she, too, was dead, and there were many things, once speakable, that Joey would never know. Though he grew used to the sandstone house without her in it, he still found it strange, back in his Manhattan apartment, that she never called on Saturday mornings the way she used to, with her playful, self-mocking account of her week. The dead are so feeble they can't even telephone. The phone's silence more than any other conveyed the peace of the dead, their final and, as it were, hostile withdrawal.

The real-estate appraiser, an old high-school classmate, stood in his gray suit in the cobwebbed cellar, next to the rickety oil furnace, among the paint cans and rusty hot-air ducts, and said to Joey, "Seventeen years here alone. It took a lot of guts."

Yes, she had been brave, he could now afford to see, all those years alone, alone but for the animals she fed, and the presences on television. Over the telephone, even when reporting an insomniac night of breathlessness and terror, she had tried to keep it light for his sake, and mocked herself, mocking her very will, at the age of eighty-five, to live. "It's strange," she confessed to her son, "but I really don't intend to die. Though a lot of people would like me to."

"Really? Who?"

"The real-estate developers. The neighbors. They think it's time for this old lady to move over and make some room."

"Do they really?" He was grateful she had not included him among the many who wished her dead.

"Really," she mocked. "But I have a responsibility here. The place still needs me."

"We all need you," Joey said, sighing, giving up. The fate of the place was another unspeakable matter. She wanted the place to go on and on, unchanged, as it was in her idea of it.

He had scanned her in vain for some sign of sunset resignation. She had choked down her pills and vitamins to the end, and her fear of life's sensations' ceasing had seemed pure. The last time he had visited, on a cool fall day, she came outdoors to supervise his planting, in two arcs by a curve of the cement walk, two dozen tulip bulbs she had ordered from a catalogue. At first he had arranged the bulbs point down, and then realized that the point was what would grow upward, toward the sun. His mother had stood there on her unsteady feet, in her gaudy bathrobe, looking down; the sight of the fat cream-white bulbs nested in the turned red earth startled a kind of grunt out of her. "Oh, how dear they look," she said. To Joey she added, as his encouraging mother, "How nicely you do things."

In all of her leavings that came to light he was most touched by her accounts—her tax forms and used checkbooks, meticulously kept, even though her tiny backward-slanting hand had become spasmodic and shaky. (Could that big pencilled handwriting on the back of the enlarged photograph have been hers after all, at the age of thirteen?) She had kept, on a large pad of green paper, spreadsheets of her monthly expenses, ruled off by hand at the beginning of each month. The last entries had been made the day before the morning of her death. This financial and mathematical niceness of hers was something quite unpredictable, like a musical passion in a banker. Among the stored sheets of figures were several drawn up before they moved, with lists of expenses side by side—taxes, heating, utilities, upkeep. Absurdly small amounts they now seemed, having loomed so large in that price-frozen wartime world. By her calculations, their reduced costs in the little sandstone house, and the projected rentals of their eighty acres to the neighboring farmers, would save them five hundred dollars—a third of her husband's salary. It had never really occurred to Joey that their move here had had a practical side. When he came to sheets showing how the money for his college education could be squeezed out among their other expenses, he couldn't bear to keep reading.

Gradually, through the stark months of a winter that was, according to the forecasters, unseasonably cold, and then unseasonably warm, he reduced the house to its essence, removing every trace, even a rusty pencil sharpener screwed to a windowsill, of his life and the four lives that had ended. Here on this patch of now uncarpeted wood his grandfather had fallen, having convulsively leaped from the bed where, a year later, his widow would breathe her last. Here, in the bedroom adjacent, his father one midnight had sat up with such pains in his chest that he finally asked his wife to call the ambulance. He had died in the ambulance. Here in this same space Joey had lain sleepless, wondering how to tell his mother of his next divorce. Here on the other side of the wall he would lie after a date, his head still whirling with cigarette smoke and the girl's perfume. Here on the worn linoleum his mother had died, at the base of a wall she had the Amish carpenters make of old chestnut boards, boards left in the barn from the era before the blight, to cover the rough stones exposed when the big kitchen chimney had been removed. The rooms had a soft beauty, empty. The uncovered pine floorboards drank the sunlight. Joey looked through the curtainless windows, seeing what his mother had seen—the sloping old orchard to the north, the barn and road and fields to the east, the lilac bushes and bird feeder and meadow to the south, the woods and the tall blue spruce to the west. Each day the sun would set behind the woods, in a blood-red blazon of concentric fire.

On his final cleanup visit, Joey found floating in the bathroom toilet something devil-like—a small dark stiff shape, in size between a mouse and a rat, its legs connected by webs of skin. A flying squirrel. It had come down from the attic and drowned, sick and thirsty from the d-Con. Joey remembered watching at twilight, that summer he moved the stones, a pair of flying squirrels sail, as if sliding swiftly on a wire, from the attic window over to the blue spruce. The house had stood empty the previous summer, before his family had moved in, and this pair had moved in ahead of them.

He had bought a padlock for the cellar bulkhead, and closed the house with a key, having installed new locks. The house was ready for sale in the spring. But in the meantime, as he lay awake in his apartment three hours away, its emptiness called to him. It needed him. Only he understood it. Suppose a fire, or local vandals, jealous of the price the place would fetch ... Housing developments were all around, and even Philadelphians were moving into the area. His mother had made a shrewd investment, buying back paradise.

Those weekends alone in the house, sorting, cleaning, staying away from the motel until moonlight had replaced sunlight on the floors, Joey had discovered himself talking aloud, as if in response to a friendly presence just behind the dry old wallpaper, within the thick stone walls. Weeknights, his own rooms, suspended above Manhattan's steady roar, with an ornamental piece of porch bannister hidden at the back of a closet, seemed to be flying somewhere. He felt guilty, anxious, displaced. He had always wanted to be where the action was, and what action there was, it turned out, had been back there.

The Other Side of the Street

"For that," his lawyer told Rentschler, "you need a notary public. In this state they're the ones who handle car title changes." Rentschler hadn't lived in his home state for forty years, and only his mother's death had brought him back. He was taking possession of his meagre inheritance, cleaning out her sad, crammed apartment. Rentschler lived far to the west, and the climate and the vegetation and even the quality of light here in Pennsylvania seemed alien. The afternoon light was dying at the windows; the leafless trees in the courtyard below were sinking into a well of darkness, with a silvery November glitter, as if after an ice storm, gleaming on their upper twigs. He looked in the phone book under Notaries Public, and the address 262 Chestnut Street, Hayesville, leaped to his eye. A woman, Georgene R. Mueller. She answered the phone and sounded excessively cheerful and helpful; but perhaps that was just the regional manner, which Rentschler had slowly lost. He suggested that, late as it was, their transaction must wait until tomorrow. But she told him, going that extra mile, the way the inhabitants of this part of the world did, "No, I'm open here until eight. A lot of the people, you know, can't get to you except in the evenings. You'll need the car title, the insurance card, your own driver's license, and what we call the Short Certificate.

It'll say 'Short Certificate—Letters Testamentary' across the top."

"Yes, I have those. My lawyer gave me plenty."

"Now let me tell you how to find my house. You come out the Ephrata Pike—"

"I know," Rentschler interrupted. "I used to live across the street, at two sixty-one."

"Did you, though? What did you say your name was?"

He told her, but it rang no bell. "It was a long time ago," he apologized. "Just after the war. I was a child. We moved when I was twelve."

"Is that an honest fact? Well, it's still a house to be proud of. The Brubakers sold it, you know." This name meant nothing to him. "A younger couple has bought it, and sold off the back half of the lot."

"Really? It wasn't that big a lot in the first place." The vegetable garden had been down there, and his mother's rows of peonies, and the asbestos-shingled chicken house his grandfather had had built, and the little fenced-in yard where his grandmother used to behead chickens with a hatchet, on a stained old stump. Within the chicken house there was a liquid clucking, and a musty stench of chicken dung, and there were fascinating glass eggs scattered about in the straw to give the stupid hens the idea of laying.

"Well, I know," Georgene Mueller sighed, "but that's how they do things these days. They crowd the houses in. This is considered a desirable neighborhood."

"It always was," Rentschler told her. "My grandparents bought it back in the Twenties. If you really don't mind, I'll be there around seven. I should get a bite to eat first; I've been lugging junk all day." There was no need to tell her all this, but perhaps he was gaining back the garrulous local manner.

* * *

He knew the way in his bones, but was slightly confused by the traffic lights, which had multiplied in Hayesville since he was last there. A mall spread itself where there had been fields. A new high school, flat and low, reminded him of an airport. Along the low side of Chestnut Street, the trees had been cut down and the curb pushed back. Without the trees, his old street had a bareness that made the houses—some frame, some brick—appear exposed and shabby. Along the low-side curb fresh erect NO PARKING signs had sprouted; he parked anyway. The cement retaining walls on the other side of the street had developed bulges and cracks since he was a child—or else a child never noticed such things—and the long flights of steps, with iron-pipe railings, up to the porches of the houses had a gaunt, cockeyed look. To a child's eyes these steps had appeared grand. You climbed them and found magical pleasures at the top: a squeaking porch glider from which to watch the traffic go by below, a plushy front parlor with its shade drawn and a tinted big goblet of hard candy on a polished end table, a back yard with a double garden swing in a kind of bower of hollyhocks and morning glories, and a cement walk going back, straight as an arrow, toward the alley where the ice plant was. Beyond the alley had been a large vacant lot where in the summer travelling amusement parks set up their tents and rides and gambling games, and two girls in white cowgirl outfits sang at night.

Rentschler had lived on the low side of the street, with his family's yard sloping down to the truck garden and the chicken house. The elevated houses across the street had seemed to be more alive than his, more packed with blessings. At 260, next door to the similar house with a lighted PUBLIC NOTARY sign in the window of a glassed-in front porch, had lived the Emmelfosses. Wilma Anna had been a girl a year older than he; she always went to school in fussy dresses such as the other girls wore only to Sunday School. At Christmastime Wilma Anna's front parlor acquired a big long-needled evergreen; he remembered the sticky rich scent of pine sap, and the tree ornaments so antique he wondered if elves had made them, and the expensive department-store look of the brightly wrapped presents. The furniture in Wilma Anna's house all matched and wore doilies, and shelves of polished knickknacks were hung on the walls; the lampshades had tassles. When the Christmas tree was crowded in, the parlor seemed a magical cave you had to wriggle into, holding your breath.

At that time, an old woman had lived next door, at 262. Rentschler had forgotten her name. She wore cotton housedresses that buttoned down the front—a figure of fun and dread, living alone. At Halloween, she turned off all her lights and wouldn't come to the door when children rang the bell in their costumes. As Rentschler climbed the steps, his heart beat harder; he rang a bell beneath where a small rectangular light glowed. With his hand on the storm-door latch, he could feel the house tremble as its owner approached from the back, walking through the rooms. The old woman was dead, he kept telling himself.

A woman younger than he came to the door. Hayesville women beyond a certain age were of two types only: overweight or wiry. Georgene Mueller was one of the wiry ones, with a quick darting head of tight solid-black curls, and eyeglass frames of several colors and substances. Her mouth seemed to be a mechanism that functioned whether or not she was paying attention to it. "I didn't hear the ring for a second, I was just finishing putting in the dishes and watching the first part of the news; it almost makes you feel sorry for Mr. Gorbachev, he must wonder what's going to happen next, and Mr. Bush can do no wrong it seems, everything he touches turns to gold."

"That could change," Rentschler said, a bit lost amid the wide perspectives she had so readily opened up.

"Yes, the way the world is now, especially with these Arabs," she said, nevertheless moving past him toward her seat of business. Her desk and typewriter were set up in the sun porch, under several framed empowering certificates.

"I'm the man who called about an hour ago—"

"About the car title," she finished for him. "I recognize your voice." An out-of-state voice, he supposed he had now. He handed her the papers he had assembled. Not quite challengingly, she said, "You had no trouble finding me, I suppose."

"No, but there are more traffic lights than I remember."

"And still it's a tangle down at the corner at five o'clock. And even on Saturdays and Sundays now. It's the new mall toward Quarrytown has done it."

"Is the quarry still there? We used to swim in it, and ice-skate on it when it was cold enough. A lot of winters, though, it never did quite freeze. It was frustrating, if you had the skates, since they wouldn't fit next year." His own mouth seemed to be running a lot. It excited him to be on this side of the street, the other side, looking through this woman's windows at his old house, with its steep-pitched roof and plump porch pillars. To Rentschler as a child the front of the house had been a face—the two bedroom windows a pair of eyes close together, and the porch roof a sort of mustache, and the door and windows gleaming teeth. The striped awning in summer became another sort of teeth. He now had the view of the house that the crabby old lady had had. She often must have seen him go in and out the front door. Old women living alone look out their windows.

Rentschler's mother, it occurred to him, must have often looked out of hers, down into that stony courtyard.

"The hole in the ground is still there, but I believe they've fenced it off. Too dangerous. A boy drowned twenty or so years ago." And in Rentschler's childhood, too, it was said that a boy had drowned, twenty or so years before. Dead children haunt the earth, to scare the living into obedience. "Everything's here," the woman said, "except I need your registration card. This is the certificate the state gives you, but there's also a little card."

"Maybe it's in my mother's car. She didn't drive too much, toward the end."

Georgene Mueller did not offer sympathy. Death to her was a matter of paperwork. Yet her advice was kind. "You look in your mother's glove compartment," she said, as to a child, "and I'll bet you'll find the little card I'm talking about."

"I don't know," he said rising. "She was pretty, uh, out of it the last year or so."

"That's how they get. My mother did too. They go back."

Rentschler understood the local expression: "going back," for regressing, for turning senile. No natural process went unnamed in Hayesville. Nature was the great spectacle; people sat on their porches to watch it go by.

He went outdoors, into the cool misty night, on the deeply familiar street. On these very sidewalk squares, Wilma Anna and he had laid out hopscotch courts with colored chalks, and played with a rubber heel that if thrown wrong would bounce and bobble into the gutter, where the water from the ice plant ran. He found the registration card immediately, in the blue Velcro-fastened folder the automobile manufacturer provided. The dead try to take care of us. His mother had been depressed toward the end but not senile. Precise instructions regarding her funeral had been folded in her upper left-hand desk drawer, with her bank books and tax forms. His heart swelled in his chest at the unaccustomed effort of climbing the cement steps again. He wondered if people who lived on this side of the street lived longer, from the exercise. The land was flat where he lived now, with snow-tipped mountains unreal in the distance.

As the notary typed away at her long, pale-green forms, he sat beside her desk, looking across the street, and told her, "We used to have a hedge, all around. In a kind of pattern, with raised pieces at intervals; we had this funny heavy long trimmer you cranked, to make the teeth go back and forth. It took two people to operate it, my mother and grandfather usually. And bushes, we had a lot of bushes to trim. The front yard looks pretty bare now." *Stop talking,* he told himself.

"When they widened the street, they pushed back the sidewalks on that side."

"Yes, and took down the horse chestnuts. We used to collect them."

"Children do," she said, still typing.

Rentschler held his tongue, helpless to convey to her the peculiar wealth of a wagonful of horse chestnuts in their glossiness, their faint punky smell, their oval spots of pallor like the belly on a teddy bear. "The place was a lot of work to keep up," he felt compelled to volunteer. "But that wasn't why we moved. My father lost his job in '45 because a returning veteran took it back and we had to move down to Wilmington, where there was work. My mother moved back to the area when my father died, since she had a sister still living here, to this apartment in town she always hated, though she never complained. I suppose she would have liked to live with me, but I had a wife at the time."

"There's a lot of heartbreak," Georgene Mueller admitted, frowning into the desk light as she rubbed the green form with a typewriter eraser. "It's a handsome house. Even without the shutters and the awnings. They came down about ten years ago, my husband and I were here already."

"I used to wish I lived on this side of the street," Rentschler confessed. "It seemed, I don't know, more fun over on this side, even though the houses were smaller."

"This sun porch is a Godsend," the woman said. "Without it, I'd have no place to set up shop. In the dead of winter, you'd be surprised how the sun warms it up—I have an electric heater but hardly ever have to turn it on." With a smart twirl of the platen she freed the paper from the typewriter. She sorted out the duplicates, with a grimace of effort pressed her notary seal into the original and carbon copies, and gave him back the cards and papers she didn't need. Yes, he remembered, this was how people did things in Pennsylvania: seriously, thoroughly. Life had weight here. The total, her fee and the commonwealth's, came to twenty-nine dollars. She clipped his checks to her papers and showed him the envelope in which she would send his application for title transfer to Harrisburg first thing in the morning. At the conclusion of her instructions, she asked, "Would you like to see the house?"

Rentschler had been gazing so steadily at the house across the street that it took him a second to realize she meant her own. "Sure," he said. "I've never been in it before. The old lady who lived here when I was a kid hated kids." The swish of traffic was slackening on Chestnut Street, and there were no lights on at the front of his old house, just an unsteady upstairs phosphorescence indicating the presence of a television set, or perhaps an aquarium with a flickering bulb. From that lonely house he would cross Chestnut Street and come play with Wilma Anna. In her back yard there was an enchanted, luxurious plaything, a white wooden swing, two facing seats suspended in a frame upon which morning glories had been encouraged to grow. She in her starchy little dress would swing forward as he swung back, and then backward as he swung toward her, her face in the sun-dapple utterly solemn and dimly expectant, the way girls' faces were, her upper lip lifted to expose a wet gleam of teeth.

Georgene Mueller's living room, as wide as her house minus the width of a set of unused stairs, contained the usual goblet of candy on an end table, next to a sullen brown plush sofa. Noticing the direction of his eyes, she said, "Have a piece. That's what it's there for."

He removed the fragile glass lid, with its round red-tinted knob. The candy was not hard, in twists of cellophane, but leftover Halloween candy: three-tone corn kernels, grinning pumpkins, and conical witches' hats, chewy but not too gummy for his bridgework. For twenty-nine dollars, he figured he could sneak three or four, while his hostess moved into the next room. "When Jake left," she was saying, as if Rentschler knew who Jake was, "I was so mad I took the little savings account we had and blew it on the dining room; the people before us had had it as such a dull dark room and Jake always said it was good enough, we ate in the kitchen anyway."

The room was not dull now. Spanishness was the theme, from a wrought-iron chandelier with violet candles to wall mirrors with wide baroque frames of encrusted fake silver. Artificial beams had been placed along the ceiling, descending to jutting oaken brackets as if in a California mission, above panels of three-dimensional imitation stonework; behind the mirrors a silvery wallpaper was patterned in blown-up Victorian steel engravings, like a Max Ernst collage repeated over and over. Magical caves: that was how the houses over here had always seemed to him. "Lovely," Rentschler said, through the chewy Halloween candy. "Really striking."

She pondered his verdict and the walls of the room, where a few prints of staring deer, shadow-boxed in velvet, completed the effect. "It was a fancy of mine," she said. "That's one blessing about being alone, you can do what you want."

Yes—you grow into the spaces the absent have left you. Rentschler had already noticed how, with the distant pressure of his mother's existence lifted, his personality had begun to expand, distorting into a shape that half frightened him. His new talkativeness, for instance—a reaching out, where he had always taken pride in being self-reliant, going west like a tight-lipped pioneer, becoming an alien. "How long have you lived here, altogether?" he asked this other solitary. Her solid-black hair was tightly curled and her movements were brisk, even twitchy, with reserves of energy waiting to be tapped.

"Thirteen years, it'll be. For the last seven I've supported myself. It's hard," she said, "but you make do. Your mother made do, too, I don't doubt. I have to rent out my upstairs here, I couldn't get by without the extra. This is my bedroom—do you mind passing through? I thought you'd like to see the back yard."

"I would, yes. I used to play in the back yard next door."

"She keeps it up real nice. Flowers back to the alley like her parents always had, and she just had that garden swing painted again. She cares for it like it's a real antique."

Rentschler was lost. "Who does?"

"Why, Wilma Anna!"

"You mean she's still *here*?"

"Oh sure. Still here. All alone. She never married. Though lately she has a boy friend comes calling, I never noticed one before. She goes to movies now, and shows in town. I don't think she's home now even, or you could go say hello."

"Wilma Anna Emmelfoss. I can't believe she's still here. That was fifty years ago we used to play together."

"Her mother went quick, but her dad, oh, he lingered something dreadful."

"You wouldn't believe what a pretty little girl she was, always in these dresses that seemed very fancy to everybody else. We were only children, the two of us."

"She still dresses nice. For her work, you know. She sells advertising for the paper in town. There, you can see her swing through the kitchen window."

Leaning over an aluminum sink, Rentschler could barely make out a patch of white in the darkness, and a blurred white framework around it: the arbor that had sheltered them as children, swinging back and forth, back and forth, a sulky quizzical look on Wilma Anna's careful face, with its wide forehead and pointed chin, flickering through shadows and sun quicker than the eye could sort out. "Yes, I see it," he said politely.

"And here's my pride and joy," said his hostess. "My little piece of heaven." She led him out the back door, and they stared up the rise of her trim back yard, with a center walk of cement arrowing back to the alley. Rentschler's heart seemed to swell again, pumping too hard. These secret yards, straight and narrow, had been the essence of the happiness on this side of the street: lush flower beds along the walk, a patch of lawn with some lawn furniture, a shed containing hoses and rakes, an apple tree or two to represent an orchard, low fences of picket or playground wire, each quarter-acre in strict parallel with one's neighbors', and the far end holding a garage and opening onto the freedom of the alley. Rentschler inhaled Hayesville happiness; he saw his entire life, past and to come, as an errant encircling of this forgotten center. His childhood back yard—the bloody stump, the frightened sad stupid chickens, the vegetable rows that always needed weeding—had been comparatively sad and disorderly. His family had not quite had the Hayesville secret. It was right that they had been forced to move.

He inhaled the moist darkness again and listened dimly to Georgene Mueller's detailing of the flowers she cultivated, the quince tree whose fruit she made jelly of, the storage shed and stone bench she had ordered from a supply house—her single life stubbornly exerting its pressure back against the pressure of the world.

Returning to the gaudy kitchen, with plaid Formica on all the counters, Rentschler looked once more at Wilma Anna's white embowering swing, and tried to imagine her life here, all those static years: it was unimaginable, like the life of a tree. For his mother's solitude, Rentschler felt largely responsible, and amid the undercurrents of this encounter he was acquiring a hallucinatory responsibility for this woman's—at least, a touch of guilt at the tug of her tight dyed curls, her undischarged energy. But in regard to Wilma Anna's majestically rooted life he felt nothing but wonder.

On the way out, he was going to avoid the tempting candy, but the notary public said, "Take some. It'll just go stale otherwise. The children don't come around like they used to. A lot of the parents don't let them out, what with the maniacs you read about who put poison and things in the treats." She had suddenly become querulous, and tired. They moved in silence together through the darkened sun porch; the slight fever of their intimacy, which had peaked in the back yard, had subsided. Rentschler felt dismissed. Stepping into the glittery November chill, he was dazzled to see the house on the other side of the street ablaze; the porch light and front-room lamps were lit up as if to welcome a visitor, a visitor, it seemed clear to him, long expected and much beloved.

Tristan and Iseult

THE OUTWARD APPEARANCES of these women told him almost nothing: some of the prettiest and daintiest turned out to have cold fingers and a merciless touch, whereas some of the plainest, with doughy humorless faces and rimless glasses, enveloped him in velvet sensations. Today's (a total stranger, as was always the case; the turnover was terrific, suggesting an overheated profession susceptible to stress, pregnancy, and tempting offers from rival establishments) led her customer with a nunnish severity to her little, heavily equipped room and offered him, as she settled him on his back, only the most grudging small talk. Yet as soon as she touched his mouth he knew that he was home, that she was a rare one, one he could trust not to hurt him more than necessary. The threat of pain was the mystical spice to these liaisons, the Heaven-sent menace that on both sides of the relationship concentrated the attention.

Heaven here was a ceiling of acoustical tiles, perforated irregularly in order to entertain trapped eyes like his. The angelic music was from an "easy listening" station—every third tune, it seemed to him, that nonsensical croon about Key Largo, Bogie and Bacall, here's looking at you, kid, have it all. . . .

"Turn your head toward me, please." Occasionally, one of her bare forearms brushed his ear or nose, stirring up in a small, pollenlike cloud the scent of spank-

154

ing clean female flesh. Because of AIDS, they wore surgical masks now, and disposable plastic gloves. Death has always been the possible price of contact, but as contacts have multiplied, so have possibilities, forming a continuous moist membrane for viral self-advancement. She worked along his lower gum line, pausing periodically to wipe one of her oblique, needle-sharp instruments on a napkin folded on the plastic tray beside her, next to his head. Some women he had had in the past used his chest as a table, resting their tools on his paper bib—making a small, unprofessional joke, he felt, of their bodily intimacy. This one would never so trespass. Though his open mouth, with its rim of teeth, and the round plastic tray, with its serrated edges, might closely alternate in the field of her attention, she would never imply that they were interchangeable. The tray was merely a thing, whereas the mouth was connected to nerves and a soul—to an ego inside a thing. A sensitive, self-solicitous thing. Her touch, as it methodically travelled along, magnified his tiny dental surfaces, transforming the bumps and crevices of enamel and its porcelain counterfeit into a continuous plane of now dim, now vivid nervous apprehension. Her voice descended: "A little sore tissue under these bridges. Don't be afraid to get up in there with the floss."

Silently, in prayer's shouting inner voice, he assured her that he henceforth would not be afraid, would *not*. He did not speak for fear of dislodging the muttering saliva ejector, which was shaped like a question mark. Sometimes his roving eyes flicked into her own, then leaped away, overwhelmed by their glory, their—as the deconstructionists say—*presence*. His glance didn't dare linger even long enough to register the color of these eyes; he gathered only the spiritual, starlike afterimage of their living gel, simultaneously crystalline and watery, behind the double barrier of her glasses and safety goggles, above the shield-shaped paper mask hiding her mouth, her chin, her nostrils. So much of her was enwrapped, protected. Only her essentials were allowed to emerge, like a barnacle's feathery appendages—her touch and her steadfast, humorless gaze.

"Now, away from me a little. Not quite so much. Perfect."

Perfect. Would that he were. She more than anyone knew how imperfect he was. How rotten, in a word. Sinking beyond the reach of shame, he relaxed into her exploration and scarification of lower molars, corrupt wrecks just barely salvaged from the ruin of his years of heedless, sugar-oriented consumption. Doughnuts, candied peanuts, Snickers bars, licorice sticks, chocolate-coated raisins ... *Mea culpa, domina.*

Her attentions, pricking and probing on the ticklish edge of pain, formed as it were a cradle of interwoven curves, from the plump meat of the ball of her thumb tangent upon his upper lip to the arc of her masked face bent an inch or two above his nose. Woven of long soft strands of tactful touch and unstated, clinical thought, she was a kind of basket inverted above him, a woven hut, a yurt; her staring black pupils were the size of the perforations in the acoustic ceiling. She was seeing, and forgiving even as she saw, a side of himself he had never had to face—a microbe-ridden, much-repaired underside. She had an angle on him that he was spared. Other people in general possess this, this instant purchase on the specifics of an exterior self mercifully vague in its self-perception. But their case, his and hers, seemed extreme, like something from a supermarket tabloid or a Harlequin romance. Serenely she presided above his supine abasement. Done with the lowers, she told him to sit up and "have a good rinse." He spit. Blood, his blood, appeared in the ecru bowl animated by centripetal water. His blood was stringy and spitty and dark. He was even more loathsome than in his humblest moments he had dreamed.

And still she returned to the bout, tackling his uppers, commanding him to open wider. At her faintly more aggressive tone, a sense of counter-striving invaded his body; he seemed to arch upward in the chair, fitting himself with a distinct push into her ministrations. Her flesh, as it touched his, had a resilience slightly greater than that of a cigarette pack, a warmth a bit less than that of a flashlight face, a humidity even more subtle than that of laundry removed five minutes too soon from the dryer. She was made for him, of the same imperilled and fallible substance, yet also woven of Heaven, unpossessable, timeless, inviolate, though focused in her every atom upon him, indeed nonexistent but for him, like air made blue by our own vision, and burned into life by our lungs.

"How're you doin'?" she asked.

Had he betrayed, by some groan or tensing, discomfort? Had the transfixed state of his soul translated somatically into resistance or involuntary spasm? "Fine." It felt like a lie—less than the whole story—or like a vow, which is also too simple. Now another mangy pet of the easy-listening stations slid into the room, an arrangement of "The Girl from Ipanema" shorn of the troubling, too-rapid lyrics, which he had once been told were much more suggestive in Brazilian Portuguese.

"Just a little more," she promised lullingly. "Then we'll polish and floss."

"Unnh," he consented, like a ditto mark under his previous, mendacious yet sincere monosyllabic avowal.

And in her flurry of searching out the last potentially disastrous plaque in the remotest crannies of his upper left molars her spirit intertwined with his. She leaned deeper in; he felt the parallel beams of her gaze like lasers vaporizing his carious imperfections; their bodies became mere metaphor. Timeless moments passed in rhythmic scraping. Then she pulled back and straightened up, her face a mask, her eyes noncommittal. He was clean. He was done. She had done him. "You may rinse," she said.

The polishing, with its playful caress of microscopic grit, and the flossing—quick, brusque, nimble around and under the bridges—felt anticlimactic. Without the threat of pain, their encounter became small, much as the childish perpetrators of giant agitated shadows, in an attic or a summer-camp shack, shrink when the candle is put out. She did not use that agonizing machine some of the women used, the Cavijet, a high-pressure nozzle with a high-pitched whine, an icy needle on your inflamed nerves. It would have been a cheap effect. The pain, to have meaning, should come purely from her. "Nice," he said, working his bruised lips over his teeth, as ideal as they could ever be. "How did I look, over-all?"

"Uh—do you smoke or drink a lot of tea?"

"No. Why?"

Her mask and goggles were off; she blushed. It was thrilling, to see emotion tinge that prim, professional face. She cared. She had to care, after all. How could she go through these motions and not care? "I just wondered," she said, turning away in, at last, embarrassment. "You have a fair amount of staining."

"Maybe that's my age. Normal deterioration."

She shook off the idea—it was heretical, perhaps; there existed no normal deterioration in her belief system—and wrote on a chart in his folder, and inscribed a small slip for him to take down to the front desk. Then . . . then she turned and faced him. Her eyes in the TV-screen-shaped rectangles of her glasses were distinctly, earthily hazel—green flecked with gold and rust above her rosy cheeks, cheeks whose thin skin could no longer conceal the circulating heat of her blood.

She hesitated to speak, then took the plunge. "There's a bleaching process that's pretty safe and effective," she said, with a lilt reined in just short of ardor.

There was, but she wouldn't be the one to witness the shining results. The woman was always a stranger. You never had the same one twice. The principle lay between the two of them like a sword. Otherwise, it wouldn't be sublime. It wouldn't be hygiene.

George and Vivian

I. *Aperto, Chiuso*

"THERE'S ONE—it says *aperto*!"

"Where?" Allenson asked, knowing perfectly well. There was a tense gullible nerve in his young wife that it amused him to touch.

"Right there! We went right by! Mobil, just like at home! I can't believe you did that, darling!"

"I didn't like the look of it. Too many ugly trucks."

Vivian explained to him, with the complacency of a knowing child, "You're just nervous because you don't know how to say 'Fill 'er up.' But if we don't get gas soon we'll be stuck by the side of the road, and then what'll you say?"

"I'll say, '*Scusi*,'" he said.

In the several years of their secret affair, Vivian, George Allenson's third wife, had had ample opportunity to observe how little, in relation to his second wife, he was to be trusted; but he had not expected her, once *they* were married, to perceive him as untrustworthy. He was twenty years older, also, and he had not imagined that this superiority in time spent upon the earth might be regarded as a deficit—in eyesight, in reaction time, in quality of attention. Throughout their vacation trip to Italy, Vivian was vocally nervous in the car, sitting beside him clutching the map while he, with growing confidence and verve, steered their rented subcompact Fiat through the Italian traffic, from one lovely old congested city to another. He was even mastering the Italian trick of turning a two-lane highway into a three-lane by simply passing anyway, right into the teeth of the oncoming traffic. Whenever he did this, she shrieked, and now she was worried about their running out of gas, and kept urging him into gasoline stations. Far as they had driven, from Venice to Ravenna to Verona, they had not yet replenished the tankful that came with the car.

"I'll turn gracefully to you," he elaborated, in the mellow baritone that even a smidgeon of Italian brings out in the male voice, "and say, *'Mi scusi, mia cara.'* Actually, honey, we've got plenty of gas. These little Fiats go forever on just a liter."

He was nearly sixty, and she nearly forty, and as these irrevocable turning-points approached, both of them, perhaps, were showing their nerves. They were headed toward Lake Garda on a day's trip out of Verona. Their Veronese hotel room was not merely expensive but exquisite, provided with real antiques and a balcony view of roof tiles and *campanili* whose various bells rang the hours in a ragged procession of tollings. The Allensons had developed a daily routine—two continental breakfasts in the room, delivered with much waiterly fussing and musical clatter, followed by a walking excursion to a church or two, a Roman amphitheatre, or a castle converted into an art museum, and then their return to the room and a lunch of fresh fruit bought en route and some thriftily saved breakfast rolls, the elemental economy of this lunch suggesting an even less expensive entertainment, in the languor of the sunny hour, on one or the other of their little Empire-style beds. This routine was intimate and strict, so it was with trepidation and potential irritability that they had set out, this morning, in the neglected car to brave the narrow unmarked streets and the helter-skelter of buzzing, thrusting Italian vehicles.

On their last excursion, which had brought them from Vicenza to Verona by way of the S-11—an inescapable green line on Vivian's map—Allenson had managed almost immediately to take a wrong turn that headed them up into the hills, through pastel flocks of villagers attending mass, between flowering hedgerows and fields dotted with sheep, on a winding upward road that offered, it seemed to him, no place to turn around. Her resentment of his failure to follow the route so clear and plain right there on her lap became shrill, and he risked their lives by angrily ducking into a dirt lane and backing out into the road. On their descent back through the village, which she retrospectively identified, on the map, as Montecchio Maggiore, Vivian confessed, by way of making up, how pretty it all was. And it was true, his blunder had in a minute uncovered a crystalline cisalpine charm bared by none of their mapbound excursions, including one in the very next hour, to Soave, at the end of a little spur that crossed the A-4.

Soave, hitherto to them merely a name on a bottle of cheap white wine, was an old walled town; they parked outside the gates and walked along the main street. Outside the town's main bar, a crowd of men had gathered after mass, and one of them abruptly presented Vivian, as she passed, with a red carnation. Allenson, a step behind her, was startled to see his wife accept the gift with an instantaneous broad smile and the appropriate gracious gesture of bringing the flower to within a few inches of her chest. *"Grazie,"* she said, managing nicely that little flirted tail of an "e" which Allenson always had trouble pronouncing.

Perhaps women are biologically conditioned to accept flowers, even from total strangers on the street. Vivian was dark-haired and somewhat stately of figure; but for her chunky, practical running shoes, she might have been Italian. Allenson reflexively reached toward his pocket to pay for the flower, but no charge was exacted. The man, in a suit but unshaven, matched Vivian's smile with an equally broad one of his own and responded, *"Prego, signora,"* ignoring her husband.

Allenson quickened his step to place himself by her side. When they had put behind them the crowd of loitering, chattering men, Vivian asked him, "What did it mean?" For all her criticism of his driving and deportment she expected him to know everything, to be wise.

"Damned if I know. Look—those little girls have carnations, too."

"Does it mean I'm a Communist or something?"

There were election posters all over Italy, and some of them did show a carnation. "Left of center, at the worst, I would think. Communism's had it, even here. Maybe it's just something they do for tourists."

"I think we're the only ones in town."

It was true, entering the walled town at Sunday noon felt as if they were trespassing in a large living room full of happy families. Allenson's eyes, moving on from the little pre-adolescent, carnation-carrying girls, had received the equivalent of a flower: seen from behind, a father and daughter strolled with their arms about each other's waists, the gray-haired father, in his possessive fond grip, apparently unaware that his long-haired daughter had grown to be as tall as he and voluptuous, her mandolin-shaped bottom just barely contained in a leather mini-skirt. These skirts, taut swatches exposing the full length of thigh, had been all over Venice, moving up and down the stepped bridges that crossed the canals. As a child wants to reach out and pat balloons, to verify their substance, Allenson had mentally reached out. Perhaps Vivian was right, he was not trustworthy; he wanted to be forever a young lover. He had left his anti-hypertensive pills at home, and she—rather chemically, he thought—credited to that his rejuvenated sexual energy. But, broken loose from the routines of work and old friendships, one is, as a tourist, immersed in youth, unable to ignore how the world's population is renewing itself. Even Vivian was old, relatively.

Allenson really couldn't understand why, after these many kilometers in which he had not crashed into anything, she seemed still not to like his driving. The car's five gears (six, with reverse) did sometimes still jumble under his hand, so that he tried to start in third or to move straight from first to fourth, but within a day he had satisfied himself that, in Italy as elsewhere, a subtle camaraderie of the road mitigates the chances of collision. Amid an incessant buzzing of motorcycles, and between onrolling walls of double-van trucks, understandings were being reached, tolerances arrived at. Even at the most frantic mergers, he felt a Latin grace and logic; the drivers of Italy, though possessed of a gallant desire to maximize the capacity of their engines, were more civilized than the Calvinistic commuters of Westchester and Long Island. "Relax," he told Vivian, on the road to Lake Garda. "Enjoy the scenery."

"I can't. You'll take some crazy wrong turn like you did outside Vicenza."

"What if I do? It's all new to us. It's all Italy."

"That's the problem."

"I thought you loved it here."

"I do, when we stop moving."

"You know, Vivian, I could start to resent all this criticism. Elderly men have feelings, too."

"It's not you, you're doing great, considering."

"Considering what?"

"Considering," she said, "you're driving on an empty gas tank."

Sirmione, even in early May, was full of other tourists. "The kids are here," the couple said, continuing a joke that had developed in Venice and continued into Ravenna, where every basilica and baptistry seemed crammed, beneath the palely shimmering Byzantine mosaics, with packs of sight-sated, noisily interacting schoolchildren. Even the vast Piazza San Marco wasn't big enough to hold the boisterous offspring of an ever more mobile and prosperous Europe.

The small fortress at Sirmione offered views of the lake and, most fascinatingly, of the process of laying roof tiles. Three men labored gingerly on a roofed pitch beneath the fort's parapets. The oldest stood on a dizzying scaffold and guided onto his platform each wheelbarrow-load of tiles and cement hoisted by a crane in the courtyard; the youngest slapped mortar along the edge where roof met parapet; the middle-aged man crouched lovingly to the main task, of seating each row of tiles on gobs of mortar and tapping them, by eye, into regularity. "Doesn't that seem," Allenson asked his wife, "a tedious way to make a roof? What's wrong with good old American asphalt shingles?"

"They're ugly," Vivian said, "and these roofs are beautiful."

"Yeah, but acres of them, everywhere you look. How much beauty do you need? The cement must dry up and then everything slips and slides and cracks. I wonder when this roof last had to be done like this. Probably last summer."

Catullus had summered here, a monument down by the dock informed them. A hydrofoil from Riva hove splashily into view, and they ate two toasted *panini con salami* at an outdoor café. When Allenson closed his eyes and lifted his face to the sun he had a dizzying sensation of being on the old workman's scaffold, suspended at a killing height, thousands of miles from home, on a small blue planet, and soon to be dead, as dead as Catullus, his consciousness ceasing, his awareness of sun and of shade, of the voices of the excited kids around them. His brief life was quite pointless and his companion no comfort. She was a kid herself. He opened his eyes and the tidily trashy, overused scenic charm of the lakeside washed in, displacing his dread.

"What are you thinking?" Vivian asked him, her voice on edge, as if they were already back in the car.

"How nice it is here," he answered. He added, "And what a dreamboat you are."

"Why do you lie?" she asked.

He felt no need to answer. People lie to be merciful. They drove west to Decenzano, then north to Salò and along a road that twisted high above the lake. "Do you *have* to accelerate around the corners?" she asked.

"There's a guy pushing me behind."

"Let him pass."

"There's no place to pass."

"Then let him go a little slower. He can see you're not Italian."

"How?"

"From the haircut. Why do you feel you have to pretend you're an Italian driver?"

"No comprendo," he said. *"Sono italiano. Sono un ragazzo."* In a lavatory in Venice he had studied a graffito that read HO FATTO L'AMORE CON UN RAGAZZO VENEZIANO E STATO BELLISSIMA. *"Con mia cara,"* he added. *"Con,"* with its coarse meanings in other languages, turned out to be an indispensable Italian word. *Cappuccino con latte. Acqua minerale con gas. Panini con salami.* The little Fiat emitted a satisfying squeal of tires as Allenson surged around a hairpin curve. The grille of the tailgating Ferrari switched back and forth in the rearview mirror like an exasperated beast in a cage.

"I'm getting sick to my stomach," Vivian said.

"Stop looking at the map. Look out the window. Enjoy the beauty you're so crazy about."

The most beautiful moment, for him, had occurred in Venice, as they were walking back to the hotel, up over a little bridge, past a place where the long black coffin-like gondolas waited in the canal while their drivers gloomily played cards. The dollar had become so weak that Americans were timid of gondola rides, and the Allensons had contented themselves with hearing, as they walked around after dinner, the astounding male voice of a gondolier, as open and plaintive as that of a woman, but enormous: it would swell from a distance into an operatic climax only a few yards away as a line of gondolas slid and tapped past and then slowly would subside, still audible long after the gondolas, with their burden of swaddled passengers, had vanished between the high, angled house walls. The water in the canal would tremble into stillness. The passengers were usually Japanese. This evening, as the Allensons crossed a little piazza and approached the passageway to their hotel, a tall Japanese girl cried out, "No! Wait!" The two syllables of English, somehow like a cry in a language Allenson only half understood, brimmed with a sweet anguish that electrified the air and arrested all motion but hers. Tall for her race, glimmering in a white dress, the young woman, her straight sleek hair utterly black in the half-light—that stagy indoors-outdoors atmosphere of Venice—raced across the flat stones at the canal's edge while the gondoliers called to one another like awakened birds. She had lost something, Vivian speculated at Allenson's side, and indeed the contralto cry had been as of someone violated, fatally penetrated. But, no, she wanted to give something, to a mustachioed young gondolier who, to receive it, gallantly made his way back across the narrow canal by stepping on other gondolas. The two of them reached out each an arm to touch hands, while imaginary music swelled, and in her strangely electrifying, passion-filled voice the Japanese girl said, in this language that belonged to neither her nor him, "Your mon-ey." A tip. Some yen disguised as lire. The Japanese were flooding the world with money, as once Americans did. The Japanese had become rich and, with it, sexy. So beautiful, so far from home, her voice rising like a Madame Butterfly's in this echoing stage set of a city. Her cry vibrated in Allenson's bones until he at last fell asleep in the hotel bed.

"Darling, you *must* stop the car," Vivian said, in a voice drained of all flirtation and wifely tact. "I'm about to throw up."

He looked over. She did look greenish, under the tan she had acquired drinking cappuccini in sunny piazzas. Within a few hundred yards he found a space by the side of the road, beside a steeply descending woods, and pulled over. Other cars whizzed by. A few wrappers and empty plastic bottles testified to previous visitors. The lake showed its sparkling green-blue through the quivering tops of poplars. On the other side of the road a high ochre wall restrained the hillside. Vivian sat still, eyes shut, like a child trying to hold down a tantrum. Feeling unappreciated, Allenson got out of the car, slammed the door, and inspected this unscenic piece of Italy—the litter, the linked fence, the flowering weeds. Such unpampered roadside nature reminded him of America; his stiff old heart cracked open and peace entered, and with it, for the ten-thousandth time, a desire to reconcile with his wife, whoever she was. Vivian had opened the car window a crack, to permit communications. "Want to come out for some air?" he asked.

She shook her head curtly. "I want to go back. I want to get off this fucking twisty road."

"What about Riva?" They had intended to drive to Riva at the head of the lake.

"Fuck Riva."

"Honey, your language," he said, slightly stirred, along the lines of the Japanese girl's thrillingly pitched exclamation in Venice. He loved it when women *let it out*. "Would you like to drive?"

"You know I'm scared of the gears."

"Then just relax and let me drive."

"O.K., but don't be so macho." Her voice softened on "macho." "I beg you," she added. *"Prego."*

"Smooth as silk," he promised. The exchange had conferred youthful status on him; he got back into the car bouncily. "Stop looking at the map," he told her. "That's what gets you sick."

On the way back toward Salo, Vivian cried out, "What a lovely little church! Darling, could you please stop?"

There was a space of cobblestones beside an array of white metal tables, and he pulled in. "See," she said, in a placating tone meant to match his new docility. "If you go slow enough, we can see things."

The ancient little church had a patchily Romanesque façade. The rounded front portal was open, and to enter they parted a thick red curtain. Within, they were embraced by the watery cool of village Catholicism—a stony deep scent like that of a well, a few guttering candles, some unfathomably murky frescoes. The hard-pressed tourist couple welcomed the emptiness, the vaulted silence between the entrance and the pale Virgin who was making a gentle disclaiming gesture beside the altar. Vivian was so moved she fed a thousand-lira bill into one of the offering boxes. From the church they went next door to sit at one of the white tables. A girl just barely in her teens came to them shyly, nervously, as if they were the first customers of her career. Allenson ordered cappuccino for Vivian, *limonata* for himself. Both were good, as Hemingway might have said. Dear old Hemingway, Allenson thought—looking for the good life in hotels and cafés, roaming Europe like a bison on a tenderly grassy plain, nibbling, defecating, showering love on headwaiters and contessas.

From the white tables one looked level across the road at the masts of some fishing boats and through them at the glittering turquoise water receding to the misty blue mountains of the far shore. Once again, the best had proved to be the unforeseen. On her map Vivian discovered that they were in Maderno. She found the church in her guidebook, in the smallest of types. " 'Sant' Andrea,' " she read. " 'Shows remains of Roman and Byzantine architecture, especially in the pillar capitals, doors, and windows. A yet older church,' it says, 'seems to be incorporated in the building.' "

" 'Yet older.' " Reading over her shoulder, Allenson said, "We should go see D'Annunzio's house. It's just down the road."

She looked at him distrustfully. "Who was D'Annunzio?"

"You dear child," said Allenson. "He was just about the most famous writer since Byron. I mean famous-famous, not literary-excellence-famous. I'm a little vague about exactly why. Kind of a pre-Hemingway, fond of big gestures. A great womanizer. Didn't you see the article on his house a while back in *Art & Antiques*? It looked like a Turkish harem."

"That *would* appeal to you," Vivian said.

"And there are gardens," he dimly remembered. "We passed the sign to it just here"—he stabbed the map—"in Gardone Riviera. We'll nip in to look at it, and then drive straight back, and be back in the hotel in time to have tea in the bar. Maybe he'll give us those little English biscuits again."

"Gas," Vivian said. "We *must* get gas, George."

Con gas. "There'll be a station on the way to D'Annunzio," he promised.

But there wasn't. The distance was so short he shot past the turnoff, and had to back around, awkwardly and dangerously, while Vivian shrieked and clamped her eyes shut. Once safely parked, they walked uphill, following signs to *Il Vittoriale degli Italiani.* It was two o'clock, and the sun had become hot. "What's a *'vittoriale'*?" she asked him.

"I don't know. Some kind of victory?"

"I thought the Italians never had that sort of victory. That was part of their charm."

"We'll see," he promised.

But at the entrance, with its ticket booth and desultory souvenir stands, the guard was explaining something to a bulky, displeased Italian family. *"È chiusa,"* Allenson heard him say. The ending was feminine. *"La casa?"* he asked, at a venture.

"La casa, il museo," the guard said, and a torrent more, of which Allenson took the drift to be that the grounds and gardens were, however, open. The day was Monday, which presumably explained the split. *Aperto, chiuso:* Italy was a checkerboard.

"You're in luck," Allenson told his wife. "The house full of pillows is closed. Only the outdoors is open."

"Is it worth seeing?"

"It must be, or they would shut everything up at once. Do you want to go in or not, dear?"

Vivian gave her first sign of D'Annunzio-induced panic. Her dark eyes, aswarm with resentments, made an effort to read her husband's face. "You want to," she said. "You think it'll be sexy."

"I want to do what *mia cara* wants," Allenson said. He pointed out, "We won't be here soon again. Maybe never." Wednesday, they were flying home.

"How much is it?"

Allenson glanced at the *biglietteria* and said, "Five thousand a head. A cappuccino in Venice cost nine. It's only money; we're making memories." *Your mon-ey:* yen passed through the reaching hands, the coffinlike gondolas bumping.

"Let's see what the other people do."

The Italian family, with abundant disgruntled dialogue between the husband and wife, while their two fat children reddened in the sun, decided to enter; but inside the gates, on the long paved walks and surreal stark stairways, where the Allensons kept encountering them, the man was heard more than once to be exclaiming in disbelief, as he surveyed the sunstruck *vittoriale,* "*Cinque mila!*"

To Allenson, it was worth it. The views of the lake, of the forest plunging down into the lake, were worth it. The only slightly aged grandiosity was worth it. The place had the feeling of an American sacred place—the home of Daniel Chester French, for instance, or Roosevelt's Hyde Park—in which history has scarcely had time to cool. One's parents, in boaters and white linen, might have been guests here, filling the terraces with the clamor of their youthful frivolity. An old scarlet roadster was displayed behind glass—*L'automobile dell'impresa di Fiume.* "The empress of Fiume?" Vivian asked.

"I don't quite think so. Something that happened at Fiume?" Stairways led upward, past closed house and museum doors, into the surrounding woodland, where a mountain stream had been tricked into forming a gold-fish pond. The atmosphere was pampered, enchanted, sinister. The couple came to a shelter wherein a large old-fashioned motorboat was suspended in memorial drydock; around the walls of the boathouse maps and photographs tried to explain the great *impresa* of Fiume, but only in Italian. It was a secret the Italians had among themselves; it involved a number of men, centered about short, bald, goateed, baggy-eyed D'Annunzio, wearing the clothes of an aviator. Maps showed dotted lines heading across the Adriatic and back. "What *hap*pened?" Vivian demanded in her impatient, car-riding voice.

"I don't know, darling. It was a heroic exploit, in the car and then the boat."

"It feels evil."

"Don't be silly. In the First World War, the Italians were on the Allied side, remember? Read Hemingway. They were fighting the Austrians."

"Then what were they doing in Yugoslavia?"

"It was Austrian at the time, maybe." History, his fragile knowledge of it, was crumbling under him.

From the boathouse a concrete path led further upward, to a bizarre and solemn structure, a two-story mausoleum. The lower portion, entered through open arches, had the same watery smell as the little Romanesque church, but the only holy objects were graven names, names of *i Tredici*—the Thirteen—and more inscrutable printed information concerning Fiume. Upstairs, in a circle, elevated sarcophagi, blazing white, thrust their pointed corners, like little marble ears, into the blank blue Mediterranean sky. In the center of the circle, on square columns twice as tall as the others, the largest sarcophagus loomed. Vivian seemed bewildered—dazed and lost in the white brilliance, in the angles of unrelieved marble. "He must be in there," Allenson said to her, pointing to the center.

"Your hero?" she said.

"He isn't my hero. Please. Relax."

"And who's in all these others?"

"His companions in the thing of Fiume. The Thirteen."

"You mean *men* are in all these boxes? Where are their wives? Why aren't they buried with their families?"

Allenson shrugged. Her insatiable questions, like a child's, were wearing him down, numbing his brain.

She announced, "This is the most hateful place I've ever been. I can't stand it. It's Fascist. It's Hitler. I keep thinking of all the dead Jews."

"Honey, it wasn't that war. Italy was on our side. D'Annunzio died in 1938, it says right here. The grandeur of all this, I don't know—maybe it *was* Mussolini who financed it. He wasn't thought to be all that bad at first—he made the trains run on time. Don't blame me, I was just a child in Pound Ridge."

"I can't *stand* it," Vivian said. "If I have to stand a minute longer here in the blinding sun listening to you defend this Nazi I'll scream. I'd like to blow it up. I wish I'd brought a can of spray paint so I could write graffiti all over it. I'm surprised nobody has."

"Vivian dear, you're being quite amazingly stupid. He wasn't a Nazi, he was a poet, a *fin-de-siècle* dandy. You don't know the details of it, and I don't, either. When we get back home, I'll do some research."

"If you ever mention this hideous man to me again, I'll ask for a divorce."

He winced a smile, here in the sun. "You think the judge will find it sufficient grounds?"

She would not smile back. "Think of it—real men in those boxes, their bones. Hideous male bonding, right through to the afterlife."

"I don't know, isn't there a kind of innocent pomp to it? I find it rather touching."

"As touching as what you did to Claire."

Claire had been his second wife. Allenson blinked, and said, "What *we* did to Claire, you could say."

"*Men*, I mean," Vivian pleaded, desperately gesturing

upward, out of the depths of a millennial oppression. "Putting themselves in pompous marble boxes, ruining all this woodland, the lovely view. Oh, I *hate* it. I can't stand you standing there smirking and loving it."

"I don't exactly love—" But his wife, with an angrily shut face, from which tears were trying to escape, dodged past him and through the shadows of the motionless memorials—the Thirteen basking in their indecipherable glory—as if through a maze, and ran down the stairs, where the portly family was with difficulty ascending, to get their *cinque mila*'s worth.

Maybe a baby would calm her down, Allenson thought. She was approaching the age of now or never, as far as pregnancy was concerned. But the concept of one more dependent, its little life sticking out past his into the future like a diving board, made him dizzy.

Vivian was waiting for him at a landing lower down, leaning against a stone balustrade. "Sorry," she said. "I lost it." In the cooling sunlight he saw that she, like a real Italian beauty, had a few fine dark hairs on her upper lip.

This vulnerable touch softened him. "You're right, of course. There is something creepy about this place."

"There's still more. There's a whole navy down there, the sign says."

"Nave," Allenson read. "A ship. How can there be a ship?"

But there was one, with a mast and cabin and funnels, breasting the treetops, below them. A kind of gigantic centaur, its back half a deck imitated in stone, the foredeck apparently real, and all the tons of it heroically dragged up the hillside to rest incongruously among the poplars and the ink-dark cypresses. It would have helped his marriage, he knew, to forgo this wonder, but the boy in him couldn't resist heading down the steps, and setting foot on the marble deck, and then the wooden deck, and looking over the rail at the ocean of trees, the poplar leaves flickering like tiny whitecaps. Returning up the stairs, he was short of breath, and his legs felt heavy. "It's a toy," he told Vivian. "It's all toys."

"Just like war," she said.

"Oh, come on," he begged. "I didn't build it. I'm just an American tourist, like you." Imitating a dutiful husband, he escorted her down, past the closed mansion with its Art Deco doors, past the red roadster used in the mysterious *impresa*, out of this maze with its dead Minotaur. Yet, at the entrance, he couldn't resist asking, "Want to buy any souvenirs?"

"Drop dead," she suggested, and walked away from him toward the car. He bought five postcards, including one showing D'Annunzio *nel suo studio (dans son bureau, in his study, in seinem Studierzimmer)* wearing a three-piece fuzzy gray suit, a handkerchief in his pocket, a stickpin in his cravat, the veins in his very bald head bulging with concentration, his little lips pursed. He looked sickly. A rich life was catching up with him. Now his body was back there, pressed against the sky, dry as a flattened lizard.

Vivian stood far down the narrow sidewalk toward the parking lot. Ignominiously, in her furious sulk, she had had to wait beside the Fiat, since he had the keys. "That was fun," he told her. "Just as well the house and museum were closed, they might have been too much."

"I'd rather have fun at Auschwitz," she said.

"Cut it *out*. O.K., the guy had a good self-image. That's no crime. That doesn't mean Auschwitz. The fucking trouble with your generation, all you know about history is Auschwitz and the A-bomb, and all you know about politics is you don't want them to happen again. Oh dear, no, anything but that! I keep telling you, he was on our side. You've got the wrong guy."

"Maybe you've got the wrong girl. You *had* a wife

just like you, why didn't you stick with her? Claire would have loved going to Nazi shrines."

"She might have," he admitted. Claire had been game, and never quarrelsome. Silence had been her weapon, and a serene, blameless inner absence.

Vivian persisted, her dark eyes flashing. "You want a new woman. Claire and I were a set, we went together. Wife, mistress. I bet you've already got her picked out. It was somebody you saw in Venice. You began to act funny in Venice." Female intuition, he thought, what a nuisance it is. The possibility of yet another woman secretly thrilled him, but the practicalities of it were overwhelming.

"Vivian, please. I'm nearly sixty. I'm ready for my sarcophagus. As my prospective widow, I hope you paid close attention up there. It's just what I want. Only you can leave out those thirteen other guys."

She grudgingly laughed, beginning to let the sore spot heal. Back on the main road, she said, "Look, George, there's an *aperto.*"

He slowed and pulled into the gas station. "How did you say we say, 'Fill 'er up'?"

"*Il pieno, per favore.* That's what the guidebook says."

But no one came out of the little office, and no other cars were at the pumps. Allenson got out into the sun and shrugged at Vivian through her window. "*Chiuso,*" he said.

Another car pulled in, and a small Italian woman in black got out, and looked around. Allenson caught her eye. "*Chiuso?*" he said again, with a more tentative intonation. She favored him with a stream of Italian and did not seem disappointed when his face showed total incomprehension.

Allenson had noticed, beyond the empty office, a boy in gray jeans and a Shell T-shirt washing a car, with an air of independence of this establishment. But now he came over and spoke to the woman, and showed her something about the pump. She smiled in sudden eager understanding, performed some action Allenson could not see, seized the handle of the gasoline pump, pumped, and drove away.

The boy approached Allenson. "Is automatique," he said. "Ten-thousand-lira note, then pump."

"Ah, *comprendo, comprendo. Molto grazie.*" He explained to Vivian, "You deal with the pump directly. You feed it lire." He found the right denomination of bill in his wallet, and with a curt mechanical purr the slot sucked it in. Gasoline then flowed from the nozzle into his tank, rather briefly. Ten thousand lire—nine dollars—bought just a few liters.

"More!" she shouted from within the Fiat. "Here's more mon-ey!" She pushed ten-thousand-lira notes out through her half-open window, and the pump avidly sucked them up, turning money into movement, into married romance.

When he got back behind the wheel, Vivian, momentarily satisfied, said, "It's strange he had to explain it to the woman, too. She was Italian."

"It's a tough country," George Allenson pronounced, from his height of experience. "Even the natives can't figure it out."

II. *Bluebeard in Ireland*

"YES, THE PEOPLE are wonderful," George Allenson had to agree, there in Kenmare. His wife, Vivian, was twenty years younger than he, but almost as tall, with dark hair and decided, sharp features, and it placed the least strain on their marriage if he agreed with her assertions. Yet he harbored an inner doubt. If the Irish were so wonderful, why was Ireland such a sad and empty country? Vivian, a full generation removed from him, was an instinctive feminist, but to him any history of unrelieved victimization seemed suspect. Not that it wasn't astonishing to see the eighty-room palaces the British landlords had built for themselves, and touching to see the ruins—stone end walls still standing, thatched roofs collapsed—of the hovels where the Irish had lived, eaten their potatoes and drunk their whiskey, and died. Vivian loved the hovels, inexplicably; they all looked alike from the outside, and, when it was possible to enter a doorless doorway or peek through a sashless window-hole, the inside showed a muddy dirt floor, a clutter of rotting boards that might once have been furniture, and a few plastic or aluminum leavings of intruders like themselves.

Vivian could see he was unconvinced. "The way they use the language," she insisted, "and leave little children to run their shops for them."

"Wonderful," he agreed again. He was sitting with his, he hoped, not ridiculously much younger wife in the lounge of their hotel, before a flickering blue fire that was either a gas imitation of a peat fire or the real thing, Allenson wasn't sure. A glass of whiskey whose one ice cube had melted away added to his natural sleepiness. He had driven them around the Dingle Peninsula today in a foggy rain, and then south to Kenmare over a narrow mountain road from Killarney, Vivian screaming with anxiety all the way, and it had left him exhausted. After a vacation in Italy two years ago, he had vowed never to rent a foreign car with her again, but he had, in a place with narrower roads and left-handed drive. During the trickiest stretch today, over fabled Moll's Gap, with a Mercedes full of gesturing Germans pushing him from behind, Vivian had twisted in her seat and pressed her face against the headrest rather than look, and sobbed and called him a sadistic fiend.

Afterwards, safely delivered to the hotel parking lot, she complained that she had twisted so violently her lower back hurt. What he resented most about her attacks of hysteria was how, when she recovered from them, she expected him to have recovered, too. For all her feminism she still claimed the feminine right to meaningless storms of emotion, followed by the automatic sunshine of male forgiveness.

As if sensing the sulky residue of a grudge within him, and determined to erase it, she flashed there by the sluggish fire an impeccable smile. Her lips were long and mobile but thin and sharp, as if—it seemed to him in his drowsy condition, by the gassy flickering fire— her eyebrows had been duplicated and sewn together at the ends to make a mouth. "Remember," she said, offering to make a memory of what had occurred mere hours ago, "the lady shopkeeper out there beyond Dingle, where I begged you to stop?"

"You in*sisted* I stop," he corrected. She had said that if he didn't admit he was lost she would jump out of the car and walk back. How could they be lost, he had argued, with the sea on their left and hills on their right? But the sea was obscured by fog and the stony hills vanished upward into rain clouds and she was not persuaded; at last he had slammed on the brakes. Both of them had flounced out of the car. The dim-lit store looked empty, and they had been about to turn away from the door when a shadow materialized within, beyond the lace curtains—the proprietress, emerging from a room where she lived, waiting, rocking perhaps, watching what meagre channels of television reached this remoteness. He had been surprised, in southwestern Ireland, by how little television there was to watch, and by the sound of Gaelic being spoken all about him, in shops and pubs, by the young as well as the old. It was part of his own provincialism to be surprised by the provincialism of others; he expected America, its language and all its channels, to be everywhere by now.

This was indeed a store; its shadowy shelves held goods in cans and polyethylene packets, and a cloudy case held candies and newspapers bearing today's date. But it was hard for the Allensons to see it as anything but a stage cleverly set for their entrance and exit. The village around them seemed deserted. The proprietress—her hair knotted straight back, her straight figure clad in a dress of nunnish gray—felt younger than she looked, like an actress tricked out in bifocals and a gray wig, and she described the local turnings as if in all her years on a cliff above the sea she had never before been asked to direct a pair of tourists. There was a grave ceremoniousness to the occasion that chastened the fractious couple. To pay her for her trouble, they bought a copy of the local newspaper and some bags of candy. In Ireland, they had reverted to candy, which they ate in the car—Licorice Allsorts for him, for her chocolate-covered malt balls called Maltezers.

They had got back into the car enhanced by the encounter, the irritating currents between them momentarily quelled. Yet, even so, for all those theatrically precise directions, Allenson must have taken a wrong turning, for they never passed the Gallarus Oratory, which he had wanted to see. It was the Chartres of beehive chapels. In Ireland, the sights were mostly stones. Allenson found himself driving endlessly upward on the north side of the Dingle Peninsula, and needing to traverse the Slieve Mish Mountains to avoid Tralee, and being tailgated by the Germans on Moll's Gap, while Vivian had hysterics and he reflected upon the gaps between people, even those consecrated to intimacy.

He had had three wives. He had meant Vivian to see

him into the grave, but unexpected resistances in her were stimulating, rather than lulling, his will to live. In his simple and innocent manhood he had taken on a swarming host of sexist resentments—men were incompetent (his driving in foreign lands), men were ridiculous (his desire to see, *faute de mieux*, old Ireland's lichened gray beehive huts, dolmens, menhirs, and ruined abbeys), men were lethal. Two years ago, out of sheer political superstition, this youthful wife had become furious in Gabriele D'Annunzio's estate above Lake Garda, all because the world-renowned poet and adventurer had enshrined himself and his thirteen loyal followers in matching sarcophagi, lifted up to the sun on pillars. Men were Fascists, this had led Vivian to realize. She proved to be violently allergic to history, and her silver-haired husband loomed to her as history's bearer. So he had, for their next trip abroad, suggested Eire, a land whose history was muffled in legend and ignominy. Just its shape on the map, next to Great Britain's spiky upstanding silhouette, suggested the huddled roundness of a docile spouse.

"You insisted," he repeated, "and then we got lost anyway, and saw none of the sights. I missed the Gallarus Oratory."

Vivian brushed his resentful memory away, there by the hotel fire. "The whole countryside is the sight," she said, "and the wonderful people. Everybody knows that. And all day, with you jerking that poor Japanese compact this way and that like a crazy teenaged hood, I couldn't enjoy looking out. If I take my eye off the map for an instant, you get us lost. You're not getting me back into that car tomorrow, I tell you that."

Itching to give the fire a poke, he gave it to her instead. "Darling, I thought we were going to drive south, to Bantry and Skibbereen. Bantry House in the morning, and Creagh Gardens in the afternoon, with a quick lunch at Ballydehob." Allenson smiled.

"You're a monster," Vivian said cheerfully. "You really would put me through a whole day of you at the wheel on these awful roads? We're going to *walk*."

"Walk?"

"George, I talked it over with a man in the office, the assistant manager, while you were putting on a shirt and tie. He couldn't have been sweeter, and said what the tourists do in Kenmare is they take walks. He gave me a map."

"A map?" Another whiskey would sink him to the bottom of the sea. But would that be so bad? This woman was a talking nightmare. She had produced a little map, printed by photocopy on green paper, showing a pattern of numbered lines surrounding the phallic thrust of the Kenmare estuary. "I've come all this way to take a walk?" But there was no arguing. Vivian was so irrational that, because her predecessor wife had been called Claire, she had refused, planning the trip, to include County Clare, where the good cliffs and primitive churches were, and off whose shore part of the Spanish Armada had wrecked.

Next morning, the devil in him, prompted by the guidebook, could not resist teasing her. "Today's the day," he announced, "to drive the Ring of Beara. We can see the Ogham Stone at Ballycrovane, and if there's time take the cable car to Dursey Island, the only such wonder in this green and wondrous land. The blessed roadway meanders, it says here, through mountainous coastal areas providing panoramic views of both Bantry and Kenmare bays. A famous stone circle there is, and just two miles further, the ruins of Puxley's mansion! A mere hundred and forty kilometers, the entire ring is claimed to be; that's eighty-eight miles of purest pleasure, not counting the cable car."

"You must be out of your gourd," Vivian said, using one of those youthful slang expressions that she knew he detested. "I'm not getting back into any car with you at the wheel until we head to Shannon Airport. If then."

Allenson shrugged to hide his hurt. "Well, we could walk downtown to the local circle again. I'm not sure I grasped all the nuances the first time."

It had been charming, in a way. They had driven up a little cul-de-sac at the shabbier end of Kenmare and a small girl in a school jumper had been pushed from a house, while her mother and siblings watched from the window, and shyly asked for the fifty-pence admission. Then through a swinging gate and up a muddy lane the couple had walked, past stacks of roof tiles and a ditch brimming with plastic trash, arriving at a small mown plateau where fifteen mismatched stones in a rough circle held their mute pattern. He had paced among them, trying to unearth in his atavistic heart the meaning of these pre-Celtic stones. Sacrifice. This must have been, at certain moments of heavenly alignment, a place of sacrifice, he thought, turning to see Vivian standing at the ring's center in too vividly blue a raincoat.

"We're walking," she agreed with him, "but not back to those awful rocks that got you so excited, I'll never know why. It's *stupid* to keep looking at rocks somebody could have arranged yesterday for all we know. There are more of these supposedly prehistoric beehive huts today than there were a hundred years ago, the nice young man in the office was telling me yesterday. He says what sensible people who come to Kenmare do is take long walks."

"Who is this guy, that he's become so fucking big in my life suddenly? Why doesn't *he* take you for the walk, if that's what's on his mind?"

Did she blush? "George, *really*—he's young enough to be my son." This was an awkward assertion, made in the sweep of the moment. She could be the mother of a twenty-one-year-old, if she had been pregnant at nineteen; but in truth she had never borne a child, and when they were first married, and she was in her mid-thirties, she had hoped to have a child by him. But he had ogreishly refused; he had had enough children—a daughter by Jeaneanne, two sons by Claire. Now the possibility had slipped away. He thought of his present wife as racily younger than himself but her fortieth birthday had come and gone, and since the days when they had surreptitiously courted, in the flattering shadows of Claire's unknowing, Vivian's face had grown angular and incised with lines of recurrent vexation.

The young man in the office—a kind of rabbit hole around the corner from the key rack, in which the Irish staff could be heard scuffling and guffawing—was at least twenty-five, and may have been thirty, with children of his own. He was slender, black-eyed, milky-skinned, and impeccably courteous. Yet his courtesy carried a charge, a lilt, of mischief. "Yes, and walking is the thing in these parts—we're not much for the organized sports that are the custom in the States."

"We passed some golf courses, driving here," Allenson said, not really wanting to argue.

"Would you call golf organized?" the assistant manager said quickly. "Not the way I play it, I fear. As we say, it's an ungrateful way to take a walk."

"Speaking of walks—" Vivian produced her little green map. "Which of these would you recommend for my husband and me?"

With his bright-black eyes he looked from one to the other and then settled on looking at her, with a cock to his neatly combed head. "And how hardy a man would he be?"

Wifely to a fault, Vivian took the question seriously. "Well, his driving is erratic, but other than that he manages pretty well."

Allenson resented this discussion. "The last time I saw my doctor," he announced, "he told me I had beautiful arteries."

"Ah, I would have guessed as much," said the young man, looking him benignly in the face.

"We don't want to start him out on anything too steep," Vivian said.

"Currabeg might be your best option, then. It's mostly on the level road, with fine views of the Roughty Valley and the bay. Take an umbrella against the mist, along with your fine blue coat, and if he happens to begin to look poorly in the face you might hail a passing motorcar to bring in the remains."

"Are we going to be walking in traffic?" She sounded alarmed. For all her assertiveness, Vivian had irritating pockets of timidity. Claire, Allenson remembered, drove on a motor scooter all over Bermuda with him, clinging to his midriff trustfully, twenty years ago, and would race with the children on bicycles all over Nantucket. Jeaneanne and he had owned a Ford Thunderbird convertible when they lived in Texas, and would commonly hit a hundred miles an hour in the stretch between Lubbock and Abilene, the top down and the dips in Route 84 full of watery mirages. He remembered how her hair, bleached blond in Fifties-style streaks, would whip back from her sweaty temples, and how she would hike her skirt up to her waist to give her crotch air, there under the steering wheel. Jeaneanne had been tough, but her exudations had been nectar, until her recklessness and love of speed had carried her right out of Allenson's life. The loss had hardened him.

The assistant manager appeared to give Vivian's anxiety his solemn consideration; there was, in his second of feigned thought, that ceremonious touch of parody with which the Irish bring music to the most factual transactions. "Oh, I judge this off-time of year there won't be enough to interfere with your easiness. These are high country roads. You park at the crossing, as the map shows clearly, and take the two rights to bring you back."

Still, Allenson felt, their adviser felt some politely unspoken reservation about their undertaking. In their rented car, with its mirrors where you didn't expect them and a balky jumble of gears on the floor, while Vivian transparently tried to hold her tongue from criticism, he drove them out of Kenmare, past a cemetery containing famous holy wells, over a one-lane hump of a stone bridge, up between occluding hedgerows into the bare hills whose silhouettes, in the view from the Allensons' hotel room, were doubled by the mirroring sheen of the lakelike estuary. They met no other cars, so Vivian had less need to tense up than on the ring roads.

The map in her lap, she announced at last, "This must be the crossroads." A modest intersection, with barely enough parking space for one car on the dirt shoulder. They parked in the space and locked the car. It was the middle of a morning of watery wan sunshine. A bite in the breeze told them they were higher than in Kenmare.

On foot they followed a long straight road, not as long and shimmering as the straightaways in Texas, yet with something of the same potential for mirage. They crossed a stream hidden but for its gurgle in the greenery. A house being built, or rebuilt, stood back and up from the road, with no sign of life. Land and houses must be cheap. Ireland had been emptying out for ages. Cromwell had reduced the Irish to half a million, but they had stubbornly bred back, only to be decimated by the potato famine two centuries later.

At first, Vivian athletically strode ahead, hungry for hovels and unspoiled views. She had brought new running shoes on the trip—snow-white, red-chevroned, bulky with the newest wrinkles of pedal technology. They were not flattering, but, then, compared with Jeaneanne's, this wife's ankles were rather thick. Her feet looked silly, under the hem of her bright-blue raincoat, flickering along the road surface, striped like birds. Where were the real birds? Ireland didn't seem to have many. Perhaps they had migrated with the people. Famines are hard on birds, but that had been long ago.

The hedgerows thinned, and after the invisible stream the road had a steady upward trend. He found himself overtaking his young wife, and then slowing his pace to match hers. "You know," she told him, "I really *did* twist my back in the car yesterday, and these new sneakers aren't all they were advertised. They have so much structure inside, my feet feel bullied. It's as if they keep pushing my hips out of alignment."

"Well," he said, "you could go barefoot." Jeaneanne would have. Claire might have. "Or we could go back to the car. We've gone less than a mile."

"That's all? I wouldn't *dream* of telling them at the hotel that we couldn't do their walk. This must be the first right turn already, coming up."

The T-crossing was unmarked. He looked at the green map and wished it weren't quite so schematic. "This must be it," he agreed, uncertainly, and up the road they went.

A smaller road, it continued the upward trend, through emptier terrain. Irish emptiness had a quality different from that of Texas emptiness, or that of the Scots Highlands, where he and Claire had once toured. The desolation here was intimate. Domes of stone-littered grass formed a high horizon, under roiling clouds with blackish centers. There was little color in anything; he had expected greener grass, bluer sky. The landscape wore the dull, chastened colors of the people in the towns. It was a shy, unassuming sort of desolation. "I suppose," Allenson said, to break the silence of their laborious walking, "all this was once full of farms."

"I haven't seen a single hovel," Vivian said, with a querulousness he blamed on her back.

"Some of these heaps of stones—it's hard to tell if man or God, so to speak, put them there." Jeaneanne had been a liberated Baptist, Claire a practicing Episcopalian. Vivian was from a determinedly unchurched family of ex-Catholic scientists whose treeless Christmases and thankless Thanksgivings Allenson found chilling. Strange, he thought as he walked along, he had never had a Jewish wife, though Jewish women had been his best lovers—the warmest, the cleverest.

"It said in the guidebook that even up in the hills you could see the green places left by the old potato patches but I haven't seen a single one," Vivian complained.

Time passed wordlessly, since he declined to answer. He hadn't written the guidebook. The soles of their feet slithered and scratched.

Allenson cleared his throat and said, "You can see why Beckett wrote the way he did." He had lost track of how long their forward-plodding silence had stretched; his voice felt rusty. "There's an amazing amount of nothingness in the Irish landscape." On cue, a gap in the clouds sent a silvery light scudding across the tops of the dull hills slowly drawing closer.

"I *know* this isn't the road," Vivian said. "We haven't seen a sign, a house, a car, *any*thing." She sounded near tears.

"But we've seen *sheep*," he said, with an enthusiasm that was becoming cruel. "Hundreds of them."

It was true. Paler than boulders but no less opaque, scattered sheep populated the wide fields that unrolled on both sides of the road. With their rectangular purple pupils the animals stared in profile at the couple. Sometimes an especially buoyant ram, his chest powdered a startling turquoise or magenta color, dashed back among the ewes at the approach of these human intruders. Single strands of barbed wire reinforced the stone walls and rotting fences of an older pastoralism. Only these wires, and the pine poles bearing wires overhead, testified that twentieth-century people had been here before them. The land dipped and crested; each new rise revealed more sheep, more stones, more road. A cloud with an especially large leaden center darkened this lunar landscape and rained a few drops; by the time Vivian had put up their umbrella, the sprinkle had passed. Allenson looked around for a rainbow, but it eluded his vision, like the leprechauns promised yesterday at Moll's Gap, in the droll roadside sign LEPRECHAUN CROSSING.

"Where *is* that second right turn?" Vivian asked. "Give me back the map."

"The map tells us nothing," he said. "The way it's drawn it looks like we're walking around a city block."

"I *knew* this was the wrong road, I don't know *why* I let you talk me into it. We've gone miles. My back is killing me, damn you. I *hate* these bossy, clunky running shoes."

"You picked them out," he reminded her. "And they were far from cheap." Trying to recover a little kindness, Allenson went on, "The total walk is four and a half miles. Americans have lost all sense of how long a mile is. They think it's a minute of sitting in a car." Or less, if Jeaneanne were driving, her skirt tucked up to air her crotch.

"Don't be so pedantic," Vivian told him. "I hate men.

They grab the map out of your hands and never ask directions and then refuse to admit they're lost."

"Whom, my dear, would we have asked directions of? We haven't seen a soul. The last soul we saw was your cow-eyed pal at the hotel. I can hear him now, talking to the police. 'Ah, the American couple,' he'll be saying. 'She a mere raven-haired colleen, and he a grizzly old fella. They were headin' for the McGillycuddy Reeks, wi' scarcely a cup of poteen or a pig's plump knuckle in their knapsacks.' "

"Not funny," she said, in a new, on-the-edge voice. Without his noticing it, she had become frantic. There was a silvery light in her dark eyes, tears. "I can't walk another step," she announced. "I can't and I won't."

"Here," he said, pointing out a convenient large stone in the wall at the side of the road. "Rest a bit."

She sat and repeated, as if proudly, "I will not go another step. I can't, George. I'm in agony." She flipped back her bandanna with a decisive gesture, but the effect was not the same as Jeaneanne's gold-streaked hair whipping back in the convertible. Vivian looked old, worn. Lamed.

"What do you want me to do? Walk back and bring the car?" He meant the offer to be absurd, but she didn't reject it, merely thinned her lips and stared at him angrily, defiantly.

"You've got us lost and won't admit it. I'm not walking another step."

He pictured it, her never moving. Her body would weaken and die within a week; her skin and bones would be washed by the weather and blend into the earth like the corpse of a stillborn lamb. Only the sheep would witness it. Only the sheep were watching them now, with the sides of their heads. Allenson turned his own head away, gazing up the road, so Vivian wouldn't see the calm mercilessness in his face.

* * *

"Darling, look," he said, after a moment. "Way up the road, see the way the line of telephone poles turns? I bet that's the second right turn. We're on the map!"

"I don't see anything turning," Vivian said, but in a voice that wanted to be persuaded.

"Just under the silhouette of the second little hill. Follow the road with your eyes, darling." Allenson was feeling abnormally tall, as if his vision of Vivian stuck in the Irish landscape forever had a centrifugal force, spilling him outward, into a fresh future, toward yet another wife. What would she be like, this fourth Mrs. Allenson? Jewish, with a rapid, humorous tongue and heavy hips and clattering bracelets on her sweetly hairy forearms? Black, a stately fashion model whom he would rescue from her cocaine habit? A little Japanese, silken and fiery within her kimono? Or perhaps one of his old mistresses, whom he couldn't marry at the time, but whose love had never lessened and who was miraculously unaged? Still, in a kind of social inertia, he kept pleading with Vivian. "If there's no right turn up there, then you can sit down on a rock and I'll walk back for the car."

"How can you walk back?" she despairingly asked. "It'll take forever."

"I won't walk, I'll run," he promised. "I'll trot."

"You'll have a heart attack."

"What do you care? One male killer less in the world. One less splash of testosterone." Death, the thought of either of their deaths, felt exalting, in this green-gray landscape emptied by famine and English savagery. British soldiers, he had read, would break the roofbeams of the starving natives' cottages and ignite the thatch.

"I care," Vivian said. She sounded subdued. Seated

on her stone, she looked prim and hopeful, a wallflower waiting to be asked to dance.

He asked, "How's your back?"

"I'll stand and see," she said.

Her figure, he noticed when she stood, had broadened since he first knew her—thicker in the waist and ankles, chunky like her aggravating shoes. And developing a bad back besides. As if she were hurrying to catch up to him in the aging process. She took a few experimental steps, on the narrow macadam road built, it seemed, solely for the Allensons' pilgrimage.

"Let's go," she said combatively. She added, "I'm doing this just to prove you're wrong."

But he was right. The road branched; the thinner piece of it continued straight, over the little hill, and the thicker turned right, with the wooden power poles. Parallel to the rocky crests on the left, with a view of valley on the right, the road went up and down in an animated, diverting way, and took them past houses now and then, and small plowed areas to vary the stony pastures. "You think those are potato patches?" he asked. He felt sheepish, wondered how many of his murderous thoughts she had read. His vision of her sitting there, as good as a corpse, kept widening its rings in his mind, like a stone dropped in black water. The momentary ecstasy of a stone smartly applied to her skull, or a piece of flint sharp as a knife whipped across her throat—had these visions been his, back in that Biblical wilderness?

Now, on the higher, winding road, a car passed them, and then another. It was Sunday morning, and unsmiling country families were driving to mass. Their faces were less friendly than those of the shopkeepers in Kenmare; no waves were offered, or invitations to ride. Once, on a blind curve, the couple had to jump to the grassy shoulder to avoid being hit. Vivian seemed quite agile, in the pinch.

"How's your poor back holding up?" he asked. "Your sneakers still pushing your hips around?"

"I'm better," she said, "when I don't think about it."

"Oh. Sorry."

He should have let her have a baby. Now it was too late. Still, he wasn't sorry. Life was complicated enough.

The road turned the third right on their map gradually, unmistakably, while several gravelled driveways led off into the hills. Though Kenmare Bay gleamed ahead of them, a tongue of silver in the smoky distance, they were still being carried upward, dipping and turning, ever closer to the rocky crests, which were becoming dramatic. The sheep, now, seemed to be unfenced; a ram with a crimson chest skittered down a rock face and across the road, spilling scree with its hooves. In what could have been another nation, so far away it now appeared, a line of minuscule telephone poles marked the straight road where Vivian had announced she would not move another step. Overhead, faint whistling signalled a hawk—a pair of hawks, drifting motionless near the highest face of rock, hanging in a wind the Allensons could not feel. Their thin hesitant cry felt forgiving to Allenson, as did Vivian's voice announcing, "Now I have this killing need to pee."

"Go ahead."

"Suppose a car comes?"

"It won't. They're all in church now."

"There's no place to go behind anything," she complained.

"Just squat down beside the road. My goodness, what a little fussbudget."

"I'll lose my balance." He had noticed on other occasions, on ice or on heights, how precarious her sense of balance was.

"No you won't. Here. Give me your hand and prop yourself against my leg. Just don't pee on my shoe."

"Or on my own," she said, letting herself be lowered into a squatting position.

"It might soften them up," he said.

"Don't make me laugh. I'll get urinary impotence." It was a concept of Nabokov's, out of *Pale Fire*, that they both had admired, in the days when their courtship had tentatively proceeded through the socially acceptable sharing of books. She managed. In Ireland's great silence of abandonment the tender splashing sound seemed loud. *Pssshshshblipip.* Allenson looked up to see if the hawks were watching. Hawks could read a newspaper, he had once read, from the height of a mile. But what would they make of it? The headlines, the halftones? Who could know what a hawk saw? Or a sheep? They saw only what they needed to see. A tuft of edible grass, or the twitch of a vole scurrying for cover.

Vivian stood, pulling up over the quick-glimpsed thicket of her pubic hair her underpants and pantyhose. A powerful ammoniac scent followed her up, rising invisible from the roadside turf. *Oh, let's have a baby*, he thought, but left the inner cry unexpressed. Too late, too old. The couple moved on, numbed by the miles that had passed beneath their feet. They reached the road's highest point, and saw far below, as small as an orange star, their Eurodollar Toyota compact, parked at a tilt on the shoulder of their first crossroads. As they descended to it, Vivian asked, "Would Jeaneanne have enjoyed Ireland?"

What an effort it now seemed, to cast his mind so far back! "Jeaneanne," he answered, "enjoyed everything, for the first seven minutes. Then she got bored. What made you think of Jeaneanne?"

"You. Your face when we started out had its Jeaneanne look. Which is different from its Claire look. Your Claire look is sort of woebegone. Your Jeaneanne look is fierce."

"Darling," he told her. "You're fantasizing."

"Jeaneanne and you were so young," she pursued. "At the age I was just entering graduate school, you and she were married, with a child."

"We had that Fifties greed. We thought we could have it all," he said, rather absently, trying to agree. His own feet in their much-used cordovans were beginning to protest; walking downhill, surprisingly, was the most difficult.

"You still do. You haven't asked me if *I* like Ireland. The Becketty nothingness of it."

"Do you?" he asked.

"I do," she said.

They were back where they had started.

Farrell's Caddie

WHEN FARRELL SIGNED UP, with seven other aging members of his local Long Island club, for a week of golf at the Royal Caledonian Links in Scotland, he didn't foresee the relationship with the caddies. Hunched little men in billed tweed caps and rubberized rain suits, they huddled in the misty gloom as the morning foursomes got organized, and reclustered after lunch, muttering as unintelligibly as sparrows, for the day's second eighteen.

Farrell would never have walked thirty-six holes a day in America, but here in Scotland golf was not an accessory to life, drawing upon one's marginal energy, it *was* life, played out of the center of one's being. At first, stepping forth on legs one of which had been broken in a college football game forty years before, and which damp weather or a night of twisted sleep still provoked to a reminiscent twinge, he missed the silky glide and swerve of the accustomed electric cart, its magic-carpet suspension above the whispering fairway; he missed the rattle of spare balls in the retaining shelf, and the round plastic holes to hold drinks, alcoholic or carbonated, and the friendly presence on the seat beside him of another gray-haired sportsman, another warty pickle blanching in the brine of time, exuding forbearance and the expectation of forbearance, and resigned, like Farrell, to a golfing mediocrity that would poke its way down the sloping dogleg of decrepitude to the level green of death.

Here, however, on the heather-rimmed fairways, cut as close as putting surfaces back home, yet with no trace of mower tracks, and cheerfully marred by the scratchings and burrows of the nocturnal rabbits that lived and bred beneath the impenetrably thorny, waist-high gorse, energy came up through the turf, as if Farrell's cleats were making contact with primal spirits beneath the soil, and he felt he could walk forever. The rolling treeless terrain, the proximity of the wind-whipped sea, the rain that came and went with the sud-denness of thought—they composed the ancient matrix of the game, and the darkly muttering caddies were also part of this matrix.

That first morning in the drizzly shuffle around the golf bags, his bag was hoisted up by a hunched shadow who, as they walked together in pursuit of Farrell's first drive (good contact, but pulled to the left, toward some shaggy mounds), muttered half to himself, with those hiccups or glottal stops the Scots accent inserts, "Sandy's wha' they call me."

Farrell hesitated, then confessed, "Gus." His given name, Augustus, had always embarrassed him, but its shortened version seemed a little short on dignity, and at the office, as he had ascended in rank, his colleagues had settled on his initials, "A. J."

"Ye want now tae geh oover th' second boosh fra' th' laift," Sandy said, handing Farrell a 7-iron. The green was out of sight behind the shaggy mounds, which were covered with a long tan grass that whitened in waves as gusts beat in from the sea.

"What's the distance?" Farrell was accustomed to yardage markers—yellow stakes, or sprinkler heads.

The caddie looked reflectively at a sand bunker not far off, and then at the winking red signal light on the train tracks beyond, and finally at a large bird, a gull or a crow, winging against the wind beneath the low, tattered, blue-black clouds. "Ah hunnert thirhty-eight tae th' edge o' th' green, near a hunnert fifty tae th' pin, where they ha' 't."

"I can't hit a 7-iron a hundred fifty. I can't hit it even one forty, against this wind."

Yet the caddie's fist, in a fingerless wool glove, did not withdraw the offered club. "Siven's what ye need."

As Farrell bent his face to the ball, the wet wind cut across his eyes and made him cry. His tears turned one ball into two; he supposed the brighter one was real. He concentrated on taking the clubhead away slowly and low to the turf, initiating his downswing with a twitch of the left hip, and suppressing his tendency to dip the right shoulder. The shot seemed sweet, soaring with a gentle draw precisely over the second bush. He looked toward the caddie, expecting congratulations or at least some small sign of shared pleasure. But the man, whose creased face was weathered the strangely even brown of a white actor playing Othello, followed the flight of the ball as he had that of the crow, reflectively. "Yer right hand's a wee bit tae into 't," he observed, and the ball, they saw as they climbed to the green, was indeed pulled to the left, into a deep pot bunker. Furthermore, it was fifteen yards short. The caddie had underclubbed him, but showed no sign of remorse as he handed Farrell the sand wedge. In Sandy's dyed-looking face, pallid gray eyes showed like touches of morning light; it shocked Farrell to suspect that the other man, weathered though he was, and bent beneath the weight of a perpetual golf bag, was younger than himself—a prematurely wizened Pict, a concentrate of Farrell's diluted, Yankeefied Celtic blood.

The side of the bunker toward the hole was as tall as Farrell and sheer, built up of bricks of sod in a way he had never seen before, not even at Shinnecock Hills. Rattled, irritated at having been unrepentantly under-clubbed, Farrell swung five times into the damp, brown sand, darker and denser than any sand on Long Island; each time, the ball thudded short of the trap's lip and dribbled back at his feet. " 'it at it well beheend," the caddie advised, "and dinna stop th' cloob." Farrell's sixth swing brought the ball bobbling up onto the green, within six feet of the hole.

His fellow-Americans lavished ironical praise on the tardily excellent shot but the caddie, with the same deadpan solemnity with which Farrell had repeatedly struck the ball, handed him his putter. "Ae ball tae th' laift," he advised, and Farrell was so interested in this quaint concept—the ball as a unit of measure—that his putt stopped short. "Ye forgot tae 'it it, Goos," Sandy told him.

Farrell tersely nodded. The caddie made him feel obliged to keep up a show of golfing virtues. Asked for his score, he said loudly, in a stagey voice, "That was a honest ten."

"We'll call it a six," said the player keeping score, in the forgiving, corrupting American way.

As the round progressed, through a rapid alternation of brisk showers and silvery sunshine, with rainbows springing up around them and tiny white daisies gleaming underfoot, Farrell and his caddie began to grow into one another, as a foot in damp weather grows into a shoe. Sandy consistently handed Farrell one club too short to make the green, but Farrell came to accept the failure as his own; his caddie was handing the club to the stronger golfer latent in Farrell, and it was Farrell's job to let this superior performer out, to release him from his stiff, soft, more than middle-aged body. On the twelfth hole, called "Dunrobin"—a seemingly endless par 5 with a broad stretch of fairway, bleak and vaguely restless like the surface of the moon, receding over a distant edge marked by two small pot bunkers, with a pale-green arm of gorse extending from the rabbit-undermined thickets on the left—his drive clicked. Something about the ghostly emptiness of this terrain, the featurelessness of it, had removed Farrell's physical inhibitions; he felt the steel shaft of the driver bend in a subtle curve at his back, and a corresponding springiness awaken in his knees, and he knew, as his weight elastically moved from the right foot to the left, that he would bring the clubface squarely into the ball, and indeed did, so that the ball—the last of his new Titleists, the others having already been swallowed by gorse and heather and cliffside scree—was melting deep into the drizzle straight ahead almost before he looked up, his head held sideways, as if pillowed on his right ear, just like the pros on television. He cocked an eye at Sandy. "O.K.?" asked Farrell, mock-modest but also genuinely fearful of some hazard, some trick of the layout, that he had missed taking into account.

"Gowf shot, sirr," the caddie said, and his face, as if touched by a magic wand, crumpled into a smile full of crooked gray teeth, his constantly relit cigarette adhering to one corner. Small matter that Farrell, striving for a repetition of his elastic sensations, topped the following 3-wood, hit a 5-iron fat and short, and skulled his wedge shot clear across the elevated green. He had for a second awakened the golf giant sleeping among his muscles, and imagined himself now cutting a more significant figure in the other man's not quite colorless, not quite indifferent eyes.

Dinner, for this week of foreign excursion, was a repeating male event, involving the same eight Long Island males, their hair growing curly and their faces ruddy away from the arid Manhattan canyons and air-conditioned offices where they had accumulated their small fortunes. They discussed their caddies as men, extremely unbuttoned, might discuss their mistresses. What does a caddie want? "Come on, Freddie, *'it* it fer once!" the very distinguished banker Frederic M. Panoply boasted that his had cried out to him as, on the third day of displaying his cautious, successful, down-the-middle game, he painstakingly addressed his ball.

Another man's caddie, when asked what he thought of Mrs. Thatcher, had responded with a twinkle, "She'd be a good 'ump."

Farrell, prim and reserved by nature, though not devoid of passion, had relatively little to offer concerning Sandy. He worried that the man's incessant smoking would kill him. He wondered if the tips he gave him were too far below what a Japanese golfer would have bestowed. He feared that Sandy was becoming tired of him. As the week went by, their relationship had become more intuitive. "A 6-iron?" Farrell would now say, and without word would be handed the club. Once he had dared decline an offered 6, asked for the 5, and sailed his unusually well-struck shot into the sedge beyond the green. On the greens, where he at first had been bothered by the caddie's explicit directives, so that he forgot to stroke the ball firmly, Farrell had come to depend upon Sandy's advice, and would expertly cock his ear close to the caddie's mouth, and try to envision the curve of the ball into the center of the hole from "an inch an' a fhingernail tae th' laift." He began to sink putts. He began to get pars, as the whitecaps flashed on one side of the links and on the other the wine-red electric commuter trains swiftly glided up to Glasgow and back. This was happiness, bracketed between sea and rail, and freedom, of a wild and windy sort. On the morning of his last day, having sliced his first drive into the edge of the rough, between a thistle and what appeared to be a child's weathered tombstone, Farrell bent his ear close to the caddie's mouth for advice, and heard, "Ye'd be better leavin' 'er."

"Beg pardon?" Farrell said, as he had all week, when the glottal, hiccuping accent had become opaque. Today the acoustics were especially bad; a near-gale off the sea made his rain pants rattle like machine guns and deformed his eyeballs with air pressure as he tried to squint down. When he could stop seeing double, his lie looked fair—semi-embedded. The name on the tombstone was worn away. Perhaps it was merely an ancient railroad right-of-way marker.

"Yer missus," Sandy clarified, passing over the 8-iron. "Ere it's tae late, mon. She was never yer type. Tae proper."

"Shouldn't this be a wedge?" Farrell asked uncertainly.

"Nay, it's sittin' up guid enough," the caddie said, pressing his foot into the heather behind the ball so it rose up like ooze out of mud. "Ye kin reach with th' 8," he said. "Go fer yer par, mon. Yer fauts er a' in yer mind; ye tend t' play a hair defainsive."

Farrell would have dismissed his previous remarks, as a verbal mirage amid the clicks and skips of windblown Scots, had they not seemed so uncannily true. "Too proper" was exactly what his college friends had said of Sylvia, but he had imagined that her physical beauty had been the significant thing, and her propriety a pose she would outgrow, whereas thirty-five married years had revealed the propriety as enduring and the beauty as transient. As to leaving her, this thought would never have entered his head until recently; the mergers-and-acquisitions branch had recently taken on a certain Irma Finegold, who had heavy-lidded eyes, full lips painted vermilion, and a curious presumptuous way of teasing Farrell in the eddies of chitchat before and after conferences, or in the elevator up to the boardroom. She had been recently divorced, and when she talked to Farrell she manipulated her lower lip with a pencil eraser and shimmied her shoulders beneath their pads. On nights when the office worked late—he liked occasionally to demonstrate that, well-along though he was, he could still pull an all-nighter with the young bucks— there had been between him and Irma shared Chinese meals in greasy takeout cartons, and a joint limo home in the dawn light, through the twinned arches and aspiring tracery of the Brooklyn Bridge. And on one undreamed-of occasion, there had been an invitation, which he did not refuse, to delay his return to Long Island with an interlude at her apartment in Park Slope. Though no young buck, he had not done badly, it seemed to him, even factoring in the flattery quotient from a subordinate.

The 8-iron pinched the ball clean, and the Atlantic gale brought the soaring shot left-to-right toward the pin. "Laift edge, but dinna gi' th' hole away," Sandy advised of the putt, and Farrell sank it, for the first birdie of his week of golf.

Now, suddenly, out of the silvery torn sky, sleet and sunshine poured simultaneously, and as the two men walked at the same tilt to the next tee, Sandy's voice came out of the wind, "An' steer clear o' th' MiniCorp deal. They've laiveraged th' company tae daith."

Farrell studied Sandy's face. Rain and sleet bounced off the brown skin as if from a waxy preservative coating. Metallic gleams showed as the man studied, through narrowed eyelids, the watery horizon. Farrell pretended he hadn't heard. On the tee he was handed a 3-wood, with the advice, "Ye want tae stay short o' th' wee burn. Th' wind's come around beheend, bringin' th' sun with it."

As the round wore on, the sun did struggle through,

and a thick rainbow planted itself over the profile of the drab town beyond the tracks, with its black steeples and distillery chimneys. By the afternoon's eighteen, there was actually blue sky, and the pockets of lengthening shadow showed the old course to be everywhere curvacious, crest and swale, like the body of a woman. Forty feet off the green on the fourteenth ("Whinny Brae"), Farrell docilely accepted the caddie's offer of a putter, and rolled it up and over the close-mown irregularities within a gimme of the hole. His old self would have skulled or fluffed a chip. "Great advice," he said, and in his flush of triumph challenged the caddie: "But Irma *loves* the MiniCorp deal."

"Aye, 't keeps th' twa o' ye taegither. She's fairful ye'll wander off, i' th' halls o' corporate power."

"But what does she see in me?"

"Lookin' fer a father, th' case may be. Thet first husband o' hers was meikle immature, an' also far from yer own income bracket."

Farrell felt his heart sink at the deflating shrewdness of the analysis. His mind elsewhere, absented by bittersweet sorrow, he hit one pure shot after another. Looking to the caddie for praise, however, he met the same impassive, dour, young-old visage, opaque beneath the billed tweed cap. Tomorrow, he would be caddying for someone else, and Farrell would be belted into a business-class seat within a 747. On the home stretch of holes—one after the other strung out beside the railroad right-of-way, as the Victorian brick clubhouse, with its turrets and neo-Gothic windows, enlarged in size— Farrell begged for the last scraps of advice. "The 5-wood, or the 3-iron? The 3 keeps it down out of the wind, but I feel more confident with the wood, the way you've got me swinging."

"Th' 5'll be ower an' gone; ye're a' poomped up.

Take th' 4-iron. Smooth it on, laddie. Aim fer th' little broch."

"Broch?"

"Wee stone fortress, frae th' days we had our own braw king." He added, "An' ye might be thinkin' aboot takin' early retirement. Th' severance deals won't be so sweet aye, with th' coomin' resaission. Ye kin free yerself up, an' take on some consults, fer th' spare change."

"Just what I was thinking, if Irma's a will-o'-the-wisp."

"Will-o'-the-wisp, d' ye say? Ye're a speedy lairner, Goos."

Farrell felt flattered and wind-scoured, here in this surging universe of green and gray. "You really think so, Sandy?"

"I *ken* sae. Aye, ye kin tell a' aboot a mon, frae th' way he gowfs."

The Rumor

FRANK AND SHARON WHITTIER had come from the Cincinnati area and, with an inheritance of hers and a sum borrowed from his father, had opened a small art gallery on the fourth floor of a narrow brown building on West 57th Street. They had known each other as children; their families had been in the same country-club set. They had married in 1970, when Frank was freshly graduated from Oberlin and Vietnam-vulnerable and Sharon was only nineteen, a sophomore at Antioch majoring in dance. By the time, six years later, they arrived in New York, they had two small children; the birth of a third led them to give up their apartment and the city struggle and to move to a house in Hastings, a low stucco house with a wide-eaved Wright-style roof and a view, through massive beeches at the bottom of the yard, of the leaden ongliding Hudson. They were happy, surely. They had dry Midwestern taste, and by sticking to representational painters and abstract sculptors they managed to survive the uglier Eighties styles—faux graffiti, Germanic-*brut* expressionism, cathode-ray prole-play, ecological-protest trash art—and bring their quiet, chaste string of fourth-floor rooms into the calm lagoon of Nineties eclectic revivalism and subdued recession chic. They prospered; their youngest child turned twelve, their oldest was filling out college applications.

When Sharon first heard the rumor that Frank had left her for a young homosexual with whom he was having an affair, she had to laugh, for, far from having left her, there he was, right in the lamplit study with her, ripping pages out of *ARTnews*.

"I don't think so, Avis," she said, to the graphic artist on the other end of the line. "He's right here with me. Would you like to say hello?" The easy refutation was made additionally sweet by the fact that, some years before, there had been a brief (Sharon thought) romantic flareup between her husband and this caller, an overanimated redhead with protuberant cheeks and chin. Avis was a second-wave appropriationist, who made colored Xeroxes of masterpieces out of art books and then signed them in an ink mixed of her own blood and urine. How could she, who had actually slept with Frank, be imagining this grotesque thing?

The voice on the phone gushed as if relieved and pleased. "I know, it's wildly absurd, but I heard it from two sources, with absolutely solemn assurances."

"Who were these sources?"

"I'm not sure they'd like you to know. But it was Ed Jaffrey and then that boy who's been living with Walton Forney, oh, what does he call himself, one of those single names like Madonna—Jojo!"

"Well, then," Sharon began.

"But I've heard it from still others," Avis insisted. "All over town—it's in the air. Couldn't you and Frank do something about it, if it's not true?"

"*If,*" Sharon protested, and her thrust of impatience carried, when she put down the receiver, into her conversation with Frank. "Avis says you're supposed to have run off with your homosexual lover."

"I don't have a homosexual lover," Frank said, too calmly, ripping an auction ad out of the magazine.

"She says all New York says you do."

"Well, what are you going to believe, all New York or your own experience? Here I sit, faithful to a fault, straight as a die, whatever that means. We made love just two nights ago."

It seemed possibly revealing to her that he so distinctly remembered, as if heterosexual performance were a duty he checked off. He was—had always been, ever since she had met him—a slim blond man several inches under six feet tall, with a narrow head he liked to keep trim, even in those years when long hair was in fashion, and frosty blue eyes set at a slight tilt, such as you see on certain taut Slavic or Norwegian faces, and a small precise mouth he kept pursed over teeth a shade too prominent and yellow. He was reluctant to smile, let alone laugh. He was vain of his flat belly and lithe collegiate condition; he weighed himself every morning on the bathroom scale and, if he weighed a pound more than yesterday, skipped lunch. In this, and in his general attention to his own person, he was as quietly fanatic as—it for the first time occurred to her—a woman.

"You know I've never liked the queer side of this business," he went on. "I've just gotten used to it. I don't even think any more, who's gay and who isn't."

"Avis was *ju*bilant," Sharon said. "How *could* she think it?"

It took him a moment to focus on the question, and realize that his answer was important to her. He became nettled. "Ask *her* how," he said. "Our brief and regrettable relationship, if that's what interests you, seemed satisfactory to me at least. I mean, the moving parts all functioned. What troubles and amazes me, if I may say so, is how *you* can be taking this ridiculous rumor so seriously."

"I'm *not*, Frank," she insisted, and then backtracked. "But why would such a rumor come out of thin air? Doesn't there have to be *some*thing? Since we moved up here, we're not together so much, naturally; some days when I can't come into town you're gone sixteen hours. . . ."

"But, *Sha*ron," he said, like a teacher restoring discipline, removing his reading glasses from his almond-shaped eyes, with their stubby fair lashes. "Don't you *know* me? Ever since that time after the dance when we parked by the river? How old were you? Seventeen?"

She didn't want to reminisce. Their early sex had been difficult for her; she had submitted to his advances out of a larger, more social, rather idealistic attraction: she knew that together they would have the strength to get out of Cincinnati and, singly, or married to others, they would stay. "Well," she said, enjoying this sensation, despite the chill the rumor had awakened in her, of descending with Frank to a deeper level of intimacy than usual, "how well do you know even your own spouse? People are fooled all the time. Peggy Jacobson, for instance, when Henry ran off with the au pair, couldn't believe, even when the evidence was right there in front of her—"

"I'm *deeply* insulted," Frank interrupted, his mouth tense in that way of his when making a joke but not wanting to show his teeth. "My masculinity is insulted." But he couldn't deny himself a downward glance into his magazine; his tidy white hand jerked, as if wanting to tear out yet another item that might be useful to their business. Intimacy had always made him nervous. She kept at it. "Avis said two separate people had solemnly assured her."

"Who, exactly?"

When she told him, he said, just as she had done, "Well, then." He added, "You know how gays are. Malicious. Mischievous. They have all that time and money on their hands."

"You sound jealous." Something about the way he

was arguing with her strengthened Sharon's suspicion
that, outrageous as the rumor was—indeed, *because* it
was outrageous—it was true.

In the days that followed, now that Sharon was alert
to the rumor's vaporous presence, she imagined it
everywhere—on the poised young faces of their staff, in
the delicate negotiatory accents of their artists' agents,
in the heartier tones of their repeat customers, even in
the gruff, self-preoccupied ramblings of the artists
themselves. People seemed startled when she and Frank
entered a room together: the desk receptionist and the
security guard in their gallery halted their daily morning
banter, and the waiters in their pet restaurant, over on
59th Street, appeared especially effusive and attentive.
Handshakes lasted a second too long; women embraced
her with an extra squeeze; she felt herself ensnared in a
net of unspoken pity.

Frank sensed her discomfort and took a certain malicious pleasure in it, enacting all the while his perfect innocence. He composed himself to appear, from her angle,
aloof above the rumor. Dealing professionally in so much
absurdity—the art world's frantic attention-getting
grotesquerie—he merely intensified the fastidious dryness
that had sustained their gallery through wave after wave
of changing fashion, and that had, like a rocket's heat-
resistant skin, insulated their launch, their escape from
the comfortable riverine smugness of semi-Southern, pu-
ritanical Cincinnati to this capital of dreadful freedom.
The rumor amused him, and it amused him, too, to notice
how she helplessly watched to see if in the metropolitan
throngs his eyes now followed young men as once they
had noticed and followed young women. She observed
his gestures—always a bit excessively graceful and precise—distrustfully, and listened for the buttery, reedy tone
of voice that might signal an invisible sex change.

That she even in some small fraction of her was willing to believe the rumor justified a certain maliciousness on his part. He couldn't help teasing her—glancing over at her, say, when an especially lithe and magnetic young waiter served them, or, at home, in their bedroom, pushing more brusquely than was his style at her increasing sexual unwillingness. At last away from the countless knowing eyes of their New York milieu, in the privacy of their Hastings upstairs, beneath the wide Midwestern eaves, she would on occasion burst into tears and strike out at him, at his infuriating impervious apparent blamelessness. He was like one of those photorealist nudes, merciless in every detail and yet subtly, defiantly not there, not human. "You're distant," she accused him. "You've always been."

"I don't mean to be. Sharon, you didn't use to mind my manner. You thought it was quietly masterful."

"I was a teenaged girl. I deferred to you."

"It worked out," he pointed out, lifting his hands in an effete, disclaiming way to indicate their large bedroom, their expensive house, their joint career. "What is it that bothers you, my dear? The idea of losing me? Or the insult to your female pride? The people who started this ridiculous rumor don't even *see* women—women to them are just background noise."

"It's *not* ridiculous—if it were, why does it keep on and on, even though we're seen together all the time?"

For, ostensibly to quiet her, and to quench the rumor, he had all but ceased to go to the city alone, and took her with him even though it meant some neglect of the house and their still-growing sons.

Frank asked, "Who *says* it keeps on all the time? I've *never* heard it, never once, except from you. Who's mentioned it lately?"

"Nobody."

"Well, then." He smiled, his lips not quite parting on his curved teeth, tawny like a beaver's.

"You bastard!" Sharon burst out. "You have some stinking little secret!"

"I don't," he serenely half-lied.

The rumor had no factual basis. But might there be, Frank asked himself, some truth to it after all? Not circumstantial truth, but some higher, inner truth? As a young man, slight of build, with artistic interests, had he not been fearful of being mistaken for a homosexual? Had he not responded to homosexual overtures as they arose, in bars and locker rooms, with a disproportionate terror and repugnance? Had not his early marriage, and then, ten years later, his flurry of adulterous womanizing, been an escape of sorts, into safe, socially approved terrain? When he fantasized, or saw a pornographic movie, was not the male organ the hero of the occasion for him, at the center of every scene? Were not those slavish, lapping, sucking starlets his robotlike delegates, with glazed eyes and undisturbed coiffures venturing where he did not dare? Did he not, perhaps, envy women their privilege of worshipping the phallus? And did he not, when the doctor gave him his annual prostate exam with a greased finger, have to fight getting an erection, right there in a passive curled position on the examining table? But, Frank further asked himself, in fairness arguing both sides of the case, can homosexual strands be entirely disentangled from heterosexual in that pink muck of carnal excitement, of dream made flesh, of return to the pre-sexual womb?

More broadly, had he not felt more comfortable with his father than with his mother? Was not this in itself a sinister reversal of the usual biology? His father had been a genteel Fourth Street lawyer, of no particular effectuality save that most of his clients were from the same social class, with the same accents and comfortably narrowed aspirations, here on this plateau by the swelling Ohio. Darker and taller than Frank, with the same long teeth and primly set mouth, his father had had the lawyer's gift of silence, of judicious withholding, and in his son's scattered memories of times together—a trip downtown in the Packard to buy Frank his first suit, each summer's one or two excursions to see the Reds play at old Crosley Field—the man said little; but this prim reserve, letting so much go unstated and unacknowledged, was a relief, after the daily shower of words and affection and advice that Frank received from his mother. As an adult he was attracted, he had noticed, to stoical men, taller than he, gravely sealed around an unexpressed sadness. His favorite college roommate had been of this saturnine type, and his pet tennis partner in Hastings, and artists he especially favored and encouraged—dour, weathered landscapists and virtually illiterate sculptors, welded solid into their crafts and stubborn obsessions. With these men he became a catering, wifely, subtly agitated presence that Sharon would scarcely recognize.

Frank's mother, once a fluffy belle from Louisville, had been gaudy, strident, sardonic, volatile, needy, demanding, loving; from her he had inherited his "artistic" side, as well as his blondness and "interesting" almond-shaped eyes, but he was not especially grateful. Less—as was proposed by a famous formula he didn't know as a boy—would have been more. His mother had given him an impression of women as complex, brightly colored traps, attractive but treacherous, their petals apt to harden in an instant into knives. A certain wistful passivity had drawn him to Sharon and, after the initial dazzlement of the Avises of the world faded and fizzled, always drew him back. Other women asked more than he could provide; he was aware of other, bigger, hotter men they had had. But with Sharon he had been a rescuer; he had slain the dragon of the Ohio; he had got her out of Cincinnati. What more devastatingly, and less forgivably, confirmed the rumor's essential truth than the willingness of the one who knew him best and owed him most to entertain it? Sharon's instinct had been to believe Avis even though, far from running off, he was sitting there right in front of her eyes.

He was unreal to her, he could not help but conclude: all those years of cohabitation and husbandly service were now thanklessly dismissed because of an apparition, a shadow of gossip. On the other hand, now that the rumor existed, Frank had become more real in the eyes of José, the younger, slier of the two security guards, whose daily greetings had subtly moved beyond the perfunctory; a certain mischievous dance in the boy's velvety features had come to enrich their employer-employee courtesies. And Jennifer, too, the severely beautiful receptionist, with her neo-hippie bangs and shawls and serapes, now treated him more relaxedly, even offhandedly. She assumed with him a comradely slanginess—"The boss was in earlier but she went out to exchange something at Bergdorf's"—as if both he and she were in roughly parallel bondage to "the boss." Frank's heart felt a reflex of loyalty to Sharon, a single sharp beat, but then he, too, relaxed, as if his phantom male lover and the weightless life he led with him in some nonexistent apartment had bestowed at last what the city had withheld from the overworked, child-burdened married couple who had arrived fifteen years ago—a halo of glamour, of debonair mystery.

In Hastings, when he and his wife attended a suburban party, the effect was less flattering. The other couples, he imagined, were slightly unsettled by the Whittiers' stubbornly appearing together, and became disjointed in their presence, the men drifting off in distaste, the women turning supernormal and laying up a chinkless wall of conversation about children's college applications, local zoning, and Wall Street layoffs. The women, it seemed to Frank, edged, with an instinctive animal movement, a few inches closer to Sharon and touched her with a deft, protective flicking on the shoulder or forearm, to express solidarity and sympathy.

Wes Robertson, Frank's favorite tennis partner, came over to him and grunted, "How's it going?"

"Fine," Frank gushed, staring up at Wes with what he hoped weren't unduly starry eyes. Wes, who had recently turned fifty, had an old motorcycle-accident scar on one side of his chin, a small pale rose of discoloration, which seemed to concentrate the man's self-careless manliness. Frank gave him more of an answer than he might have wanted: "In the art game we're feeling the slowdown like everybody else, but the Japanese are keeping the roof from caving in. The trouble with the Japanese, though, is, from the standpoint of a personal gallery like ours, they aren't adventurous—they want blue chips, they want guaranteed value, they can't grasp that in art value has to be subjective to an extent. Look at their own stuff—it's all standardized. Who the hell but the experts can tell a Hiroshige from a Hokusai? When you think about it, their whole society, their whole success really, is based on everybody being alike, everybody agreeing. The notion of art as an individualistic struggle, a gamble, as the dynamic embodiment of an existential problem—they just don't get it." He was talking too much, he knew, but he couldn't help it; Wes's scowling presence, his melancholy scarred face and stringy alcoholic body, which nevertheless could still whip a backhand right across the forecourt, perversely excited Frank, made him want to flirt.

Wes grimaced and contemplated Frank glumly. "Be

around for a game Sunday?" Meaning, had he really run off?

"Of course. Why wouldn't I be?" This was teasing the issue, and Frank tried to sober up, to rein in. He felt a flush on his face, and a stammer coming on. He asked, "The usual hour? Ten-forty-five, more or less?"

Wes nodded. "Sure."

Frank chattered on: "Let's try to get Court Four this time. Those brats having their lessons on Court One drove me crazy last time. We had to keep retrieving their damn balls. And listening to their moronic chatter."

Wes didn't grant this attempt at evocation of past liaisons even a word, just continued his melancholy, stoical nodding. This was one of the things, it occurred to Frank, that he liked about men: their relational minimalism, their gender-based realization that the cupboard of life, emotionally speaking, was pretty near bare. There wasn't that tireless, irksome, bright-eyed *hope* women kept fluttering at you.

Once, years ago, on a stag golfing trip to Portugal, he and Wes had shared a room, with two single beds, and Wes had fallen asleep within a minute and started snoring, keeping Frank awake for much of the night. Contemplating the unconscious male body on its moonlit bed, Frank had been struck by the tragic dignity of this supine form, like a stone knight eroding on a tomb—the snoring profile in motionless gray silhouette, the massive, scarred warrior weight helpless as his breathing struggled from phase to phase of the sleep cycle—from deep to REM to a near-wakefulness that brought a few merciful minutes of silence. The next morning, Wes said Frank should have reached over and poked him in the side; that's what his wife did. But he wasn't his wife, Frank thought, though he had felt, in the course of that night's ordeal, his heart make many curious motions, among them the heaving, all but impossible effort women's hearts make in overcoming men's heavy grayness and achieving—a rainbow born of drizzle—love.

At the opening of Ned Forschheimer's show— Forschheimer, a shy, rude, stubborn, and now elderly painter of tea-colored, wintry Connecticut landscapes, was one of the Whittier Gallery's pets, unfashionable yet sneakily sellable—none other than Walton Forney came up to Frank, his round face lit by white wine and his odd unquenchable self-delight, and said, "Say, Frank old boy. Methinks I owe you an apology. It was Charlie Whit*field*, who used to run that framing shop down on Eighth Street, who left his wife suddenly, with some little Guatemalan boy he was putting through CCNY on the side. They took off for Mexico and left the missus sitting with the shop mortgaged up to its attic and about a hundred prints of wild ducks left unframed. The thing that must have confused me, Charlie came from Ohio, too—Columbus or Cleveland, one of those. I knew it began with a C. It was, what do they call it, a Freudian slip, an understandable confusion. Avis Wasserman told me Sharon wasn't all that thrilled to get the word a while ago, and you must have wondered yourself what the hell was up."

"We ignored it," Frank said, in a voice firmer and less catering than his usual one. "We rose above it." Walton was a number of inches shorter than Frank, with yet a bigger head; his gleaming, thin-skinned face, bearing smooth jowls that had climbed into his sideburns, was shadowed blue here and there, like the moon. His bruised and powdered look somehow went with his small spaced teeth and the horizontal red tracks his glasses had left in the fat in front of his ears.

The man gazed at Frank with a gleaming, sagging lower lip, his nearsighted eyes trying to assess the damage, the depth of the grudge. "Well, *mea culpa, mea culpa,* I guess, though I *didn't* tell Jojo and that *poisonous* Ed Jaffrey to go blabbing it all over town."

"Well, Wally, thanks for filling me in," Frank said resonantly. Depending on what type of man he was with, Frank felt large and straight and sonorous or, as with Wes, gracile and flighty. Sharon, scenting blood amid the vacuous burble of the party, pushed herself through the crowd and joined them. Frank quickly told her, "Wally just confessed to me he started the rumor because Charlie Whitfield downtown, who *did* run off with somebody, came from Ohio, too. Toledo, as I remember."

"I said Cleveland or Columbus," Wally murmured, not sure Frank was being satirical.

Sharon asked, "What rumor, honey?"

Frank blushed. "You know, the one that said I ran off with a boy."

"Oh, *that* rumor," Sharon said, blinking once, as if her party mascara were sticking. "I'd totally forgotten it. Who could believe it," she asked Wally, "of Frank?"

"Everybody, evidently," Frank said. It was possible, given the strange willful ways of women, that she *had* forgotten it, even while he had been brooding over its possible justice. If the rumor were truly quenched—and Walton would undoubtedly tell the story of his "Freudian slip" around town, as a self-promoting joke on himself—Frank would feel diminished. He would feel emasculated, if his wife no longer thought he had a secret.

Yet that night, at the party, Walton Forney's Jojo came up to him. He seemed, despite an earring the size of a faucet washer and a magenta stripe in the center of his "rise" hairdo, unexpectedly intelligent and low-key, offering, not in so many words, a kind of apology, and praising the tea-colored landscapes being offered for sale. "I've been thinking, in my own work, of going, you know, more traditional. You get this feeling of, like, a dead end with total abstraction." The boy had a bony, humorless face, with a silvery line of a scar under one eye, and seemed uncertain in manner, hesitant, as if he had reached a point in life where he needed direction. That fat fool Forney could certainly not provide direction, and it pleased Frank to imagine that Jojo was beginning to realize it.

"All that abstract-expressionist fuss about *paint*," he told the boy. "A person looking at a Rembrandt knows he's looking at *paint*. The question is, What *else* is he looking at?"

As he and Sharon drove home together along the Hudson, the car felt close; the heater fan blew oppressively, parchingly. "*You* were willing to believe it at first," he reminded her.

"Well, Avis seemed so definite. But you convinced me."

"How?"

She placed her hand high on his thigh and dug her fingers in, annoyingly, infuriatingly. "*You* know," she said, in a lower register, meant to be sexy, but almost inaudible over the roar of the heater fan. The Hudson glowered far beneath them, like the dark Ohio when he used to drive her home from a date across the river in honky-tonk Kentucky.

"That could be mere performance," he warned her. "Women are fooled that way all the time."

"Who says?"

"Everybody. Books. Proust. People aren't that simple."

"They're simple enough," Sharon said, in a neutral, defensive tone, removing her hand.

"If you say so, my dear," Frank said, somewhat stoically, his mind drifting. That silvery line of a scar under Jojo's left eye ... lean long muscles snugly wrapped in white skin ... lofts with a Spartan, masculine tang to their spaces ... Hellenic fellowship, exercise machines ... direct negotiations, between equals ... no more dealing with this pathetic, maddening race of *others* ...

The rumor might be dead in the world, but in him it had come alive.

Falling Asleep Up North

Falling asleep has never struck me as a very natural thing to do. There is a surreal trickiness to traversing that in-between area, when the grip of consciousness is slipping but has not quite let go and curious mutated thoughts pass as normal cogitation unless snapped into clear light by a creaking door, one's bed partner twitching, or the prematurely jubilant realization *I'm falling asleep*. The little fumbling larvae of nonsense that precede dreams' uninhibited butterflies are disastrously exposed to a light they cannot survive, and one must begin again, relaxing the mind into unravelling. Consciousness of the process balks it; the brain, watching itself, will not close its thousand eyes. Circling in the cell of wakefulness, it panics at the poverty of its domain—these worn-out obsessions, these threadbare word-games, these pointless grievances, these picayune plans for tomorrow which yet loom, hours from execution, as unbearably momentous. Consciousness, that glaring fruit of evolution, that agitation of electrified molecules, becomes a captivity—a hellish churning in which the insomniac is as alone as Satan, twisting and turning and boring a conical hole in the darkness, while on all sides the wide world blessedly, obliviously snores.

One such night breeds another; wearily stumbling through the day, you arrive back in bed at last and the same electric barrier has been switched on, the same invisible shell bars the way into sleep. From over twenty years ago I recall a spell of such sleepless nights ending. It was in 1967, a year of riot and expanding quagmire but in my own tiny corner of North American domestic life noteworthy for Expo 67, a world's fair in Canada to which my wife and I had promised to take our many small children. Our launching pad for the drive to Montreal was my wife's parents' summer house in Vermont, an old farmhouse up a dirt mountain road so steep that in one section, unless you had floored the accelerator at the bottom and made a wild, fishtailing run for it, the car wheels would begin to spin in the gravel near the top and you had to back down and try again. The house was surrounded by pine woods reputed to be haunted by bears, and my father-in-law, a theologian so liberal he considered both Paul Tillich and Reinhold Niebuhr to be neo-orthodox, had been accustomed by years of delicate health to having poised around him a household at all points respectfully alert to his comfort. It made for a lot of tiptoeing and unexpressed tension. Yet I couldn't really blame bears or my father-in-law for my insomnia. Maybe it was the hard bed—a horsehair mattress supported by ropes laced through the maple side rails—or the stark moon-drenched mountaintop silence, or some internal romantic conflict whose terms I have forgotten. I was a passionate creature in those years, with surges of desire shaking my bones like loose bolts in the undercarriage of the old Ford Fairlane we bounced up the gravelly hill. My wife felt so sorry for me in my sleeplessness that, on the second morning, she begged a sleeping pill from her mother.

Her mother said of course. She thought nothing of it. Sleeping pills were a dime a dozen to her. She was, as theologians' wives tend to be, an oddly free spirit, her one eye on permanent wink from the irritating smoke of the cigarette constantly in her mouth, and she had reached that happy advanced age when medical science no longer scruples at prescribing addictive drugs. My in-laws' medicine cabinet—nicely made of yellow oak, with a mirror whose bevelled edge threw prismatic rainbows around the sunny country bathroom, into the long metal tub, diagonally across the bare plaster walls and nappy guest towels—brimmed with chemical ease. Carefreely she waved me toward the bottle holding the two-tone capsules that induced sleep. I accepted one, and, later, stole two more, scarcely believing that a single pill could quell the turmoil of my midnight brain.

Do I remember this right? Why would I have felt the need to steal what was as blithely given as I have described? A certain affection that existed between my mother-in-law and me clings to the incident, heightening the gloss of the green-and-white capsules, inviting me to linger here in the shade of the prose as it evokes those unexpected bathroom rainbows; they were one of the few elegancies of the austerely furnished, oft-robbed house. Once the snowmobile became common, annual break-ins occurred. Before, the house's remoteness had protected it all winter. Heavy vines, as I recall, hung from the shingled eaves, darkening the long side porch. In the room behind this porch there was a big wooden loom gnawed by porcupines hungry for the salt that had come off people's hands when people still used looms. There were also shelves of abandoned books, including an old-fashioned encyclopedia whose weathered spines I once, in my Vermont idleness, rubbed with chalk, so the identifying letters—*A-Ang, Nev-Ost*—could be read again, and the obsolete texts, on crinkled pages smelling of refrigeratorlike winter isolation, systematically consulted.

She was sexy, my mother-in-law, with her thinning

gray hair, permed in tight curls against her scalp, and her quick-heeled, slightly tottering walk, leaving a smoke trail behind her in a room like a bit of sky-writing. Her handwriting was squiggly, too—crackling with energy. There was a current between us that did not exist, strangely, between her lovely, voluptuous daughter and me, or (I felt) between her distinguished husband and her.

Come to think of it, the sleeping pill in my imagined hand may have come from her husband's cache. This was the drug-happy Sixties, and the two of them had pills to put them to sleep and pills to wake them up, pills to get their bowels working and pills to reverse the effect, pills that played upon their nervous systems as fluently as a harpist's fingers upon the taut, color-coded strings. Old age, as encapsulated in the sunstruck, prismatic medicine cabinet, looked like a party: all bets were off, the sky was the limit. With those of us still of child-bearing, child-rearing age, the medical world was stingier, asking us to tough it out and maintain chemical purity, for the good of the race. Our doctors smugly denied us sleeping pills, and tranquillizers, however hard we begged. We *were* allowed, though, the Pill itself—the anti-conception tablets that had brought on the sexual revolution that might have been what was keeping me awake. Those pills came on toylike little cardboard wheels, twenty-one to a cycle, encoding for women from Berkeley to Burundi when to take and when to skip. Once, a woman I had slept with for a few glorious days of sexual tourism handed me, as we parted forever, with a little laugh, her emptied pill-disc. We had made love at the end of her cycle. We would never make a baby. She was, like my former mother-in-law, tiny—just five feet tall. Small women, my tall mother used to say, make the world go round. The very thought of it turned her forehead and throat red with indignation. My limited experience has borne this out: small women are the best, more concentrated. This woman's parting laugh was debonair, brave, and sad, for we had done something unforgettable for each other, tourists or not.

Yet I don't seem to have taken my mother-in-law's sleeping pill, because when my wife and I packed up the car and left Vermont I was still groggy with insomnia; its glaze lay on everything, giving the summer day and the flatness of Quebec a hallucinatory shimmer. Vermont and extreme upstate New York seem the end of the world, a final thinning, and then north of them there appears this great city, with fancy restaurants and cathedrals and smartly turned-out women speaking two languages. Temporary villages had been constructed around the city to accommodate visitors to the fair: rows and miles of little boxes set down in muddy, flat areas that had perhaps been golf courses or rugby fields. We arrived toward evening, the four children cramped and hungry but steeled to have an exceptional time, in an actual foreign country, at an international exposition whose photographs had been in all the papers. It was raining. We must have eaten, somewhere—not fancy Montreal cuisine but friendly, fast food. What I remember is getting into my assigned corner of our thin-walled box, with rain drumming on the flat roof close above my head, and, while my children were still bumping around and disputing their territorial claims in this new world, falling headlong into the most delicious sleep of my life. This little rented box somewhere north of reality, my dependents all clustered around me, was the entrance at last to the heavily defended underground kingdom of sleep.

Can this be right? Why wouldn't I have taken the sleeping pill the night before, back in Vermont, and been well rested? Perhaps I have compressed, in the way of a rememberer, two separate bouts of insomnia, on two different trips to Vermont. I didn't seem to need the pill in Montreal. Still, I certainly am right about falling so satisfyingly, so ravenously asleep in the little temporary cabin; sleep had become delicious, edible, a huge piece of shadowy cake I couldn't wait to devour, toppling into its crumbly depth without hesitation.

(We fall *into* something, falling asleep, not *out* of things. Dreams are already there, beckoning; were sleep an unpopulated void, as null as a dead television screen or the surface of the moon, no one would want to go there. The great gleaming pond of the night would be full of floating ephemerids, each clinging in terror to his or her bubble of wakefulness.)

So unusually well rested, I was able to captain a successful raid upon the wonders of Expo 67; we got into the early-morning line for the Russian pavilion with its marvellous miniature hydroelectric dam, and devoted the day to the lesser and duller pavilions, including the Canadian one—housed in what I remember as an array of giant tree stumps—and lingered at night with takeout cartons on a grassy bank so as to gain admission, with less than an hour's wait, to our own national pavilion, a Buckminster Fuller geodesic dome touchingly devoid of imperial boasting or menace, in this era of rising Vietnam crisis. Instead, the dome was gaily filled with Raggedy Ann dolls and giant images of movie gods— the United States made weightless for its visit to the moon two years in the future. And then back we went to the box in the mud for another night of blissful (as the phrase is) sleep.

Perhaps I like exiguous wooden shelters. In New Hampshire, once, I fell asleep under a Ping-Pong table while a game was being played. Again, there were many children about—mine, and those of the male friend whose ski house we were in, and some friends of our mingled children. We had skied all day, one of the more strenuous mountains, Wildcat or Cannon. After our returning and having a drink and eating, an irresistible avalanche of sleepiness overtook me. Since every square foot of the little house seemed to be occupied by a person or a piece of furniture, I crawled under the Ping-Pong table and fell asleep on the cement floor while the paddles and the celluloid ball hollowly clicked overhead. It was a triumph of a sort, I could not help thinking at the time, something for *Believe It or Not*; yet my host was noticeably displeased. Just as he needed to fill his little house with furniture of all sorts—aluminum and plastic kitchen chairs in the living room, lopsided hassocks, driftwood lamps, odd bits of carpeting distributed on the cement floor like postage stamps in a messy drawer—so he needed to cram his hours with activities. He couldn't take a bath without reading a magazine in the tub; he couldn't drive a car without turning on a symphony or a language tape. He had planned, after our day of skiing, an evening of organized games, and I, as the only other adult male, had been important to his plans. The pressure of his expectations may have been part of the weight of the psychic avalanche that had swept me away.

Possibly this memory also belongs to the Sixties; it wears the psychedelic polychrome of that decade—there may have been a Peter Max poster on the wall, along with the obligatory New Hampshire mountainscapes and hunting scenes—and not the yellowing, sickly tint of the Seventies. But it seems later than 1967: my children are bigger, to judge from the ponderous scuffling of their feet as they race around the Ping-Pong table, and my wife, though still there, somewhere far above the table top, has a decaying presence, a dim feminine phosphorescence on the edges of the memory. My host finds her lovely and voluptuous, I happen to know, and perhaps it is this awareness—a knowledge, as in the Montreal cabin, that everyone was accounted for and taken care of—that has released me to oblivion.

Yet my host emanates sulky waves of disappointment that assault me as I fitfully wake and stir beneath the celluloid battering of Ping-Pong racket. He is somewhere near his prime—freshly divorced, resolutely bachelor. His felt displeasure leads me to reflect, as I shift position on the friendly cool cement, where perhaps a square of shag carpeting has drifted to pillow my cheek, on my role in his life: it is, I see for the first time clearly, that of an entertainer, of a hired jester, of someone expected to pay for his access to this jumbled ski house, with its electric heat and flimsy partitions, in coin of an unflagging willingness to participate in whatever games have been scheduled. Up to this moment, year after year, I have been willing; I don't know what has come over me—this miraculous sleepiness, this refusal to come out from under the Ping-Pong table. It is, in Sixties style, a protest of a sort, this I also see. But I can't stop making it, and fall asleep again, on my little island of cement, as if on a towering column of cotton.

Becoming a bachelor, my friend and host—Franz, he shall be called—acquired open access to the women I had to covet in secret, in the town we lived in, to the south. What a strain it was, always being in love! I seem to recall a costume party, where my wife and I were dressed in matching outfits—as Louis XVI and Marie Antoinette, or as a fork and a spoon—and Franz was escorting a fresh divorcée, she dressed as a Spanish male, with a black hat from whose circular rim small black wool balls hung. Her eyes, also black, looked at me from beneath the row of swaying balls, and her teeth showed in a teasing bite of a smile, as if to say, "Yours, too, could be this freedom." And, again, after volleyball, in the summer sweat of it, and the long day's light, having had drinks on Franz's porch, all of us couples at last guiltily hurrying home to give the children Sunday supper, yet one lone woman lingering on the porch, lighting up another cigarette with a cocky twist of her pony-tailed head, the rusty old porch glider giving off a squeak beneath her, her glance flicking past mine like a cocky flick of ash, her thighs thrusting from her little denim skirt with a somehow unnatural gloss, as of plastic piano keys that have replaced gaps in the original worn ivory. Both these women Franz was taking from me were little, with small bright bones, solid hips, and pulses beating as rapidly as birds' breasts.

Yet I once saw him, when we were all younger still— could it have been the innocent Fifties?—after a Christmas party that had left us all drunk, crying tears because my wife was mine instead of his. I was driving, she was sitting between us, and drops of bright water, I could see in the snowy streetlight, were falling from the tip of his nose, one after another. I had to love him, for that.

As for the era of my falling asleep under the Ping-Pong table: On second consideration, from the jaundiced tint of the memory, and the hormone-laden heaviness of my children's feet, it must be later than I thought. It must be the early Seventies after all. It can't be the mid-Seventies, for by then I had cast myself adrift from my family and was exploring such bastions of freedom as laundromats and art-movie houses.

My clear-eyed present wife, once when I asked her how I had seemed to her in the midst of that dear old crowd, said, "Oh, like a dog who doesn't know he's being kicked."

"Really?" I thought about it. The image had a truthful ring that put me on the defensive. "I sound rather sweet," I said.

Masochism is as unfashionable now as aggressiveness was twenty years ago, but that's all right. Realities don't need to be named to exist. Being kicked is a stimulus, and when the stimuli stop, we fall asleep. Insomnia is no longer one of my issues. As we age, the distinction between being asleep and being awake blurs. My grandmother used to fall asleep in a rocking chair, between one rock and the next. Once in a great while—too rousing a rental video, or a cup of coffee the hostess solemnly swore was decaf—I enter the old terrain, the three-o'clock twists, the four-o'clock disbelief that this is happening to me. It is thrilling, in a way, like reading Kierkegaard again, or Maritain. I console myself that I am storing up fatigue toward the next night.

And I rarely make it north of Massachusetts now. At a certain stage in life, which we pass into as if crossing the unguarded border between two friendly countries, the drift becomes southerly—toward New York, Washington, Florida. Going north, it turns out in retrospect, was a lot of unnecessary effort. An old buck can curl up and call it a day anywhere.

The Brown Chest

IN THE FIRST HOUSE he lived in, it sat up on the second floor, a big wooden chest, out of the way and yet not. For in this house, the house that he inhabited as if he would never live in any other, there were popular cheerful places, where the radio played and the legs of grown-ups went back and forth, and there were haunted bad places, like the coal bin behind the furnace, and the attic with its spiders and smell of old carpet, where he would never go without a grown-up close with him, and there were places in between, that were out of the main current but were not menacing, either, just neutral, and neglected. The entire front of the house had this neglected quality, with its guest bedroom where guests hardly ever stayed; it held a gray-painted bed with silver moons on the headboard and corner posts shaped at the top like mushrooms, and a little desk by the window where his mother sometimes, but not often, wrote letters and confided sentences to her diary in her tiny backslanting hand. If she had never done this, the room would have become haunted, even though it looked out on the busy street with its telephone wires and daytime swish of cars; but the occasional scratch of her pen exerted just enough pressure to keep away the frightening shadows, the sad spirits from long ago, locked into events that couldn't change.

Outside the guest-bedroom door, the upstairs hall,

having narrowly sneaked past his grandparents' bedroom's door, broadened to be almost a room, with a window all its own, and a geranium on the sill shedding brown leaves when the women of the house forgot to water it, and curtains of dotted swiss he could see the telephone wires through, and a rug of braided rags shaped like the oval tracks his Lionel train went around and around the Christmas tree on, and, to one side, its front feet planted on the rag rug, with just enough space left for the attic door to swing open, the chest.

It was big enough for him to lie in, but he had never dared try. It was painted brown, but in such a way that the wood grain showed through, as if paint very thinned with turpentine had been used. On the side, wavy stripes of paint had been allowed to run, making dribbles like the teeth of a big wobbly comb. The lid on its brown had patches of yellow freckles. The hinges were small and black, and there was a keyhole that had no key. All this made the chest, simple in shape as it was, strange, and ancient, and almost frightening. And when he, or the grown-up with him, lifted the lid of the chest, an amazing smell rushed out—deeply sweet and musty, of mothballs and cedar, but that wasn't all of it. The smell seemed also to belong to the contents—lace tablecloths and wool blankets on top, but much more underneath. The full contents of the chest never came quite clear, perhaps because he didn't want to know. His parents' college diplomas seemed to be under the blankets, and other documents going back still farther, having to do with his grandparents, their marriage, or the marriage of someone beyond even them. There was a folded old piece of paper with drawn-on hearts and designs and words in German. His mother had once tried to explain the paper to him, but he hadn't wanted to listen. A thing so old disgusted him. And there were giant Bibles, and squat books with plush covers and a little square mottled mirror buried in the plush of one. These books had fat pages edged in gold, thick enough to hold, on both sides, stiff brown pictures, often oval, of dead people. He didn't like looking into these albums, even when his mother was explaining them to him. The chest went down and down, into the past, and he hated the feeling of that well of time, with its sweet deep smell of things unstirring, waiting, taking on the moldy flavor of time, not moving unless somebody touched them.

Then everything moved: the moving men came one day and everything in the house that had always been in a certain place was swiftly and casually uplifted and carried out the door. In the general upheaval the week before, he had been shocked to discover, glancing in, that at some point the chest had come to contain drawings he had done as a child, and his elementary-school report cards, and photographs—studio photographs lovingly mounted in folders of dove-gray cardboard with deckle edges—of him when he was five. He was now thirteen.

The new house was smaller, with more outdoors around it. He liked it less on both accounts. Country space frightened him, much as the coal bin and the dark triangles under the attic eaves had—spaces that didn't have enough to do with people. Fields that were plowed one day in the spring and harvested one day in the fall, woods where dead trees were allowed to topple and slowly rot without anyone noticing, brambled-around spaces where he felt nobody had ever been before he himself came upon them. Heaps and rows of overgrown stones and dumps of rusty cans and tinted bottles indicated that other people in fact had been here, people like those who had posed in their Sunday clothes in the gilded albums, but the traces they left weren't usable, the way city sidewalks and trolley-car tracks were usable. His instinct was to stay in the little thick-walled country house, and read, and eat sandwiches he made for himself of raisins and peanut butter, and wait for this phase of his life to pass. Moving from the first house, leaving it behind, had taught him that a life had phases.

The chest, on that day of moving, had been set in the new attic, which was smaller than the other, and less frightening, perhaps because gaps in the cedar-shingled roof let dabs of daylight in. When the roof was being repaired, the whole space was thrown open to the weather, and it rained in, on all the furniture there was no longer room for, except up here or in the barn. The chest was too important for the barn; it perched on the edge of the attic steps, so an unpainted back he had never seen before, of two very wide pale boards, became visible. At the ends of each board were careless splashes of the thin brown paint—stain, really—left by the chestmaker when he had covered the sides.

The chest's contents, unseen, darkened in his mind. Once in a great while his mother had to search in there for something, or to confide a treasure to its depths, and in those moments, peeking in, he was surprised at how full the chest seemed, fuller than he remembered, of dotted-swiss curtains and crocheted lap rugs and photographs in folders of soft cardboard, all smelling of camphor and cedar. There the chest perched, an inch from the attic stairwell, and there it stayed, for over forty years.

Then it moved again. His children, adults all, came from afar and joined him in the house, where their grandmother had at last died, and divided up the furniture—some for them to carry away, some for the local auctioneer to sell, and some for him, the only survivor of that first house, with its long halls and haunted places, to keep and to assimilate to his own house, hundreds of miles away.

Two of the three children, the two that were married, had many responsibilities and soon left; he and his younger son, without a wife and without a job, remained to empty the house and pack the U-Haul van they rented. For days they lived together, eating takeout food, poisoning mice and trapping cats, moving from crowded cellar to jammed attic like sick men changing position in bed, overwhelmed by decisions, by accumulated possessions, now and then fleeing the house to escape the oppression of the past. He found the iron scales, quite rusted by the cellar damp, whereon his grandmother used to weigh out bundles of asparagus against a set of cylindrical weights. The weights were still heavy in his hand, and left rust stains on his palm. He studied a tin basin, painted in a white-on-gray spatter-pattern that had puzzled him as a child with its apparent sloppiness, and he could see again his grandfather's paper-white feet soaking in suds that rustled as the bubbles popped one by one.

The chest, up there in the attic along with old rolled carpets and rocking chairs with broken cane seats, stacked hatboxes from the Thirties and paperback mysteries from the Forties, was too heavy to lift, loaded as it was. He and his younger son took out layers of blankets and plush-covered albums, lace tablecloths and linen napkins; they uncovered a long cardboard box labelled in his mother's handwriting "Wedding Dress 1925," and, underneath that, rumpled silk dresses that a small girl might have worn when the century was young, and patent-leather baby shoes, and a gold-plated horseshoe, and faithful notations of the last century's weather kept by his grandfather's father in limp diaries bound in red leather, and a buggy-whip. A little box labelled in his mother's handwriting "Haircut July 1919" held, wrapped in tissue paper, coils of auburn hair start-lingly silky to the touch. There were stiff brown photo-graphs of his father's college football team, his father crouching at right tackle in an unpadded helmet, and of a stageful of posing young people among whom he fi-nally found his mother, wearing a flimsy fairy dress and looking as if she had been crying. And so on and on, until he couldn't bear it and asked his son to help him carry the chest, half unemptied, down the narrow attic stairs whose bare wooden treads had been troughed by generations of use, and then down the slightly broader stairs carpeted decades ago, and out the back door to the van. It didn't fit; they had to go back to the city ten miles away to rent a bigger van. Even so, packing eve-rything in was a struggle. At one point, exasperated and anxious to be gone, his broad-backed son, hunched in the body of the U-Haul van, picked up the chest single-handed, and inverted it, lid open, over some smaller items to save space. The old thin-painted wood gave off a sharp *crack*, a piercing quick cry of injury.

The chest came to rest in his barn. He now owned a barn, not a Pennsylvania barn with stone sides and pegged oak beams but a skimpier, New England barn, with a flat tarred roof and a long-abandoned horse stall. He found the place in the chest lid, near one of the little dark hinges, where a split had occurred, and with a few carefully driven nails repaired the damage well enough. He could not blame the boy, who was named Gordon, after his paternal grandfather, the onetime football player crouching for his picture in some sunny autumn when Harding was President. On the drive north in a downpour, Gordon had driven the truck, and his father tried to read the map, and in the dim light of the cab failed, and headed him the wrong way out of Westches-ter County, so they wound up across the Hudson River, amid blinding headlights, on an unfathomable, exitless highway. After that egregious piece of guidance, he could not blame the boy for anything, even for failing to get a job while concentrating instead on perfecting his dart game in the fake pubs of Boston. In a way not then immediately realized, the map-reading blunder righted the balance between them, himself and his son, as when under his grandmother's gnarled hands another stalk of asparagus would cause the tray holding the rusty cylindrical weights to rise with a soft *clunk*.

They arrived an hour late, after midnight. The unloading, including the reloading of the righted chest, all took place by flashlight, hurriedly, under the drumming sound of rain on the flat roof.

Now his barn felt haunted. He could scarcely bear to examine his inherited treasure, the chairs and cabinets and chinaware and faded best-sellers and old-fashioned bridge lamps clustered in a corner beyond the leaf-mulcher and the snow-blower and the rack of motorcycle tires left by the youngest son of the previous owner of the barn. He was the present owner. He had never imagined, as a child, owning so much. His wife saw no place in their house for even the curly-maple kitchen table and the walnut corner cupboard, his mother's pride. This section of the barn became, if not as frightening as the old coal bin, a place he avoided. These pieces that his infant eyes had grazed, and that had framed his parents' lives, seemed sadly shabby now, cheap in their time, most of them, and yet devoid of antique value: useless used furniture he had lacked the courage to discard.

So he was pleased, one winter day, two years after their wayward drive north, to have Gordon call and ask if he could come look at the furniture in the barn. He had a job, he said, or almost, and was moving into a bigger place, out from the city. He would be bringing a friend, he vaguely added. A male friend, presumably, to help him lift and load what he chose to take away.

But the friend was a female, small and exquisite, with fascinating large eyes, the whites white as china, and a way of darting back and forth like a hummingbird, her wings invisible. "Oh," she exclaimed, over this and that, explaining to Gordon in a breathy small voice how this would be useful, and that would fit right in. "Lamps!" she said. "I love lamps."

"You see, Dad," the boy explained, the words pronounced softly yet in a manner so momentous that it seemed to take all the air in the barn to give them utterance, "Morna and I are planning to get married."

"Morna"—a Celtic name, fittingly elfin. The girl was magical, there in the cold barn, emitting puffs of visible breath, moving through the clutter with quick twists of her denim-clad hips and graceful stabs of her narrow white hands. She spoke only to Gordon, as if a pane of shyness protected her from his hoary father—at this late phase of his life a kind of ogre, an ancestral, proprietorial figure full of potency and ugliness. "Gordon, what's this?" she asked.

The boy was embarrassed, perhaps by her innocent avidity. "Tell her, Dad."

"Our old guest bed." Which he used to lie diagonally across, listening to his mother's pen scratch as her diary tried to hold fast her days. Even then he knew it couldn't be done.

"We could strip off the ghastly gray, I guess," the boy conceded, frowning in the attempt to envision it and the work involved. "We *have* a bed," he reminded her.

"And this?" she went on, leaving the bed hanging in a realm of future possibility. Her headscarf had slipped back, exposing auburn hair glinting above the vapor of her breath, in evanescent present time.

She had paused at the chest. Her glance darted at

Gordon, and then, receiving no response, at the present owner, looking him in the eyes for the first time. The ogre smiled. "Open it."

"What's in it?" she asked.

He said, "I forget, actually."

Delicately but fearlessly, she lifted the lid, and out swooped, with the same vividness that had astonished and alarmed his nostrils as a child, the sweetish deep cedary smell, undiminished, cedar and camphor and paper and cloth, the smell of family, family without end.

His Mother Inside Him

ALLEN Dow had been fearful, in childhood, of his mother's unhappiness, which would vent itself in sudden storms of temper that flattened the other occupants of the house into the corners and far rooms. Once he saw his father cowering under the dining table while his mother, red-faced with fury, tried to get at him to slap him again. Allen never forgave her for that—for her doing it, for his seeing it. Though he learned to get around her—indeed, no one was better at getting around her; he was her only child, her confidant, her charmer, her prince, amusing and politic—he remained wary of the rage inside her that he had been permitted to glimpse. She made him nervous, and nervousness became his mode. All the complaints of nervousness—skin rashes, stammering, asthma, insomnia—were his. It took him decades of living hundreds of miles beyond her reach to begin to breathe, to sleep, and to speak normally. The women who drew close to him in the course of his life tended to suffer, and it took no great insight of his to imagine why his heart was, in regard to their sufferings, rather aloof and cool, if not faintly exultant. Whereas with the sufferings of a child or of a man—a man cowering under the table as an alternative to hitting back, or a child helplessly watching—he was quickly empathetic. He resented it, then, when, after her death, people (second cousins, Lutheran ministers) fondly remarked on how much he, as he approached sixty, resembled his mother.

He couldn't see it. He looked in the mirror. The fair skin, yes—freckled in his childhood, now pocked by spots of sun damage. Though her hair looked brown and had early turned gray, she had been one of nature's redheads, and when he had grown a beard, it had come in reddish. And there was a vexed something about his forehead—a rather low forehead like his mother's, for all their intellectual pretensions. When her temper flared, a pink V had appeared between her eyebrows; he had no temper to speak of, but there was a pink roughening of his skin exactly between his eyebrows. Otherwise—nose, mouth, ears—he saw no resemblance.

His ears were the "Hofstetter ears"—small-lobed, protuberant at the tops, like a lemur's. He had inherited them from his grandmother, his mother's mother; a photograph existed of her and her eleven brothers and sisters posed in black together, all with variants of these ears, sticking out white against the black. His mother's ears, while the rest of her body had dwindled in old age, had grown larger and come to look just like her father's, with big, flat, dull-colored lobes. As a little boy, Allen, crayoning on the floor, had often looked up and admired the impressive ears of his grandfather as the old man tilted back his head to bring the newspaper print into focus. His mother, he felt, had identified more with her father than with her mother, a tiny industrious woman toward whom her daughter had felt a compound of admiration, exasperation, and pity—somewhat the way, perhaps, in which Allen regarded his own father. His mother's father figured in the vividest of her family tales of the past—the man returning from a tavern down a straight dirt road and greeting with harsh drunken words the little girl who had run up the road to meet him; the man, younger, working in the woods, sawing and burning trees for the "charcoal business" with his bride's brothers; younger still, slender and unmarried, the man walking miles up and down the local hills to teach at a one-room schoolhouse. The walk took him daily through the farm where a certain young woman, the baby of her large family, spied him out and created a reason, one day of deep snow, for them to meet. We are all the result of sexual events, and their faded heat still warms us. Allen's mother had implanted him with a set of images that entwined, flourishing and fading, among those he had acquired with his own senses.

It surprised him, unpleasantly, when his mother's laugh, its unmistakable sly cry and shy trailing-off, came out of his mouth. And it irritated him to detect, in the workings of his brain, an increasing amount of the fanciful, self-defeating obliquity that had irritated him in her. In conversation she always resisted simple concurrence, and would nimbly take a contrary position, as if to make life, for herself and her partner in dialogue, more interesting. This curious courtesy was generally wasted, Allen had long ago observed, on the world, yet he felt in his own dealings an increasing tendency in the same direction; he couldn't help himself, the pull of the contrary was too strong, and there was too much justice lurking in the case not being presented.

For instance: When his second wife was negotiating the price of the suburban spread where they would consolidate their married status, he found himself in the mental position of the sellers, who were desperate to move to California, and he kept proposing to his wife a worse bargain than the one she eventually managed to strike. "Whose side are you on?" she asked in exasperation, and he felt his mother inside him itching to embark on a discourse as to the small- and mean-mindedness of taking anything as simple as a single side, this being the root of all wars and exploitation.

There was something very vulgar and un-Christian, this inner voice urged, about any display of self-interest. Yet in some sense, too, he was arguing *against* his mother, for she had been, in her rural realm, a considerable acquirer of acreage, adding slice after slice of neighboring property as "protection" for the acreage already possessed. She had done this, in her later years, with Allen's money, even though he hated land—its weediness, its erosiveness, its taxability. Or, rather, he felt about land, as about his mother, ambivalent, she having planted in him the idea that land was sacred, a piece of Mother Earth, endlessly valuable, and the last thing that the vulgar self-interest-seekers of the world would manage to take from you.

So within him his mother was battling his mother, and his sensible, hard-headed wife was the exasperated recipient of a double message. His first wife, too, had been fond of land; she still queened it over a tract his diligence had supplied. It seemed to be his circular fate to settle one woman after another on a sizable property and then move on, momentarily free, until the next female real-estate developer locked him into her plans. If he had not, in his wish to avoid his mother's temper, totally tamed his own, it might have angered him to contemplate. But, then, his mother's contrarian voice within him urged, where would he have lived, but for these landed women? On the streets? In the trees?

When his mother died, he became the sole custodian of hundreds of small mental pictures. In the most recent, he and she were moving in and out of hospitals, stooped and slow, like one of those elderly couples in which the man looks a generation younger. Hospitals, all glossy and abounding in exits and entrances and eccentric minor characters, seem made to be sitcom sets, and his mother and he laughed at the same places in the script. When the big, black, male nurse insisted on cutting her toenails, and washing her ticklish feet, Allen laughed at her account of it, while thinking secretly that it had needed to be done. Her sphere of effective supervision had so shrunk that even her feet were out of it.

Yet she looked, with her white hair flung about unpinned on her pillow, attractively wild, and the brick cityscape out the hospital windows took her back to her own city days, when she and his father had travelled through the state's small cities as his father's employer directed. Allen preferred her city self, the young woman predating his birth, whose aura of nervous grace clung to the young mother who would take him on the trolley car into town, to buy him a jacket for Sundays, or shoes in which he could see the bones of his feet move in an eerie green space at the bottom of a fluoroscope; or she would take him to a dance lesson, or a piano lesson, or the office of a city doctor, redolent of raincoats and Mercurochrome. Sometimes, when he thought back on it, it had been *she* who was going to the doctor, for female reasons that belonged to the dark subterrain of her unhappiness.

When she was dead and her input had ceased, he wondered about her unhappiness. Had the two of them imagined it? Her life had been no worse than most lives and better, surely, than many. Being a woman had no doubt frustrated her, keeping her at home, tying her to the fortunes of men less intelligent than herself, denying her a career. Perhaps something timid within her, even a lazy and self-indulgent something, had held her back from joining the women of her generation who did manage to make their own lives, as schoolteachers and saleswomen if not as artists and executives. This idea— that she was lazy and self-indulgent—came from her; all of Allen's ideas came from her, save the male, boyish idea of *getting away*, of getting out into unheated, unmediated space. Even that, in truth, had been her idea; she had once taken him up on the little hill, Shale Hill, that overlooked their town and told him that some day he would leave all this, he would fly free.

She was in him not as he had been in her, as a seed becoming a little male offshoot, but as the full tracery of his perceptions and reactions; he had led his life as an extension of hers, a superior version of hers, and when she died he became custodian of a specialized semiotics, a thousand tiny nuanced understandings of her, a once commonplace language of which he was now the sole surviving speaker.

Finding human relations difficult, she had turned to nature for comfort, and now, as he aged, the vast, restless natural presence, the birds and blossoms in their seasons and the chromatic tunings of air and weather, pressed upon him as he paced the suburban acreage where his present wife had installed him. His mother had had a nature-lover's hatred of smoking and drinking—her father had come home drunk and cruel from the tavern—and Allen had relinquished both habits years ago. She didn't smoke or drink but had loved to eat, and her middle-aged corpulence embarrassed him as well as her. In the hospital, looking back upon her life, she had confessed only one regret, with a fleeting expression of disgust: "I'm sorry I let myself get fat."

But then, in the sentences that followed, as an excuse, she had described the irresistible apple pie à la mode served in the basement cafeteria of a downtown department store where she had worked for a few Christmases—the delicious crust, the cinnamon on the crust, the creaminess of the vanilla or even fudge-ripple ice cream on top of that. The store had been the classier though smaller of the two major downtown emporiums, both rendered defunct by the rise of suburban malls; inside the revolving doors, gusts of candy-sweet perfume had swamped his youthful senses, and Christmas tinsel shivered everywhere, and carols were chiming from high on the walls, and toward the rear of the first floor, across from the stairway leading down to the clattering, fragrant cafeteria, a lending library had held, each jacket proudly wrapped in cellophane, the new Ellery Queen mystery, the new Thurber collection. Trembling tracks of wire carried money and receipts around the ceiling to an unseen cashier's office and back again—or was this in the big hardware store in the next block? Were pneumatic tubes used here, spitting out, with a stunning thump and crash, cylinders colorfully padded at both ends with thick felt? His mother would have known; she could have shared with him the vanished texture of this lost world, the world she had brought him to life within, a world of glamorous drugstores, with marble counter tops, and movie houses that were exotic islands of air-conditioning, with paper icicles dripping from the marquee. The entire old downtown that had held such wonders was not just dilapidated but wiped out—replaced by blank-faced buildings holding only the gray minions of government and finance. He wandered a world without features, just grass and sky, as in Brazil's remotest Mato Grosso, the last of his tribe, silent and hungry.

Hungry—he could not stop eating. After a full dinner, while his wife loaded the dishwasher, he would rummage rather frantically in the breadbox and the cupboards, scarcely conscious of what he was doing, and stuff his mouth with cookies, peanuts, raisins. On weekend mornings, in a strange daze he would find himself in the kitchen, not remembering how he got there, and consume half a bag of potato chips, or a safe-dish of leftover microwaved peas. Food, all the other sirens having grown faint and hoarse with age, now sang to him penetratingly—the edginess of food; the friability; the saltiness or sweetness of it in the ardent moment of first contact with his membranes; the ruminative pulverizing and liquefying and incorporating of it, like an act of memorization or of mathematical comprehension. Eating was a way, his only remaining way, of intersecting with the world. People guessed; his Christmas presents tended to be edible—boxes of giant cashews, of pricey conglomerate nuggets of chocolate, nuts, and caramel—and at dinner parties, he was the one somehow elected to take a second helping, to gratify the hostess. Allen Dow was getting fat. Just five pounds overweight, as he saw it, though he could have lost fifteen without looking thin. Each day proved to be not quite the one in which to eat less. Though he woke to a stomach ache, and vowed moderation, as the sun grew higher the cry from an emptiness within was too sharp, too persistent. As the last of a jar of sugared peanuts, or of a nicely buttered blueberry scone, disappeared into his insides, smothering the suppressed panic there—not so much the fear of death as the sensation that his life was too *small*—he smiled to think that his mother had reached this point at the age of thirty, whereas he was all of sixty. As they tell you in seventh-grade health class, girls develop more rapidly than boys.

Baby's First Step

GLENN MORRISSEY had been an utterly faithful husband until, at the age of thirty-six, he broke his leg playing touch football on the Mall in Washington, D.C., where he lived, as a lawyer employed by the Bureau of Weights and Measures. A heavy young black man had been standing on the sidelines, watching the scrimmage of lawyers and lobbyists and bureaucrats who each fall Sunday assembled down near the Hirshhorn for their afternoon tussle, and since he seemed to be alone, and the sides were uneven, he was invited to play. Assigned to cover Glenn on an out-and-in button-hook pass pattern, he slipped on the soft earth in changing direction and fell against Glenn's braced leg as the ball spiraled toward them. Glenn heard the bone pop—a muscle-muffled *snap*. But the young black picked himself up and scrambled back to the defensive huddle without even an apology, and it took a while for the other players to believe that Glenn, still lying there astonished, was truly injured and could no longer play. He hopped off the field and induced a close friend, Bud Jorgenson, a red-bearded specialist in ethnic art for the Smithsonian Institution, to help him hop the two blocks down 7th Street to his parked car. Glenn drove it back one-footed to his home in Adams-Morgan, a neo-colonial of powdery brick with a sideways view of Rock Creek Park. His wife, Stacey, was out back, giving the roses their fall pruning; she laughed when she saw him hopping toward her and heard his aggrieved voice cry out, "Look what those bad boys did to me!" It was only an hour later, after a trip to Sibley Memorial Hospital and a reading of his X-rays, that she took his injury seriously. His right tibia had been fractured vertically, splitting off the exterior tuberosity, with a messy involvement of the interosseous cartilage that would necessitate an operation, a week in the hospital, and three months in a cast.

Still, Glenn didn't consciously hold Stacey's underreaction against her—she was right; he was a boyish hypochondriac who had cried wolf too often—or the fact that that very night, with him settled and doped in his hospital bed, she went alone to a cocktail party at the Romanian Embassy, where the hors d'oeuvres were famously lavish. He no more had it in him to blame his wife for anything than he would blame himself; he knew her from the inside out—every motive, every reaction—just as he knew himself. In fact, he found her *more* predictable than he did his own self, which still had some depths and twists that took him unawares. You land, it seemed to him, on the shore of your own being in total innocence, like an explorer who was looking for something else, and it takes decades to penetrate inland and map the mountain passes and trace the rivers to their sources. Even then, there are large blanks, where monsters roam.

Being hospitalized, for the first time in his life— measuring out in pills his capacity for pain, sleeping on his back, submitting his most intimate functions to the care and scrutiny of nurses, learning shamelessness and becoming intensely, solicitously conscious of his own body, as well as doing all the forced entertaining, of doctors and visitors, that a hospital patient must do—opened up a new side of his being, a new stretch of potential. He took it all pretty well, was his verdict on himself. He was less of a sissy than he had thought. And then he endured being on crutches, having to carry his papers and possessions in a canvas tote bag while keeping his grip on the sponge-wrapped rungs of the crutches as he levered himself up and down stairs. He compressed, as it were, his physical activity, at home and the office, into a restricted yet still-effective mold—a smaller, more considered version of his previous life, which had been lived without proper appreciation of the miraculous powers of his body.

The late-winter day came when his orthopedist removed the last of a series of gray, itchy, odorous, scribbled-upon casts and pronounced him whole again. Glenn could hardly believe, even though he had taken a few experimental steps in the doctor's office, that he was free to walk on no more support than his own fallible bones. He felt, without the crutches, dizzyingly tall, and oddly vaporous below the waist. He was floating, he was gliding, and when he stepped into the waiting room he thought the other patients were looking up at him as if at a man on stilts. "Baby's first step," he joked, to a woman whose stare seemed especially nonplussed. But her expression remained stupid, and he realized that she didn't see anything extraordinary about him—just a man walking on his own two legs, as most men do.

That night, he and Stacey had a dinner party to attend, at the home of one of the bureau's chief calibrators; as Glenn stepped into the house he seemed still to be miraculously gliding, like Fred Astaire across a polished ballroom floor. He kissed his hostess with particular warmth; he was back among the living, the ambulatory. The party seemed to be his coming-out party, and he the belle of the evening, to whom every-

thing, as to Shakespeare's Miranda, was new. The unknown woman in finespun metallic red sitting next to
him at the dinner table was, he realized, alive just as he
was; her thorax held the same complex of arteries and
veins pounding with blood, clean and unclean, bluish
and bright.

"Do I know you?" he asked her, sliding into his chair.

"We met in the living room." Her smile was dazzling,
in a lipstick that also seemed metallic. "I'm the wife of
your host's brother. My husband and I live in the Midwest."

"The Midwest's a big place."

Vast areas seemed to lie all about him, waiting to be
explored. This woman contained patches of ambivalence and vacancy, he realized. We all hold uncertainties yearning to be clarified. There is more play in the
human situation than he in his old innocence had
dreamed.

"The Minneapolis–St. Paul area," she said.

"Twin Cities," he said, pleased with himself. "I love
the way people from there pronounce it—so quickly, all
those syllables. How do you stand the winters?"

"We go underground. We have skyways. Our feet
never touch the snow."

There was a sparkle, a shimmer, to the skin of her
face, its microscopic epidermal grain, as well as to her
red dress and her lipstick. Even the transparent fuzz on
her upper lip sparkled as it lifted in the tension of a
smile. He felt her rising to the challenge his inner space
presented to her; she somehow sensed, Glenn was convinced, his recent initiation, via suffering, into a free-
masonry of human exploration and exchange. Their
conversation, as the courses came and went by candlelight and the wine glasses were rhythmically refilled,
became so heated that they had to keep reminding
themselves to turn to the dinner partner on their other

side, for courtesy's sake. Her knee momentarily rested against his healed knee without apparent awareness; to emphasize a point she smartly tapped the back of his hand. How delightful she was, how wonderfully quick to perceive and respond, to parry and thrust! As they sat side by side at the dining table, Glenn kept picturing their two chests full of pumping blood, two barrels brimming with mystery.

"Are you in Washington for long?"

"The National Gallery and all those others—I could be happy here forever! But I must fly back tomorrow, on United at eleven-forty. My husband is going on to New York on business first thing in the morning. Our twelve-year-old daughter takes riding lessons and is doing dressage in a show and would never forgive me if I weren't there. She'd be in psychoanalysis forever. You know how it is—one of those moments that won't come again."

"I know," he said, not sure, in his rapture with her, that he did.

The next day, on the excuse of some research at the Library of Congress, he took a taxi to National Airport to see his dinner-mate off. Dressed in a trim travelling suit, carrying a small navy-blue overnight bag whose many-compartmented capacity was left limp by her gossamer party clothes, she did not seem surprised to see him. In the human clutter of the obsolescing old airport, with its spaces and shops like those of a railroad terminal, and its traffic of robed and sandalled visitors from all points of the globe, they walked back and forth, Glenn still marvelling at the ease with which his healed leg carried him. With every step, he seemed to be floating. The caged volume of her chest hung beside his; they had their arms about each other's waists like teenagers lounging back from the beach. As they walked, he carried her bag, which seemed weightless, and she talked about her children's activities—the girl's equestrian lessons, and the two boys' hockey practices, which took place at ungodly hours at a distant rink. "The sacrifices one makes! But you *must*, because some day they will be gone." The message was clear: she was committed, her life was a thousand miles away. The lapel of her travelling suit held a small brooch of cloisonné enamel, like a badge of membership in a society whose insignia he could not quite make out. The club of secret dissatisfaction.

He thought of kissing her, but here, in this international clutter, this traffic, it would have been awkward; it was enough to have her head beside his shoulder, so close he could smell on her the morning dew of her face lotion. She was nervous about missing the plane, and he should be back in his office. At the first boarding call, they reported to her gate; he passed her feather-light suitcase into her hand; they hugged, pressing their chests together; he bent his face to her shoulder and kissed the padded cloth. "Will you forget me?" she asked hurriedly in his ear, in a voice gone husky.

"Why would I do that?"

"You'll have all those others."

"What others?" he asked.

"You'll see." Adroitly she backed off and melted into the boarding line; Glenn missed some of the expressive nuances of her darting, apologetic farewell gestures, for his eyes, amazingly, had mustered tears. More gratifying still, in the few seconds of their embrace he had felt behind his fly the furtive pang of an erection commencing, the tingling throb of the areolar spaces embarking upon engorgement. He was alive, he was full of passion—a barrel waiting to be tapped.

They never met again; she had been a false dawn. Perhaps every major campaign in life needs a false start, a dry run, a resetting of the compass. Riding lessons in Minneapolis were a mere obstructive detail; the possibilities had been established. In the carnival of Washington, with its constant demonstrations, its litter of yesterday's placards, its picketing maniacs and widespread dangerous neighborhoods, there is room for romance and anarchic adventure. All those women, the wives underemployed and the employed women usually single, and all those demure side streets, frothy with flowering azalea and cherry, and the constant parties, and the seething of political gossip, of discontent, of official turnover and hoped-for advancement. War is a well-known aphrodisiac, and Washington is always at war. As the men rise and fall on the ladders of power, women are stimulated to take chances. The touch of Southern indolence in the air helps. Los Angeles and New York, by comparison, are too much in love with work—sex, like lunch, is tightly harnessed to business.

Stacey's best friend was a similarly lean, attractive, exercise- and cause-conscious mother of two, named Andrea Jorgenson. Bud was her husband; he travelled to third-world countries for the Smithsonian, bringing back sculptures made mostly, it seemed, of hair and straw. Andrea had appeared to Glenn rather opaque and standardized hitherto; now, as he turned upon her the powerful beam of his new knowledge—we are all full of warm darkness, unformed and inquisitive—her bones began to glow. It was a simple series of knight's moves, on the skewed chessboard of L'Enfant's city plan, to give her his ear at a party or two (his head bowed like that of a doctor listening to her heartbeat with a stethoscope), and then to indicate with a minute pressure of his hand during a fund-raising ball that a certain unspoken path was open, and then to suggest that, now that her children were both in boarding school and she was working toward a Ph.D. at Georgetown University,

she write a paper, with his help, on the failure of met-
rication in the United States. From there it was just a
few pushed pawns to lunches *à deux* downtown, and finally to his afternoon infiltration of her home and occu-
pation of her bed. Bud was off in Mali and Chad,
dodging civil wars.

Glenn had been in the Jorgensons' house in Woodley
Park many times, as a married guest of the couple, but
had never seen it in the quiet of the day, as a possessor
of sorts. These chairs and tables, curtains and rugs had
all been selected and tended by a sensibility akin to
Stacey's yet distinctly other. The bathroom had little be-
ribboned jars of potpourri set about, and pink toilet paper with a quilted texture, and a padded seat to match,
and a long-handled brush and a loofah on the sill where
the bathtub met the tiles, so he felt invited to picture
Andrea scrubbing and buffing herself to a subepithelial
rosiness, within a sloshing pond of suds. The tub and
sink were of some black substance like polished slate or
lava, and large mirrors here and there made the sight of
one's naked body unavoidable. Andrea was a closet
sybarite, just as Stacey was a closet ascetic, though,
seeing the two women side by side at a lunch table, one
would think them identical.

Andrea fancied not the prim pastel bed linen Stacey
preferred but splashy hot-colored floral patterns. She
provided, once, in his honor, purple satin sheets, which
were disconcertingly slippery; the pillows squirted out
from under their bodies like greased pigs. On the walls,
even in the bedroom, hairy, hollow-eyed masks stared
down, and on bookshelves and table tops carved fertility symbols thrust buttocks in one direction and breasts
in the other. The violence of the African artifacts made
Glenn slightly uncomfortable. Andrea's absent husband
seemed to be present in them, staring through the eye-
holes of grimacing masks.

Strange to say, part of the pleasure of Andrea's house was leaving it behind. Glenn would slip out the back door, stride quickly, purposefully along the side of the house like a meter reader up from the basement, and, with relaxing breath, walk the slant sidewalk to his car, parked for discretion's sake in the next block of hushed Washington homes—their gables politely looking the other way, their neo-classic porchlets void of daytime visitors, their walls of powdery or painted brick and plantings both lush and trimmed all conspiring with him to keep his secret, as he, a white man in a business suit, exercised his American right to walk wherever he wished.

One day after three months of such visits, he must have, in his post-coital relaxation, confided something admiring about the décor, because Andrea said, with a jarring vehemence, "God, if Bud brings back one more Ashanti fertility doll or Bambara antelope headdress, I think I'll scream. I honestly think I might leave him if he gets any more African."

Glenn was jarred because he wanted to think that Andrea's marriage, like his own, was basically happy. "Really?"

"Really. What I'm *really* scared he's going to bring back from these trips is AIDS. The whole continent is lousy with it. I'm terrified of sleeping with him."

"But—do you think he . . . ?"

He didn't finish; she snorted at his delicacy. "People do," she said, her angry gesture taking in their naked bodies, on the wrinkled sheet, with its dangerous-looking pattern of red roses and green thorns. "It's human nature, darling."

"You know, that didn't come home to me until I broke my leg last year." He went on, as if selling her husband back to her, "Bud was so nice that day; he was the only one who cared. Not even Stacey cared." The accident had happened in the fall; this was May, on the verge of uncomfortable summer heat; soon, people would be leaving the District for the mountains, for the shore. "Where would you go if you left him?"

The question was idle, but her answer was not. Andrea propped herself up on an elbow to give it. Though they had closed the Venetian blinds, the bedroom was still bright, the sharp spring sunlight clamoring at the windows like a noisy pack of children. Her face—her fine, lean, well-cared-for face, whereon sun and chronic social animation had engraved tiny wrinkles, at the corners of her eyes and mouth—confronted him with that female openness and depth of interrogation which remind men of the dark, of the ocean, of the night sky, of everything swallowing and terminating. But her manner of speaking was girlish, embarrassed, offhand. "With you somewhere?" She primly wrapped the top of the sheet around her breasts and settled her mussed fair head back on the pillow to hear his answer.

Again, there was a muffled *snap*. He had entered more new territory, barren stretches of disappointment and recrimination, under skies gray with tears. He tried to picture it—her in a house of his, them in a house of theirs—and couldn't. What he liked possessing was a woman's accoutrements—her clothes, her blue overnight bag, her distant daughter's riding lessons, her husband's appointment calendar, her exotic black-tubbed bathroom, her entire *nest*. What he wanted was for women to stay put, planted in American plenty, while he ambulated from one to another carrying no more baggage than the suit on his back and the car keys in his pocket. In the years to come, long after Andrea had sunk back angrily into her nest of roses and hairy masks, Glenn experienced a light-headed bliss whenever his feet glided across an illicit threshold, on what felt like stilts.

Playing with Dynamite

ONE ASPECT OF CHILDHOOD which Fanshawe had not expected to return in old age was the mutability of things—the willingness of a chair, say, to become a leggy animal in the corner of his vision, or his sensation that the solid darkness of an unlit room was teeming with presences about to bite or grab him. Headlights floated on the skin of Fanshawe's windshield like cherry blossoms on black water, whether signifying four motorcycles or two trucks he had no idea, and he drove braced, every second, to crash into an invisible obstacle.

It had taken him over fifty years to internalize the physical laws that overruled a ten-year-old's sense of nightmare possibilities—to overcome irrational fear and to make himself at home in the linear starkness of a universe without a supernatural. As he felt the ineluctable logic of decay tightening its grip on his body, these laws seemed dispensable; he had used them, and now was bored with them. Perhaps an object *could* travel faster than the speed of light, and we each have an immortal soul. It didn't, terribly, matter. The headlines in the paper, trumpeting news of campaigns and pestilences, seemed directed at somebody else, like the new movies and television specials and pennant races and beer commercials—somebody younger and more easily excited, somebody for whom the world still had weight. Living now in death's immediate neighborhood, he was developing a soldier's jaunty indifference; if the bathtub in the corner of his eye as he shaved were to take on the form of a polar bear and start mauling him, it wouldn't be the end of the world. Even the end of the world, strange to say, wouldn't be the end of the world.

His wife was younger than he, and spryer. Frequently, she impatiently passed him on the stairs. One Sunday afternoon, when they were going downstairs to greet some guests, he felt her at his side like a little gust of wind, and then saw her, amazingly much reduced in size, kneeling on the stairs, which were thickly carpeted, several steps below him. He called her name, and thought of reaching down to restrain her, but she, having groped for a baluster and missed, rapidly continued on her way, sledding on her shins all the way to the bottom, where she reclined at the feet of their astonished visitors, who, no strangers to the house, had knocked and entered. "She's all right," Fanshawe assured them, descending at his more stately pace, for he had seen, in watching her surprising descent, that she had met no bone-breaking snag in her progress.

And indeed she did rise up, as resiliently as a cartoon cat, pink with girlish embarrassment, though secretly pleased, he could tell, at having so spontaneously provided their little party with a lively initial topic of discussion. Their guests, who included a young doctor, set her up on the sofa with a bag of ice on the more bruised and abraded of her shins, and held a discussion which concluded that she had caught her heel in the hem of her dress, unusually long in that year's new fashion. A little rip in the stitching of the hem seemed to confirm the analysis and to remove all mystery from the event.

Yet later, after she had limped into bed beside her husband, she asked, "Wasn't I good, not to tell everybody how you pushed me?"

"I never touched you," Fanshawe protested, but without much passion, because he was not entirely sure. He remembered only her appearance, oddly shrunk by perspective on the stairs in their downward linear recession, and the flash of his synapses that imaged his reaching out and restraining her, and his dreamlike inability to do so. She blamed him, he knew, for not having caught her, for not having done the impossible, and this was as good as his pushing her. She had become, in their recent years together, a late-blooming feminist, and he accepted his role in her mind as the murderous man with whom she happened to be stuck, in a world of murderous men. The forces that had once driven them together now seemed to her all the product of a male conspiracy. If he had not literally pushed her on the stairs, he had compelled her to live in a house with a grandiose stairway and had dictated, in collusion with male fashion-designers, the dangerous length of her skirt and height of her heels; and this was as good as a push. He tried to recall his emotions as he watched her body cascade out of his reach, and came up with a cool note of what might be called polite astonishment, along with a high hum of constant grief, like the cosmic background radiation. He recalled a view of a town's rooftops covered in snow, beneath a dome of utterly emptied blue sky.

His wife relented, seeing him so docilely ready to internalize her proposition. "Sweetie, you didn't push me," she said. "But I did think you might have caught me."

"It was all too quick," he said, unconvinced by his own self-defense. With the reality of natural law had faded any conviction of his own virtue. Their guests that afternoon had included his wife's daughter, by an old and almost mythical former marriage. He could scarcely distinguish his stepchildren from his children by his own former marriage, or tell kin from spouses. He was polite to all these tan, bouncy, smooth-skinned, sure-footed, well-dressed young adults—darlings of the advertisers, the "now generation"—who claimed to be related to him, and he was flattered by their mannerly attentions, but he secretly doubted the reality of the connection. His own mother, some years ago, had lain dead for two days at the bottom of the cellar stairs of a house where he had allowed her to live alone, feeble and senile. He was an unnatural son and father both, why not a murderous husband? He knew that the incident would live in his wife's head as if he had in fact pushed her, and thus he might as well remember it also, for the sake of marital harmony.

At the Central Park Zoo, the yellow-white polar bears eerily float in the cold water behind the plate glass, water the blue-green color on a pack of Kool cigarettes (the last cigarettes Fanshawe had smoked, thinking the menthol possibly medicinal), and if a polar bear, dripping wet, were to surface up through his empty bathtub tomorrow morning while he shaved, the fatal swat of the big clawed paw would feel, he suspected, like a cloud of pollen.

Things used to be more substantial. In those middle years, as Fanshawe gropingly recalled them, you are hammering out your destiny on bodies still molten and glowing. One day he had taken his children ice-skating on a frozen river—its winding course miraculously become a road, hard as steel, hissing beneath their steel edges. As he stood talking to the mother of some other young children, his six-year-old son had fallen at his feet, without a cry or thump, simply melting out of the lower edge of Fanshawe's vision, which was fastened on the reddened cheeks and shining dark eyes, the perfect teeth and fascinatingly shaped and mobile lips of Erica Andrews, his fellow-parent. A noise softly bubbled up through the cracks in their conversation; the little body on the ice was whimpering, and when Fanshawe impatiently directed his son to shut up and to get up, the muffled words "I can't" rose as if from beneath the ice.

It developed that the boy's leg was broken. Just standing there complaining about the cold, he had lost his balance with his skate caught in a crack, and twisted his shinbone to the point of fracture. How soft and slender our growing skeletons are! Fanshawe, once his wife and the other woman and their clustering children had made the problem clear to him, carried the boy in his arms up the steep and snowy riverbank. He felt magnificent, doing so. This was real life, he remembered feeling—the idyllic Sunday afternoon suddenly crossed by disaster's shadow, the gentle and strenuous rescue, the ride to the hospital, the emergency-room formalities, the arrival of the jolly orthopedic surgeon in his parka and Ski-Doo boots, the laying on of the cast in warm plaster strips, the drying tears, the imminent healing. Children offer access to the tragic, to the great dark that stands outside our windows, and in the urgency of their needs bestow significance upon life; their fragile lives veer toward the dangerous margins of the narrow path we have learned to tread.

"It wouldn't have happened, of course," his first wife said, "if you had been paying attention to him instead of to Erica."

"What does Erica have to do with it? She was the first one to realize that the poor kid wasn't kidding."

"Erica has everything to do with it, as you perfectly well know."

"This is paranoid talk," he said. "This is Nixon-era paranoid talk."

"I've gotten used to your hurting me, but I'm not going to have you hurting our children."

"Now we're getting really crazy."

"Don't you think I know why you decided to take us all ice-skating, when poor Timmy and Rose didn't even have skates that fit? It was so unlike you, you usually just want to laze around reading the *Times* and complaining about your hangover and watching *The Wide World of Golf.* It was because you knew the Andrewses were going. It was to see her. Her or somebody else. That whole sleazy party crowd, you don't get enough of them Saturday nights any more. Why don't you go live with them? Live with somebody else, anybody except me! Go. Go!"

She didn't mean it, but it was thrilling to see her so energized, such a fury, her eyes flashing, her hair crackling, her slicing gestures carving large doomed territories out of the air. At that age, Fanshawe saw now, we are creating selves, potent and plastic, making and unmaking homes, the world in our hands. We are playing with dynamite. All around them, as he and his first wife stood hip-deep in children, marriages blew up. Marriage counsellors, child psychiatrists, lawyers, real-estate agents prospered in the ruins. Now, in old age, it remained only to generate a little business for the mortician, and an hour's pleasant work for the local clergyman. Just as insurance salesmen had at last stopped approaching him, and the movie-makers had written him out of audience demographics, so the armies of natural law, needed all over the globe to detonate dynamite where it counted, had left him to wander in a twilight of inconsequence.

In early August, a pair of birds decided they had to build a nest on the Fanshawes' porch. If he could trust his eyes and his mother's battered old bird-book, they were house finches, or else bay-breasted warblers too far north. Something must have gone wrong with their biological clocks. It was too late in the season for nesting, but, even more willful than children, they persisted, while warbling back and forth furiously, in piling up twigs and wands of hay on the small shelves created by the capitals of his porch pillars. The twiggy accumulations blew off, or Mrs. Fanshawe briskly knocked them off with a broom. She tended to be less sentimental than he. It was her clean white porch, and her porch boards that would be spattered with bird shit. But the warblers kept coming back, as children keep demanding to go to an amusement park or to buy a certain kind of heavily advertised candy until finally, adult resistance worn down, they have their way. A pillar next to the house afforded shelter enough from the wind; the twigs and grass accumulated, and from its precarious pile the stone-colored head of the female bird haughtily stared down one afternoon when the Fanshawes returned from a day in town shopping. She had her nest. The warbling ceased. The male had vanished. Then, after two weeks, the female, it dawned on the Fanshawes, had also vanished. Vanished without a warble of goodbye. Something had not worked. All the time she had been in the nest, her stony profile had radiated anger.

Getting out the stepladder, Fanshawe fetched down an empty, eggless nest, its rim tidily circled round with guano, its rough materials worked in the center to a perfect expectant cavity. A nest in vain. Whatever had those birds been thinking of? His impulse was to save the nest—his mother had always been saving birds' nests, setting them in bookshelves, or on top of the piano—but his wife held out an open garbage bag, as though the innocent wild artifact were teeming with germs. *Birds' nests shouldn't go in garbage bags*, he thought, but dropped it in. *We're in this together*, he thought, as in the shade of the porch his wife stared up at him with her shining dark eyes, trying to control her impatience as he wrestled with his sentimental scruple.

* * *

At Fanshawe's fifth (at a guess) birthday party, a piece of cake had mysteriously vanished from the plate in front of him and reappeared in his lap. He had never touched it; it was an authentic miracle, there in the candlelight and childish babble. He could still see it lying on his corduroy lap, the cake peeping out from its inverted dish. It had been a chocolate cake with caramel icing of a type only his mother had ever made for him, its sugary stiffness most delicious where the icing between the layers met the outside layer in a thick, sweet T. A few years later, lying in bed with a fever, he had seen a black stick, at a slight angle, hop along beyond the edge of the bed, as if in one of the abstract sections of *Fantasia*. In those years, the knit of the physical world was stretched thin, and held a number of holes. When he was in the fourth grade, his new glasses vanished from his pocket, in their brown round-ended metal case, and a week later, cutting across a weedy vacant lot thinking of them and of how hard his father would have to work to buy him another pair, he looked down, and there the case was, like a long egg in the tangled damp grass. Inside it, the glasses had become steamy, as if worn by an overexcited, myopic ghost. Perhaps this was less a miracle than the transposed birthday cake, but the fact that he had been thinking of them *at that very moment* made it the strangest of all. Could it be that our mind does, secretly, control the atoms? On the strength of that possibility, Fanshawe had never quite broken his childish habit of prayer. Yet, as a child, staring at a model airplane that had unaccountably come unglued during the night, or confronting the bulging shadows at the head of the stairs, he found it hard to think of God and Jesus; the supernatural seemed no more elevated in its aims than a Walt Disney animated feature.

That curious cartoon lightness and jumpiness had returned to the texture of his life. Fanshawe would find himself in a room with no knowledge of how he got there—as if the film had been broken and spliced. As he lay in bed, the house throbbed with footsteps, heard through the pillow; they fell silent when he lifted his head. Perhaps it had been his heartbeat, stealthy as a burglar.

In the sedate neighborhood where he now lived, everyone was old, more or less. For years he had watched the neighbor to his right, a widower, slowly deteriorate, his stride becoming a shuffle, his house and yard gradually growing shabbier and shaggier, inch by inch, season by season, in increments as small as those, visible only to stop-action camerawork, whereby a flower blooms. The two men would converse across the fence from time to time; Fanshawe once or twice offered to do some pruning for his neighbor. "No thanks," would be the answer. "I'll get to it, when I'm feeling a little more lively." We look ahead and see random rises and falls; the linear diminishment so plain to others is invisible to us.

One Saturday morning, a fire engine appeared along his neighbor's curb, though there was no sign of smoke. The fireman, who had moved up the front walk with some haste, stayed inside so long that Fanshawe grew tired of spying. An hour later, with the fire engine still parked there, its great throbbing motor wastefully running, a small foreign convertible appeared, and a fashionably dressed young woman—all things are relative, perhaps she was forty—uncoiled rapidly out of the lowslung interior, flashing her long, smooth shins in their glossy pantyhose, and clicked up the flagstone walk. This was his neighbor's daughter, who explained to Fanshawe later, at the party after the funeral, that her father had been found by the cleaning lady, sitting up in his favorite chair, shaved and dressed in a coat and tie as if expecting a caller. So that was death, Fanshawe realized—a jerky comedy of unusual comings and goings on a Saturday morning, followed in a few days by a funeral and a yellow For Sale sign on the house next door.

"Thank you for being such a good neighbor to my father," the daughter said. "He often mentioned it."

"But I wasn't," Fanshawe protested. "I never did a thing for him. I just let him"—he suppressed the word "deteriorate"—"go his way."

Why had the dead man benignly lied? Why had the cleaning lady called the fire department and not the police? And why had the fireman never shut off his engine, discharging carbon monoxide and consuming fossil fuel at taxpayer expense? Fanshawe didn't ask; there were too many mysteries to pursue.

He often felt now, going through the motions of earthly existence—shaving, dressing, responding to questions, measuring up to small emergencies—that he was enacting a part in a play at the end of its run, while mentally rehearsing his lines in the next play to be put on. It was repertory theatre, evidently. When he remembered how death had once loomed at him, so vivid and large it had a distinct smell, like the scent of chalk dust up close to the schoolroom blackboard, he marvelled, rather patronizingly, at his timorous earlier self. When had he ceased to fear death—or, so to speak, ceased to *grasp* it? The moment was as clear in his mind as a black-and-white-striped gate at a border crossing: the moment when he first slept with Erica Andrews.

How inky-black her eyes seemed, amid the snowy whiteness of the sheets! There was snow outside, too, hushing the world in sunstruck brilliance. Meltwater tapped in the aluminum gutters. There had been a feeling of coolness, of freshly laundered sheets, of contacts never before achieved, by fingertips icy with nervousness. He had peeled off her black lace bra—her back arched up from the mattress to give him access to the catches—almost reluctantly, knowing there would be a white flash that would obliterate everything that had existed of his life before. She had smiled encouragingly, timorously. They were in it together. Her teeth were, after all, less than perfect, with protuberant canines that made the bicuspids next to them seem shadowy. The pupils of her shining eyes were contracted to the size of pencil-leads by the relentless light; he had never seen anything so clearly as he saw her now—the fine mechanism of her, the specialized flesh of her lips, the tripwires of her hair. He got out of the bed to lower the shade, the sight of her was such a dazzlement.

A dull-reddish bird, a female cardinal, was hopping about on the delicately tracked-up snow beneath the bird feeder a story below, pecking at scattered seed. A whole blameless town of roofs and smoking chimneys and snow-drenched trees stretched beyond, under an overturned bowl of blue light that made Fanshawe's vision wince. He drew the curtain on it and in merciful twilight returned to where Erica lay still as a stick. He heard his blood striding in his skull, he felt so full of life. Sex or death, you pick your poison. That had been forever ago. She was still younger and spryer than he, but all things were relative. He did not envy those forever-ago people, for whom the world had such a weight of consequence. Like the Titans, they seemed beautiful but sad in their brief heyday, transition figures between chaos and an airier pantheon.

The Black Room

"I DON'T *want* to go," said Lee's mother, though she had already agreed to go, in the too-bright, teal-blue silk dress that had come out of the cedar closet where it had hung for all the decades in which she had been too fat to wear it. Her weight loss was not a good sign, Lee felt, though as a boy and then as a man and then as a middle-aged man he had hoped for it. Less of a mother, he had thought, would be more—more chic, more manageable. But now that she was in her eighties and her clothes hung loose on her and her skin hung loose above her elbows, he was frightened. He wanted her bulk back.

He tried joking: "It's the chance of a lifetime." She didn't smile, so he tried backing out: "You don't have to go. I'm the one who's interested, so I'll go alone."

Yet it had been her idea. She had heard that their old house in the city of Alton was being sold; the then-young couple who had bought it, Marine Lieutenant Jessup and his wife, had enlisted in a retirement community and placed the house on the market. Embarrassingly, Lee felt, his mother had phoned the Jessups and explained how much it would mean to her son if he, on one of his monthly visits from New York City, might come by. Neither she nor he had entered the house since that drizzly November day forty-seven years ago when the movers had cleared out their furniture, damaging the cane-back sofa and breaking two plates of Philadelphia blueware in the process. The family, which had numbered five then, climbed into a newly bought second-hand Chevrolet and drove twenty miles in the rain to the unimproved farmhouse that Lee's mother had settled on as the site of her long-deferred self-fulfillment. She said now, "That Alton house nearly killed me and I swore I'd never set foot in it again."

"You've made your point. Forty-seven years is as good as never. You've put the house in its place, Mother."

"Your grandfather was always convinced that Jessup had slipped Jake Oberholz a fifty, to persuade us to accept the eight thousand." Lee had heard it all before: Oberholz had been their real-estate agent, and Jessup had been fresh out of the Marines, a quiet war hero, slim and blond and tall in Lee's memory of him, and in a white dress-uniform. He had seen him once, in the front hall, from the height of a twelve-year-old, while the sale was still being negotiated. The whole thing had gone on over Lee's head; he could scarcely believe it was happening, this abandonment of the only house he had ever lived in.

"Well, you didn't want the place," he pointed out. "Jessup did. Come on. We can't not go now, after you've got us invited. You shouldn't have set this up if you didn't want to go."

"I was trying," the old woman said primly, "to please my only child."

They had maneuvered themselves out of the back door of the sandstone farmhouse, and were halfway across the yard to Lee's BMW. His mother's car was stored in the barn. Her cardiologist had forbidden her to drive, though she occasionally did, to the 7-Eleven at a crossroads two miles away, "to keep the engine from seizing up," she said. They walked slowly, her hand heavy on his arm; even a little exertion left her short of breath, though she didn't stop talking: "I don't know why you always spite me by loving that house so."

"I don't say I love it. I was born there, is all."

"It was too much house—my father's vanity made itself a monument the day he bought it. He bought it when I was off at college, without even telling me. I never could feel at home there. Neither could Mother. We weren't city people. It nearly killed her, trying to keep it clean, up to city standards. It had a peculiar dust in it, that clung everywhere."

He had heard this before, too, but its implausibility still made him laugh. "Well, you showed it," he told her. "You escaped its clutches."

"I don't know why you've always resented our moving. Honest to goodness, Lee, I added years to all of our lives by getting us out of Alton. The only city person among us was your father."

"I was just a child, Mother. I was in no position to resent anything. I'm still not."

But was she right? Had he loved the house in Alton, all these years, just to spite her? It was a long, narrow-faced brick house, on a wider lot than most along the street. In his childhood the bricks had been painted pale yellow and the trim dark green. There was a front porch, a side porch, and an upstairs porch, and the yard had held cherry trees, a walnut tree, a birdbath, a bed of lilies of the valley, and a vegetable garden that his grandfather turned with a shovel every spring.

"I can take it or leave it, seeing the house," he said. "This trip wasn't my idea, remember." They were skimming along a highway lined with ranch houses; it had been a winding asphalt road the first time he had travelled it, with an occasional dirt lane leading off to a barn, a silo, and a square stone farmhouse just like theirs.

"I had to, seeing as it was our last chance. They were always inviting us, those first years. On every Christmas card. Then they stopped asking. I thought I'd get through life without ever having to see those rooms again. I like your idea, of you going in alone. You could drop me off at Weisbach's Drug Store for half an hour."

His mother's fanciful distortions and quick little visions had always struck him as a higher form of truth. This trip *was* his idea, somehow; she had read his mind and set it up to please him. He said, truthfully, "Without you, Mother, it'd be no fun."

"I could sit at the counter and have one of those sundaes. You have to say this for Luther Weisbach—he didn't stint on the butterscotch."

"Mother, I don't think it's still called Weisbach's. And drugstores don't have counters any more."

The road surface wore a moist shine. It was a soft late-September day, the sunshine golden and the towering trees misty. A barn whose red side had said JESUS SAVES in fading letters year after year was suddenly gone, replaced by a Japanese-style building with wide eaves and staggered shingles—a golf-course clubhouse.

"You weren't such a child," his mother said, picking up another thread of her mental web. "You were thirteen. If we'd stayed there you'd still think of yourself as a child. That house made everybody in it childish. As long as I was in that house, I was my parents' daughter."

The Depression had thrown them all together—his parents and his mother's parents. The Crash took his grandfather's savings, and then his father had been laid off from his job in Pittsburgh. Lee had been born into this wealth of disappointments and had been a happy child. All four adults had conspired to make him happy, as if his happiness might yet reverse their fortunes. They had scraped by, with various jobs. The war had come along and helped. With their modest war profits, his mother had finagled the change of houses, moving them to what his father had called "the sticks." Now, with his grandparents and father long dead, the sticks—raspberry canes and sumac and wild grape and poison ivy—were moving ever closer to the little farmhouse, as his mother's strength waned. For decades she had wielded the clippers and scythe like a man, and had ridden the power mower hour after hour, bouncing in widening circles around the lawn. Now reluctant teenagers did the mowing, when they could be recruited from the countryside; Pennsylvania held fewer and fewer farm children, accustomed to physical work. His mother's house, stuck in the past, smelled of dust balls and mouse droppings. The plumbing and heating, brand-new in 1946, had become antique. Yet she insisted, "That Alton house was never healthy. The coal furnace made a gas that sat on my chest whenever I'd lie down."

Lee laughed again, for they had reached the far end of his old street, and he was heading home.

This neck of Alton had a small-town quality, many of the houses free-standing on lots adorned by hydrangeas and rhododendron bushes, and even the semi-detached houses solid and well kept up. The vacant lots of Lee's childhood had been filled in, and the street had been widened at the expense of a row of sycamores whose blotched bark and buttony seed-pods had seemed oddly toylike to him, as if God were an invisible playmate. On the uphill side, a tall row of semi-detacheds held fascinating little guttered spaces between them, passageways sexual in their intimacy, with a thin slice of sky at the top. Even widened, Franklin Street from its far end had a contained, narrowing look. In the side of Lee's vision his mother's hand fumbled in her black pocketbook and darted one of her nitroglycerin pills into her mouth. "Don't be nervous," he told her.

Over her teal-blue dress she had donned, though the day was unseasonably warm, an old-fashioned wool overcoat in a broad plaid, with a fox-fur collar. Her thick head of chestnut hair had been one of her youthful glories; Lee remembered from childhood the witchy, dripping tent her hair made after she had washed it, a towel worn over her shoulders as it dried. Now this hair, gone in the last decade from iron-gray to a gauzy white, let pink scalp show through, and she wore indoors and out a round knit cap on her head, bigger than a beanie but not quite a beret. Her ankles and feet were so swollen she could no longer squeeze her feet into anything but running shoes; she had chosen a vivid, several-striped pattern. From the days when she had been a young beauty and her father had still had money, she retained a taste for attention-getting clothes. Lee tried to repress his embarrassment, as he had when he was an adolescent and she was a vivacious, overweight, countrified woman, her sun-reddened hands and forearms scored by the scratches of raspberry and greenbrier thorns. "Why would I be nervous?" she asked sharply.

It was he who was nervous. Parking the car, he rubbed the tires against the curb, which the street improvement had left higher and whiter than it had been. Getting out of the car, he felt eerily tall in this setting of his earliest days. The houses across the street, with their trees and telephone poles, presented the same silhouettes, though on this side the sunshine struck down strangely through the absence of sycamores, and the Jessups had taken away the waist-high box hedge that had shielded the front yard from sidewalk traffic. Sidewalk traffic, of course, was a thing of the past; it belonged to the Depression, to door-to-door salesmen walking on foot and people running to catch clanging trolley cars. The pale new curb of the widened street was so high that his mother couldn't get the door of the BMW to swing open, and he had to repark it, his stomach nervously pinching. Entering this house again, this paradise at the far end of his life, seemed a trespass.

The brick front walk, which had had little ant cities of mounds like coffee grains between the bricks, had become glaring concrete. The distance across the porch to the front door, which he remembered as large and full of peril—for the porch had thick brick walls that might conceal a crouching beast—had dwindled to two strides. The door, with its letter-slot lid saying MAIL and its bevelled-glass window, had been replaced by an opaque panelled door, though the leaded sidelights and tinted fanlight holding the house number, 303, remained above. Jessup, who greeted them inside the door, had grown shorter than Lee, but his hair was still close-cropped and blond, and his figure had a military trimness. Mrs. Jessup, whom Lee had never met, was like a bride on a wedding cake, perfect of her kind, though grown plump and blue-haired. She had dimples, and bifocals, and cheeks as round and bright as if rouged. The Jessups greeted Lee cordially, but saved their real ardor of welcome for his mother, whose shrunken figure seemed in the corner of his vision to be engulfed by their courteous bodies. His eyes were darting about, desperate to light on something familiar and cherished.

"What a *nice* idea this is," said the former Marine. "I must say, you folks have waited to the very last minute. As soon as we get a buyer, we're out of here, as the young people say."

"Well, my father used to tell me, 'Don't be so impatient, Elsie. Good things keep.' "

Her charm—Lee tended to forget that about his mother. When pulled out of the sticks and put to the test of social encounter, she rose to the challenge. "I love your lemon-yellow wallpaper," she told the elderly couple. "This was always such a dark hall, with the two big gloomy radiators. I never knew why there had to be *two*; on winter days it was the warmest spot in the house. Lee used to lie on the floor, drawing, where we all had to step over him."

The flattened texture and faded plum color of the carpet that had lain at the edge of his drawing pad returned to his mind's eye out of the past, along with the diagonal beams of dust-laden light that came in the sunparlor windows and broke on the wide oak arms of his grandfather's favorite chair. The sun parlor was gone, swallowed up by Jessup's office; he had used the GI Bill to become an attorney. Lee was tempted to open the shut office door on the chance that his grandfather was still sitting there, in the slices of sunlight, his head tilted back in that ostentatiously resigned way he had, and his hands, frail and brown as onionskin, folded across the buttons of his gray sweater as he waited for the mailman or the afternoon paperboy to bring him word of the world. His grandfather had exuded an air of graceful defeat that the boy had found endearing.

"Everything is so *right*," his mother was saying. "When we were here, everything was slightly *wrong*."

Lee knew, as the Jessups did not, that his mother distrusted rightness, in this bourgeois sense—felt herself rather above it, in fact. As her breathy voice flirted behind him, in and out of the Jessups' catering voices, he felt freed to walk ahead, looking for traces of the house he remembered. There were almost none. Renovations had come in and washed everything away, even the old touches of elegance like the elaborate spindlework headers above the wide archways into the living room, and the fluted wooden pillars that framed the archways. The ceilings, plastered in tidily overlapping semicircles, seemed lower. Instead of their old Oriental rug with its mazy border and the cane-back settee and its companion chairs—their horsehair cushions holding that musty, oystery scent country parlors have—there was fat modern furniture in pastel shades surrounding a glass table supported on wrought-iron scrolls. A semitropical Floridian luxuriance had crept into Pennsylvania interiors since the Forties. Where their Christmas tree had annually stood, between the two front windows from which Lee would watch, beyond the porch wall, the coal sliding thunderously down the chute that telescoped out from the truck, now stood a blond-stained wood cabinet holding souvenirs of the Jessups' foreign travels—beaten copper, carved ivory, Mexican pottery, New Mexican turquoise.

The "piano room" held not the old upright Chickering but a large-screen television set and a cabinet of hi-fi components. Down the dark hall that had once seemed perilously shadowy and long, beside the flight of stairs his grandfather had quaintly called "the wooden hill," the dining room quickly appeared, minus the Tiffany lampshade that had hung from the center of the ceiling, and the mahogany-veneered sideboard with the cloudy mirror, and the stained-pine corner cabinet that had held their good china, including the Philadelphia blueware whose broken plates had been one of the costs of the move from Alton. In this room, on a strip of wooden floor between the figured rug and the doors that led out to the side porch, Lee to entertain himself would bowl, using rubber Disney dolls—Mickey Mouse and Pluto, Donald Duck and Ferdinand—for tenpins. Now wall-to-wall carpet covered the space. Staring down, trying to picture the concealed floorboards, he was overtaken for a moment by the taste of that distant time, a musty sensation, bland as a stale malt ball, of being sheltered in a low cave while great things were going on above him, in the clangorous heights where the Second World War merged with Walt Disney's busy kingdom. Beneath the notice of all the grown-up furor he would set up his battered rubber creatures and bowl them down again with a lopsided softball, whose stitches, he seemed to remember, were not real but a bas-relief imitation.

The house was quickly traversed; next came the kitchen, which he had not expected to find unchanged. Even the plumbing had been moved about, so that in place of the slate sink with its long-nosed copper faucets now bulked an electric stove with a black-faced microwave, and where the old gas stove had poured forth X-patterns of blue flame a modern stainless-steel sink had appeared, the dishwasher and trash compactor installed to one side. Rose-colored cabinets matched a giant double-doored refrigerator; the little walnut icebox, the blackened tin toaster that had sat on a gas burner like a tiny house full of chinks, the food-grinder that had clamped to the edge of the kitchen table were so thoroughly, irrevocably carted away by the years that Lee could scarcely imagine the little boy who used to reach up on tiptoe to the red-and-white recipe box on top of the icebox. The family kept its meagre cash in the tin recipe box, and he was entitled, at schoolday lunchtimes, to buy a Tastykake to eat on the walk back to elementary school.

His mother's voice was carrying on behind him. "So Mr. Oberholz came to us and said, 'It was an eight-thousand-dollar house when you bought it in 1922, and it's still an eight-thousand-dollar house in 1945.' My dad, he was such a trusting man, he believed him, just like he believed all those shysters who unloaded their stock off on him before the Crash, but me, I had a bit of the devil in me, I guess, I couldn't believe it hadn't gone up in value *at all* in twenty years. Now I read in the paper that you're asking over two hundred thousand. I still have friends in town who send me such clippings in the mail. If you can call them friends."

Lee tried to intervene. "Mother, it's only been since the nineteen-fifties that people expect to make money off of real estate. And now they're losing it again."

But Mrs. Jessup could defend herself. Putting herself on a first-name basis, she said, "Elsie, we really couldn't have paid a penny more. Even so, we went into debt, and Hank was working nights as a watchman as well as going to law school. Those were hard times." Her blush of indignation was pretty.

"It's been a kind house to us," Jessup said, in a conciliatory lawyer's voice, putting the done deal behind them. "We raised three beautiful children in it."

Back in the dining room, Lee at last found a survival of the house of his own childhood: the windows. They were still tall, gaunt four-pane windows, and the panes were still the imperfect glass whose waveriness and oval bubbles had fascinated him as a child. He would stand and move his head and watch the lines of their neighbors' house warp and undulate, as in the underwater scenes of *Pinocchio*. The oval bubbles, like immortal microbes, were still there, in the glass, though combination storm windows dulled the outlook, and the neighbors' house was a different, closer house, filling the vacant lot where Lee had played fungo and kick-the-can with Doug Rhoda and Shorty Heister and the neighborhood girls, who lived in the sexy row houses across the street and whose parents would call them home from their rickety high porches in the summer twilights, as the fireflies came out.

The tour of the downstairs completed, Mrs. Jessup politely asked, in the narrow hallway, "Would you like to see the upstairs? We moved some walls about, to accommodate the children. I doubt you would recognize much."

"I'd love to see it," Lee said, when his mother was silent. Upstairs had been the enchanted realm of sleep, of days home sick in bed, of his parents in their underwear, of his grandparents muttering behind their closed door. Ultimate realties had resided upstairs.

The party was dividing along gender lines. Mrs. Jessup conducted her own conversation with Lee's mother. "Elsie, there was something I've always wanted to ask you about," she said, drawing close enough to touch the older woman on the shoulder, next to the prickly fox-fur. "When we moved in, there were two little rooms out back, above the kitchen, looking into the back yard."

"Yes. The one on the right was Lee's room, looking toward the vacant lot."

"And the other, the one with only the one window, was painted black."

"Oh no! Was it really?"

"Yes, and we couldn't figure out what it had been used for. Had it been a darkroom, maybe, for your husband's photography?"

"Norman never took a picture in his life. I was the family photographer, with this old Kodak that had lost its viewfinder. You paced off the yards and hoped for the best."

Mrs. Jessup persisted. "It must have been for storage, then."

"Yes, we kept a few things in it. Mother's ironing board, her Singer sewing machine, an old sleigh-bed headboard and footboard that had been *her* mother's . . . But I don't remember that room as *black*."

"Well, it was. We were quite struck and puzzled, I remember, at the time."

Lee sensed an impasse. His stomach was starting to

chafe. He asked, "Mother, do you want to come upstairs?"

"No," she said. "No I don't."

"Really? Why would that be?" He darted a look at her; her face, fallen into creases with her loss of weight, seemed pale, stricken by some internal development. He felt in his own insides the effort with which she kept up the charm. She gasped before she spoke.

"You all go," she said, "and I'll spare myself the stairs and just sit and admire how bright and cheerful the Jessups have made our dreary old living room."

"Then I'll stay right with you," Mrs. Jessup said, with the firmness of a warder. "We'll have a good chat. Shall I make us a cup of tea?"

For much of his life, Lee had seen other people, attracted by his mother, draw close; but in the end, only he could follow her twists and turns. Sometimes he wondered if his personality hadn't been so exactly conformed to his mother's that it made a poor fit with anyone else's.

"Tea? To tell the truth, I never developed the taste for tea. I was a coffee drinker, up to a dozen cups a day, and now the doctors say I shouldn't drink even decaf. Coffee and ice cream and apple pie were my sins, and now I'm paying for them. Norman always used to say to me, 'You're the last person in the world, Elsie, who thinks there's such a thing as a free lunch.'"

While Mrs. Jessup coped with this pronouncement, her husband took Lee upstairs. In passing, Jessup touched the newel post, with its round knob. "Bet you recognize this."

"Yes." But in fact the knob, with its equator of beaded grooves, had seemed an unpleasant presence to little Lee—an eyeless head, a possible Martian like those in that radio play that had frightened everybody in New Jersey.

"I asked that it be left," Jessup said, with what seemed shy pride, "though Dorothy thought it didn't go with the new décor."

At the head of the main stairs there had been a windowless landing where they would gather, sitting on the steps, during air-raid drills, while Lee's father strode around the darkened neighborhood in his air-raid warden's armband and helmet. One set of three steps had led to a hall that went past Grampy and Grammy's bedroom to the guest bedroom, which overlooked the street. Another short set had led the other way, to his parents' bedroom and his own, and a third had gone up to the communal bathroom. All this awkward architecture had been smoothed into a parade of bright bedrooms to shelter, in the Jessups' prime, the couple and three growing children. Lee's grandparents' room, which even through a closed door had smelled powerfully to his childish nostrils of old shoes and old bodies and mothballed blankets and bottles of liniment, had become the Jessups' daughter's room. A kind of shrine, it still held her school pennants, a poster of a bare-armed Mick Jagger, her frilly bed coverlet, and framed photographs of herself as a child, as an adolescent with braces, as a graduating senior, as a bride in white, and as a mother in slacks posing with two small children in what Jessup told Lee was a back yard in Colorado, where she lived with her husband, an Air Force pilot. "She inherited your military gene," Lee observed.

"Born ten years later, she'd have been a pilot herself," her father boasted.

The guest bedroom, where his mother would go for her naps when she needed to get away from them all, and where Lee, when sick, would recline in a litter of picture books and cough-drop boxes, had been expanded outward, into a massive master bedroom, swallowing the hall window, whose sill had always held a potted geranium. At the back of the house, other walls had vanished as his little room with its stained and varnished wainscoting had been merged with the mysterious one next to it, and from his parents' bedroom had been carved a spacious bathroom that the Jessup sons could share. The boys' bedrooms still held traces of extensive electronic equipment. In this unfamiliar space Lee found himself remembering how the whole sleepy house would resound with the noise when his grandfather, first thing in the morning, shook down the ashes in the furnace, and shovelled in fresh coal.

"Well," he said to his host, by way of leavetaking, and in response to a certain air of self-congratulation, "I'd say you spent your forty-seven years here very well."

"It was a happy house for us."

"Good. For me, too." No longer child and young veteran, they had become two aged men who had loved the same object. One had won and one had lost, but now the winner was surrendering the prize also. Time takes all. Lee looked around once more and couldn't find himself, even in the shape of the windows. A silent hurricane had swept through this house, leaving nothing undamaged. His parents' bedroom had opened onto a side porch just like the one below, with jigsawed balusters holding up the wooden, green-painted rail. The present railing was ornamental ironwork, as if they were in New Orleans.

Downstairs, a glance told Lee that his mother was in trouble. She had slumped to one side on the sofa, and was resting a bony, veiny hand upon her chest, as if to quiet something within. Yet her face still bore a listening smile, as Mrs. Jessup finished saying, presumably of a son, "Now he's in corporate finance in Wilmington, with this wonderful Bank of Delaware."

"Mother," Lee announced, by way of rescue, "you missed a grand tour up there. They knocked out the wall between the guest bedroom and the hall and made a master suite! Grammy and Grampy's old room is full of pennants and teddy bears. Their daughter married a pilot in Colorado."

"Dorothy was saying," she responded, "that she agreed with me—this house . . . is hard on its women." She spoke in little hurried skips, struggling for breath. When she stood, she staggered one sideways step, and leaned heavily on Lee in heading to the front door. She had never taken off her plaid overcoat.

"Can't we get you anything?" Mrs. Jessup asked, her eyes and cheeks yet brighter with alarm. "Even a glass of water?"

"You've done . . . everything," was the answer. "I get . . . these spells, where my chest . . . doesn't seem to have any *depth*." She laughed in self-deprecation. "It was lovely of you to let us . . . see what all you've done. You've done . . . wonders."

The porch, as Lee escorted his mother across it, seemed as wide as he remembered it from childhood. The concrete walk glared under their shoes as they shuffled to the curb. She allowed herself to be folded into the passenger's seat, and lifted a withered hand and waved it in response to the Jessups' cheery, worried farewells. As Lee drove the car down the street, in the direction in which he would walk to elementary school eating his Tastykake, past Weisbach's Drug Store, she struggled to breathe, in intense, sharp sips; her body shook as if some invisible predator had it by the nape of the neck.

Lee asked, "Shall we go home or straight to the Alton Hospital?"

"Home." The syllable seemed all she could manage.

As he made the turn to circle the block, her hand in the side of his vision fed a pill into her mouth.

"That house," she explained. "I needed ... to get out."

"Just like always." Her retreating into ill health irritated him. His old grudge remained. "Well," he announced, putting on the blinker to signal the next right turn, which would head them out of the city, "you won't have to see that house ever again."

"That room ... was never black."

"What?"

"That's what upset me. That room was never black. Why would anybody in their right mind ... paint a room black?"

"That's what they said they were wondering."

"They imagined it. The walls had old cream-colored paper ... with blue florets ... and the wainscoting was pine, stained walnut. Mother used to do her sewing in that room, before her eyesight went."

"They couldn't have just imagined it, they must have had some basis, Mother. She was very definite."

"Yes, about everything. Maybe it was a joke. That's how those Alton people are, Lee. That's the way they were when I was a girl. Sly. Always poking fun. It made me feel bad. It made me feel crazy. That they would think ... we would have had a black room."

"How's your chest?"

"A little better. Don't you remember how the room was?"

"I don't remember ever looking in, Mother. That room frightened me. When I would go to sleep in my bed, I remember, I would turn to face that wall so that if something came through the wall I could grab it before it grabbed me."

"Oh my. And here we all thought you were such a happy child."

* * *

As Alton fell away behind them and the country roads began to sing beneath their tires, her spirits lifted. She helped him make their dinner, directing the cooking from her chair at the kitchen table, where she sat with all her pill bottles—a miniature city—at her elbow. He fried a big slice of ham, boiled up some frozen succotash, and baked two potatoes in the crusty old oven: the kind of meal she used to devour, with a heaping of ice cream to top it off. She ate half, trying to please him, and he finished up her plate, which made him feel unpleasantly full. During the night, he heard her moving about in her room, clearing her throat and gasping, on the other side of the wall. It was still dark, before dawn. He thought of going in to her, but fell back asleep instead.

In the morning, the smell of coffee rose up the stairs. It was like his grandfather stirring the furnace: life. His mother was downstairs ahead of him, in her quilted purple bathrobe, with a tent of white hair worn loose over her shoulders. Light from the back door shone through her thinning, floating hair. "Isn't coffee verboten?" he asked.

"Not to you, yet. I had a cup myself. I don't know why that woman offering me tea made me so mad."

"You were determined something would," he told her, "no matter how nice they tried to be."

"They were nice," she said tonelessly.

He had to leave right after breakfast, since it was three hours back to New York City and he had promised to take his younger daughter to her riding lesson in Central Park, while his wife went to a matinee of *Jelly's Last Jam*. His mother came outside with him and shuffled along as far as the sandstone walk allowed. She was dressed in wool-lined suede slippers, and the uncut lawn was lank and whitened by dew. Beyond the house, the sumac was turning red here and there, and the poplars showed a yellow tinge. Fall was on the way, with winter behind. What would she do, alone? They should have discussed it last night, after dinner, instead of watching television: *Golden Girls*, followed by *Empty Nest*. She had become an unreality addict.

"Wouldn't you like it," Lee asked, "if we could get somebody to stay in the house with you this winter?"

"The Jessups, maybe," she said. "They could call this their retirement home. They could clean out all my cobwebs and put in wall-to-wall polyester."

In the low morning sunshine, the eastward wall of the stone farmhouse glowed as if from within. Lee was conscious of the neglected lawn, the wild raspberry canes, the towering trees beyond as a tightening net of interwoven nature. The house seemed perilously small. So did his mother. From the concerned look on her face, he knew she was viewing him as her child, having one of his nervous stomach cramps. "It's a real problem, Mother," he weakly insisted. "It worries me. You shouldn't be alone."

She had taken to wearing her glasses less and less. The absence of frames gave her face a startled, naked look, even now, when she assumed her teasing expression. She asked, "Why would you want to kill me, making me live with somebody else? I just barely survived living with your father all those years."

He was content to be dismissed, yet couldn't make himself move off the sandstone walk, the ten yards or so to where his car was parked. This September day was beginning with high clouds, a few ribs of cirrus arched in the stratospheric cold. Some birds made a sudden flurry of noise in the old, half-dead pear tree. There was a buzzing in the air, a constant eating. The truck traffic on the Jersey Turnpike would be at its peak. "Think about it. About, you know, more ideal arrangements."

"Lee, this house *is* my ideal arrangement. Now, don't make Jenny late for her lesson. Girls love horses. Maybe that was why I resented Dad's moving us to town—it meant I couldn't ride anymore. Here. Let's see if I can make it to the road." Holding on to his arm, she kicked off her slippers and stepped off the last stone barefoot. The icy shock of the wet grass sprang a delighted laugh: life. She hobbled with him to the side of his car. Her blue-veined feet were puffy on top, like a baby's feet. "Now, I'll be fine," she recited, when they had stopped walking and she could get her breath. "I'll take my pills and try to eat more and get some strength back. I'm sorry I let those city folk get the better of me yesterday. I had wanted so *not* to act up."

She lifted her weightless, onionskin hand from his arm and found a footing on the uneven lawn which held her upright while he got into his BMW and started the engine. Seen through the open car window, in the morning light, her face looked defenseless around the eyes, the delicate skin owlish. "I'm sorry," she said solemnly, "I let myself be so frightened."

"You mean of the bla—?"

She was startlingly quick to touch his arm again, to stop his mouth. "Don't even *say* it!"

Cruise

ISLANDS kept appearing outside their windows. Crete, Ogygia, Capri, Ponza. Calypso, who had became Neuman's cruisemate, his wife at sea, liked to make love sitting astride him while gazing out the porthole, feeling between her legs the surging and the bucking of the boat. Her eyes, the color of a blue hydrangea, tipped toward the violet end of the spectrum in these moments. Her skin was as smooth as a new statue's. He called her Calypso because the entire cruise, consisting of sixty-five passengers and forty crewpersons, was marketed as a duplicate of the tortuous homeward voyage of Ulysses, though everyone including their lecturers kept forgetting which port of call represented what in *The Odyssey*. Were the cliffs of Bonifacio, a chic and slanty tourist trap on the southern tip of Corsica, *really* the cliffs from which the giant, indiscriminately carnivorous Laestrygones had pelted the fleet with rocks, sinking all but the wily captain's dark-prowed hull? Was Djerba, a sleepy hot island off the Tunisian coast, distinguished by a functioning synagogue and a disused thirteenth-century Aragonese fort, *really* the land of the Lotus Eaters?

"Well, what is 'really'?" their male lecturer asked them in turn, returning a question for a question in Socratic style. "Τί ἐστιν ἀλήθεια? Or, as the French

290

might put it, *'Le soi-disant "Ding an sich," c'existe ou non?'* "

Their on-board lecturers were two: a small man and a large woman. The man preached a wry verbal deconstructionism and the woman a ringing cosmic feminism. Clytemnestra was her idea of a Greek hero. Medea and Hecuba she admired also. She wore gold sickles around her neck and her hair was done up in snakes of braid. Our lovers—cruel and flippant vis-à-vis the rest of humanity in their ecstasy of love newly entered upon—called her Killer. The male lecturer they called Homer. Homer sat up late in the ship's lounge each night, smoking cigarettes and planning what he was going to say the next day. He looked wearied by all his knowledge, all his languages, and sallow from too much indoors. Even while trudging up and down the slippery, scree-ridden slopes of archaeological digs, he wore a button-down shirt and laced black shoes. The lovers felt superior to him, in the exalted state brought on by repeated orgasms in the little cabin's swaying, clicking, cunningly outfitted space. *"Aiiiieeee!"* they cried. *"Aiae, aiae!* We are as gods!"

There were rough seas between Malta and Djerba. Neuman threw up, to his own surprise and disgust. He had thought, on the basis of several Atlantic crossings in gigantic passenger liners, that he was seaworthy. Calypso, who in her terrestrial life had been raised on a Nebraska wheat farm and not seen the ocean until she was twenty-one and unhappily married, had no mal-de-mer problem; when he bolted from their table in the seesawing dining room she stayed put, finished her poached sea-trout, helped herself to his squid stew, ate all of the delicious little Maltese biscuits in the bread-basket, and ordered caramelized *pomme Charlotte* for dessert, with Turkish coffee. In the tranquillity of her stomach she was indeed as a goddess—Calypso, the daughter of Thetis by Oceanus. Fleeing the dining room, Neuman held acid vomit back against his teeth for the length of his run down the second-deck corridor; when he got into his own bathroom he erupted like a fountain, disgustingly, epically. Ah, what is man but a bit of slime in the cistern of the void?

"You poor baby," she said, descending to him at last. Her kiss smelled of caramel and brought on a minor attack of gagging. "I think I'll spend the night back in my own cabin," she told him. "After a spot of anisette."

"Don't go up to the lounge," he begged, feeble and green-faced yet sexually jealous. "There's a hard-drinking crowd up there every night. Hardened cruisers. Good-time Charlies. Tonight they're having a sing-along, followed by a showing of *Casablanca*. Whenever they show *Casablanca* on one of these boats, all hell breaks loose."

"I'll be fine," she told him, her complicated blue eyes drifting evasively to the porthole, which was black but for the dim glow of the starboard lights and a diagonal slap of spray at the nadir of an especially sickening flop into watery nothingness. "Just because we have good sex," she told him, firmly, "you don't own me, buster. I paid for this cruise with my own money and I intend to have a good time."

She was one of the new women and he, despite his name, one of the old men. Female equality struck him as a brutish idea. Just the idea of her having a good time—of trying to milk some selfish happiness out of this inchoate hyperactive muddle of a universe—doubled and redoubled his nausea. "Go, go, you bitch," he said. His stomach, like a filmy jellyfish floating within him, was organizing itself for a new convulsion, and he was planning his dash to the toilet once she had removed the obstacle of her trim, compact body, in its chiton of starched blue linen, belted with a rope of gold.

She had good sturdy legs, like a cheerleader's without the white socks. Hips squared off like small bales of cotton. Narrow feet in gilded sandals. "Easy come," he told her queasily, with false jauntiness, "easy go."

They had sized each other up at the start, in the ruins of Troy. She was standing in khaki safari slacks and a lime-green tennis visor on Level VIIa, thought to be Priam's Troy if anything on this site "really" was, and he was down in Level II, not far from where Schliemann and his racy Greek wife, Sophia, had discovered and surreptitiously hidden a hoard of golden treasures from the middle of the third millennium before Christ. Now it was all a mess of mounds and pebbles and blowing grasses and bobbing poppies and liquid-eyed guides and elderly Americans and tightly made limestone walls most probably too small to have been the walls of fabled Troy. "Can this be all there was?" Homer was murmuring to their group. "*Est-ce que c'est tout?* A little rubbly village by the marshes? Schliemann decided, '*Es ist genug.* This was Troy.' " The poppies bobbed amid the nodding grasses. The rubble underfoot had been trod by Cassandra and Aeneas, venerable Priam and ravishing Helen.

The destined lovers' glances met, and remet; they measured each other for size and age and signs of socio-economic compatibility, and he carefully climbed through the levels to edge into her group. Their group's guide, a local Turk, was telling about the Judgment of Paris as if it had happened just yesterday, in the next village: "So poor Zeus, what to do? One woman his wife, another his daughter, straight from head—*boom!*" He hit his fist against his broad brown brow. "Each lady say she the absolute best, *she* deserve golden apple. So Zeus, he looking around in bad way and see far off in Mount Ida, over there, you can almost see"—he gestured, and the tourists looked, raking with their eyes the vacant plains of Troy, vast if not as windy as in the epic—"he see this poor shepherd boy, son of King Priam, minding own business, tending the sheeps. His name, Paris. Zeus tell him, 'You choose.' 'Who, me?' 'Yes, you.' " The American tourists, broiling in the sun, obligingly laughed; the guide smiled, showing a gold fang. " 'Oh boy,' Paris think to self. 'Problem.' One lady offer him much riches, Hera. Another say, 'No, have much glory in battle and wars, thanks to me.' That was Athena, daughter straight from Zeus's head. Third say, Aphrodite say, 'No, forget all that. I give you most beautiful woman in world to be your wife.' And Paris say, 'O.K., you win. Good deal.' "

By now Neuman had drawn level with his tennis-visored prey. He murmured in her ear, "The 'O.K.' that launched a thousand ships." A gravelly American witticism, here in this remote archaic place. He liked her ear very much, the marble whiteness and the squarish folds of it. It was feminine yet no-nonsense, like her level gaze.

She had sensed his proximity. The soul has hairs, which prickle. In profile Calypso barely smiled at the pleasantry, then turned to appraise him, calculating his physical and mental compatibility and the length of the cruise ahead of them. Nauplia, Valletta, Bonifacio, Sperlonga. O.K. As if by destiny, without planning it, they arrived at the lounge for pre-dinner drinks at the same moment. With utmost diffidence they chose the same banquette and, their increasingly excited recountings of their separate pasts far from finished, asked to be seated at the same dining table, as the sleek white cruise ship slipped off the tight-fitting Dardanelles and slipped on the sequinned blue gown of the Aegean.

* * *

Malta, a fairy-tale island. Everything was sand-colored—a series of giant sand castles unfolded as they wormed into the harbor. Groggy from one of their sea-borne nights of love, Neuman and Calypso, strolling slightly apart from the sixty-three other cruisers, wandered hand in hand through the bustling streets of Valletta, where every swivel-hipped pedestrian wore a dark scowl. The prehistoric Maltese blood had been suffused with centuries of Italian immigration. The palace of the grand masters of the famous persecuted Knights was gloomy with tapestries, and the ruins of the temples of Tarxien were so ancient and their purpose was so conjectural that one went dizzy, right there in the roof-less maze of it all, under the blazing overhead sun.

In the harbor of Marsaxlokk, the little fishing boats had painted eyes on the prows; Neuman wondered, though, if they were sincerely magical or just painted on to keep tourists happy. So many things were like that now—the hex signs on Pennsylvania barns, the beef-eater costumes at the Tower of London. The world had become a rather tatty theme park, its attractions trumped-up and suspect. A little rusty playground existed here in Marsaxlokk, and Calypso got on one of the swings, and Neuman gave her a push, both of them fighting the sadness welling from underneath—a black sludge leaking up through the grid of the "x"s in Maltese place-names, a dark liquid sliding beneath the progress of the tightly scheduled days, the certainty that the cruise would one day be over. They were both between divorces, which was worse than being between marriages. Their spouses had point-blank declined to come on this educational cruise, and these refusals hung in the air like the humming in the eardrums after a twenty-one-gun salute. In the heat of Malta, on the hike from the bus up to the standing stones of Hagar Qim, her pink hand in his felt as sticky as a child's.

Marvels—marvels!—began to beset them. Mrs. Druthers, a grossly overweight widow from Caldwell, New Jersey, who maneuvered herself about on metal arm crutches (very gallantly, everybody agreed, especially when she, several days before, had leveraged herself all the way to the top of the hilltop fortress of Mycenae, through the celebrated Lion Gate and along the lip of the great shaft tomb) exhaustedly sat down on one of the stones of Hagar Qim in her sand-colored raincoat and simply vanished. Vanished! A concerted search led by the ship's captain and the Maltese secret service failed to uncover her whereabouts, though a rubber crutch-tip turned up in a crevice, and a local archaeologist said there seemed to be one more stone than usual, somehow.

Then, at sea, the captain's Bolivian fiancée, with her striped poncho and bowler hat, began to dress diaphanously and to drape herself at the U-shaped bar with the ship's purser for hours at a time, while the stern-visaged captain steadfastly steered the ship. The purser was a grave, mustached young man given to exceedingly slow calculations, as he turned dollars into drachmas and dinars; lachrymosely reading a French translation of John Grisham by the ship's bathtub-sized pool while his surprisingly muscular body acquired a glowering, narcissistic tan, he had been thought by the passengers to be a still-closeted gay. Now he was revealed as a Lothario, a Prometheus flying in the face of authority, and all the female passengers began to need to have their money changed and their accounts audited; they found on the office door a sign saying HOURS/HEURES/HORAS/STUNDEN but not giving an hour, the blank space left blank.

One night, long after midnight, the passengers turned and moaned in their dreams as the ship made an unscheduled stop in mid-Mediterranean; the captain was putting his rival ashore on a barren rock, crinkled like papier-mâché, east of Ustica. Then in a rage he reduced his fiancée to the form of a bright-green parrot and wore her on his epauletted shoulder when he descended, fiery-eyed, from the bridge. He was an erect middle-aged Samothracian, very proud, his uniform very clean. The parrot kept twisting its glistening small head and affirming, with a croak and a lisp, *"Sí. Sí."*

But most marvellous was what happened to old Mr. Breadloaf. He was the oldest passenger, well into his eighties. His mouth lacked a number of its teeth but he smiled nevertheless, at a benign slant; his white countenance was rendered eerie by the redness of the sagging lids below his eyes, like two bright breves on an otherwise unaccented page. From Djerba, a group including the elderly gentleman passed over to the Tunisian mainland on a ferry noisome with Mercedes-Benz diesel trucks. A bus met the cruise passengers and carried them through miles of olive groves to the ruin of a Roman city in Gigthis. Here, close to the sea, pale stones—pavements, steps, shattered columns, inverted Corinthian capitals—still conveyed the sense of a grid; milling about in their running shoes and blue cruise badges, the Americans could feel the presence of an ancient hope, an order projected from afar. AVRELIO VERO CAESARI GIGTHENSIS PUBLICE, an upstanding reddish stone stated. Killer stood on a truncated pillar and, with a jaunty diction originally designed to capture the attention of inner-city students, translated it for them: "I, the emperor Aurelius, be sending you this boss little Roman town, with its forum and shops and public baths and spiffy grid street-plan, as a sample of what the power of Rome can do for *you*. Yo, guys, get with the program!"

Dinnertime was nearing; the bus drivers, slim men with two-day beards, smoking over in the dunes, were letting their Arabic conversation become louder, as a sign of growing impatience. The blue sky above them was turning dull; parallel shadows were lengthening in the orderly ruins. But as the tourists began to gather and to straggle toward the bus through the collapsed arcades of limestone, Mr. Breadloaf, standing alone in a paved space like a slightly tilting column, was transfigured. He grew taller. His cane dangled down like a candy cane, and his knobby old hand released it with a clatter. His irradiated white face spread out along a smiling diagonal bias. His wife of fifty-six years, hard of sight and hearing both, stared upward in habitual admiration. Her husband's radiance was by now quite diffuse, and his disturbing eyelids were smeared into two thin red cloudlets near the horizon, above the storied wine-dark sea. Mr. Breadloaf had become a sunset—the haunting end to a day satisfyingly full of sights.

As the ancients knew, nothing lasts. The lovers' supernal bliss was disturbed on the eleventh night by Calypso's repeated sniffing. "There's a funny smell in this cabin," she said. "Worse than funny. It's terrible."

Neuman felt insulted. "Do you think it's me?"

She bent down and sniffed his chest, his armpits. "No. You're normal masculine. Nice." She dismounted him gingerly and walked, nude, around his cabin, opening doors, bending down, sniffing. Glimmers from the starboard lights, bounced back by the waves, spotlit now her squarish buttocks, now the crescent of her shoulders and the swaying fall of her hair, unbound from its pins of spiralled gold wire. Her voice pounced: "It's in here, down low." She was at his closet, in the narrow corridor to his bathroom. "Oh, it's *foul*."

They turned on the light. There was nothing there but his shoes, including a pair of sandals he had bought in a row of shops near Houmt Souk. "One dollar, one dollar," the Tunisian outside had been chanting, but when

Neuman went inside and was trapped in a rear room between walls of worked leather and horsehair fly whisks and souvenir mugs with a picture of the Aragonese fort on them, men kept tapping him and thrusting sandals in his face and saying, "Thirty-five dollars, only thirty-five." He had panicked, but as he crouched to barrel his way through the scrum and back into the open a voice had said, "Ten," and he—as keen as Odysseus to avoid unnecessary violence—had said, "It's a deal." The sandals were beige and cut rather flatteringly, he thought, across his instep. He had worn them once or twice to the ship's pool, which had been deserted since the Grisham-reading purser had been marooned for hubris.

Calypso held the sandals up close to her pretty white Doric nose, with its sunburned nostril wings. "Ugh," she said. "Fish. Rotten fish. They used fish glue to hold the soles on. Throw them *out*, honey."

Her tone reminded Neuman unpleasantly of his land wife, his legal wife, thousands of air-miles away. "Listen," he told her. "I paid good money for those sandals. I risked my hide for them; suppose one of those guys in the back room had pulled a knife."

"They were poor Tunisians," she sniffed, "trying to make a sale to a disgusting rich Westerner. You like to dramatize every little encounter. But you're wrong if you think I'm going to keep making love to a man whose cabin smells of dead fish."

"I didn't even notice the smell," he argued.

"You're not immensely sensitive, I can only conclude."

"If you were really as carried away by me as you pretend, you wouldn't have noticed."

"I *am* carried away, but I'm not rendered absolutely insensible. Drop those sandals overboard, Neuman, or do the rest of this cruise by yourself."

"Let's compromise. I'll wrap them in a plastic shirt bag and tuck them under my dirty laundry."

She accepted his compromise, but the relationship had taken a wound. The islands seen through the port-hole kept coming, faster and faster: Stromboli, Panarea, Lipari, Sicily. In the Strait of Messina, they held their breaths, between the Scylla of having loved and lost and the Charybdis of never having loved at all.

On Corfu, supposedly the land of the obliging Phae-acians, who turned Ulysses from a scruffy castaway into a well-fed, well-clad guest worthy of being returned to the island where he was king, Calypso took a dislike to the Achilleion Palace, built in 1890 to humor the Empress Elizabeth of Austria's extraordinary fondness for Achilles. "It's so *pseu*do," she said. "It's so *Ger*-man."

Her dislike of his sandals' fishy smell still rankled with Neuman. "To me," he said, "this grand villa in the neoclassical style has a lovely late-Victorian charm. Statues without broken noses and arms, for once, and infused with a scientific sensibility. Who says the nine-teenth century couldn't sculpt? See how with what charming anatomical accuracy the boy and the dolphin, here in the fountain, are intertwined! And look, darling, in Ernst Herter's *Dying Achilles*, how the flesh of the tendon puckers around the arrow, as it were erotically! Scrap the 'as it were.' It *is* erotic. It's *us*."

But she was harder to beguile, to amuse, each day. In anticipation of the injury that her susceptible, vain, and divine nature would soon suffer, she was trying to make their inevitable parting her own deed. No longer riding the boat's rise and fall, she huddled deep under the blankets beside him as the wistful scattered lights of coastal Greece and benighted Albania slid away to port. Just the sun-kissed pink tip of her Doric nose showed, and when he touched it, it, too, withdrew into the cara-pace of blankets.

At the Nekromanteion of Ephyra, once thought to be the mouth of Hades, they were led, in stark sunlight, through the maze that credulous pilgrims had long ago traced in the dark, in an ordeal that took days and many offerings. The modern pilgrims were shown the subter-ranean room where the priests shouted oracles up through the stone floor of the final chamber. The stones smelled of all those past lives, stumbling from birth to death by the flickering light of illusion.

In the little fan-shaped lecture hall, with its feeble slide projector and slippery green blackboard that re-sisted the imprint of chalk, Homer tried to prepare them for Ithaca. His sallow triangular face was especially melancholy, lit from beneath by the dim lectern bulb. The end of the journey meant for him the return to his university—its rosy-cheeked students invincible in their ignorance, its demonic faculty politics, its clamorous demands for ever-higher degrees of political correctness and cultural diversity. "ΚΡΙΝΩ," he wrote on the black-board, pronouncing, "*krino*—to discern, to be able to distinguish the real from the unreal. To do this, we need *noos*, mind, consciousness." He wrote, then, "ΝΟΟΣ." His face illumined from underneath was as eerie as that of a jack-in-the-box or a prompter hissing lines to sty-mied thespians. "We need *no-os*," he pronounced, scrabbling with his invisible chalk in a fury of insertion, "to achieve our *nos-tos*, our homecoming." He stood aside to reveal the completed word: ΝΟΣΤΟΣ. In after-thought he rapidly rubbed out two of the letters, created ΠΟΝΤΟΣ, and added with a small sly smile, "After our crossing together of the sea, the *pontos*."

And the marvellous thing about Ithaca was that it *did* feel like a homecoming, to the quintessential island, green and brimming with memories and precipitous: *ithaki*, precipitous. The bus taking them up the hairpin road to the monastery of Kathara and to Ulysses' *soi-disant* citadel repeatedly had to back around, with much labored chuffing of the engine and tortured squealing of the brakes. Had the driver's foot slipped, Calypso and Neuman, sitting in the back holding hands, would have been among the first tourists killed, the bus sliding and tumbling down, down in Peckinpahish slow motion, over the creamy white crags of Korax down to the wooded plateau of Marathia, where loyal Eumaeus had watered his pigs and plotted with the returned monarch his slaughter of the suitors—the suitors whose only fault, really, had been to pick up on the languishing queen's mixed signals. The lovers' hands gripped, as tightly as their loins had gripped, at the thought of the long fall with death—*aiae!*—at the end.

But the driver, a tough local kid called Telemachus, drove this route all the time. In the monastery, bougain-villea was in bloom and a demented old blind monk waggled his hand for money and occasionally shrieked, sitting there on a stone bench intricately shaded by grapevines. "At home, he'd be homeless," Neuman shyly said.

"Somehow," she said, unsmiling, "it offends me, the suggestion that one must be insane to be religious." A dirty white dog slept before a blue door, a blue of such an ineffable rightness that Calypso photographed it with bracketed exposure times. Below them, the cruise ship was as white as a sliver of soap resting on the bottom of a sapphire bathtub whose sides were mountainsides.

The bus went down a different way, and stopped at the sunny, terraced village of Stavros. Here in a small park a bust of Odysseus awaited them. Neuman posed for Calypso's camera beside it; though Neuman had no bronze beard, there was a resemblance, that of all men to one another. Wanderers, deserters, returners. Now in a mood of terminal holiday the Harvard graduates posed for the Yale graduates, and vice versa, while those marginal cruise passengers from Columbia and the University of Chicago looked on scornfully.

Calypso and Neuman drifted away from the square with its monuments and taverna, and found a small store down a side street, where they bought souvenir scarves and aprons, baskets and vases for their spouses and children. He said, thinking of the grip of her loins, so feminine yet no-nonsense, "I can't bear it."

"Life is a voyage," Calypso said. "We take our pleasure at a price. The price is loss."

"Don't lecture me," he begged.

She shrugged, suggesting, "Stay with me, then, and I'll make you divine. This was the last gasp of your youth. With me, you will be eternally youthful and never die."

Neuman would never forget the electric, static quality she projected, there with her arms full of cloth and her hands full of drachmas, staring at him in the wake of this celestial challenge with irises as multiform as hydrangea blooms. Did her lower lip tremble? This was as vulnerable as the daughter of Oceanus could allow herself to appear. The disconcerted mortal defended himself as best he could, by distinguishing the real from the unreal: "I am a mere man. Only gods and animals can withstand the monotony of eternity, however paradisiacal."

She snapped her profile at him, with a wisecrack: "So now who's lecturing?"

By mutual agreement they slept, on this last night at sea, in separate cabins. But at four in the morning, Aurora Mergenthaler, their melodious chief stewardess, announced to every cabin over the loudspeaking system that the ship was about to pass through the Corinth Canal. The project, cherished by Periander and Caligula, and actually begun by Nero, had been taken up by a French company in 1882 and completed by the Greeks in 1893. The canal is four miles long, twenty-four yards wide, and two hundred sixty feet at the highest point. Dug entirely by hand, it transformed the Peloponnesus from a peninsula into an island.

In the dark of the hour, the walls of earth slid by ominously, growing higher and higher. There seemed to be many horizons, marked by receding bluish lights. The ship, formerly so free, plodded forward in the channel like a blinkered ox. The damp upper deck was surprisingly well populated by conscientious cruisers, some wearing ghostly pajamas, others sporting fanciful jogging outfits, and still others fully dressed for disembarkation on the mainland at Piraeus. Personalities that had grown distinct over the days now melted back into dim shapes: shades. Calypso was not among them. Or if she was—and Neuman searched, going from face to face with a thrashing heart—she had been transformed beyond recognition.

Grandparenting

THE FORMER MAPLES had been divorced some years before their oldest child, Judith, married and had a baby. She was living with her husband, a free-lance computer programmer and part-time troubadour, on the edge of poverty in Hartford. Joan Maple, now Joan Vanderhaven, told Richard Maple over the phone that she and Andy, her husband, were intending to go down from Boston for the birth, which was to be induced. "How ridiculous," said Ruth, Richard's wife. "The girl's over thirty, she has a husband. To have her divorced parents both hovering over her isn't just silly, it's cruel. When I had my first baby I was in Hawaii and my mother was in Florida and that's the way we both wanted it. You need *space* when you're having a baby. You need *air*, to *breathe*." Remembering her own, efficiently natural childbirths, she began to pant, demonstratively. "Let your poor daughter alone. It's taken her ten years to get over the terrible upbringing you two gave her."

"Joan says Judith wants her there. If she wants Joan she must want me. If I let Joan go down there alone with Andy, the baby will think Andy's the grandfather. The kid will get—what's the word?—imprinted."

Ruth said, "Nobody, not even an hour-old infant, could ever think Andy Vanderhaven is one of your family. You're all ragamuffins, and Andy's a fop." Richard had long ago grown used to Ruth's crisp way of seeing things; it was like living in a pop-up book, with no dimension of ambiguity.

But the thought of letting his first grandchild enter the world without him near at hand was painful. Judith had been born in England, and had been tightly swaddled when he first saw her—a compact package with a round red face. She was the first baby he had ever held; he had thought it would be a precarious experience, shot through with fear of dropping something so precious and fragile, but no, in even the smallest infant there was an adhesive force, a something that actively fit your arms and hands, banishing the fear. The hot wobbly head, the wandering eyes like opaque drops of celestial liquid, the squinting little face choleric and muscular with the will to live. *We're in this together, Dad,* the baby's body had assured him, *and we'll both get through it.*

And they had, through diapers and midnight feedings, colic and measles, adolescent tears and fits of silliness, flute lessons and ski lessons, grade school and high school, until at last, ceremoniously attending an entertainment by the graduating seniors, Richard had been startled by how his daughter, one of a leggy troupe of leotarded dancers, had in synchrony with the others struck a conclusive pose and stared unsmiling out at the audience. All their eyebrows were raised inquisitively. They were asking, *What are we?* And the answer, from the silently stunned audience, had become: *Women.* Richard had never before quite so distinctly seen his daughter as a body out in the world, competing, detached from his own. And now her body was splitting, giving birth to another, and he'd be damned if he'd let Joan be there having their baby all to herself.

Driving down Route 86 into the blinding splinters of a sunset, he heard the disc jockey crow, "Get your long johns out of the mothballs, Nutmeg Staters, we're going to flirt with zero tonight!" It had been a dry January so far, but what little snow had fallen had not melted, because of the cold; tonight was to be a record-setter. The station played country music. Hartford had always struck him as a pleasantly hick city, a small forest of green-glass skyscrapers on the winding road to New York; when you descended out of the spaghetti of overpasses, there was a touching emptiness, of deserted after-hours streets and of a state capital's grandiose vacancies. It was a city with nobody in it, just a few flitting shadows, and some heaps of plowed snow. The hospital complex included a parking garage, but he circled the inner-city blocks until he found a free meter. Not yet six o'clock, it was quite dark. Richard hurried through the iron air to the bright lights of the warm hospital spaces. He was the last of this particular extended family to arrive, and the least. A receptionist and her computer directed him to the correct floor, and after he had sat in the waiting room long enough to skim the cream from two issues of *Sports Illustrated*, Joan hurried out to him from some deeper, more intimate chamber of the maternity wing like a harried hostess determined to make every guest, however inconsequential, feel welcome.

She had put on weight with her contentment as Mrs. Vanderhaven—Andy evidently didn't impose the slimming stress of her first marriage—and wore a beltless yellow dress, with small flowers, that seemed old-fashioned, a back-to-nature dress from the Sixties. Her face, broader than he remembered it, was rosy with the event overtaking her—she was becoming a grandmother—and the tropical warmth of the hospital air. "We didn't know if you'd be coming or not," she explained.

"I said I would," Richard protested, mildly.

"We didn't know if Ruth would let you."

"How would she stop me? She thought it was a terrific idea. 'Give them all my love,' she said."

Joan shot him a quick, blue-eyed glance, uncertain, as she often had been, of how ironical he was being. She seemed in the years since they were married to have lost her eyelashes, and her hair had turned gray above her wide brow. Factually she said, "They broke the waters an hour ago, and now we're just sitting around waiting for the contractions to take hold. Judy is in good spirits, though a little apprehensive." This last description seemed to fit Joan as well; she was shy with him. Their telephone conversations, which on the excuse of the children had persisted long into their second marriages, had dwindled these last years; months of silence between them went by now, and he did not know when he had last been as alone with her as he was in this hotly lit waiting room, with its rows of plastic chairs in alternating colors and its yammering television set up near the ceiling. It was the Sunday of the Super Bowl, and the announcers were revving up; even the female members of the news teams were supposed to be excited. Joan had been bending over awkwardly, to look him in the face, with her hands braced on her thighs, and now, perhaps in response to a pang in her back, she suddenly sat down, in the plastic chair next to his. His chair was dirty cream in color, hers scuffed orange. The molded shapes were for narrow people, and Richard and Joan had to edge away to avoid touching rumps.

"Who wouldn't be apprehensive?" he asked. "And who is 'we'?" He had taken off his overcoat but was still wearing a tweed sports jacket, and uncomfortably felt the heat of her proximate body.

But Joan seemed to be rapidly relaxing. "Oh," she said, "Paul, and Paul's sister—she's a nurse, as you know, but not at this hospital, but they let her come sit with us, in the pre-delivery room—and Andy and me. And of course Judy and the little stranger."

"Some crowd," he said. "How's Paul acting?"

His son-in-law, whose blond hair was already thinning in front, wore a pony tail, and had always seemed to Richard insolently tall, as if he had just drawn himself up a few extra inches in a kind of full-body sneer. Richard had never quite known what the word "weedy" meant, applied to a person, but Paul Wysocki had helped him to understand. A weedy person was a tall dry stalk you wanted to pull up and throw away. Richard was surprised the marriage had lasted five years.

"*Won*derfully," Joan said, with defensive emphasis. "*Very* tender with Judy, and very confident. He didn't miss a single birthing class, you know, and is all set to breathe with her. He brought her favorite book of poems, E. E. Cummings, to read to her as a distraction if she needs it."

"How do you read E. E. Cummings aloud? All those staggered letters and open spaces."

"We heard him himself do it, don't you remember? The year he gave the Norton Lectures."

Cummings had been a small, quite bald man in a tuxedo, very precise in manner, reading everything— Wordsworth, Dante, his own prose and poetry—in a fluting voice that never faltered or slipped, up there on the cavernous stage of Sanders Theatre. Richard and Joan had stood together in line in the Cambridge winter to get into the theater, whose vast neo-Gothic space was murmurous and steaming with student excitement. For an instant he and this plump elderly woman beside him became a pair of worn binoculars focused on that animated bright-headed homunculus lodged deep in the transparent mass of lost time. He was jointly and privately theirs, fluting Wordsworth's Immortality Ode, stanza after stanza, while the student audience around them grew restless, wadded in place with hundreds of overcoats.

Joan went away, promising she'd be back. She did not invite him to join the crowd around Judith, nor did he want to. He took the elevator down to the cafeteria, to have a cup of coffee and a lemon Danish. Something about hospital cafeterias freed him from all dietary restraints. If it was bad for you, they wouldn't be selling it. He called Ruth, collect. "Well, I'm here, honey. Nothing much is happening yet."

He liked calling his wife, because her voice over the phone had a throaty, shapely quality he didn't easily hear when they were face to face; it was a young voice, the voice of their old courtship—secretive, urgent, humid. Yet what she said was typically crisp: "Well, of course not. Whoever said anything *would* happen? You could be stuck there for days. Where are you staying?"

Richard smiled; she always asked that, as if his staying in any hotel or motel without her were a kind of infidelity. "At a Best Inn just off 84. I thought I should grab a room before I came here. It's going to be record cold tonight. Is it zero yet in Boston?"

"How would I know? I was watching *Sixty Minutes*—a *fas*cinating exposé of the pharmaceutical companies, and now I've missed the conclusion, thanks to you. Mike Wallace was being absolutely relentless with some wishy-washy Squibb CEO."

"I don't think, once they induce, it takes days."

"Well, I never thought I'd wind up a grass widow while my husband runs around watching his children have children. How is Joan? As darling as ever?"

"I only saw her a minute. They're in some other room timing Judy's contractions, and I'm outside in the waiting room reading old *Smithsonian*s."

"How un*fair*," Ruth said, and it sounded as though she was, at last, touched.

"No, Joan understands. I don't need to be in the same room with that willowy Pole."

"But you love Judith so."

"All the more reason, not to get her distracted."

After hanging up, he went back into the cafeteria and bought an Almond Joy. He hadn't had one for years. He had returned for less than a minute to his perusal of out-dated magazines when Joan came back. "Where *were* you? Judy's pace has picked up and she's gone into the labor room." His former wife's cheeks bore a hectic, spotty flush; with her wiggly gray hair and waistless figure she was looking like one of those art-loving Cambridge ladies Cummings had written about sardon-ically but who had shown up at his reading anyway, decades ago, among the hot-bodied undergraduates. "The doctor says Paul and I can stay with her, but not Andy. Andy hates waiting rooms, he thinks they're full of germs, and the nurses said why not wait in Judy's room? It has a television set. We thought maybe you'd like to go in there, too." Joan looked slightly alarmed at the idea, as if her two husbands hadn't known each other for years, through thick and thin. "Judy's worried about you sitting out here alone."

"Well, we don't want to worry Judy, do we? Sure, why not?" Richard said, and let her lead him down the corridor. Her hair looked less gray from behind, and bounced as it used to when she would wheel her bicycle ahead of him along the diagonal walks of Harvard Yard.

Andy was sitting in the room's one leather chair, reading a prim little book from the Oxford University Press, with a sewn-in bookmark. He was wearing gold half-glasses and looked up like a skeptical schoolmas-ter. Richard told him, "Keep reading, Andy. I'll just cower over here in the corner." Joan hovered uneasily, her hands held out from her body as if she were in a chain dance with invisible partners.

"Dick," she said, pointing, "there's a chair that looks at least half comfortable."

Andy looked up over his glasses again. "Would you like the chair I'm sitting in, Richard? It's all one to me."

"Absolutely not, Andy. Survival of the fittest. To the victor belong the spoils, or something. What's that cute little book you're reading? *The Book of Common Prayer?*"

It amused him that Joan, a clergyman's daughter to whom the concept of God seemed not only dim but oppressive, had married such a keen churchman. Andy was an Episcopalian the way a Chinese mandarin was a Confucian, to keep his ancestors happy. He showed Richard the little anthology's jacket: *West African Explorers.* "But astonishing," he said, "the faith some of these poor devils had. They were all walking straight into malaria, of course."

"You two will be all right, then?" Joan asked.

Her husband didn't respond, so Richard took it upon himself to reassure her. "Happy as clams. Let us know when the baby comes or dinner is served, whichever comes first."

After listening to Andy turn pages and sniff for a while, and staring out the window at a paved, snow-dusted space crossed now and then by a human shadow hunched against the cold, he asked the other man, "Mind if I turn on the TV? We're missing some great commercials."

"That football game? You watch such things?"

"The Super Bowl, I generally do. Andy, how can you call yourself an American and not watch the Super Bowl?"

"I don't call myself an American," Andy said, and sniffed, "very often."

Richard laughed. This was fun, he had decided. If he were at home, Ruth would have him watching *Nature* on PBS. One team wore white helmets, and the other helmets were bronze in color. One quarterback threw passes like darts, neat and diagrammatic, and the other kept scrambling out of his crumbling pocket of protection to toss high wobbling balls, butterflies up for grabs. "What a catch!" Richard cried out. "Did you see that, Andy? One-handed, six inches off the Astroturf!"

"No, I didn't see it."

"It was a miracle," Richard assured him. "A once-in-a-lifetime miracle. There—you can see it on replay!"

Joan kept checking on them every half-hour or so. On one trip, she brought them doughnuts, and on another, Styrofoam bowls of chicken-noodle soup on a tray of nubbly recycled cardboard. "The cafeteria is closing," she explained.

"Crackers, did you remember crackers for me?" Richard asked.

"Salt and starch, Dicky boy," Andy said. "You still eat that crap?"

Joan blushed. "As a matter of fact, I did," she said to her former husband, and produced two packets of saltines from a pocket of her shapeless dress with its little yellow flowers. "I wasn't going to give them to you unless you asked."

Andy explained to him, "Already, there's enough sodium in this canned soup to add five points to your blood pressure."

"Go! *Go!*" Richard yelled at the screen, where a running back, his bronze helmet lowered, his brown calves pumping, was driving three tacklers backward to gain the yard needed for a first down.

Andy eventually stopped trying to read his book, and

put on his distance glasses, the better to follow his ad-hoc roommate's football commentary. Richard found himself wildly partisan for the bronze helmets—the more Eastern of the two teams, and the one with the scrambling quarterback and some butter-fingered ends. They were down by ten points at the half. The half-time show seemed very long and overpopulated and was based on nostalgia for a brand of Seventies rock that both men had been too old to appreciate the first time around. Richard went out and found a vending machine and brought back four dollars' worth of candy bars and snacks in little waxed-paper bags. Andy ate a few cheese curls, wiping his fingers on his handkerchief afterwards. Joan came in, her eyes the electric blue they used to be after a bath, and told them, "They're coming faster now." The contractions.

"How many points is that?" Andy asked when the bronze-helmeted quarterback was sacked behind his own goal line.

"Just two. Last chance at the cheese curls."

"No thanks. All yours."

"How about a strawberry-flavored Twizzler?"

"God, no."

Richard wondered if Andy was this fastidious in bed. Perhaps that was what Joan had needed—a man to draw her out, to make her feel relatively liberated. "No matter where I go," she had once complained to Richard, not only of their sex, "you're there ahead of me."

"Wow," Andy said, of a long, fluttering pass that found the receiver's fingertips, and stayed in his grip despite a lethal blind-side hit.

"That seems to be the name of the game now," Richard explained. "Trying to strip the ball. It's amazing, what passes for legal with the pros. Watch what happens *after* the tackle." For how long, he wondered, had Joan and Andy been sleeping together before he had known? Saying she needed interests outside the home, she had joined the Episcopal choir, and would come back from Thursday-night rehearsals later and later, creeping between the sheets with a stealthy rustle as loud as a thunderclap. Even if he was asleep, her sudden warm body, with its cold toes and beery breath, would waken him. Andy sang bass, though you would have taken him for a tenor.

"Survival of the fittest," Andy said now, smiling to himself.

A quick slant, another fluttering pass completed, a brilliant cut-back through a hole opened for a nanosecond by an all-pro offensive tackle, and then that big fullback tucking his head down and writhing over the goal line: the Eastern underdogs were back in the game. An interception early in the fourth quarter, by a lineman who almost lumbered off in the wrong direction, and the score was tied. Andy, who was well into it by now, cheered, and Richard offered him a palm-up hand for a slapped five. "My goodness," Joan said, once more entering the room. "Sorry to interrupt the fun, guys, but I have news."

"No!" Richard said, suddenly terrified, as when sometimes in the movie theatre a vast pit of reality and eventual death opened underneath him, showing the flickering adventure on the screen to be a mere idle distraction from his life, a waste of minutes while his final minute was rapidly approaching.

"Yes," Joan said, complacently.

"What sex?"

"Paul wants to give you the particulars himself."

"What a tease she is, huh, Andy? Tell me at least the weight."

"Big. The whole process was big—amazing, seeing it from that side. The afterbirth!" Her eyes rolled up, picturing it; then she gave her nervous clergyman's-daughter laugh, to recall herself from so intimate a sharing, and said sharply to her present husband, "Andy, you must be starving."

Paul came in a minute later, looking so tall he seemed stretched by a transcendent pull from the ceiling. His pale face and lank woman's-length hair were damp with the exertions of vicarious labor. He stabbed at Richard's chest with a recklessly extended hand, and, when Richard took it, said in his soulful troubadour manner, "Your dear, brave daughter has given birth to Richard Leo Wysocki."

It was one of those prepared sentences, like Armstrong's when setting foot on the moon, that came out stilted and hard to understand. They had named his grandson after him. Paul and Judith must have planned this ahead of time, in the event that it was a boy. "My God. You didn't have to do that," Richard said, he feared ungraciously.

Visiting hours were long over. Out of sight, medical procedures had closed protectively around the mother and baby. Paul would stay, to see his wife settled into her room, but he gave the grandparent-figures permission to go. "The Super Bowl is still tied!" Richard protested.

Andy said curtly, "It'll be in all the papers tomorrow. Joan and I are leaving."

Richard had to admire how carefully Andy wrapped his gray wool scarf around his neck, holding it in place with his chin while he inch by inch shrugged his overcoat up to his shoulders. Joan reached out as if to help her husband, and then, sensing Richard's watching, suppressed the wifely gesture. "Don't forget your book," she told Andy instead. "And your *Wall Street Journal*."

Paul said, "Mr. Maple, we'll be moving Jude"—he called Judith "Jude," as in "Hey Jude," rather than *Jude the Obscure*—"in here, but if you wanted to finish watching the Super Bowl I bet it's on in the lobby downstairs. I don't think they want you to stay on this floor." Already, he seemed more mature, and slightly stooped.

"That's fine, Paul—the party's over. I'll go with the other old folks. Tell Judith I'll try to swing by tomorrow morning before I head back to Boston. Think that would be O.K.?"

"Visiting hours don't begin until one, but I would think, sure," Paul answered—rather grudgingly, Richard felt. He tailed the Vanderhavens out through the hospital corridors. Joan had acquired a mink coat since her marriage to him; its glinting collar set off becomingly her lightly bouncing hair, with its elusive texture between frizzy and wavy. Her hair was tightly curly elsewhere, and in the Sixties she had managed a pretty good Afro, for a white woman. On the other side of the glass hospital doors, the dark civic vacancy of Hartford brimmed with sheer cold. No one else moved on the streets; Richard's eyes and nostrils stung, and within a minute the tips of his thumbs were aching in their thin leather gloves. Across the street, the hospital parking garage glowed with an aquarium dimness, and the booth where the men took the tickets was empty. To the striped cross-bar was attached a sign that in large red letters stated that the garage closed at nine-thirty.

"Oh, *damn*!" Andy cried, and stamped his foot on the snow-muffled asphalt. Both Richard and Joan laughed aloud, the gesture was so petulant and ineffective. Their laughter rang in the brittle cold as if off the rafters of a deserted church. Andy asked, "Why didn't anybody *tell* us?"

"I bet they thought you could read," Richard said. "It's probably printed right on the ticket."

Joan said, "I'm sorry, darling. It's my fault. I was just so excited about becoming a grandmother I wasn't noticing anything."

"And I don't see any taxis anywhere," Andy said. "Damn, *damn!*" He wore an astrakhan hat that made him look like a toy soldier, and every word from his mouth was a streaming white flag.

"Where are you?" Richard asked Joan.

"I think it's called the Morgan. It's the only decent hotel downtown."

That sounded more like Andy than the egalitarian Joan he had known. He said, "Don't despair. I'll take you in my car, and you can take a taxi back here in the morning."

"That'd be lovely," she said, swinging her body to keep warm, so that her coat shimmered in the faint streetlight. "Where are *you?*"

"Good question. I parked on the street, but *I* was so excited I didn't really think where. I remember I had to walk slightly uphill." He headed down the nearest slant of sidewalk, beside Joan in her mink, while Andy tailed behind them. The street came quickly to a dead end, next to what seemed to be a boiler plant, a windowless brick building housing a muffled roaring of heat, and again Richard had to laugh. Joan did, too.

Andy whined, "Let me go back to the hospital and have them phone for a cab."

"Don't be such a sissy. Think of yourself as a West African explorer," Richard said. His face was blazing in the cold and his thumbs in his thin gloves were quite numb. "It has to be around here somewhere. A gray Taurus, with three bridge stickers on the windshield. I remember noticing a row of boarded-up shops and wondering if kids looking for drugs were going to smash my windows."

"Great," Andy said. "Come on, Joan, let's head back. This is a mugger's paradise."

"Nonsense," Joan pronounced. "Everybody's too cold to mug." She was still a liberal at heart. She turned and said, "Richard, *think*. What kind of shops? Did you cross any big streets? From what angle did you approach the hospital?"

Her hopeful voice, which he had first heard in a seminar on the English Romantics—a dozen callow male faces around an oaken conference table, and hers, shining—summoned up in him a younger, student self. Ruth was so much more decisive and clear-headed than he that he rarely had to think. A grid began to build in his mind. "One street over," he said, pointing, "and then, I think, left." Joan led the way, he and Andy numbly following; she was the friskiest of the three, perhaps because she had the warmest coat. They had not walked ten minutes before he recognized his car— its three stickers, its pattern of road-salt stains. It had not been broken into. The shops he vaguely remembered were on the *other* side of the street, oddly. He was pleased to hear the door lock click; he had known it to freeze in weather warmer than this.

Joan got into the back, letting Andy have the seat by the heater. The engine started, and as the car rolled along the silent, glazed streets, she put her face up between the two men's shoulders, talking to Richard. "The baby. When they come out—I've never seen this described—they have an expression on their faces, a funny little bunchy look of distaste. He looked just like Judith when we'd try to give her prunes. Then there's a gush of water, and the rest of the baby slips out like nothing, trailing this enormous spiralled umbilical cord, all purply and yellow."

"Joanie, please," Andy said, readjusting his muffler.

She went on, inspired, to Richard, "I mean, the *apparatus*. You think of the womb as a kind of place for transients, but it's a whole other life in there. It's a lot to give up." He understood what she meant; as always, she was groping for the big picture, searching for the hidden secret, in keeping with all those sermons she had had to sit through as a child. Life is a lesson, a text with a moral.

Whereas Andy listened to her as one does to second wives, in confidence that the search is over. Or that there is no search. He patted her hand, where it rested in its mink sleeve next to his shoulders. "I shouldn't have let you watch," he said. "It's going to give you bad dreams."

"I wouldn't have missed it for the world," she said, a bit indignantly, Richard felt.

"Tell me one more thing," he begged. "Who the hell is Leo?"

"*His* father—didn't you know? They're not like we were—this may be their only child, or male child at least, and they had to load him up."

Andy told Richard, "Go right up there, and then you have to go left—it's a one-way street. You can let us off at the corner and we'll walk up to the entrance."

"I wouldn't *dream* of it. I'll circle the block and let you off right under the marquee. Right under the damn doorman's nose."

Joan's hand touched his shoulder. "When you see Judith tomorrow morning, give my love. We're going to hurry right back in the morning, Andy has a meeting at ten."

Richard thought of kissing her good night, but their faces were probably still icy, and his neck didn't turn as easily as it used to.

* * *

His room at the Best Inn was on the ground floor, its wall-to-wall shag carpeting laid over concrete poured right on grade. The walls seemed subterranean, breathing out a deep freeze, their surface cold to the touch. The baseboard heating was ticking but unequal to its task. Richard hadn't thought to throw pajamas in with tomorrow's fresh shirt; he shivered in his underwear between the clammy sheets, got up, robbed the other twin bed of its skimpy blanket and bedspread, and finally draped his overcoat on top of himself. Still, the cold pressed in upon him from the walls like a force that wanted to compress his existence to nothing, that wanted to erase this temporary blot of heated, pumping blood. *It's a lot to give up,* Joan had said of the womb, and indeed the cosmic volume of lightless, warmthless space hostile to us is overwhelming. He felt, huddled up, like a homunculus frigidly burning at the far end of God's indifferently held telescope. He was a newly hatched grandfather, and the universe wanted to crush him, to make room for newcomers. He did fall asleep, a little, and his dreams, usually so rich in suppressed longing and forgotten knowledge, were wispy, as if starved by his body's effort to maintain body temperature.

In the morning, checking out, groggy and still chilled, at the front desk, he complained of the lack of heat; the youthful clerk, fresh arrived from a cozy bed elsewhere, shrugged in scant apology and said, "We don't get a night like last night very often. Four below, on my mom's porch."

By daylight the hospital looked different: more bustling, yet more shabby and temporary, a factory of healing staffed by weary people working half in the dark. A Hartford *Courant* Richard bought with his tea—no more coffee, he vowed; keep that blood pressure down—said that his team of bronze-helmeted heroes had lost in the last thirty seconds, to a forty-seven-yard field goal. Miracles are cheap.

When, at last, against the strict rules, they let him in to see his daughter, Judith looked unexpectedly neutral after her ordeal—neither drained nor jubilant, sick nor well, older nor younger than her age of thirty-one. She was wearing a hospital johnny under Joan's old powder-blue bathrobe, and sitting on the edge of the bed. She had been feeding the baby, and the nurses had taken him back to the nursery. "I don't know, Dad," she said. "It was a little weird. They put this thing in my arms this morning and it's like I had no idea what to do with it. I hardly even knew which end was up. I was afraid I'd drop it and felt very, you know, awkward."

He sat down in the big leather chair Andy had taken last night and smiled paternally. "You'll stop feeling awkward very quickly."

"Yeah, that's what Paul says." Paul, the know-it-all. From just the way in which Judith pronounced his name, he had won an undeserved promotion. Richard found himself more jealous and resentful of Paul and the baby than of Andy. Judith said, "He's a great father already."

"Maybe it's an easier role. There isn't all that—that apparatus. Maybe you're still feeling the baby is part of yourself, like a foot. I mean, how much feeling can you work up right off the bat toward a foot? How did the actual—what's the word—birthing go?"

Judith from infancy on had been a sturdy, independent sort, a little opaque in her feelings, with something of her mother's detached honesty. "Good," she said. "It was good. Paul was great, with the breathing. At one point he began to sing, and got all the nurses laughing. But they were wrong about the Lamaze method. It hurt. They kept saying it was just pressure, but it *hurt*, Dad."

Warmth swarmed to his eyes, at the thought of his daughter in pain. He blinked and stood and kissed her lightly on her forehead, that wide pale brow that from the start, love her as much as he could, held behind it her secrets, her sensations, her identity. "I should go. The nurses want to do something to you."

"Look at him around the corner. See who you think he looks like. Mom thinks he looks like Grandpa, the way his mouth has a little pinch in the middle, and turns down at the ends."

"Sounds like Andy's mouth to me. You don't suppose he's the real grandfather, do you?"

It took Judith a moment to put it together and to realize that her father was being ironical. She was as groggy as he was; he had been compressed in the night, and she had been split in two. He told her, "Your mother by the way said to give her love. Andy was rushing her back to Boston bright and early, as soon as they could spring their car from the garage, where it got trapped last night."

"She told me all about it. She was in, she and Andy, right after breakfast. She talked him into it, I guess."

Richard laughed. "It's going to be hard to keep up with your mother, in the grandparenting business."

"Yeah. You should see *her* hold the baby. *She* knew which end was up."

To him, too, it seemed clear, when a nurse brought his grandson to the window, that this reddish grapefruit, with its frowning closed eyes and its few licks of silky hair, pale like its father's, was a human head, and that the tiny lavender appendages on the other, unswaddled end were toes. "Want to hold him?" the nurse, who was young and black, asked him through the glass.

"Do I dare?"

"You're the grandpap, aren't you? Grandpaps are special people around here."

And the child's miniature body did adhere to his chest and arms, though more weakly than the infants he had presumed to call his own. Nobody belongs to us, except in memory.

JOHN UPDIKE

Call 1-800-793-BOOK (2665) to order by phone and use your major credit card. Or use this coupon to order by mail.

Fiction:

__THE CENTAUR	449-21522-9	$5.95
__COUPLES	449-20797-8	$5.95
__MARRY ME	449-20361-1	$5.99
__MEMORIES OF THE FORD ADMINISTRATION	449-22188-1	$5.99
__A MONTH OF SUNDAYS	449-20795-1	$4.95
__PIGEON FEATHERS	449-21132-0	$4.95
__ROGER'S VERSION	449-21288-2	$6.99
__S.	449-21652-7	$5.99
__TOO FAR TO GO	449-20016-7	$5.99
__TRUST ME	449-21498-2	$5.95
__THE WITCHES OF EASTWICK	449-20647-5	$6.99
__RABBIT, RUN	449-20506-1	$5.99
__RABBIT REDUX	449-20934-2	$5.99
__RABBIT IS RICH	449-24548-9	$5.99
__RABBIT AT REST	449-21962-3	$5.99

Nonfiction:

__SELF-CONSCIOUSNESS	449-21821-X	$5.95

Name_____

Address _____

City_____ State_____ Zip _____

Please send me the FAWCETT BOOKS I have checked above.

I am enclosing	$____
plus	
Postage and handling*	$____
Sales tax (where applicable)	$____
Total amount enclosed	$____

*Add $4 for the first book and $1 for each additional book.

Send check or money order (no cash or CODs) to:
Fawcett Mail Sales, 400 Hahn Road, Westminster, MD 21157.

Prices and numbers subject to change without notice.
Valid in the U.S. only.
All orders subject to availability.   UPDIKE